# GOOD
# SOUTHERN
# WITCHES

edited by J.D. Horn

CURIOUS BLUE PRESS

# Good Southern Witches

**Published 2021 by Curious Blue Press**

**Contact: Editor@CuriousBluePress.com**

# Contents

# Editor's Note

Some of the stories in this collection include elements of violence, violence against children, sexual assault, consensual sex, and profanity.

It is a book about witches after all.

For my uncle, Roy Horn.

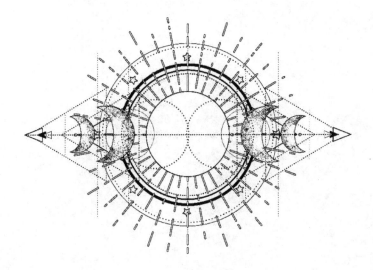

# Preface: All of Them Witches

While collecting the stories for this anthology, I found myself considering my lifelong fascination with the occult and contemplating how my obsession with witches came to be. I was born in the mid-1960s, just as the occult was taking the world by storm—again—some years after Raymond Butler's initiation, Gerald Gardner's demise, and Sybil Leek's decision to quit High Street in favor of America.

Already for two television seasons Samantha Stevens had been trying to pass as a mortal suburban housewife, and teen-aged Sabrina Spellman, four years in Archie Comics trying to pass as a mortal high school student. On my first birthday, a gift from Angelique Bouchard led to the death of Jeremiah Collins, and six months later, Rosemary Woodhouse was choking down tannis root smoothies and perusing the *oeuvre* of J.R. Hanslet.

Wilhelmina W. Witchiepoo babysat me, and I entered first grade with Miss Tickle, though I was too young to join the Adventurers Club. Sarah was initiated, Satan opened his school for girls, and everyone danced to "The Mephisto Waltz" until "Rhiannon" hit the charts.

All this is to say, as with many early-edition Gen Xers, my formative years were steeped in magic, both light and dark, but I believe with me, more so than with most of my cohort, these wild seeds fell on fertile ground. Still, a decade ago, when I began writing what would become my first published novel, a story about a dysfunctional family of witches from Savannah, I never imagined the witch would play such a central role to my writing career. Witches, both real and imaginary, have been very, very good to me.

The most accessible of supernatural entities, arguably even more so than ghosts, the witch is a wildflower, ready to thrive anywhere she chooses to take root.

i

She might be a force of nature, a mother, a maiden, a crone. Or she might not be a *she* at all, manifesting instead as a non-binary person, or a young boy looking to understand how he fits in in a man's world. She is the knowing outsider, the cunning killer, the healing center, the avenger of the disenfranchised, and patriarchy's perennial scapegoat.

Sometimes she acts as a window on other realities. Sometimes she stands as the dam holding these alien realities back.

In this volume, she's dug her roots deep into the soil of the American Southeast. Here, you'll find Baba Yaga reimagined as a Southern socialite, Kentucky granny witches, Texas water witches, Tennessee tricksters, North Carolina guardians, Georgia killers, Mississippi virgins, and Louisiana whores.

This collection is a love letter to the witch, in all her glorious and fearsome incarnations, because—you have to admit—even when she's wicked, she's still damned good.

Books such as this are created with a very specific reader in mind: a reader who is searching for just such a book. So, whether you found these stories, or they found you, when you've finished reading, go take a long look in the mirror—you might just see a witch staring back at you.


J.D. Horn,
February 2021

# BABY

## BY R. A. BUSBY

The baby bit hard into my flesh and held there.

It dug into the left side of my womb with a pinprick pinch, sharp and determined. Lying in bed, cheek hot against the old pillowcase redolent of hair and bleach, I imagined the embryo floating through a warm-wet universe, a creature small as a salmon's egg with tiny biting jaws that tore into the dark walls of my flesh and ate itself a cave to grow inside.

It nestled there, a pearl as red as sin.

But whose?

🐀

Jess and I had come here to this wild wooded place about half a year ago. I'd grown up where the desert runs in an ancient, wrinkled playa all the way to limestone mountains stark and grey as a curse. The only green came from creosote bushes that suck the water from the dry earth so nothing grows around them, and the leaves smell just like rain.

But a few months into our almost-marriage, Jess got an itch to move back to West Virginia to be with his people. That was ironic. He'd come out in the desert to be away from his people. Hell, Vegas was the farthest away he could live and still afford the rent. By that point, though, the COVID had struck, and folks were unemployed. Home with his brothers Mike and Grady, Jess explained, he could pick up jobs where an extra hand was always needed—construction, landscape, road crew. That sort of thing.

What could I say? When Jess first met me, I was squeaking by in a shitty studio in a truck town near Vegas and knew I wasn't going anywhere. I'd been three credits short of an

1

associate degree when Daddy got cancer, and the mercy was that it was fatal. There'd be no handwringing about spending his savings on chemo. Daddy saved it all for hospice. In the meantime, his help would be on me.

I first noticed Jess when I stopped in at Gibby's one day after work for a beer, and he ambled up to the bar. He had a devilish grin and long hair, tousled and gold-red like turmeric, thumbs hooked inside his waistband, fingers framing whatever lay below.

"So," he asked. "What is it you do?"

For a minute, I toyed with my straw. "I'm an aesthetician."

Jess gave a half-smile that was almost a laugh, and I saw one tooth was nicked a little in the corner. He said, "What the hell's an aesthetician?" When I explained aestheticians did skin care, laser treatments, and hair removal, he smiled a little wider. "Gotcha," he said. "Fancy word for a pussy groomer."

Yeah, I know what you're thinking. And you're right.

But oh, for the moment, he did put things from my mind. The job. The degree I'd never get. The powdery sand drifting in eddies along the chain-link fence to blow inside so the windowsills were always gritty. The hateful glare from the bone-tailed pit bull chained in the neighbor's backyard. The gold poison needles of the cholla. The high, sweet stink of decay in the house where my father lay dying.

So yeah. Between the fingers and the tousles and the nicked-tooth smile, Jess put things from my mind just fine. And before long, he and I were talking about marriage. Or at least I was. No big affair. A justice of the peace. My dad to give me away. That's all I asked.

But asking ain't getting.

Daddy died before the COVID hit. As it turned out, he never got to spend his money on hospice. Walking to his door after work one day, I simply knew. Between one step and another, really. The air around fell still, and no birds sang beneath the white pearl sky that cold December day.

My key was halfway in his lock. Breathing too hard, I yanked it out, letting the moment before opening the door just spin out and breathe. In some college course I'd taken once, the professor had mentioned an experiment with a cat in a box. The cat, she explained, was both alive and dead. You couldn't be sure until you opened the lid and made it happen this way or that. At the time, this had seemed like obvious bullshit. The cat was dead, or it was not. That was all.

I'd been wrong. After a time, I put the key back in, and I found out.

🐈

After the funeral, there wasn't much left, but there'd not been much to begin with. What there was, I socked away in the empty Chock Full o'Nuts can where Daddy kept his grocery money and put it on the back of my shelf.

Now there was just me. And Jess. And when our wedding day came, I guessed I'd be walking down the aisle all alone.

Alone. That was truer than I knew.

Maybe it was the grief of those times, but I have to say, it took me too long to figure out Jess liked nothing more than to put some kind of daylight between me and the people I loved. I didn't have much family left other than my cousin Tracy, but I did have friends. Within a year or so, those ties would all be gone.

Jess went about it strategically, almost never saying anything straight. It was always some sideways remark like, "That Amie, man. I don't know," or "Krystal. Wow." Then his mouth would twist in a kind of soft regret as if the world had once again confirmed his basic cynicism. When I asked what he meant, he'd give a shrug and tinker with the car. And there I'd be, standing alone in the house wondering just what I had missed seeing in Amie or Krystal.

As for my heart-friends and relatives, Jess was persistent as a dripping faucet. He'd turn from a show about a McMansion bottle-blonde and ask if she didn't look like my cousin. "You know—the one who does those Coddled Cook

3

things?" he asked. "Where she pretends to invite you to a party just so you'll buy a frying pan, and she gets a commission?" Jess kept nibbling away, little bits here, little bites there, until he got what he wanted.

That's how I was pretty sure, despite its strange conception, this baby might be his.

The nibbling, you know.

🐈

"Every child's a changeling," Jess's mother remarked the first time I met her. "Oh, they might have their daddy's eyes, but they're changelings all the same. Trust me."

I did.

I hadn't expected to like Mama. Jess sure as hell didn't. "You just want to stay outta her way," he'd muttered. We were near Memphis, and I could tell from the restless tapping on the U-Haul's wheel that Jess was in a mood full of pissoff. He'd had to sit in the right-hand lane behind the eighteen-wheelers for fifty miles and it was rasping him badly, Jess being a person who liked to dart in and out of traffic like a needle set to zigzag.

He kept on. "Out there in the woods by herself in that old doublewide and five cats." Jess shook his head, orange-gold curls tumbling. "Crazy bitch."

"Whatever happened to your daddy, anyway?" I asked, staring out the window. "You never talk about him."

Jess shot me a bitter glance, and his lips tightened. "Fuck him. He wasn't exactly a good guy. Quick with his hands until he decided to just fade away to nothing. At the end, he walked out on us. Literally."

"What do you mean?"

Jess gripped the steering wheel. "He got up one night and walked out of the house. I watched from my bedroom window and saw him cross into the woods like he was answering a call from the trees. He kept right on going until the shadow ate him up, and none of us ever laid eyes on him again. Simple as that." He paused. "But what bugged me were his boots."

"His boots?"

"They were the only thing he wore. Otherwise, he was naked as the day he came screaming out of Grandma."

I had nothing to say to that.

The signs for Memphis came more thickly now. Gas. Food. Services. "We're living down the road? From your mama?"

"Close enough. Grady's lending us his old place." From there, Jess fell silent.

I'd never had a mother. I didn't really know what that was like. After Mama died, Daddy'd had a string of girlfriends over the decades. Sweet women with understanding faces, secretaries and nurses. Women who help.

Women like me.

I'd never seen myself that way until right then in the U-Haul outside Memphis, and I thought, *But it's good to help folks. Nothing wrong in helping. God, the world needs help. We all do. That's why we're in this shit anyway. No one helps anyone.*

But.

But still.

🐾

Mama's place lay deep in the forest. Grady's old place— our place now—was closer to the main road, but Mama's trailer was down a winding dirt path wending through the trees and underbrush.

The land was richly green. Light came through the leaves in dappled dots like upflung coins that hovered in the air. The soil was dark and rich with leafloam, and the tree roots were skirted in velvet. On their bark clung horizontal mushrooms like the spread tails of Thanksgiving turkeys, and the place spoke of emerald growing things.

"Piece a shit," said Jess, and kicked aside a coffee can of flowers in his way. I set the can back on the step. Beside the screen sat a broad grey rock, flat as an ironing board, and on it leaned a grocery bag with peaches from the tree, wilting leaves still clinging to the stems.

5

The interior door opened on a woman with long silver hair and spotted-leather skin stretched over bones. From her hands dangled a tangled vine covered with fruit that resembled lantana but probably wasn't.

"Well," she said through the mesh. "Look what the cat dragged in."

"Glad to see you too, Ma," muttered Jess.

She paused there a moment, considering. For a second, I figured she would close the door, but then her eyes, faded grey and gimlet-sharp, stared into mine.

Into me.

Mama gave a nod. "Well. You comin' in? Enter of your own free will, as they say," she said, opening the rusty screen, and there we were.

On the way, I grabbed the fruit bag. "I found these by your door," I explained. She peered over the half-glasses she wore.

"A gift," said Mama after a moment. "For some help. Just put it on the counter."

After that, my feet found their way to Mama's more than I'd have thought. The forest called, and all that summer, I longed to plunge my head inside that verdant tunnel and run for miles and miles to feel the earth spring up and breathe in air so green. In that sweet hypnotic rhythm, time ceased to tick and the world was not a separate thing.

The path ran through the wood, and no matter what, the forest found a way to wind me through trees asleep in a morning mist until I stood at Mama's porch and she was there inside.

And always when I arrived, I'd find things outside her door. A stack of bloody-butcher ears in summer. Gala apples. Jellies glowing in the sunlight. In early autumn, a tiny corn dolly sitting by herself, faceless head peeping from beneath a green husk bonnet. At first, the rock on Mama's porch had looked to me like an ironing board. Now it felt like something older and darker. A place of offering. Of gifts.

We'd go into the forest, Mama and I, starting on the track behind the trailer that wound past a tamped-down circle in the grass and a car part pile on which a white cat lounged. Though we always walked to the right, I noticed there was a left-hand path, more overgrown, feeding farther into the vale. *His daddy went that way*, came the unbidden thought.

"Now," Mama told me one September. "We're sang hunting. Head into that patch, Ginny." She wagged a thin finger at a leggy upcropping. "Go on," she nodded.

"Isn't that poison ivy?"

Mama snorted. "Don't you remember that old saw about 'leaves of three'?"

"They all look like leaves of three."

"Then learn to count to five," Mama said, and handed me a stick. We dug till the earth fell away. Reaching into the ground, she pulled out a small brown root in the shape of a man.

"This boy has himself a pecker," Mama chuckled, pointing at the place where a smaller root stuck out at a junction. "That'll fetch good money."

Mama and I worked awhile at digging sang, and at last I asked, "Who leaves those things at your door, anyway? Those gifts?"

She paused, tugging on a long thin runner gently, as if it were an umbilical cord. "Women I help."

"But what do you do?"

With a grunt, Mama poked at the dirt with her stick. "I get them what they need," she answered. "Or I try. So long as it hurts no one. They come to me, and together, we ask."

Thinking about Daddy and Jess, I said bitterly, "Asking ain't getting. And getting what you want isn't always so good."

Mama's hands brushed down her jeans, leaving a dark earth-trail across her thighs. "So, you've figured that out?" she said. "'Bout time. But I didn't say getting what you *want*, girl. I

7

said getting what you *need*. And you often do get that. Just not the way you imagined. But you get it."

Over time, I learned the names of things, their look and their lore. I brought home morels with long thin caps folded like a human brain, hen-o-the-woods that grew on the oaks, and dark black berries in a pail.

And in exchange, I started to leave gifts for Mama on the stone. A china pot and Earl Grey tea. A catnip plant and fishing-pole toy. Tens and twenties fashioned into flowers, cranes, and fish I'd hoarded from the coffee-can money Daddy left.

"What did you mean?" I asked once. "About changelings?"

She paused a bit, remembering. "Heh. I did say that, didn't I? That first day. It was mostly to twit Jess, but yes. You can grow a child right beneath your heart and not figure out till later the only bit in common is a name."

I thought about her boys leaving her alone in an empty house with cats. I thought about her son calling her a crazy bitch.

Over her glasses, Mama peered at me. "You're a lonely little thing, aren't you?" she asked, not unkindly. "But if you suppose you can birth yourself a lifelong companion, think again."

The rightness of her hit me so hard I didn't know what to say, so I didn't.

"Children are wild magic," she continued. "Not a single one is yours. Folks assume you can mold them like God making Adam from the clay." She paused a minute. "And look how that turned out."

"It sounds lonely."

Mama scoffed. "The world's lonely." Then she shot a quick little glance, sharp and assessing. "And you only have children for a while. One hot minute, and then they're gone.

But listen. Sometimes you birth them, sometimes you get them, and sometimes you find them," she said. "But sometimes…"

"What?"

"Sometimes they find you."

🐈

Jess was home when I got back. As the days started to grow thin and cold, he worked less and less. By now, I had regulars who came for off-license haircuts and homemade facials, and that helped, but for months, we'd drawn hard on the money socked away for my college fund while Jess brooded on the couch.

"First," he said as soon as the door closed, "quit traipsing off to Mama's. Start helping around here." He jerked his chin at the dishes. "No more running about in the woods. That is, if that's really what you're doing. And speaking of help, you'll be glad to know I found this." He lifted his hand. Between his fingers dangled the envelope from the can where I'd kept Daddy's money.

🐈

It ended exactly like you'd suppose.

Or maybe not.

As that glorious green summer faded into fall and the leaves left, I stayed in the house and did chores, washed dishes, and washed them again. I folded shirts into precise squares and arranged them by color. Once or twice, hanging wash on the line, I would spot Mama lingering at the borders of the wood. I'd wave a hand to her and she to me, and I'd try to ignore that ache in my chest and the anger in my throat, so during the day, I hardly spoke at all, and at night, my mind wandered to the woods. I dreamed of Jess's father and his boots.

The house became too close for Jess and me. We scratched up against each other, poked one another with knees and elbows, danced around in doorways, opened cabinets in faces. Heaving himself from the couch one day, Jess paced to the fridge and peered inside.

"I gotta get the fuck away from here," he muttered.

"Sorry?"

"I have got," he said, biting the words, "to get the *fuck* away from here. You hear?" With a jingle of keys, he was out and gone. When he came back, he reeked of sweat and beer and a shampoo we didn't own.

Yeah, I know what you're thinking. And you're right.

In the forest grows an orange tangled plant the color of turmeric. Devil's hair, Mama named it. A parasite. It finds trees and inserts tendrils in the wood to suck it dry while the seed lives on and waits for another host.

I wondered what I'd have left to me when Jess was gone for good.

The next morning on November eve, I spotted a note tucked into my shoe, written in shaky and angular old woman's cursive.

"Come on by," it said. "Tonight."

🐾

Outside, the air was crisp as an apple. Jess had rolled in an hour ago, talking softly, supposing me asleep. As he murmured into the phone, his voice low, I noticed that lazy way he lounged against the wall, fingers dangling below his waistband, and said to myself, *Not long before he walks on out of here. Not long at all.*

He eased into bed, shifting a bit, and I waited until his breath took on that rasping sound of sleep. From above, the moon stared down round-bellied and full as the door clicked shut. Not looking back, I turned down the path to Mama's and wondered if Jess was watching from the window.

As I came to the trailer, I heard singing.

A circle of women had gathered in the field, that tamped-down spot I'd noticed by the dark and looming trees. Together they stood, hands lifted to the moon. I recognized a few. I'd styled their hair. The women wore it loose now, flowing down to their butt-splits, for each one was mother-bare and damn the autumn cold. And as I froze in place, I saw them reach to the sky and heard them call out the names of their need, and the cry was taken up and passed around until it became the need of them all.

Mama saw me. It was dark, and I'd drawn behind the pile of rusty parts where the white cat always sat in the sun patch, but Mama's eyes fixed on mine all the same. I froze like a deer at a cracked stick, for I had no idea what they would do, those mother-women with their wild long hair.

*eat me     welcome me in*
*or both*

I held my breath in that suspended time. And in my head, I heard Mama ask me plain as dirt, "You comin'?"

They welcomed me in. I raised my hands and called out what I needed.

🐈

"Shh," I whispered to Jess when I eased back into bed. My breasts pressed against his back, my nipples tight and cruel. I rolled him over, felt below. He came mostly awake and murmured assent, arching to the dark indifferent sky. "Your skin is cold," said Jess, but then found himself occupied by other things.

I was cold. So cold.

I warmed up soon.

🐈

In college, this professor—not the cat one—made an offhand remark that stuck. "Maternity," the professor said, "can be proven by evidence of the senses. Paternity, though? We're never so sure about that." This struck me as funny at the time and still does. When you see a baby head framed by the taut diamond of a woman's vagina, there's not much doubt it's coming out from her. But who put it in there to begin with? That's somewhat less than clear.

Jess wandered off when I was four months pregnant. Ever since that night, he'd found reasons to stay late and leave early. A job, he said. Some appointment. I let him walk away. There was less and less of him each passing day, like he was fading.

One afternoon, I found Grady sitting uncomfortably on the porch steps, twisting a worn snapback cap and looking up like a kicked dog. Jess had taken up with an old girlfriend, Grady said. From high school. Lived out in Bolivar. They'd been off and on for a long old time.

"And, well," muttered Grady, trying not to look at my belly, "Not like you were married or nothing."

I did indeed know what to say to that, but I didn't. "So," I said instead. "You'll be wanting your house back."

Grady stared at the ground, plump cheeks red in the thin daylight. "Well," he said. "I suppose, yeah. No real rush. I guess you'll go back home?"

"I guess so," I said, and let that spin out in the silence.

🐾

I did go home. In Mama's field, I got myself a small used trailer and put it where she wanted, by the woods. "You'll like it there," said Mama, and I did. From time to time, Mama ate supper at my place or hers, or we played cards with her friend Marylou, whose eyebrows were drawn with brown pencil, or hung out with the other women from the group. Passing each other at the park, a church social, or on the police station sidewalk selling bake sale cookies, we'd simply smile and nod.

And once a month, we'd gather in the field beneath the moon.

As the wheel of the year turned, I waxed and grew until my belly swelled like a second moon itself, all round and white. Mama lay hands on my bulge and probed. "Feels like a girl. 'Bout damn time," she sniffed, and shooed the cat from the couch so I could sit down, my legs splayed out to make room.

The funny thing about having a daughter is this. Before she's born, she's got all the eggs she'll ever have. Those eggs might drop during her period, grow into a child, or just stay put, but no matter what, before that daughter's born, her eggs are there. So while I carried her, I carried half my grandchild. And when my mother was pregnant with me, my child was inside her, at least my half. I imagined us, grandmother, mother, and child, nested inside each other like Russian dolls, each coming into the world through that taut diamond door.

And one dark night, she came. All that day, I'd cranked around the house, logy and restless, the child rising and dropping like a bowling ball in thick water. The moon rose above us, fat and bright in the field, and the women gathered and sang.

With a sudden clutch, something inside heaved and shifted down. I stumbled to my knees in the middle of the circle, hands grasping at grass as I saw the child was coming then and there. There would be no time for the doctor.

My back bent like a bow, and she pressed hard to get out. All that week, the bones of my pelvis had crunched and wiggled around, jangly and jury-rigged, as if held in place with spit and bubble gum. "Well, naturally," said Mama, pointing to her crotch. "There's no bone joining things together there. Only tough tendon that gets soft when the baby's due." She chuckled. "With Jess, I walked around like those thumb puppet toys where you push the base and the elastic holding them up goes slack, and they tumble down in pieces just like that."

Drawing in a breath, I sensed the women clustering around, telling me to breathe, to breathe, and with a shock, I remembered I remembered I

saw

*it*                    *them*

That thing in the forest. That first time.

13

That night when I'd raised hands to the sky and called my need, the women passed a cup from hand to hand and drank, and when the vessel came to me, Mama touched my wrist and said, "You sure you wanna? You don't have to, you know. This ain't Kool-Aid." She chuckled. "It wears off quickly enough, and no hangover, but until then…you'll feel like flying." I nodded and took it. When I raised the cup to my lips, I tasted fresh hexwort rank with a scent like semen.

And then the song, the song, the song was all around me and inside me, and

*then*

*there was a space and*

Above, dark tree-spears pierced the stars. The cosmos wheeled overhead, and a thousand years unfolded in the dark as I lay in the loam that tore apart my flesh and fed it to the trees and thirsty earth until I was the tree. Till I was thirsty earth.

And shadow.

Long eons later, I half-rose, gripping ground for balance. I shivered in the cold, but my head was clear as air. I knew where I was and when.

I'd flown far from the circle. The women had vanished by now, and I was deep in the forest alone. Through the trees glowed the little kitchen light over the sink in Mama's trailer, but it seemed far away, set at an unfamiliar wrong angle.

Between one step and another, I knew. The other way into the woods. Jess's father's path. I'd come down there. Seeking something.

And something sought me too.

As I tottered to my feet, I heard it move. The dark thing in the woods. The air grew thicker, sultry and close as it does in dreams when you try to run, my feet tangling and stubbing in the roots that clustered like conspirators trying to drag me down, and all the while the thing was

*Watching me. It's watching me it's*

Snap.

A stick-crack. A brush of a branch.

Low, nearly inaudible, a murmur came like a chant arising from the ground. A growl. In the back of my throat I tasted blood and the electric black-brown tang of musk. I wheeled about, trying to find an escape, but the presence was everywhere, above me and around, behind and before.

Then it blotted out the stars.

I turned and saw. My eyes slid over a shifting, formless shape I could not see with my eyes, not with my eyes—crude fleshy balls—but oh, good God, I saw it with my mind, with my blood, with some ancient sense I saw it, not with eyes, and I could only think

*so many so many oh there are so many not one but many many*

They were old, as old as earth and older. I would have called them by their name, but there was none.

They could not be named or even worshiped.

But, oh.

They could be asked. Oh yes. They could be asked.

I opened my arms to them. "Yes," I said. "I do."

There was a thrumming in my ears and the tang of copper pennies on my tongue. Between my legs, a flesh-scent rose like earth and sweat and death and holy things, and they were in me, in me, in me.

Or I was in them.

Or both.

R.A. Busby

On my knees in the field, held close by the women as I heaved and screamed, I pulled the baby out. With a cry, I reached between my legs and felt her head, the angle of her tiny jaw, and with a gush, the child slid out and tumbled on the grass, thick blue cord still throbbing with our blood, and I thought, *oh god she has no head she has no head she's just a thing*, for writhing at my knees was a grey ball streaked with gore, this creature that had slithered out of me.

But maternity can be proven by evidence of the senses.

Then Mama, with her deft hands, pierced the sac around the baby with a thumbnail, and the child kicked, sending a gush of water flowing into the grass. It smelled like desert rain. Like creosote.

"Born in the caul," said Marylou, breasts hanging down as she bent to gather the child. "That's a mark of second sight." Peering between the baby's legs, Marylou proclaimed, "A girl. A girl for her and all of us." She elbowed Mama. "'Bout damn time, don't you think?"

"Hmph. Can't say I didn't try," said Mama with a shrug.

Someone had taken the old crocheted afghan from the couch and wrapped it over my shoulders as they handed her to me. The child lay at my breast, nibbling my nipple with her tiny gums, and wearily I looked at her.

"Who is she?" I said, only half-aware, and Mama grasped my hand.

"Why," she said, "she's what you need. She's yours." Then she added, "For a while."

Just then the child unlatched, the weak and early milk dribbling down her chin, and smiled to see me. Her mouth was filled with tiny golden pinpricks, sharp tight clusters that grew along the ridges of her jaw like cholla thorns in place of human teeth.

I breathed in the desert smell of her, so strange, so marvelous, and brought her closer to my heart. She was mine, this child, this gift. For a while, at least.

In the moonlight, I could see her two eyes staring into mine. Into me.

My daughter's eyes were silver. Like the moon.

"Mama," she said, tiny lips moving. "Mama."

———————

R.A. Busby is author of several short stories including "Bits" (*Short Sharp Shocks* #43), "Cactusland" (*34 Orchard* #2), "Holes" (*Graveyard Smash*), and "Street View" (*Collective Realms* 2). She spends her spare time running in the wilderness with her dog and finding strange things to write about.

# PUTTING DOWN ROOTS

## BY KEILY BLAIR

Eliza returned to Ider, Alabama for the first time in twelve years, two days after her older sister's funeral. With the windows of her sedan rolled down, the air hummed, alive with heat and the songs of cicadas. The smell of rotting apples in the abandoned orchard and wet soil rose into the air, pervading her senses. Memories crept to the front of her mind, and she pushed them back down. She dabbed at the sweat on her face with a tissue, careful not to smudge her makeup. The tissue brushed against the stud in her left nostril, pulled at the ring in her brow. Despite her efforts, a single tear, black with mascara, ran down her face and plopped onto the tattoo of thorns circling her wrist.

The tattoo had been Ruth's idea. Her late sister thought they needed something edgy, rebellious—a reward for finally ditching Ider and striking it out on their own. A bracelet of rose thorns seemed perfect at the time—roses were Maw Maw Pearl's favorite. They'd kept in touch, she and Ruth, even after splitting up, calling monthly and meeting up once a year for coffee and for Eliza to talk about her schooling and then work in graphic design. Ruth never said much, just smiled and nodded. Not once had she mentioned Ider in those twelve years. Neither of them had.

Ruth had returned to the tiny, old house Maw Maw Pearl had raised them in, only to die. Maw Maw Pearl called Eliza to share the dreadful news during one of their weekly calls, revealing that Eliza missed the funeral. Ruth's wish for cremation wound up buried away like her body in the family

18

plot. Eliza, furious, packed her bags and headed to Ider with barely a word to her wife.

The long drive mellowed the rage. A hollowness formed inside Eliza, eating at her core. She grabbed a makeup removal wipe from her purse. As she worked to strip her face of the dark makeup she'd selected, her phone rang.

"I've been trying to call you for hours," Heather, her wife, said.

"I'm sorry," Eliza said.

"Are you okay? Do you need me to come there? It's only two hours away. Just send me the address."

"No," Eliza said.

It was too quick, too sharp. Silence hovered between them.

"Pearl wouldn't like that," Eliza said. "You know how she is."

Heather snorted back a surly laugh.

"You dressed up like you were going to some emo high schooler's Halloween party."

"It was stupid. I was angry."

"I know," Heather said. "Just call me if you need me. Please? Don't play Stone Girl today, okay?"

Eliza eyed the tattoo of a ring on her left ring finger. She sucked in a shaky breath.

"No Stone Girl," she said. "Just soft, squishy Eliza."

Once the call ended, Eliza stepped out of the car. The moment her feet touched the ground, she shuddered. Southern roots reached deep into Ider's soil so that Eliza's steps carried the weight of those tendons, straining to pull her into the earth along with her late sister. Ider called to her blood and made it sing with the slow, steady rhythm of the old hymns. There was a reason she'd never shared it with anyone, even her own wife.

There was a reason she and Ruth swore to never return.

Tall bushes lined the pathway, spotted with fragrant pink roses—her grandmother's favorite. One for each woman in the family, supposedly. A fresh one occupied a space near the

19

steps, right across from an empty space that would belong to Maw Maw Pearl once she finally "went to Jesus," as she liked to say. Fresh manure and potting soil lined the space under the new rose bush, their pungent odor reaching Eliza several yards out.

Maw Maw Pearl waited for Eliza in her wooden rocking chair—the same one Eliza and her sister had carved their initials into as children, right next to the initials of their mother, aunt, and two cousins. Her wrinkled hands closed a thick, red book and folded together in her lap. The sweet, earthy aroma of fresh-cut grass enveloped Eliza, and the sun caressed each section of exposed skin. Eliza's careful, slow steps kicked up little clouds of dust that clung to her ripped jeans—the same style of jeans that Maw Maw Pearl had beaten her with a belt over when she was a teenager.

Eliza eyed the patches of sweat that stained Pearl's yellow, floral print dress and ran down her face like the condensation on a glass of sweet tea. How long had Pearl sat in the sun, waiting for her? Another smell hit her, and she recognized it as that of a cooling cherry pie on the windowsill. A flash of guilt, hot and sharp, cut through Eliza. She'd made the extra effort to wear all her piercings, wear revealing clothes to show off her tattoos. Pearl's heart would break when she moved closer.

"Welcome home," Pearl said.

She flashed a smile that reached her eyes and concealed her crooked teeth from view, though it was only Eliza standing close enough to see. The neighbors would register the two of them as dots on the horizon. The miles that ran between each farm saw to that.

Eliza held out her arms for an embrace, smile shaky and unsure. Pearl rose on unsteady legs to pull her into a tight hug.

"I'm so sorry about Ruth," Pearl said. "I'm just glad she was here when it happened. We had a place for her in the family lot."

Eliza swallowed a lump in her throat. Tears pricked her eyes like thorns. She stepped away and swiped at them.

"I loved my sister," she said.

Ider was poison. It grabbed at Ruth's roots and ate away at her until nothing was left. Eliza would never let it snag her the way it took the others. The moment she'd done her duty and said goodbye to Ruth, she'd return to the city and forget that Ider existed. She'd answer the weekly calls from Pearl like a good granddaughter and only return for one final visit when Pearl kicked the bucket. That much, she didn't say.

"There's something I'd like you to see," Pearl said.

She opened the door, and Eliza, puzzled, stepped into the small house. The scent of the cherry pie filled the entire house. Her gaze searched for the unfamiliar object, raking over the TV, her late grandfather's favorite armchair, the overstuffed couch, the little girl—

"Maw Maw?" Eliza asked.

Her own voice surprised her, a child's voice. She knew, didn't she? Those eyes, the hair, the shape of the jawline. It was all Ruth.

"This is your niece," Pearl said. "Her name is Leah."

Eliza raced out of the house and turned a corner on the porch that surrounded the structure. She kneeled on the worn, wooden floorboards that creaked under her weight, panting. The humid air barely registered against the sudden cold sweat coating her skin. The memory of fire laced across her back, right along a scar from where Pearl's belt buckle broke the skin.

"Eliza?" Pearl asked.

Her voice rose into the air, a plea that calmed Eliza immediately. She knew better than to cry in front of Pearl. She wiped the sweat on her forehead against her sleeve, sucking in deep, careful breaths. When was the last time she'd had a panic attack?

She turned the corner to confront her sister's image once more.

"Hi, Leah," she said.

Leah's eyes dropped to the floor. Pearl's arm wrapped around her in a tight grip.

21

"It's so wonderful that you're home, Eliza," Pearl said. "You'll set a good example for Leah, won't you?"

🐾

"She can't stay here," Eliza said.

Leah's cries drifted downstairs. The young girl trudged off to bed an hour ago, and her sobs hadn't ceased since. Eliza sipped at the herbal tea Pearl made, tasting the hints of rose and citrus.

"Why on earth not?" Pearl asked.

Her hands worked a ball of dough, kneading and pulling. Eliza's guarded gaze observed those old, weathered hands, recalling the time Pearl hacked away at her hair with a pair of sewing shears after a boy had commented on how pretty it looked. Pearl had tugged and tugged while Eliza shrieked in pain. Those hands couldn't have Leah.

"I've been trying for a baby. Taking in my sister's daughter is natural. It's like a gift from God." The word soured on her tongue.

Pearl hesitated.

"You should've never left Ider," she said. "Looks like you've forgotten God frowns upon sinners. Children need to be raised in a stable home with a God-fearing family. Especially young girls if they're to become the flowers society asks them to be."

Eliza's jaw clenched. In Pearl's eyes, women were flowers—delicate things of beauty meant to be seen, not heard. Before she could respond with words she'd likely regret, Pearl set down the dough and turned to her.

"Tell you what," she said. "One night. Spend one night at home, and if you want her, you can have her. I'll sign over custody without a fuss. Just do an old woman a favor and let her spend some time with her lost lamb."

Eliza recognized the tone. Pearl's voice always softened once she caused a hurt—burn the flesh, apply the salve.

"I don't want to stay here."

"Just one night to let me pray on it," Pearl said. "Who knows? This girl might be the key for your repentance."

Eliza sighed, holding her head in her hands. "One night. I need to call Heather."

Pearl's careful smile slipped at the name, but she said nothing.

🐈

Eliza woke in the night to a sharp, terrible pain. She fought through the cobwebs of sleep, stumbling to her feet. A howl of pain rose from her chest as she fell onto the bed once more, toes curled in agony. Pain danced up from her feet to her calves, almost as though something moved just under the skin.

She fumbled for the lamp next to her bed just as a light came on in the hallway. Footsteps creaked toward her. The light turned on, and Eliza hurried to investigate the source of the pain.

Dark, purple splotches covered her feet. She bit her lip to hold back another scream as the skin appeared to move. Parasites? Had she picked up something on that last vacation with Heather?

"Eliza?"

The small voice snatched her attention. Eliza covered her feet with a blanket.

"Go to bed, Leah," she said. "I'm okay. Just some bad dreams."

The girl waited at the doorway, Ruth's eyes staring out from her face, as knowing as Ruth's had always been.

"Please," Eliza said.

Leah shrugged and returned to her room, but Eliza didn't remove the covers until the door closed. She bolted from bed onto her aching feet. Every movement in the old house led to creaks and groans. Twelve years ago, Pearl would've woken up from any of those sounds. Now, she appeared to sleep through anything.

Eliza cast a glance over her shoulder to make sure that no one followed her. A lump rose in her throat, sending her into a fit of gagging and coughing. Her empty teacup rested on the counter, and she grabbed it and filled it with water from the tap. She swallowed hard, quick gulps, but the thing in her throat rose anyway. Another cough shook her body, sending a spray of water and pink onto the floor. This time, when she coughed, her hand shot out to catch the object lodged in her throat.

A wad of fragrant pink petals.

They scattered as her hand fell to her side. Her voice, frantic, grew to a shout. "Maw Maw!"

The floorboards above the kitchen creaked as Pearl shifted out of bed. Eliza listened for more movement, but the old woman moved like a ghost. Her arms wrapped around her chest, only for pinpricks of pain to follow. She lifted her black shirt to find rows of thorns sprouting from her skin, sharp and wet with blood. Fingers plucked at the thorns, attempting to pull them free. They refused to budge, attached firmly to their fleshy prison. Blood oozed from tiny cuts in her hands as the thorns shredded them.

Before she could scream again, a hand clapped over her mouth.

"Hush, Eliza," Pearl said.

She guided Eliza with surprising strength through the front door. The screen slammed behind them, and Eliza broke free. Blood soaked through her shirt, casting a dark stain. Her breaths came in rapid pants.

"Maw Maw," Eliza said. "What's going on? What's happening to me?"

"The same thing that happened to your mother," Pearl said. "And Ruth. You can't leave Ider, dear. None of us can."

She swept her arm outward, drawing Eliza's eyes to the rose garden.

"In time, we all return home, and it won't let us leave again."

"This is crazy," Eliza said.

Pain surged through her legs, buckling them under her. A wet, tearing sound accompanied the protrusion of two dark objects from each foot. Her fingers reached to grasp them, pulling in frantic, twisting motions without a second thought. Flesh bloomed around them, blood running down her heels. Fingernails dug into the objects for purchase. They were hard, rough, yet somehow flexible. She bent and twisted them until Pearl smacked her hands away.

"You're putting down roots, dear," Pearl said. "Best to leave them alone if you want to remain strong and healthy like your mother and Ruth."

She swept out her arm once more, gesturing to the two bushes at the end. This time, Leah stood in the doorway, rubbing her eyes.

Eliza shoved Pearl aside and limped over to Leah. She grasped the young girl by the shoulders.

"You get out of here," she said. "The moment you can fend for yourself, leave this place, and never come back."

Leah's gaze drifted down toward the bloody footprints Eliza left behind, eyes growing wide. "You're like Mama."

"So are you," Eliza said. "This will happen if you leave and return. Ider wants to take everything from you, and you won't let it. Swear to me."

Leah's voice was small. "I swear."

Eliza loosened her grip on Leah's shoulders after one final squeeze. She turned to face Pearl, whose mouth twisted into a grimace.

"You're not keeping me," Eliza said.

She ran to her car, feet sticking to the bare earth. The car's tires slumped close to the ground, deflated. A quick inspection revealed tears in each of the tires. Eliza cursed and turned to the forest at the property. Where was the town line? Where did Ider's soil end? She raced toward the trees, plowing through tall grass. As a child, she'd feared the tall grasses and the copperheads and ticks that plagued them. Now, she ran through the black night with complete abandon.

The thick, humid air whipped at her face. Adrenaline pumped through her veins, surging her forward even as the pain in her feet shot through her legs with electric intensity. Her soles stuck to the ground, and she yanked herself free with a thick, tearing sound. Blood splattered the earth each time her roots broke as though it pumped through them.

She fell to her knees, choking and coughing up wads of petals streaked with blood. Her eyes rolled in their sockets, taking in the surrounding darkness, struggling to remember.

Where was the border?

The roots stretched toward the earth, elongating and slithering out of her feet. Itchiness spread over her skin, and she lifted the sleeve of her nightshirt to find her skin darkening, hardening into bark. A low moan slipped through her lips. She struggled to her feet and took off into the night once more.

An owl hooted in a nearby tree, and small creatures scurried in the forest's underbrush. The nightshirt clung to Eliza's changing form, damp from humid air and sweat. A taste of dirt lingered on her tongue. The night didn't recognize Eliza's plight. It went on as it always had, as it had the evening Pearl brought Ruth and Eliza to the edge of the Mason property and—

The border.

*This is as far as you go,* Pearl had said. *Play as far from home as you want, but don't you dare trespass on Mason property.*

It had seemed silly back then. An electric fence surrounded the Mason property line to keep their horses in and potential trespassers out. Eliza once reached to pet one horse that came near, only to wake up on the ground with pain throbbing in her arm. It hadn't been the easiest way to find out the fence was electric, but Pearl liked them to find things out the hard way. The incident fueled Ruth's curiosity, and the sisters spent nearly an hour by the fence, touching it with blades of grass and giggling at the light shocks before Pearl caught them and beat them until their backsides were raw.

"Eliza?" Pearl's voice rang through the forest.

Eliza scrambled to her feet, hissing under her breath to hold back another cry or scream. She ran a few feet, but the pain stopped her. She trudged through the thick undergrowth, teeth gritted together in a grimace of agony. Each step stuck to the earth as the roots sought purchase in the soil. Eventually, the light of the moon shone through the thick canopy of trees. The fence lay somewhere in the dark, and Eliza would follow it until she found the end.

Then she would step over the border.

"Eliza, don't fight it."

Eliza broke free from the forest. She made her way toward the fence, only to find that her feet no longer budged. The roots stretched into the ground, worming through the earth, branching out. A scream of frustration tore from her throat. Her legs twisted, trying to uproot her body. Fingers clawed at her feet, tugging at the roots.

"It hurts if you fight it," Pearl said.

The voice came directly behind Eliza. She buried her palms in her eyes and sucked in a deep, shaky breath.

"Why, Maw Maw?"

"Disobedient daughters and wives need to be punished," Pearl said. "God asks us for obedience, and you have run straight into sin. Now, you'll be the beauty you were always meant to be. The quiet, obedient beauty."

The undergrowth rustled behind Pearl, and Leah sprang forth from it. She dashed over to Eliza in awkward strides, balancing a shovel that glinted in the moonlight. It rammed down against the roots spreading from Eliza's heels, and Eliza screamed in pain. Again and again, Leah stabbed at the protrusions, ignoring Eliza's pleas. Though the sensation threatened to bring Eliza to her knees, the roots kept her in place.

"Stop it," Pearl said.

There was a struggle, a soft thud as Pearl fell into the grass. The pain began again as Leah continued.

Finally, Eliza broke free from the ground. She collapsed forward on her hands and knees, a fiery pain searing her feet and legs. Black encroached on her vision, but she could just make out the wires of the electric fence. No time to travel the length of it. Her hands reached for the cables.

Nothing.

Eliza pushed the wire aside and rolled under the fence. The pain slipped into a dull ache as bark shed from her arms, revealing raw, red skin underneath. Wild, rapid pants slipped through her lips. The odors of dirt and blood filled her nose, and she gagged.

Leah followed.

"Leah!" Pearl said.

Leah didn't look back. She helped Eliza to her shaky feet and slipped Eliza's cellphone into her hand. Eliza, however, cast her gaze back to Pearl. Her eyes narrowed in the darkness, taking in the woman's features full of anger and hurt—a reflection of her own suffering. The scar on her back burned with phantom pain. One hand rested on Leah's shoulder, urging her toward the road. Pearl's silence hung over Eliza like a heavy curtain, weighing down each step. Together, Eliza and Leah headed home.

The wounds kept Eliza in the hospital for a long time and in physical therapy even longer. Eventually, Heather stopped asking questions, and Eliza never offered information. Grueling physical therapy, as well as caring for Leah, kept them both occupied. Pearl never showed up for the custody hearing, and Eliza and Heather adopted Leah soon after.

Eliza stroked the scars on the soles of her feet one morning while she assumed Heather slept, only for Heather to roll over, eyes still closed.

"You're doing it again," she said.

"Doing what?" Eliza threw the covers back over her feet.

"Obsessing," Heather said. "About Ider. I don't know what happened, Eliza, but can't you just call Pearl up and talk to her? Or maybe visit? I'd go with you."

Eliza's voice dropped to a whisper. "I already cut my roots," she said. "I'm never going back."

---

Keily Blair is a creative writing student at UT Chattanooga, where her nonfiction won the Creative Writing Nonfiction Award. Her fiction has appeared in magazines such as *The Dread Machine, Trembling With Fear, Night to Dawn,* and is upcoming in *Dream of Shadows* and others. She is currently at work on a fantasy novel and a collection of essays about being a person with bipolar disorder. She lives with her husband, dog, cat, and two guinea pigs. You can find more details about her work at www.keilyblair.com.

# Bad Apple

## by Louise Pieper

Truth is, Uncle Amos told me what he did, up where Whitlaw Wood rubs itself against the orchard, was a necessary evil. I believe him. He had a hard time dying and it's a rare man who lies at such a time. Besides, them woods have always been what you might call unsavory. The orchards...well, they ain't so sweet neither.

Course, there's plenty of folk happy to blame any trouble that falls on the Hollow right square on the late, but never lamented, Amos Polkinghorne the third and last of his name.

My name's Tace Bolley, and I'm his baby sister's baby girl. Mama gave the usual Mary Lou and DeeDee and Willadean and what have you to my six sisters. She called me Tace on account of wishful thinking and it meaning silent. And I guess I were always more likely to shut my mouth and try to work things out than most of my kin. Bolleys and Bridmores, Finches, Dewlaps and Mackellars—I got me a whole mess of cousins spilling out of the Hollow all the way to Averson's Cross and out west to Pine Creek.

Ain't no more Polkinghornes though.

Makes it easy work to blame trouble on Amos. Don't hardly raise a sweat to make a scapegoat of a scapegrace old man who was cold and bitter as the grave long before he was laid under his six feet of dirt. Easy, that is, 'til it comes to that quiet hour on the cusp of dawn, when Death and Sleep finish up their drinking and call for the last roll of the dice to see who gets to carry off the evening's souls.

Might raise a sweat then.

Course, most of my kin would shame the devil out of his britches, so maybe I'm wrong, and they don't let it worry them. Maybe.

I found Cousin Beulah at my back steps while the sun was busy burning the night's sweat off the grass. She let her gaze take in my work boots and my old jeans, then she raised them big doe eyes to me and said, "You got trouble in the orchard. Andy Davey's done got himself a shovel."

It was a warning, and don't think I weren't grateful for it. But Beulah's painted lips twisted over the words the way all them Finches have, and I was damned if I could tell why she'd come. Still…

"Right nice of you to let me know," I said with a nod.

"Only neighborly, cousin." She smirked and added, casual-like, "Zeke's with 'em."

Neighborly, was it? Last I minded, my cousin was sweet on Zeke Mackellar, for all he was the deputy's boy.

I grabbed my coat and pulled the door closed. Made damn sure Beulah heard the lock catch, too; I ain't green like a Bridmore. I looked away as I pushed my arms into the sleeves of my duster. Didn't want her watching my face as its cold weight settled over me.

"Zeke, huh?" I hoped my sneer would distract her from thinking too hard about wearing coats on hot days. "Ain't you got nothing better to do with him?"

She raised her shoulders, making them hollows beside her neck that always put me in mind of brittle-boned little birds.

31

"Papaw Mac sent him. He don't want that fool Andy spooking the herd." Her mouth went sly again. "Be a right shame if he got hurt. Deputy won't like it."

Truth is, the deputy'd want blood. But that was one thing and not the same as Beulah feeling beholden if she asked for my help. Well, she could smile and pout and try and sidle around what old Granny Dewlap called the proper ways. I reckoned she'd keep.

"Coming?" I asked.

She shook her head. "Don't want to get my shoes wet."

Anyone out in them fool heels was after more trouble than wet feet, you ask me, but nobody did, so I set off across the yard, leaving her to pick her way home best she could.

I'd hit my stride by the time I reached the crab apple. I checked everything was buttoned down and cleared the dry-stone wall into the orchard at a run. Felt it, though. That jolt through my feet and the answering kick from the pocket of my coat. *Malus sylvestris* giving way to *Malus pumila*, but malice all the same. Malice in the soil and in the wood.

Still, it's Idared and Grenadiers and Maiden's Blush in the lower orchard, and they're sleepy enough. Domesticated, you might say. Good for cooking, though the Blush has a crisp little bite. I laid my hand over my inside pocket and kept running.

"Orchard won't have you," Uncle Amos had told me.

"Because I'm a girl?" I'd puffed, full of indignation.

"Trees won't stay tame for none but a Polkinghorne," he'd crowed. "Papaw Jeb seen to that."

I'd tried my luck, when I was fourteen and full of warm pie, cold cider, and foolishness. An apple is an apple, I'd thought—it ain't nothing but a piece of fruit. I'd gone alone

into the orchard. Well, an apple is an apple, but an apple tree...
Turned out that was a different matter.

Uncle Amos dragged me clear before I was much worse
than half-senseless. He called me Doubtful after that, which
made him grin, but it weren't something that raised a smile with
me. Only a fool don't ever have doubts, and I'm no fool. And
once I knew how things stood I just needed to find a way to
work around it.

That's what Bolleys do. Work around and around 'til we
get what we want.

I ran through the Melbas and Melroses and Mollie's
Delicious and Shacklefords and the Westfield Seek-No-
Furthers that my great-granddaddy planted in the middle
orchard. Eating apples. The weight of their regard settled on
me the same way my uncle's hands came to press on my
shoulders some nights in my fever dreams. Cold and heavy.
Pitiless in that pause as he reckoned whether he'd rather choke
the life from me with his bare hands, or trouble to draw the
bone-handled knife he wore on his belt and drive it hilt-deep
into my back.

Uncle Amos used to laugh at the way Mama pushed me
onto him.

"She thinks I'll leave the orchard to you, Doubtful." The
old man's grin had nigh on cracked his face. "Maybe I will, all
the good it'd do. You ain't no Polkinghorne."

"Mama was," I'd reminded him. "Makes me half
Polkinghorne, don't it?"

He'd sneered. "You're a Bolley, girl, through and
through."

"I could change my name, legal-like." I'd shrugged. Lord,
I had cousins who'd married and changed their name more
often than I changed my coat.

33

"Think you can worm your way in that easy?"

Amos had laughed some more, but it got me thinking. Not on deeds and lawyers and tides of paper that drowned the truth, though plenty of my Bolley kin knew them tricks. I'd thought about apples and how you could find a worm right at the heart of the fruit. Weren't nothing the tree could do about it.

I just needed to find the way in.

Like I needed to stop whatever fool notion had taken hold of Andy Davey. I kept running, though I was blowing like a green colt put to a steeplechase. Wouldn't do to stop. The orchards ran up the side of the Hollow, and Whitlaw Wood loomed at the top, a dark smear blighting the horizon. The men'd be at the gap, where the woods and one spiteful old Kittageskee apple tree conspired between them to tumble the stones.

I'd have slowed for the gate, but the branches whispered a warning against it. The intrusion ran like poison through their leaves. The trees just about tolerated me and that only because of what I carried. As well Andy hadn't brung an axe.

I caught my foot as I vaulted the wall and stumbled into the top orchard. Didn't go down, for all I staggered, and I swear the nearest Smokehouse threw out a root hoping to trip me up. The cider trees were heavy with fruit—rare and terrible Saxon Priests and the Wolf Rivers whose kin grow wild in the back-country thickets of the Shenandoah Valley. I kept a wary eye on the great, malevolent globes of the Twenty Ounce with their broad red striping. I reckoned them stripes was nature's way of warning you off, same as with wasps and tigers.

Past those curse-weighted limbs and there's Andy himself and his fool friends prodding at the soil the other side of the wall. Zeke Mackellar hung back, looking like death eating a cracker. Figure he'd realized he was smack bang between the devil and a damn hard rock. Whitlaw Wood bristled at his back and at his feet the orchard wall tumbled down like a pretty girl's hair—all sweet invitation until you got close enough to see the shotgun she was hiding behind her.

I slowed and stepped into the blade of sunlight that lit the wall, slicing between the orchard and the woods. The heat of it struck my head, set my scalp prickling while my plait pressed heavy on my neck, like I was a dog trying to tuck its tail between its legs. I put out my hands, real calm-like.

"Morning Zeke. Andy." I nodded. "Boys."

"Tace Bolley." Andy hawked and spat onto one of the fallen rocks. The top orchard kind of... flexed. Zeke twitched like a ferret in a trap, but Andy didn't seem to notice. "We got us a problem."

"You sure do," I said, but Andy paid that no mind neither. He's like that. Narrower than the barrel of a twelve gauge. He don't like the way I dress like a man, talk like a man, like I got a right to do what I please. Don't like the way I stepped into my uncle's shoes, the way I live alone, the way I don't pay him no mind. He don't like nothing he knows about me, I reckon, and I'm glad he knows so little.

He put up his chin.

"My Luanne been having bad dreams about this here wall."

Well damn it to hell and back on a turkey because the Davey's are thick as tree stumps, but Luanne's mama was a Dewlap, and everyone knows them girls got the Sight. Sweat slicked my skin under my too-hot coat.

"Ain't nothing—" I started but Andy cut me off, shaking his head.

35

"Tace Bolley," he repeated, "you know, and I know, something ain't right. My Luanne—"

"Y'all know these woods." I cut across his molasses drawl easy as he'd nipped off my budding protest. I started scraping the ground at the base of the wall with the side of my boot. "Truth is, you don't want to be telling your little girl what Old Amos done to keep what's in there—" I nodded over their shoulders and Zeke flinched. "—out of the Hollow."

Andy pursed up his fat lips again, like to spit out the idea of my uncle doing anything that might be mistaken for a civic duty.

"But y'all know," he muttered, "old sins throw long shadows."

Zeke shivered. "Them woods ain't safe, Andy. We oughta—"

"Whitlaw Wood ain't the problem. This here wall's the problem."

Andy jabbed the shovel into the soil and the tremor it raised knocked loose another stone. Zeke cursed and the others shifted like hound dogs watching a boomer, but I couldn't spare them no mind. The ground had gone soft under the side of my boot like a cloth sack full of chitlins. I'd been hoping to turn over some dry old cat bone to convince Andy his Luanne was right, but that weren't nothing for him to worry his block head about. Instead, I'd cleared myself a green patch that weren't grass.

Uncle Amos wore that same moss-green jacket for more years than I knowed him. Nasty old thing reminded me of a mangy dog. Smelt like one, too, when it got wet. Smelt worse now.

Damned if I hadn't put him six feet down, with nine needles to keep him down, but what was that to a Kittageskee whose roots probably reached clear to Hell?

Zeke choked, catching the stench of it; that white-hot reek of putrefaction as the too-thin soil gave up its vapors to the sun's prying rays. I clapped a hand to my pocket and stepped over it, every hair on my body rising, afeared my uncle's bony hand would break through the dirt and grab me. It'd be just like the old bastard to try to pull me down.

"Shootfire!" Andy gasped. "What in hell is that kyarn stink?"

I opened my lying Bolley mouth to spill excuses about dead critters and necessary evils, anything but the truth about what that damned tree had brought to the surface. Anything but admit that my uncle's coffin, down in the cemetery, held nothing more than an Amos-weight of soil. Anything but risk Andy and his boys seeing what I'd done by the light of the last Sap Moon to the last of the Polkinghornes.

"Truth is—" I said and the soil by Andy's shovel split open, spilling a horde of jewel-bright beetles into the light. They pushed aside the dirt, clawing over each other with their hair-tufted, black legs. Fat, metal-green bodies shimmered, and them copper-covered wings looked like ancient shields pinned to emerald tanks. Common pests, I been told, but ain't much common comes out of Whitlaw Wood. Each summer they get bigger and meaner, and these were about the size of suckling pigs.

I swear I never thought I'd be glad to see one of them bugs.

I ain't never heard a man scream like Andy Davey did when one scuttled onto his boot. He laid into it with that shovel, and one of his boys, who ain't the sharpest knife in the drawer, starts up with a holler and a stomp. The other, dumber than a coal bucket, pulled out his pistol and shot the bug his friend's stomping right through his buddy's foot.

Zeke staggered back from their ruckus, and I was sore tempted to let him go, but I didn't want Beulah to witch me. I lunged, bruised my thighs on the wall, and grabbed the front of his shirt.

"Not the woods, Zeke," I said.

Them bugs reared up, waving the hooks on their skinny, chitinous legs, like they was cussing at the sky. Then they lifted their glossy copper shields and spread their wings, and I recalled there weren't nothing the apple trees liked less than jewel bugs, less it was pharaohs or coddle moths. Behind me the air pressed in, tight and angry, as if the orchard were a banshee about to start wailing.

"Hold on," I shouted, shoving Zeke down on his side of the wall.

I hit the ground hard; felt it split under me. A hot wind slammed me into the wall near to quick enough to spare me the stink of what I'd landed in. The trees shrieked and a hail of sticks pelted my head and back. I turned my face and stared straight at five flesh-tattered finger bones poking from the soil.

I ain't ashamed to own I screamed right along with them trees. Weren't a wind in the world strong enough to stop me from jerking away, grabbing up a stone and pounding it down on them bones again and again, like I was driving iron nails into soft, white pine. Uncle Amos was dead, I knowed it. There's no coming back from what I did to him. I knowed that, too.

Still, I beat him down seven times and when I was done, I piled another stone on top and then another to keep him down. I stood, to fetch a fourth, and cursed to find I was shaking worse'n I had the night the orchard gave me a walloping. I put a hand to the wall to steady myself, and Zeke said, "You reckon a twister?"

Damned if I hadn't forgot them fools was right there, on the other side of the wall.

I straightened up and looked around. The bugs were smashed or gone, blown into the woods. The boys had toppled like bowling pins, but Andy Davey was standing. He swung up that shovel and grinned right at me like he'd just won a pig, and my innards ran cold. The apple trees leaned in, and I clenched my fists to stop myself from grabbing hold of what was in my pocket.

"Shootfire, Tace Bolley," Andy said through his smile. "I ain't never heard you scream like a girl before. Guess you don't like them bugs much, neither."

I licked my bone-dry lips and croaked, "Ain't real fond, no."

"Ain't no wonder Luanne's dreams been so bad," he said.

"Ain't no wonder," I repeated, "between them big stink bugs and twisters."

I waited a breath and another. Andy shook his fool head, and one of the boys muttered something about getting his foot cleaned up. I watched the blood drip off his boot and soak easy and deep into the soil. I let my hands open, real slow, like blossoms unfurling beside me, as they helped him to his feet.

"You'll fix that wall?" Andy said.

"Oh, I'll fix it," I promised.

He nodded, like that was a tough job seen to, and I watched them shuffle off. One, two, three... I counted the bloody prints they pressed into the soil until they reached the corner of the orchards and headed into the Mackellar pastures.

Louise Pieper

Then I turned back to face the apple trees.

"That oughta fix it good," I told them. "That and the libation I'll bring y'all tonight."

Ain't nothing like fresh blood to keep that wall strong and them apples sweet.

Mama was a Polkinghorne and I knowed enough about apples to reckon the way of grafting a scion. I slipped my hand inside my coat and patted the crusted, cloth-bound organ I'd carried there since I cut it out of my uncle's chest. My name is Tace Bolley but I have the heart of a Polkinghorne.

You can be sure about that.

———————

Louise Pieper has been accused of having too many books, a weird sense of humor, and an unsophisticated palate. It's been said she's too smart for her own good, reads too much, laughs too loud, and wears too much black. It's even whispered that she was born in a tent, keeps her heart in an iron-bound box, and refers to herself in the third person... Such feckless scandalmongering—she was born in a hospital. Pieper's a librarian and lexophile who lives in Australia's bush capital. Find out more at www.louisepieper.com.

# BEATING SEVENTEEN

## BY G. LLOYD HELM

Seventeen Williams wasn't a native of Big Spring, so he was viewed with suspicion most of the time. And he had a funny name. Who gives a child a number instead of a name? But Seventeen insisted he got the name because he was the last of seventeen children, and his mother hadn't known what else to call him.

No matter what the truth was, the man had a kind of an aura about him. He was tall and skinny to the point of emaciation, with hands and feet that seemed too big for the rest of him. His eyes glistened like oily coal, and anyone who dared to look into those eyes for too long would swear they saw fires burning down deep in them.

He had a crow that often sat on his shoulder. Most everyone had seen him talking to the bird one time or another, and some even swore they had heard the crow talking back. Of course, that was probably just a story, but what wasn't a story was Seventeen's phenomenal luck with dice.

Max Tilden's general store had always doubled as sort of gamblers' refuge, but when Seventeen showed up, the place grew from a refuge to a magnet. Anyone in the whole county with money and a taste for chance began showing up at Tilden's. Some nights so many men piled into the back room, they had to kneel shoulder to shoulder around the blanket where the dice rolled.

The night always had its winners and losers, but the most consistent winner was Seventeen Williams, and the most consistent loser was Cull Potter—and that rankled Cull.

"I'm gonna beat that Seventeen," Cull Potter said one day to a trio of men sitting with their feet up on the porch rail of Tilden's General Store. "Yes, Sir. I'm gonna. I'm gonna bust his luck once and fer all." Cull's brag was empty. No one ever beat Seventeen Williams at dice, at least not for long.

"And how you gonna do that?" Jake Ellis asked, barely covering his contempt for Potter. "Seventeen's luck can't be broke. Could maybe take an ax to Seventeen hisself—naw. Wouldn't work neither. Ax'd probably slide off."

All the men laughed except Potter. His face crimsoned at the taunting. "I'll beat him. Just you wait."

"Shore ya will. You always do like you say you're gonna, don't cha?" Ellis goaded. The others laughed even more. Potter was famous for being all brag and no do.

Cull turned from the three on the porch and stomped into the store. Max Tilden had only half heard what had gone on outside, but he could see from Cull's expression the boys had called his bluff again. "Afternoon." He rolled the strong, black cigar from one side of his mouth to the other. "Right warm, ain't it?" He brushed the beads of sweat from his bald head as if to emphasize the truth of his words.

"Warm enough," Cull snapped and fell silent. Suddenly he said, "Max, do you think Seventeen's dice is loaded or somethin'?"

The question surprised the shopkeeper, so he thought a bit before answering. "Naw, I'd say not. If they are, he done it hisself. I sold him them dice to begin with, and they was good clean stock. I don't think he could load 'em without it showing. 'Sides, if they was loaded, they'd work for anybody. Only one ever wins much with 'em is Seventeen."

"I reckon. Still, it don't seem right, him being the only one wins when we shoot craps," Potter said, not quite whining.

"He ain't the only one wins. Ed and me and Jake and Theo—all of us wins some. Even you."

"Some." Potter rapped his knuckles on the counter. "But who walks out a winner alla time? Whose pockets is lined with most of the money that floats in and out of your back room?"

Max chuckled. "Yeah, I gotta say, mostly yer right."

Cull leaned on the counter for a while, deep in thought. "Max, is my credit good?"

Max took the cigar out of his mouth and looked at the chewed end as though it had begun to taste nasty. "You all that short of cash?"

"Not exactly, but I ain't got enough for what I want right now."

Max shoved the cigar back into his mouth and rolled it around, eyeing Potter. Cull paid his bills, but often long past the time they should have been. "All right, I reckon." He said at last, as though the saying hurt him.

Potter sprang to life. "Then gimme a twenty-pound sack o' flour, five-pound o' sugar, and five of dry pinto beans."

Max looked him over, then shrugged and complied.

The list went on: canned peaches and pineapple; dried apricots; the end of a bolt of calico cloth; three spools of thread; five feet of thong leather; three twists of the best chewing tobacco in the store.

If Max felt unsure of Potter before, it was nothing compared to the mistrust he felt now. "What in hell are you gonna do, Cull? Leave the country?" Tilden wasn't opposed to free spending, but the story was different when it was on his cuff.

"I'm fixin' to beat Seventeen. That's what I'm gonna do. Them dice of his may be square, but square or not, I'm gonna get his money this time 'stead of the other way round. Now, le'me see here..." Cull passed his eyes over the goods stacked on the counter. He shoved his hair back out of his face and said, "that oughta do 'er, Max—'cept one thing." He flashed his snaggle-toothed grin, and a lock of sandy hair fell back in his eyes.

Tilden knew what else Potter wanted and grimaced at the thought. "How much do ya want?"

"Two jugs," Cull said.

Tilden winced but got the jugs. "I don't hafta tell ya to be careful where you show them jugs around. Royce would nail me to this counter if some long-nose revenue agent was ta bust up his still."

"Don't worry about it." Cull winked and picked up the jugs, shaking them to see if they were full, which annoyed Tilden. "I'll bring my pick-up 'round back, and we can load this stuff."

The sun was all the way down when Cull Potter knocked on the door of Seventeen Williams' ramshackle shanty. A noise like rattling bones came from above, and Cull looked up to see Seventeen's pet perching on the point of the roof, the bird a silhouette against the darkening blue of evening.

Seventeen came to the door, and a grin split his bony face when he saw Cull held a jug of Royce's best moon in front of him. "Glad to see ya, Cull." He stepped back from the doorway and motioned Potter in. "What brings you here?"

"Just thought how I'd like to share a nip with a friend, and you come right to my mind." Potter gave a weasley grin. He placed the jug in the center of the table and sat down without being invited.

Seventeen looked at him for a moment then went and lit a coal-oil lamp. Its light shone too sulphur yellow for comfort and barely pushed the shadows out of the shack.

"Kind of ya." Seventeen sat down across from Potter and glanced at the jug. "I figured after Saturday you'd not even be talkin' to me."

Potter tried to appear shamefaced. "Reckon I was a little hot then, but—what the hell. Ain't nothin' but money. I'll get it back, maybe." Cull hoped Seventeen didn't see the gleam in his eyes or the grin that tried to come to his face.

Seventeen blinked but didn't move to drink from the jug sitting on the table between them. "Now then," he said, "what do ya really want?"

"Nothin', Seventeen. Nothin'. Just to tip a little moon with ya. Go 'head. Have some." Potter uncorked the jug and, seeing the other was still hesitant, lifted it to his mouth and swigged mightily from it. He set the jug down with a thump and wiped his mouth with the back of his hand. "Right fine moon," he said with the slightest burr in his voice.

Seventeen's heavy-lidded eyes glittered as they dipped from Potter to the jug. His big hand twitched in his lap and rose to the jug's handle. He lifted it, sniffed the mouth, then took a small sip. His eyes widened in pleasure, then he took a proper pull at the jug before placing it back on the table. "'Tis good squeeze," he agreed but then said, "Now then, what did ya really come here for?"

"You just ain't gonna believe I got no other reason, huh?"

"You don't never go 'round nowhere's unless you want something, so what is it ya want?"

Potter tried to look offended but failed. He lifted the jug and took another small taste. "Well—I'll tell ya. I figured maybe if I drink outen the same jug as you, and spend some time around ya, maybe some of your luck'll rub off on me. That's the real reason," he hesitated, "and maybe to ask ya if I could carry yer dice a while." He brought the jug to his lips and drank, then returned it to the table.

Seventeen glared at him from across the gloom, then swiped the jug up from the table and swigged. "Get some of my luck, huh?"

Cull sighed. "Yep. I figure you got more'n any man I ever seen. More'n enough for you and me both."

Seventeen laughed slow and deep. The sound sent a prickly chill up Potter's back. "I ain't got no special luck. I just tell the dice what to do, and they does it."

Potter shrugged. "Then it won't matter whether I carry 'em or not. Won't hurt you, and might help me. So how 'bout it?"

Seventeen grunted and shook his head. "One man's good luck is another's bad sometimes."

"Sometimes."

"Might be bad luck for you."

"Don't reckon it could be a lot worse."

Seventeen leaned back in his seat. "You determined to carry 'em, huh?"

"If you're willing." Cull tilted the moonshine to his mouth, watching Seventeen over the shoulder of the jug. After a moment he said, "Well? Can I carry 'em? I'll leave the jug all fer you, if ya let me."

Seventeen raked his hand over the black bristles darkening his chin. "All right. Don't think it gonna do you any good, but if ya want, all right. But don't be telling it around that I done this for ya, or everybody'll be wanting me to do it. And you make sure I get 'em back before Saturday night so's nobody sees ya give 'em back."

"Sure, sure, Seventeen. I'll do that. I'll bring 'em back to ya Saturday afternoon or maybe before." Cull tried to be ingratiating and kept his eyes lowered, not wanting Seventeen to see the look of satisfaction lurking in them.

Seventeen stood and went to a battered chest of drawers in the corner and opened the lid of the cigar box that sat on top. He took out the dice along with a Bull Durham tobacco sack. He rubbed the sack all over the dice, mumbling some words Potter couldn't discern, before returning the sack to the box. He clenched the dice in his fist and turned back to Potter. "Ain't nothing special about these dice, but they been right good to me, so don't you do nothin' to hurt 'em, and don't you lose 'em. Ya hear? I got my gran'pappy's spirit from outen that sack to protect 'em, so you don't try witchin' 'em or nothin'.

"No, sir. I won't do nothin' but carry 'em." Potter reached for the dice.

Seventeen extended his fist over the table to let the dice fall into Potter's outstretched palm. They turned up seven on the flat of Cull's hand. He closed his fist on them and shoved them into the bib pocket of his overalls.

"Thank ya a lot, Seventeen. You don't know how much I 'preciate this." He stood. "You enjoy that jug. Max says be careful how you show it around, 'cause Royce is havin' some law trouble."

"I'll be careful."

Cull almost didn't make it to the truck before he burst out in raucous laughter. He couldn't believe Seventeen could be stupid enough to let the dice leave his possession. As he started his rattley old pick-up he laughed again and shouted, "I'm gonna beat him. I'm gonna beat Seventeen."

When Seventeen heard the truck pull away, he stepped out the door, and the crow, like a piece broken free from the puzzle of the night, dropped down to land on his shoulder. Seventeen nuzzled the bird and watched Potter's taillights fade. When they disappeared, he twitched his shoulder, and the crow rose and flew in the direction Potter's truck had gone.

🖤

Iola was an old woman. Nobody really knew how old, since everyone could only remember her as bent and gray. She was a maker of hill medicines and thought to be a witch. Everyone around Traveler's Trace avowed they didn't believe in witches or potions, but if someone wanted to dig a new well, or have the blight run off their corn, or had a sick cow, or just a general run of bad luck, they would quietly slip off to see Iola. She never took money for her services, saying she had no way to spend it since she lived far up in the hills and came down only when someone brought her down to witch something for them. She charged her fees in kind—cloth, or food that would keep, or tobacco.

Cull Potter stood at Iola's door, mashing his slouch hat in his hard hands. "Miz Iola, I want you to witch something for me."

Iola's wrinkled face didn't change. The almost-smile lurking around the corners of her mouth stayed the same when she said, "You got sick animals again, boy? If you'd be a little careful about the mold in yer hay, ya wouldn't need me."

"No ma'am, it ain't that. It's kinda I been havin' a bad run of luck with the dice. I was hopin' you could maybe help me out."

The old woman went to her rocking chair, the porch groaning beneath its runners as she began to rock. "Don't hold much with gamblin'. Dice is just Lucifer's toys ta catch rascals like you."

"Yes ma'am," Potter said. "But I'll pay for ya to witch some dice for me."

She brought her chair to a stop. "What ya got to offer?"

Cull stepped off the porch to his truck and began bringing out the loot. First came the calico. Iola looked and said nothing. Cull laid the cloth on the floor of the porch and brought out some of the canned fruit. Iola's eyes widened momentarily, but she said nothing. The spools of thread followed.

"That'll do." Iola rose and ambled into the house.

Potter smiled. He had not thought to come away so cheap. He followed the old woman, taking the dice out of his pocket as he walked.

Iola stopped in the middle of the room and held out her hand. Cull extended his and showed her the dice. "I want you to make 'em so's no one can throw a natural with 'em, ner never make a point—'cept me."

She looked at the ivory-colored cubes and nodded. He dropped them into her hand.

Iola cried out and let the dice tumble to the floor. She pulled her hand to her breast as though the dice had burned her. "Those is warded," she spat out the words. "They warded strong. I ain't gonna do it, Cull. Get outa here with 'em."

Cull bent to pick up the dice, hesitated a moment in fear, but then snatched them up and held them toward Iola. "You mean you can't?" He covered his disappointment with contempt.

Iola glared at him, her eyes smoldering. "I can, but not for the little you gimme. It'll take black spellin', and black spellin' costs."

"I'll pay." He dropped the dice back into his overall pocket and went out to the truck with Iola trailing him. He unloaded apricots, thong leather, and the twists of chewing tobacco and placed them on the porch beside his other offerings.

Iola looked over them, her eyes lingering on the tobacco. She looked longingly at the twists but shook her head. "Tain't enough. They're warded with an old spirit—probably blood kin."

Cull returned to the truck and brought out the flour, sugar, and beans and dumped them on the porch.

She was tempted. Cull could see it in her eyes.

Iola took a deep breath. "Who warded them dice?"

"Seventeen Williams."

The old woman raised an eyebrow then shook her head. "Right strong. Don' know, Cull. I don't think…" Her words trailed off.

Potter had saved his hardest convincer for last. He threw back an empty tow sack and hauled the second jug of Royce's moonshine out. Iola's eyes opened wide. "Whose still?" She asked at last.

"Royce's. Good squeeze, too. I had some outen another jug."

Iola's face stayed impassive as she considered. Cull almost danced with anxiety that it wouldn't be enough.

"My outhouse needs cleanin' and fixin'." Somehow, she knew he had no more goods to trade.

"I'll do it."

She looked at him and then at the goods on the floor, munching her toothless gums together. After a bit she jerked her head in a short nod. "Tote the stuff on in. I'll get started. Might take a while."

Iola's house seemed dimmer inside than before—as if a cloud stood between it and the sun, though sunlight still streamed in through the window. A calico cat sat on the top shelf of a crowded china cabinet, washing its paws and grooming its whiskers and paying no attention whatsoever to Potter.

Iola brought out a medium-sized stewer, blackened by years of woodsmoke, and placed it on the stove. She poured liquid from a covered bucket into it, then crumbled herbs into the mix.

"Set down over yonder." She worked without looking up. "Don't be movin' around none and don't make no noise. I can't be distracted."

Potter sat in a straight back chair and looked around the room. Cobwebs hung everywhere, yet the house seemed free of dust. Bunches of herbs and drying charms dangled from a string looped from one side of the open beam ceiling to the other. More things rested in jars set neatly on the windowsills and in shelves.

Steam was rising steadily from the stewer now. Iola continued dropping bits of this and that into the brew, stirring it with a willow switch. Her lips didn't move, but a rhythmic mutter danced around her. Cull watched on, eerie prickles racing down his spine.

A warm wind ruffled the ragged curtains, and a shiny black crow glided in. The bird cawed once, startling Cull, and landed on the floor at his feet. It cocked its head to the right, then to the left as though examining Potter. Then it strutted away and fluttered up to a table near Iola's hand. She glanced at it with gleaming eyes. She patted her shoulder, and the bird hopped up to it. Iola whispered, and the crow lifted its head and began to caw over and over. It sounded disturbingly like laughter.

"That's Seventeen's bird. What's it doing here?"

"'Cause I called it. And just 'cause it hangs out with Seventeen don't make it his bird. He keepin' an eye on old Seventeen for me." Iola looked back into the stewer and stirred it. The steam hovered thick around her face.

The cat stretched, extending its claws and yawning, walked across the shelf and jumped down onto the table. Iola turned from her stew to Potter. "Bring 'em," she ordered.

Cull rose and pulled the dice out of his pocket.

"Put 'em in the midst of the table," then she pointed at a low rush-bottom stool beside the table, "set 'em down right there."

Cull did as he was told.

Iola dipped a cup full of the brew from the boiling pot and poured it into a bowl. "Hold out yer arm."

Cull did, and, with a blurringly fast movement, Iola cut him just above the wrist. Potter snatched his arm back and stared at the blood welling from the slash. "Don't jerk around," Iola screeched, extending a chipped saucer to catch a few drops of the blood. When a teaspoonful had gathered in the center of the saucer, she poured it into the bowl with the brew.

Potter was frightened now. The old woman had moved so fast. He watched the tincture of red spread through the liquid in the bowl.

Iola ignored Potter. She stared at the dice then made a salt circle around them, saying "Salt to preserve and purify." She led lines of the salt out in four ways from the circle and made smaller circles at the end of each. Within the center of the circle with the dice she drew a pentagram, then traced smaller pentagrams within each of the remaining circles. Iola examined her work carefully, grunted her satisfaction, and poured a salt circle around the whole table. The circle enclosed Potter, herself, the cat, and the crow. She inspected it closely, adding a bit more here and there and saying, "Salt to preserve and protect."

Satisfied, she focused on Cull. "Don't you leave the circle no matter what. You do and there ain't no help for you. Somethin' much worse than Seventeen's granpappy'll carry you off to shadow, and you won't never come back."

"Yes, Ma'am."

Iola carefully stepped out of the circle and retrieved a little bottle from a shelf, then returned to the circle. She inspected the area where she had stepped across making sure it was not disturbed or broken. She then opened the little bottle, wet her finger with the contents and made an X on Potter's forehead, on her own, on the cat's, and on the bird's. She carefully dripped one drop from the bottle on each die. She corked the bottle and put it in her apron pocket, then began passing her hands over the dice. The soft chant accompanying her movements grew louder with each pass. Cull couldn't understand her words, but their rhythm was compelling. He was so taken by it, a crackle of fire in the stove caused him to startle. Steam rose in great clouds from the still boiling stewer, filling the room with a pungent, minty aroma. Soon the scent faded, changing to that of soured earth and reminding Cull of the smell of a graveyard in the rain.

The room beyond the salt circle grew dim and foggy, and a nip of frost stole into Potter's body, making the hairs on his arms stand up. The graveyard smell intensified into the reek of putrefaction.

Iola swayed slowly side-to-side, though her feet seemed nailed to the floor, making Cull think of his truck's failing windshield wiper. He couldn't take his eyes off her.

Lightning flashed inside the room. It snaked around the floor and outlined the salt circle. A thread of crackling blue fire rose up and arched over them, and, when it touched the other side of the circle, thunder crashed, rattling the windows.

Iola's voice commanded, "Ghost of Octavius Williams, come to me."

The lightning aura around Iola stretched and formed two arches. In the next instant, another person faced her from outside the circle. Like Seventeen. But not him. Older. Haggard. Almost skeletal, with large and bony hands and deep-sunken eyes flecked with coal fire.

"Who calls?" Seventeen's grandfather spirit asked.

"Iola."

"Why?"

"Do you guard the dice of Seventeen?"

"If I am called."

"Guard them no more."

"Why?"

"Cull Potter asks it."

The spirit looked at Potter, and Cull felt his insides turn watery. He wanted to run but found his legs too weak to support him.

A hideous grin creeped across the spirit's face, then broke apart to release a scornful laugh that made Potter's bowels grip like a vice.

"For such a weasel as Cull Potter I do nothing."

"I command it," Iola said.

Panicked, Potter rose to flee the house. Forgetting Iola's warning, he lifted a foot to escape the salt circle, but she grabbed hold of him with the power of a bear and slammed him back onto the stool.

A horrific cackling laughter came from outside the circle. Someone—something stood at the circle's edge like a dark blot. The blot lifted a hand and pointed at Potter. It cackled again and beckoned to him.

Cull knew this was the thing worse than Seventeen's granpappy. This thing felt like the Devil himself.

"No," Potter cried. "I'll not come." Still, only Iola's skinny arm held him back from being drawn to the dark thing.

The witch's grip let go, the hand that had held him now extended toward the dark power. With her other, she touched the old spirit saying, "I command that you never guard these dice again."

The spirit's face twisted in disdain but at last said, "So be it," and disappeared.

Potter fainted.

"Wake up, Cull Potter," Iola said, shaking Potter's shoulder. "It's done. Wake up."

Cull snapped awake to see Iola's toothless face inches from his. A tiny line of tobacco stain ran from the corner of her mouth down her chin.

Potter drew back from her with a cry, nearly tipping over the chair. Iola cackled and munched her mouth together. Her chin seemed to disappear. "It's done best I can do." The merry twinkle in her eyes disconcerted Potter. "I make no promises though," she continued. "Black spellin' can always go wrong."

Cull stood, still shivering with fear. The pungent aroma of the steaming stewer lingered in the air. He reached for the dice on the table.

"No." Iola screeched and grabbed his wrist. "Touch 'em 'fore sundown and the spell's broke. Wait." She brought forth a slender willow switch and bent it like tongs, picking up the dice one at a time and placing them in the center of a piece of gray cloth. Then she folded them up in the cloth and handed the wrapped pair to Potter. "The spell'll set at sundown, but I don't know how long it'll hold. Yore blood's weak. It 'most clabbered the brew 'fore I could use it."

"It'll let me win Saturday night, won't it?" Potter demanded, greed overcoming fear.

"I reckon."

"You sure?"

"You doubtin' me?" Iola challenged, and her voice regaining a touch of the power it held when she spoke with the spirit.

"No, no, I ain't doubtin'." He started backing toward the door.

The calico cat yowled, and Cull's hair prickled. He turned in panic and ran out the door, hardly touching the porch step on the way to his truck.

Iola stepped onto the porch and shouted, "Don't you forget. You must clean and fix my outhouse soon. Soon. Or I'll hex ya for a debtor."

Iola watched the truck raise thick clouds of dust as it rattled, too fast, down the rutted road. The crow, which had been sitting on the peak of the roof, fluttered down to light on the old woman's shoulder. It ruffled its neck feathers then stroked its blue-black head against Iola's cheek making soft gurgling sounds deep in its throat.

Iola looked into the bird's glass bead eyes. "Go on." The crow lifted and flew. Iola watched it a time, then went into the house.

Potter jabbed a gray splinter into his knuckle when he knocked on Seventeen's shanty door. He held the dice, still wrapped in cloth, in his other hand. Seventeen opened the door without a word. Cull had to look away from him, the memory of the haggard image in the lightning arch still haunting his thoughts.

"Did ya enjoy the jug, Seventeen?" Potter said at last, dragging the toe of his scuffed work shoe through the dust.

"Yep. 'Twas good. Didn't even need the hair of the dog. You got my dice?"

"Yeah, yeah. They right here." Cull extended his fist.

"How come they all wrapped up?" Seventeen asked suspiciously.

"Didn't wanta get 'em messed up. I took real good care of 'em, like you said. They ain't harmed a bit."

55

G. Lloyd Helm

Seventeen stuck out his outsized paw, and Cull gave him the little gray package. "Thank ya for lettin' me carry 'em. Maybe I can win back some of my money now." Potter tried to grin but made a botch of it. "I gotta go. See ya at Tilden's tonight." He turned and hurried away, leaving Seventeen standing in the door.

Seventeen watched Potter leave then looked up. Sun glinted off blue-black feathers as the crow swooped down to land on Seventeen's shoulder. He reached up and stroked the midnight feathers, then turned into the house. He unrolled the dice and shook them in his hand as he walked to the cigar box and opened it. He dropped them in. The dice turned up snake eyes.

Seventeen blinked and picked the dice up again, rattled them in his hand and dropped them on the chest of drawers. They turned up boxcars. A smile crept across his face as he picked the dice up and returned them to the cigar box.

🐦

"You're jumpy as frog in a frying pan, Cull," Max Tilden said. "What's wrong?"

"Nothin'. I'm just ready to play. Where's Seventeen at anyhow?"

All the men turned toward the clumping sound of footsteps coming through the store. Seventeen Williams opened the door of the back room.

Max glanced at Cull and saw all the color drain from his face. "What's wrong? You all right?"

Potter managed to lift his hand and point at the shiny black crow perched on Seventeen's shoulder.

Seventeen grinned. "Max, I b'lieve I'm gonna need me some new dice."

G. Lloyd Helm—born in Arkansas, raised in California, and educated in Tennessee—has been a ne'er-do-well scribbler under the kind auspices of his long-suffering wife for more than 50 years. He has many novels for sale on Amazon and Barnes & Noble.

# THE SMOKE OVER MISSISSIPPI

## BY NATHAN LEIGH TAYLOR

*Toil, toil, twis' and turn,*
*The witch of Harrowood will watch us burn,*
*Bound t'earth and broken bone,*
*She turns our flesh t'soil and stone.*
- unknown, 1859

All that remained of Willard Yancey was his name, but she would soon take that from him too. She would take it from the lips of his children, neither of which would mourn his passing. She would take it from the heart of his wife, who would sleep peacefully at night without ever knowing she was a widow. She would take it, like she had so many others, and burn it until there was nothing left but smoke.

❧

Willard had been a reverend, not that it mattered; his was still but one soul. He was well respected, and, to the men, women, and children of Rodney who lined his pews, he was the patron saint of goodness. He was a holy man, one that would look upon their sins, then sweep them under the carpet so God couldn't see them. They'd be damned if anything as paltry as the stench of stale cigarettes or the budding bruises on his knuckles—the ones that matched those under his wife's foundation—could beg them to think otherwise. If only they knew. He wasn't the first crooked preacher to come through Rodney, though, and he wouldn't be the last. Hell, she had killed most of them.

*Alcina De'amor.*

The words danced on the wind as Willard's sermon drew to a close. It was a simple incantation, one that she had learnt almost a century ago, and it did nothing more than alter the way she was perceived. It obscured her morbid truth. She could have dressed herself as any of the horrors that lurked in Harrowood—the mess of dead and dying trees that haunted the space between Rodney and Cool Boiler Bayou, which, in turn, bled into the Mississippi River—but she knew better than most how to drag a man into the darkness. Harrowood sulked behind her as she waited in the chapel garden for Willard. He didn't know it yet, but it would be the only cigarette he had left.

She presented herself as the Lord had made her, or so Willard thought, and he followed her into Harrowood without so much as a whisper. They often did when confronted with their lust. Starving thorns bit at his arms, and roots tugged at his feet, as if they were trying to save him, but her auburn hair was like a fire in the darkness, and it guided the preacher through the browning trees, strangled by the autumn chill, towards the clearing.

The canopy of leaves separated above them, giving way to the rain and waning light which now decorated a sparse campground in the center of the clearing. Reddened stones of varying sizes formed an uninviting maw around a large bed of scorched earth, and a canvas tent, adorned with moss, stood on the northern side. A cauldron hung over a dormant fire-pit, and the carcasses of rats and crows—successful hunts in

59

Nathan Leigh Taylor

Harrowood—had been strung up to bleed. Willard slowed to a stop.

"Ma'am?" He buttoned his trousers and tightened his belt. "Ma'am, where in the good Lord's name are we?"

Dressed in nothing but the dirt of Harrowood, she turned back to look at him and smiled, "Come closer, Reverend."

Willard, under the spell of his own sin, forfeited his better judgment and stepped between the stones onto the charred ground. He had made it this far, after all, and it was a long way to come for just a walk. He stopped again, but not because he could feel his heart in his chest. Some kind of change met him on the other side of those stones, and if it hadn't been for the fetor of rot and death that almost made him spill his guts, he would have noticed the hush that now suffocated the clearing.

"Is there no place else we can go?" Willard shifted his gaze from the watchful eyes of uneaten remains, only to find her missing.

Harrowood held its breath, as if in anticipation of what would come.

ᘒ

The knife was crude, both in nature and its placement between his ribs.

It was a hunting knife, one she had made from an uneven sliver of sharpened stone, and it had served her longer than she cared to remember. It didn't go in easy. The edges were dull from regular use, and it bore through Willard's back like a shovel through dirt, jarring only briefly as it broke through bone. She'd never been very good at this part.

Barely aware of what had happened to him, Willard bent backwards under the force of the blow before dropping to his knees. He made a sound as though he was trying to scream and clawed at the rooted blade now burning inside him.

As he knelt there, looking at his bloody hand and choking on his own breath, she placed a knee between his shoulders

60

and dislodged the knife. Willard shrank beneath the pain. She would have felt pity for him, if only she could have forgotten how deliberately he had beaten his wife. She supposed that even now, with his life pouring out of the hole in his back, he wasn't thinking of his family.

"Please." Willard's voice trembled as he fought to stay among the living. "Have mercy."

"Now why would I do that?" She spoke softly as she circled her prey.

Willard looked up. The temptress who had led him to his grave was nowhere to be seen. In her stead, stood a frail young woman with dense, colorless hair that curled and coiled like wire. Her skin was no longer porcelain; it was a tapestry of scars no mortal being could have ever sustained. In that moment, she could have sworn he recognized her.

"Please, I'm a good man." Willard pleaded with both her and his God.

"None of us are blameless, Reverend," she thought of those who had come before him, "but some of us can be blamed more than others."

Before Willard could respond, she drew a neat line across his neck with the still-wet knife and watched as what was left of his life cascaded onto the ground. He hung there momentarily, as if suspended by something unseen, then, without so much as a whisper, his body followed.

If only that could have been the end of it.

🐈

*Sedit, no'Sanguinem.*

Dread consumed her, even after all this time, and her hands began to shake as she tore off a length of cloth from Willard's shirt and pressed it against the open wound on his throat. It turned from white to red as his warmth flooded the empty space between its fibers. She held it there until it was

61

heavy, and then, one after the other, she approached the stones that encircled the camp and wrung a single droplet of blood onto each of them. In unison, they hissed.

She looked at Willard, who stared back from behind petrified eyes, and convinced herself once more he deserved to be forgotten. There was something about the way he looked at her just before he died—like she was the monster, and, despite his sins, he was the victim—that gave her pause. It was as though he had seen her before, and she supposed he had, in a way.

Of course, she was familiar with the stories told to the children of Rodney to keep them from wandering into Harrowood by themselves—cautionary tales of hungry beasts and lost fiends that served their purpose in teaching them there are things to be mindful of. Willard had most likely been shown the same creatures when he was growing up, before uncovering them for his own brood when they were hardy enough. The stories twisted perfectly ordinary shadows into wretched things. They were works of fiction, but there was one story in particular that must have rung true for Willard in his final moments. She'd heard it, spoken in stifled tones by intrepid and disobedient youngsters on their way to explore Cool Boiler Bayou. It told of a lonesome but cruel monster; the Witch of Harrowood.

The witch, as they said, would lead you into the darkness and cook you up before breaking each and every one of your bones to use as toothpicks, then bury whatever was left underneath Harrowood. You would never be heard of again.

If only they knew she was one of the good ones.

As long as they weren't monsters themselves, they needn't be afraid of her at all. There were things more terrifying, more insidious, more wicked, sleeping in the room next to theirs at night, and she was certain Willard had been one of them. She hoped his wife and children would go on to live better lives because of what she had done to him. Besides, there were things much worse than her in Harrowood.

Dread rattled her once more as the bleeding stones grew impatient. Thin plumes of smoke reeked from each of them and rose upwards towards the blackened sky that now watched over the clearing. She had to finish what she had started. The hissing grew to a crescendo as she wrapped the blood-soaked rag around her head, obscuring her vision, before kneeling beside her offering. Some things were better left unseen.

*Sedit, no'Sanguinem.*

She spoke the words again, held her breath, and then waited.

The preacher would have called it the devil, but she knew better than to call it anything at all. It had cursed her with an unending suffering, one that she had both asked for and deserved, and she wouldn't be rid of it until her stake in the covenant was paid. Willard was merely one of a score of souls to replace her own.

The stone choir fell silent, and her knuckles flushed white as her nails pierced through the skin on her palms. It was there. Terror pulled at the hairs on the back of her neck as she felt it skulk around the camp in search of Willard. She had seen it once before—an undying, viscous mass of charcoal sinew that pulsated and clung to fractured limbs and a broken spine—and she had no intention of ever seeing it a second time.

There was a sickening and violent urgency as it collected what it was owed, and, from the other side of the blindfold, she heard the familiar sound of flesh being unstuck from bone, the sound of skin being torn like cloth. Then, as though her prayers had been answered, there was nothing.

Harrowood exhaled.

Nathan Leigh Taylor

❦

A cardinal punctuated the quiet that shrouded the clearing before it swept down, painting a red streak across the canvas of Harrowood, to peck at the bloody patch where Willard Yancey once lay. All that remained of him now was his name, and she set about taking that from him too.

Columns of new light broke through the canopy to investigate the remnants of the night before, as she cast her hand over the drying rag, now pulled from her eyes. A curious flame appeared on the ground beneath it, rested, and then swallowed the rag whole. Soon there wouldn't be a soul that would know to come looking for him, and she would be the only one who remembered his name. She remembered all of their names—every last one of them—and yet, somewhere along the way, she had forgotten to remember her own.

The Witch of Harrowood whispered into the smoke that rose from the burning cloth, Willard's blood like oil, and carved her penance into the tapestry of scars that covered her body as it drifted over Mississippi.

'One more…'

———————————

Nathan Leigh Taylor is an aspiring horror author based in Bristol, England, and is currently working on his first book, *Harrow*. He holds a bachelor's degree in photography, which he has never used, and during the day he works as a UX/UI designer. When he isn't writing, Nathan is reading, watching or thinking about horror. You can learn more about Nathan and his writing at NathanLeighTaylor.com.

# THAT THEY SHOULD COME UNTO ME

## BY LUCY BENNETT-GRAY

Their mama was a free spirit. She quit high school on her sixteenth birthday. Gave birth to her first, and married and divorced the baby's father within six months of that. Moved into the twenty-year-old mobile home her daddy bought and hauled onto his land three miles outside Rome, Georgia for her and her short-term husband. Dropped out of the cosmetology course she'd begged her mama to cover with the payout they got when her daddy died, just because.

She named her babies River and Rain, like the people in the glossy checkout line magazines, left the sagging trailer when she convinced an older married man to desert his family, then moved back in again when he returned to them after she bled their child away. She burned through what she got for selling up after her own mama died from emphysema, then took up with a good ole boy named Billy who made his way selling oxy and robbing the occasional gas station or convenience store.

The owner of the convenience store Billy hit up ten days before Christmas pulled out a sawed-off shotgun from beneath the counter and left Billy no choice. It was only Billy's dumb luck that an off-duty state deputy sheriff decided to come in for cigarettes that self-same instant, dropping Billy's options to less than none. Billy left both men bleeding out on the floor.

A buddy of Billy's knew of a house up on Big Four Mountain near Jellico, Tennessee that had been sitting empty since his granny died the year before. The place was rustic, off a rutted, unpaved road, with only a woodstove for heat and no running water beyond a hand pump in the kitchen, but it was the last place anybody would be likely to look for Billy.

River got his daddy's coloring, his curly blond hair and green eyes. Rain took after her father, dark red hair, and large hazel eyes whose too-steady gaze never failed to unnerve their mama. Now seven and four, neither of her babies looked like her. Maybe that's why it came so easy for her to do as Billy wanted. They took the kids with them as far as Jellico, but when Billy complained they only slowed them down, their mama didn't think twice.

Billy split enough wood for the woodstove for three days and carried it up to the porch. He taught River how to fill the stove without getting burned and how to use the kitchen hand pump. The plan was to cross into Kentucky, drop a note in the mail to the Jellico police telling them about the kids, trade cars in Lexington and head west. Late Christmas Eve, while the kids were sleeping, their mama left a note saying "Merry Christmas" next to toys she'd shoplifted from a discount store just outside Knoxville—a plastic toy tractor-trailer and a baby doll with one eye that wouldn't open—and five cans of pull-top, store brand spaghetti rings in tomato sauce.

River awoke to find their mother gone, and heavy snow falling. He threw the toy truck into the fire, just as a semi on I-75 jackknifed on black ice and rolled, bursting into flame as Billy's car skidded into it.

The old house smelled bad for a while after River burned the toy, a bit like their trailer did the time Billy's friend came over and made something they called 'meth' in the kitchen.

66

His baby sister cried but clutched her new doll to her chest. River opened a can of the spaghetti, tasted it, then decided to set it on the stove for a while to warm. The snow stopped just before sunset, and River went out to the porch to gaze out on the unbroken white.

🐾

The temperature dropped as the sky cleared.

The sun rose on a still, crystalline day. The sun set again as another front blew in, blotting out the moon. The next morning the footprints River made, leading his sister to and from the outhouse, had been erased. Still, when River went out to the front porch to take from the dwindling stack of wood, he noticed fresh tracks he hadn't made. He went as far as the edge of the porch to examine them. From what he could make out, the prints looked like they could've been left by hooves like those of the goats he'd seen the time his kindergarten class visited the petting zoo. Only these were larger and looked like the animal that made them had been walking on only two legs.

A fear, different from that of being left behind by his mama, different from what he felt watching their supplies diminish, swooped in on him. He dodged back to the woodpile, snatched up three of the rough logs, and nearly jumped back over the threshold.

He kicked the door closed behind him, then looked up to find Rain standing hand-in-hand with a man he'd never seen before. River took the whole of him in in an instant: tall, thin, black suit, black hair, blue-black eyes, and cloven hooves where feet should have been. The logs River held tumbled to the floor.

The man—for that's what the most of him looked like—released Rain's hand and drew slowly closer, solid, heavy thumps sounding with each step. He stopped and bent down, collecting the logs River had dropped, then carried them the rest of the way to the stove. He didn't use the mitt to open the stove door. He grasped the scorching handle with his bare hand but gave no sign of pain. He added the wood to the fire and closed the stove door.

He looked back at River, and all fear evaporated.

"We're…we're running out," River said, not sure how else to react. "The wood."

The man brushed his hands against each other to knock off the dirt from the logs. "You have enough." The man's eyes darted about the room, like he wanted to take in his surroundings. His gaze fixed on the doll. "No one is coming for you," he said, still staring at the doll. "No one knows you're here." He turned his face to River. "But you can come live with me. You and your sister." Without warning, he snatched up Rain's hands and began spinning her around.

River moved to pull Rain away from the stranger, but Rain began laughing.

"You'll dance beneath the moon." They spun around. "You'll take to the night sky." Spin. "You'll play games with magic." The man stopped cold and caught Rain up in his arms. He looked to River. "You'll never be cold, or hungry, or alone again. Either of you." He shifted Rain to one arm and held his free hand out to River. "You've already made your sacrifice. All you have to do is take my hand."

River didn't even think to ask. He knew the sacrifice he'd made when he burned the truck and wished Billy dead. Looking into the man's eyes, River knew it had worked. He thought he should feel guilty, but he didn't feel…guilty. He looked from the man to his sister who watched him in silence, though he could sense her willing him forward. River crossed to the man and took his hand.

The man's touch was calloused but gentle. He released River, then he lowered Rain to the floor. He knelt before her.

"Your brother has made his offering," he said. "Are you ready to make yours?"

Rain stood there, considering the man's features longer than River expected her to. At last, she nodded. The man nodded back, then stood. Rain fetched her doll and brought it to him.

"No, it must be done by your own hand," he said. "By your own wish." He went to the stove and opened its door. Rain joined him and gazed into the belly of the beast. She took one last look at the doll, then thrust it into the fire.

Miles away, in an intensive care unit just across the state line, a young woman who'd lost an eye in the Christmas Day pileup, but who'd held on till that point, breathed her last.

---

Lucy Bennett-Gray leads a blissfully uneventful life with her partner and their two dogs. She hopes one day to finish the novel she's started and set aside more times than she cares to admit.

# BIBLIOMANIWAC

## BY J.J. SMITH

"Mediocre at best," said an unfamiliar male voice coming from the client side of the customer service desk at Montgomery County Public Library.

*Is he talking to me?* wondered librarian Elizabeth Drennan, who was on her lunch break and, as was usual for her, remained at her workstation to consume both Dante's *Inferno* and a PBJ sandwich. Despite being annoyed, confused, and a little scared, Elizabeth lifted her head to see a somewhat smartly dressed man looking down at her. She said, "What did you say?"

"Mediocre at best," he replied.

Elizabeth was aware and accepted that the library attracted more than students and academics conducting research; it also was a haven for the homeless and quirky individuals who aren't generally welcome elsewhere in Washington's Maryland suburbs, so she tempered her response. "Thank you for your input. Now, I'd like to get back to my book. I only have 30 minutes for lunch."

But that didn't stop him, for he said, "I admit Dante can be entertaining, but for someone like you, someone who so loves and appreciates writing and literature to the point you've dedicated your life to it...well, Dante is kindergarten reading compared to what you should be spending your time on. So again, mediocre at best."

Elizabeth, who now felt truly nervous, didn't know what to say in response. She never got the opportunity to speak, for he said, "I've seen you working around here. Directing subordinates, inspecting the stacks… Why do you paint your toenails red?"

Fear now ran through Elizabeth, and she unconsciously tried to hide her toes by placing one sandal-encased foot over the other. As she did so, past news stories of lone women who had been attacked rushed through her mind. *I'm in the library, and it's the middle of the day, and there are people everywhere, and there are security cameras pointed at us—would he still attack me here? And if I screamed, would people help?*

However, the situation suddenly changed when, without another word, he turned away from the counter and moved toward the main exit.

Elizabeth kept her eyes focused on him as he left the library. He had frightened her so, she didn't notice he'd left the leather-bound book that now sat on the counter. Despite what had just occurred, Elizabeth's inclination to be helpful took hold, and she looked to the exit intending to shout, "Sir, you left your book!" However, she just as quickly recalled the encounter and bit her lip.

Her eyes fell to the book. She found herself immediately mesmerized by its old, weathered cover. It was leather, colored light brown, and embossed with flowers, fruit, and the heads of mythical creatures like those found on medieval royal standards. In the center was a coat of arms—at least that's what it looked like—consisting of a knight's helmet, with a blue banner underneath that crossed diagonally. The banner had designs in it, three red flowers. While the cover alone excited Elizabeth, her excitement skyrocketed when she opened the book and saw its text, and discovered it wasn't an ordinary work, not by a longshot.

The contents were handwritten in a language Elizabeth not only didn't understand, but one she had never before seen, despite her history as a librarian, which included an internship at the library of a Roman Catholic diocese while she'd pursued her master's degree. The internship provided her access to a massive number of unusual books and manuscripts, but the only thing that came to mind as she perused the pages of this new volume was the Voynich manuscript, an illustrated codex believed to date back to Renaissance Italy, hand-written in an unknown language or an, as yet, unsolved cipher. However, despite having seen scores of photos of the Voynich manuscript's pages, she couldn't remember much about it at the time, so she resolved to refresh her memory by conducting her own research as soon as she arrived home.

Library protocol directed that she should have turned the manuscript over to "lost and found," but she couldn't bring herself to. In part, because she couldn't get over what a jerk the man had been—daring to comment about her toenails—but also because she couldn't stop thinking about the manuscript, and what a find it was. *Besides, once he realizes he doesn't have his book, he'll be back for it,* she concluded while putting the book in the drawer where she kept pens, paper clips, staples, and rubber bands.

With the book so close, Elizabeth barely got any work done as she obsessed about it for the rest of the day...secretly planning what she was going to do as soon as her shift ended. That obsession made her subway ride home seem incredibly long and torturous...torturous because Elizabeth wanted to pull the manuscript from her bag and examine its pages. *But what if someone recognized it? They could call the police, and it would be taken from her,* she reasoned. *No, it's better to wait...for privacy.*

Upon entering her apartment, Elizabeth rushed through dinner, then sat at her desk where she kept her computer to access the library system's website. Information on the Voynich manuscript soon appeared, including that it was named after the book dealer—Wilfrid Voynich—who "discovered" it in 1912. She continued to scan the data when one passage jumped to her eyes: "The manuscript consists of about 240 pages, but it is clear some pages are missing. Text in the manuscript is written from left to right, and it also contains illustrations or diagrams."

Elizabeth continued to review what was known about the Voynich manuscript, and eventually wondered, *Do I have the manuscript's missing pages?* She considered that for a few seconds, then thought, *No, I think I have something better. Something new. I think I might have the 'Drennan manuscript.'* While it was a thrilling eponymous prospect to ponder, what she really wanted to do was get back to examining her manuscript, to savor the sensual feel of the vellum, to delight in the smell of the ancient pages, and to bask in the splendor and majesty of the work, even if she couldn't understand a word of it. So, that's what she did.

🐈

If Elizabeth had to describe the text, she would say hieroglyphs, cuneiform, and runes all had sex, and gave birth to gibberish. As descriptive as that was, any interested party would still have to see the manuscript to understand what she meant.

Adorning the manuscript were drolleries—illustrations in the margins. Some pages had a score or more, while other just a few. They were as subtle and as random as a doodle, or as grand as the most ornate illuminated pages of a medieval Bible. The only real difference was the subject matter. The drolleries and illuminated pages were of the blackest blasphemies, abominations Elizabeth could never herself have imagined, would never want to imagine, or felt such shame if she had.

She intuited the text described these manifestations of wickedness, and asked herself, *How diseased and depraved were the people who pictured such things?* At the same time, she did not want to know, sure such knowledge would come with a price. The text repelled her, still she couldn't look away. Even though she didn't have a clue about the language, she found herself compelled to follow each line, and as she did so, pictures formed in her head.

They started as visions flashing in her mind's eye, but by the end of each page became daydreams that played like movies. She didn't know where her confidence and knowledge came from, but she was sure her visions revealed what each page of text meant. Just when she thought the latest abomination that flashed through her brain was the nadir of sacrilege, she would turn the page and images even more shameful and maleficent would invade her consciousness— and it hurt. She feared a blood clot was forming. What began as a headache, not long after she started examining the text, developed into something more excruciating than her worst migraine. She didn't know why it was happening, but she became aware of one thing: if the agony continued, it would drive her mad.

Elizabeth was now desperate to end her "bibliomania"— she didn't know what else to call it—but was at a loss on what to do. She found while she wasn't able to take her eyes off the text, she could move her arms. Knowing her phone lay close by, she formulated a plan. She slowly moved her hand toward the phone—slowly because she felt she needed to hide her intentions, though from what she didn't know. Feelings of joy filled her as her fingers wrapped around the device. She couldn't look directly at the numbers, but using her peripheral vision combined with touch, she dialed 9-1-1.

"Nine-one-one, what's your emergency?" said a female operator.

"I can't stop reading this abomination."

"What are you saying ma'am?"

"I have a manuscript that I can't stop reading!"

"Ma'am, it's a crime to call this number for frivolous reasons, so unless you have a real emergency, don't call this number again. I'm going to terminate this call, but not before

I say that if you call again, police will be dispatched to your location to charge you." Having issued her warning, the emergency operator hung up.

But the dispatcher's threat got Elizabeth thinking. *She said if I call them back, they'll send police to arrest me. They'll force me to stop, and probably even take me in. It's not great, but at least I won't be stuck here reading this thing.*

She once again dialed the emergency number and got another operator who gave the same speech before disconnecting the call. Elizabeth dialed the number again, and again, until on the fourth attempt she got results. The emergency operator said, "Uniformed officers are being dispatched to your location. Once there, they will charge you with a violation."

Feelings of joy once again flooded through Elizabeth, but she wouldn't breathe a sigh of relief until the officers had separated her from the manuscript. *How long would it take?* her mind asked. She, of course, didn't have the answer. The only thing she was certain of was that she was trapped reading the evil tome. With no other options available, she continued reading and envisioning the violent blasphemies forced into her consciousness. Then, what she feared happened: time passed, and yet no police arrived.

*Where are they?* she asked herself as her panic grew. She didn't want to call again, but realized she had no choice. She reached for the phone, but found it was gone. *I set it on the desk. Where'd it go, and how'd it move?*

That's when he revealed himself.

From behind Elizabeth, a male voice said, "I have your phone."

Because her eyes were locked on the text, she couldn't turn to see who was speaking. She recognized him, nonetheless.

"I made a mistake by not collecting your phone earlier, so yes, the first call you made was genuine. Lucky for me bureaucrats only know how to be bureaucratic. So, I rectified my mistake, and your subsequent calls were illusions. Sorry about that, but it was necessary.

"In my defense, I didn't retrieve your phone earlier, because I didn't want to risk glancing at a page and ending up in the same predicament as you. I must admit, I didn't think you were headstrong enough to attempt an escape, but you proved me wrong. Bravo. Your boldness has earned you the truth." He said this as if he were about to impose a punishment.

"To start with, it looks like you're suffering from myiasis, a parasitic infestation. At least that's the common diagnosis in cases of myiasis, but in your situation such a diagnosis would be wrong. Yours isn't due to a parasite; it's a retributive infection caused by a curse."

His tone changed, sounding suddenly cordial. "I apologize. I realize I have you at a disadvantage. My name is Jonathan Channing. You know me as the library patron who left the manuscript." He gave her a moment to process this, then said, "I'm a low-level practitioner of witchcraft, and while it's true I have limited skills in that regard, I do have enough ability to instill an illusion in your mind. That's what I did at the library. I wanted you to believe I left, but I've been your constant companion the entire time. You've been perusing a grimoire, which is, as you're probably aware, a textbook of magic, or in this case, of black magic. It's one of the most powerful grimoires in existence. The catch is its text is only to be viewed by those who have exchanged their souls for power, and, unfortunately, the manuscript has been safeguarded by a curse that protects its secrets from the prying eyes of those who haven't made the requisite bargain."

Though she couldn't turn to face him, in her mind's eye she could see him as clearly as any of the other anathemas lingering there. He was smiling down on her with near affection.

"I needed to find a way around the curse, you see. That's where you come in." He leaned over her, his breath on her nape. "The reason you've been experiencing headaches is that any uninitiate who reads the text will pay a price—a different price for each—in your case, the earlier mentioned myiasis." He rested his hand on her shoulder. "In your studies, did you ever encounter research conducted in the 1960s on memory involving flatworms? No?" he rushed on. "Well then, I'll enlighten you.

"A researcher," he said, speaking in a stentorian voice as if lecturing a class, "conditioned some worms to cringe when he flashed a bright light over them. He then chopped them up and fed them to other flatworms that hadn't been conditioned. The result was that without undergoing the conditioning, the cannibal worms would cringe when the light was flashed. He concluded that by eating their brethren, the unconditioned worms acquired the knowledge of the conditioned worms."

Why me?" she managed, though she struggled to form the words.

"I knew this exercise would be easier if I found someone who really loves the written word. It seemed to me a librarian would best meet that requirement, so I started searching all the libraries, public, university, and, yes, even the library of the local diocese. That's where your name first came to my attention. You're still held in high regard there for your abilities. I selected you as someone who'd want to read the manuscript once it was in her possession. I just had to get it to you, make you believe I accidentally left the grimoire behind. To trick you into abandoning your natural inclination to call out to the person who left a possession behind. To forget your honesty, so you'd keep the book for yourself. Your awareness of the Voynich manuscript helped with that." He gave a dark chuckle. "I've found that work to be a godsend, if you'll pardon the term, in helping find a candidate. One could even conjecture its true purpose was to be the honey that attracts the inquisitive fly."

As he spoke, Elizabeth turned to the last page of the grimoire, causing Jonathan to pause. He stood far to her side, so he could watch her actions using his peripheral vision, making sure to never look directly at the manuscript. After a few moments, her body slumped, and he was sure the life had flowed out of her.

He produced a bag he'd sewn from cloth imbued with a spell that dampens temptation to transport the manuscript. Being careful to always look away, he covered the manuscript with it.

He grabbed a handful of hair at the back of Elizabeth's head, lifting it and pushing it forward to uncover a large hole in the top of her scalp. The hole revealed that most of the parietal bones were gone, exposing the inside of her skull, but there wasn't any brain left for her cranium to protect. Her brain, along with the parietal bones, had been eaten by what appeared to be thousands of bookworms.

🐈

Jonathan was sitting at Elizabeth's dining room table facing the dead woman. Before him sat a bowl of throbbing, writhing bookworms that contained the grimoire's evil knowledge that Elizabeth had gained and lost. "I'm sorry Elizabeth—you don't mind if I call you by your given name, do you? Because your soul was your own, you paid a price for ingesting the knowledge contained in the grimoire. These bookworms—larva really—formed in your skull with every line of text you completed, and they consumed your brain. Sorry, but like I said, I'm determined to make that information mine."

He held up a spoon he brought for the occasion and scooped up a helping of worms, shoveling it into his mouth.

The wiggling of the larva nearly made him gag, but he persevered and swallowed most of the lot, only missing those that slipped between his cheek and gum. He fished these out with his finger, and on he went to the next spoonful, and the next after that, and the next, and the next, and the next.

As he feasted, Jonathan recalled Hieronymus Bosch was rumored to have ingested hallucinogens before proceeding with some of his paintings. Quite pleased with himself, he concluded, *I now know what Bosch must have felt when he was overcome by inspiration.*

Within minutes the bowl sat empty. Jonathan reached for water to wash down the worms still squirming in the folds of his cheeks, when the first of the visions hit him. It was all there, the abominations and blasphemies, the blood-thirsty ceremonies and cruel rituals, all performed to summon malevolent spirits to do as the summoning practitioner demanded.

At first it seemed wonderful and magnificent, the font of all the power Jonathan desired. But soon it turned into an onslaught of images and a cacophony of noise, all happening at once, and none making any sense, like the intense hallucinations he'd experienced while tripping on datura. The scary kind of trip. The kind where you believe you'll never come down, and you're going to die. Before he could convince himself it was just his paranoia fucking with him, the impossible happened. From across the table, Elizabeth raised what was left of her head.

Despite not having any brains left, Elizabeth stood, and retrieved the grimoire from the desk. She stepped away and turned toward Jonathan, revealing her now pancake-white face and her droopy sleepy eyelids that gave the impression of a stroke victim. The spark of intelligence that had inspired and motivated the librarian was gone, replaced by a dull, slack-jawed lifelessness.

79

Impossibly, she stepped toward Jonathan, who would have screamed, but the activity he felt squirming in his brain robbed him of his focus. When he next saw the thing that used to be Elizabeth, it stood next to him. A flash later, the manuscript rested on the table before him, open to page one. The creature grabbed a handful of Jonathan's hair and forced his head forward, so his face hovered directly over the manuscript. He tried shutting his eyes, but the visions he was experiencing made that difficult. He really did not know if his eyes were open or closed, but soon that was all moot.

His instinct that it was no longer Elizabeth controlling the body was confirmed when it spoke. Holding Jonathan's head in a steely grip the entity said, "You fool. We allowed Bosch to maintain his sanity so he could produce. You might have done the same by consuming only a few of worms each day, but arrogant glutton you are, you ingested all the larvae in one sitting. You've opened yourself up to the entirety of the knowledge of the grimoire at once, and it is, even now, driving you mad. Your ambition has destroyed you."

Unable to stop himself, the low-level magician gazed at the text.

❧

Elizabeth Drennan, again alive, her face now glowing with a luster of intense beauty and confidence, placed the incomplete grimoire on her desk. Sensing his imminent arrival, she opened the book to the first blank page, and took a seat some distance from the tome. Soon, she heard the buzzing that heralded the swarm's readiness to return home.

As expected, he exited his body via a hole the swarm had eaten through the back of his skull. Returning, the swarm now flew straight for the open diary, smashing headfirst into the blank page like Kamikazes.

He hit the book again and again, but rather than leave a stain of insect entrails, each collision reproduced a line of the strange, handwritten text matching that of the rest of the manuscript. It took more than an hour, but eventually the pages were filled, and the room fell silent.

Elizabeth went to her desk and looked down at the text, searching for the newest illustration to adorn the book. It didn't take long to find a drollery of a man, crucified upside down, his mouth open in a perpetual scream. His eyes shifted back and forth, then locked with hers.

"Hello, Jonathan," she said. "There's no need for me to explain how I became librarian in charge of the grimoire. All you need to know is this is just the beginning for you. But you've read the text, so you must have seen enough to have some idea of what you have to look forward to in the rest of its pages. I'll drop by from time to time to see how you're doing. Until then, you hang in there."

With that, she snapped the book shut.

J.J. Smith is a writer living in the Washington, D.C. area. He's been a hard-news reporter for international news services and newspapers. After 16 years of reporting on the U.S. government, he now spends his daylight hours writing summaries of House and Senate hearings, as well as short stories. His work has appeared in the anthologies *Blood & Blasphemy*, *The Big Book of Bootleg Horror* Volumes I and IV, *Depraved Desires* Volume I, *Dark Magic: Witches, Hackers & Robots*, *Halloween Shrieks*, and *Tales from the Witch's Cauldron*, and in *Horror Bites Magazine*. J.J. is a proud Ojibwa.

"ROSA & HER GRANDMOTHER"
Heather Scheeler

# 405 FORT ERIE LANE

## BY ROD MARTINEZ

I didn't want to go trick-or-treating tonight. Every other year it was just the normal thing to do—a tradition even—and we never failed. Me, Mom, and my brother would hit every house we could before it got too dark. My brat little brother didn't like the dark, a fear that started when he was a baby.

I was born and raised in this small town, Piper, Florida. The families of most people here have been here for generations. I know Mom and Dad said they used to go to elementary school together, and pretty much knew each other all their lives. In a small town like Piper, we celebrate every holiday like a big family, and here, Halloween is huge.

Mrs. Davidson was the favorite of the whole community; everybody knew and loved her, even if we didn't appreciate how special she was. Us native Piperans, we assumed every town had a Mrs. Davidson.

We especially liked visiting Mrs. Davidson's on Halloween, because she always stocked the good stuff. She used to make her own chocolate, and everybody devoured it. She had a special recipe she wouldn't share with anyone, even if they offered to pay her.

Her treat was the easy one to pick out. She wrapped it in a sandwich bag along with a big marble, one that always reminded me of a miniature crystal ball, and a small wind-up toy—the old tin kind my grandfather said he used to play with when he was little. The last one I got from her kind of creeped me out. It seemed to wind itself up on its own sometimes,

Rod Martinez

because sometimes during the night, I'd hear it walking across the floor.

Mrs. Davidson had a special liking for me ever since I was little, and I never understood why, so at her funeral I think I cried more than anyone else did. I remember three years ago, when I was ten, she babysat me and Benny, because Mom and Dad had to go to a funeral in Tampa. I'd been in her house before but never to spend the night. All of us kids used to joke about how it looked like a haunted house on the outside, but inside she kept it so clean you could eat off the floor. The walls, carpet, wooden floor, even the huge grandfather clock that rang every half hour were so spotless my mom said it looked like the place was a model home for "Great Antiques Magazine."

Mrs. Davidson was a widow of two years. She had portraits of her husband hanging on every wall of her house. Mr. Davidson had been the math teacher at our only middle school; he would have been my teacher eventually if he hadn't retired. The day after he retired, he was admitted to the hospital and passed away. His funeral was huge, too, and they renamed the street the school is on in his honor.

Her house at 405 Fort Erie Lane, the only three-story one in the neighborhood, looked like it was built when Abraham Lincoln was President. All the kids on the block played in its front yard, but she never seemed upset about it. She even kept her pool clean for all of us to enjoy. Mrs. Davidson was the lady everyone wished was their grandma. I always thought there was something else, though. She was different—weird— but I was the only one who ever saw it.

One day after school, I was walking through her front yard when I heard a man's voice say, "Get off!" It scared me, and I jumped the picket fence onto the sidewalk. Then I got curious, so I went up to her door and peeked in. She was in the hallway, talking to a framed picture of her husband. It hit me, it was her husband's voice I heard. I remembered, because

84

he had such a unique voice, it was raspy like Rod Stewart's. Goosebumps popped up all over me, and I rushed home to tell Mom. No one ever believed me.

Then last week, tragedy struck—Mrs. Davidson died. The worst thing is, I saw it happen right in front of me and felt helpless and creeped out ever since.

She opened her front door, and her cat Sebastian—she'd adopted him soon after her husband died—flew out in a mad frenzy. Even with the cane, she moved faster than I would have trying to chase after that crazy pet. By the time I jumped the porch to run out to her, the car was already out of control and headed straight at her. The driver had swerved to miss someone on a bicycle, and, in turn, Mrs. Davidson unfortunately became the car's unintended target. The driver punched the brakes but couldn't stop in time. The worst part, just before impact, Mrs. Davidson turned to me, and our eyes locked. It was as if she knew this was going to happen, almost like it had been preordained, and she chose me as witness.

After the accident, Pastor Rivers quickly made the arrangements, and before we knew it, we were all at the Piper Community Cemetery. The whole town came. At the graveside, even mean Coach Adam couldn't stop crying. I know I'll never forget that day.

Now, here it is Halloween, the one night the whole neighborhood goes out *en masse,* but it just wouldn't be the same without the frail little old lady down the street. I chose not to go, so Mom and Benny went out for treats. I stayed home with the lights off, hoping no one would come yelling *"Trick or Treat!"*

I sat on the couch with my iPad, ready to watch Netflix movies—I love all that horror stuff—then the doorbell rang. I ignored it, giving a frustrated sigh and grabbing my glass of chocolate milk.

*Ding-dong!*

Rod Martinez

"Geez." I should'a posted the *"No candy this year"* sign
Mom told me to place on the porch. She even printed it in
color on 11 x 17 cardstock.

After the third annoying ring, I rushed to the door and
yanked it open, ready to tell the idiot off. I mean didn't they
understand that a dark house on Halloween night meant "no
candy"? I thought it was universally understood.

But as soon as the door opened full, I lost my breath at
the sight of my lone visitor. She'd pinned her gray hair up in a
bun, and she wore a dress that was unmistakably her
trademark—black with roses and vines all over.

"Hello, Kelsey. Aren't you coming over for candy this
year?" Mrs. Davidson smiled softly and reached out to touch
my hand. "I made a special batch of chocolate just for you."

"Mrs... uh...?" I stammered.

"Yes, honey, it's really me."

I almost dropped my iPad on the floor as I backed away.

"Honey, aren't you going to invite me in?" Not even a
second after she asked, her hyperactive cat Sebastian rushed in
and bumped my leg.

"Uh, sure Mrs... uh, didn't we just bury...?"

"Honey, I can explain."

"Yes, I think you need to do that," said a raspy male voice
behind me.

I spun around. Sebastian was nowhere to be found, but
Mr. Davidson stood there with his hand out like he was about
to pat my shoulder.

🐱

I didn't feel the floor when I fell. In fact, the last I
remember was seeing Mr. Davidson's hand reach for me. The
next thing I knew, I was lying on the couch in their house. Mrs.
Davidson was seated on the small ottoman next to me, and her
tall husband had a cup of hot tea in his hand.

"Kelsey, that was a nasty fall. I tried to catch you but—"

"Happy All Hallows' Eve, my dear," Mrs. Davidson said interrupting him.

I sat up just as the stupid grandfather clock did its noisy ring, a clanging reverberation I never could get used to, like someone tapped a cracked bell with a big spoon, in a big bathroom where sound bounced all over the place.

"We need to explain some things..."

"I'll say," I responded. I accepted the hot tea and sipped it. The sweet taste of honey on the brim of the cup was a welcomed one.

"Kelsey, sweetie," Mrs. Davidson said, "you know, we've been here a long time."

"Here in this house? Yeah, I bet, this house should be a historical house. But that doesn't explain—"

"No, she didn't mean how long we've been in Piper."

"Well, I'm still confused. Neither of you should be here. Not that I don't miss you but, uh...?"

"This is going to be hard for her to understand, Connie." For some reason, it had never struck me that Mrs. Davidson would have a first name.

Mrs. Davidson's huge dark watery eyes fixed on mine, like she was peering into my soul.

"Kelsey, when you were born, I saw something special in you. I mentioned it to your mother, but she couldn't quite understand what I was telling her."

"Special?" I fidgeted on the couch, as the couple exchanged a glance. Suddenly my situation seemed too surreal. Here I was sitting on a couch staring at two dead people. I moved to get up, but Mrs. Davidson eased in closer to me.

"Haven't you ever wondered about, well, the way you feel about things? The way you see and hear things other people don't."

"Yeah," I mumbled, trying to make conversation so I could get up and walk casually toward the door. I pointed. "Like that annoying bell sound on your clock over there."

"Young lady, that clock stopped working in April of 1974," the tall gray-haired man said.

"Huh? No way." I shook my head. "It chimes every thirty minutes. It's annoying."

Mrs. Davidson's focus shifted from the clock back to me. "The last time you were here with your brother and you covered your ears because of the clamor...did your little brother do the same?"

I thought back. Benny looked at me weird when I covered my ears. It was like he didn't even... "Hey...what's going on here?"

"You are of age now and are ready to know," she told me.

I placed the warm cup of tea on the old wooden table next to me. Steam still rose from it, or so I thought. Was I the only living person who'd see that too?

❦

The quick raps of knuckles on the front wooden door broke the unnerving silence. Whoever it was seemed in a hurry for the door to open. Deciding this was my chance to leave, I jumped up and rushed to the door, giving it a yank.

Standing there, staring at me was...

"Mom?"

"Honey, I was looking all over for you, Benny started crying because he thought you went out trick-or-treating by yourself. He thought you'd get more candy and—"

She was talking, but I turned and glanced back into the room, the Davidsons were gone.

"Mom, how did you know to look for me here? I didn't even come here on my own... uh, what I mean is..."

"I called Beck thinking you were at his house. He did a GPS query for your phone and told me you were here. How did you get inside? This place has been under lock and key since Connie passed away."

88

"Jeez, Beck is worse than the eleven o'clock news," I groused even though I was happy to be found.

"He's your best friend."

"Yeah, ok." I looked back at the cup, steam still rising from it. Then, just at that very second, the clock's annoying clamor sounded. I covered my ears.

"Honey, something wrong with your ears?"

I looked at Mom; I could tell that she couldn't hear it. How could I even explain this kinda thing? I moved my hands away and just accepted the noise.

"No, I'm ok, Mom. Can we just get out of here?"

"You know, if you weren't so level-headed, I'd think you were in here all alone on Halloween night looking for ghosts, or witches, or—" A glimmer of mischievous hope shone in her eyes. "Connie's chocolate recipe. You didn't happen to find it, did you?"

I laughed. "No Mom."

We walked home. Some trick-or-treaters were still out, but by now it was really dark. We crossed our lawn and went inside. Benny was snoring on the couch with a bag of candy at his feet. The chocolate stains on his face told me that he decided not to wait for me and to get to the good stuff first.

"Brat," I whispered.

"What, dear?"

"Oh, nothing Mom." I stretched out in a long yawn. I heard bones and cartilage crack.

Mom moved the bag of goodies from the sofa to the coffee table.

"I want to wake him, but then I don't," she said. "He's so peaceful."

On the table, I noticed a small paper bag with my name printed on it. I opened it and pulled out what felt like a king-sized candy bar.

Rod Martinez

"Mom, what do you know about the Davidsons? Do you know anything about where they came from? How long they lived here?"

"Why, no, Kelsey. They've always just been here."

I pulled out the candy bar. It was inside a sandwich bag with a tiny crystal ball—a real one, not just a big marble—and an old metal wind-up toy in the shape of a grandfather clock.

————————

Author of middle grade & young adult works, Rod Martinez grew up on Marvel Comics and *The Twilight Zone;* their inspiration was inevitable. Challenged by his son to write a story about him and his friends "like *The Goonies,* but in Tampa," Martinez's first novel *The Juniors* was picked up by a publisher—and the rest is history. Rod was recipient of the 2017 Jerry Spinelli Scholarship and the 2018 Professional Development for Artists Grant in Tampa, and speaks at schools, conferences, and libraries promoting love of the written word.

# BACKTRACK

## BY E.C. HANSON

A figure is following me. I know it now. I wasn't sure
before, but I have seen it—whatever it is—too many times for
this to be a coincidence. Yes, it's Halloween night. That is the
only fact that puts my mind at rest. Practically everyone wore
costumes tonight, but there is something about this figure's
appearance that makes my stomach churn.

It stands among a row of trees across the street.

With the sky officially turning dark, it blends in rather
effectively. It seems human. Or at least I hope it is. The little I
notice of the figure's body suggests a slight build; this could be
a man or a woman. I am leaning toward the latter. Not knowing
is torture. I want to barf, but it would attract too much
attention from Adam, the bratty nine-year-old boy in my
charge.

I hold my breath, thinking it will make me feel better. It
has the opposite effect. I cover my mouth and breathe
intensely through my nose. Yes, I am one of those mouth
breathers.

Adam doesn't notice how much I am struggling, because
he's busy, tapping his foot impatiently on the front stoop of a
colonial that looks like it's the birthplace of pumpkins. He
wants his candy, and he hates waiting for it. He thinks he
deserves extra candy because he dressed up as Captain
America. I would like to inform him that most people hate
Captain America.

After a middle-aged woman hands Adam a candy apple
and closes the door, he heaves it across the street near where

91

the creepy figure stood. I hate littering with a passion, but I don't hate it enough to put myself in harm's way retrieving the apple. I have my senior year to finish.

I scold Adam for being so disrespectful and ask if he's about ready to go home.

"Home? We have to cross the street soon and stop at least ten more houses before we get back to my house."

I could tell Adam about the sinister figure. How it closes in on us. How it stares at us. How it, beneath that dark hair, grins at us. The likelihood of him believing me, however, would be low. But if I did convince him a stalker had followed us around this Chattanooga neighborhood for the past fifty-four minutes, I could taint his childhood and scar him for life. I still have to tell him this is my last night of babysitting, but I'll cross that bridge when the opportunity presents itself. Or I won't tell him. I will let his parents know via text in the morning.

Technically, nothing has happened yet. I put stock in this reality and hope to crank through the next ten or so houses in no time.

The layout of our route is a rectangle shape. We are about to visit the last house on the right side of the street, which will then present us with a crosswalk to start visiting the homes on the left side. That's all there is to it. But I don't want to cross the street. That's where the figure is. It's been keeping pace with us ever since we cut through the graveyard.

I let Adam run towards the front door of a raised ranch. A mechanical spider crawls down the roof and into the front lawn. A group of kids scream. Unimpressed, Adam avoids it and approaches the front door. He puts his finger on the doorbell and holds it there for what seems like an eternity. I check my Insta feed. While I wait for it to load, I glance across the street, expecting to get a breather from the figure. I am wrong. It stands next to a neon "Yield to Pedestrians" sign. I have no clue how the figure could have gotten there so fast. I turn to check on Adam's status. He holds his bag out and receives a massive haul of candy. I look back at the street sign. The figure is gone. Its ability to appear and then vanish freaks me out.

New plan: We are not walking on that side of the street. Period. End of story.

"You should see how much that chick gave me."

"We don't refer to women as chicks," I say.

"Still! She gave me like thirty pieces. And a gross Moon Pie. Uggh."

Adam runs to the crosswalk area and stops. Four cars zoom past. I grab his arm, and he yanks it away.

"We're going back the way we came."

"What?"

Like a dialup connection, my brain freezes. I want to tell Adam that it isn't safe on the other side of the street. Unfortunately, the idea of a figure haunting the streets wouldn't scare him one bit. But the reason I don't warn him is that he will only want to go to that side more.

"We're going back this way."

"Over my dead body."

"Want me to tell your Mom you punched the dentist's sign?"

"You wouldn't?"

"I would."

Adam ponders this thought. He doesn't think I am bluffing. He also doesn't think his mother would care as much as I do.

"I'll take my chances."

Adam steps into the crosswalk. I tug him backward by his costume.

"Speaking of which, you should apologize to the dentist."

"I'm not apologi—"

"She could sue and get all your family's money."

Raised in an affluent household and too proud of it, Adam's face and body posture shifts. I have his attention, so I continue with, "As a matter of fact, you should apologize to a few others for your behavior tonight."

Adam didn't apologize to anyone for his actions. Secretly, I admired this personality trait. But his actions from this evening—punching a dentist's sign, insulting an elderly woman, etc.—were the sole reason a figure was stalking us. If I was wrong, he could, at the very least, learn a valuable lesson about human behavior.

"I'll sweeten the pot for you."

"How?" he wonders.

I know, right then and there, I will become a terrible parent. I know better than to negotiate with a child. But I have to keep him safe—not just because his parents will pay me later—and I have to figure out whether there was something to be genuinely concerned about, or if this mysterious night traveler got off on playing mental games with total strangers.

"I'll let you visit all the homes again."

He smirks. His eyes say, "Yeah, right." I nod. Something still bothers him.

"The people would know I visited. They'd remember a Captain America."

I consider telling him that most people would forget Captain America. Instead, I dig into my backpack and whip out a mask. Adam studies it and shakes his head.

"I'm not dressing up like a nun."

"Why not? You'd get more candy."

"I'd get the same amount, if not more, on the other side. And I wouldn't have to change costumes."

"If you play along," I said pulling out the matching costume nun's habit, "I'll take you to the other side of the street."

"How long would I have to be the nun?"

"Until the dentist's office."

"Then I could change back and hit up the other side of the street?"

I nod. Adam snags my mask and habit. He darts towards a tree-lined area and removes his clothes. I turn around to check on my friend—even though my enemy would be more appropriate. I don't see anything. But then a motion detector goes off under Noreen's General Store, and sure enough, the figure is back. I check on Adam. While I can barely make out his body, I can tell that he's struggling with the habit based on how much the tree branches are shaking. I return my attention to the figure. Fed up and wanting this mystery to end, I address her in a firm tone:

"What do you want?"

The figure slowly raises its right hand and points directly at me. I want to scream. I want to flee. I want to race to the cops and have this, whatever it is, arrested for holiday harassment.

"You talking to me?" Adam asks.

His question startles me. But I recoup my mental strength and lead him toward the next house.

"I make a good nun or what?"

"You do," I say.

I lie. He looks absurd. The habit is too long for him, and the mask hangs off his face awkwardly.

"How many stops to go before we reach the dentist's office?"

Eighteen minutes and an overflowing candy bag later, Adam and I cross the front lawn of the dentist's office. Whereas the place was lit up inside upon our first visit, most of the lights are out now. This allows me to relax because this dentist could very well be the figure that's stalking us. It's worth pointing out that she stood in front of the bay window and gave Adam a death glare after he punched her sign. The intensity of her expression was like nothing I had ever seen before. Perhaps Adam's insensitive act motivated her to harass us. Her body frame and wicked face make her a suspect. And now, all the lights in her business are off. Could she have wrapped up work and gone home? Yes. But could she have also closed shop, switched into some creepy attire, and followed us? Yes, she could have.

Adam hops on the front stoop and hammers on the front door.

"Would you stop? There's no one in there."

"You said I had to come here."

"Let's leave her a note."

"What should we write? 'Dentists are dumb'?"

"You're here to apologize."

"Then give me some paper and a pen."

I dig around in my backpack. I find a composition notebook, but there isn't a single pen in any of the pockets. Adam stares at me with disdain. My inability to find a pen delays his dream to cross the street.

Like an amateur boxer, Adam delivers the jab-right combo to the front door. I glance at him, using every expression on my face to ask, in the harshest way, *"Why would you even do that?"* He laughs. I dig around one last time and find a pen. I hold it up in the air and, right as I am about to announce this small success, the front door opens. Adam turns around slowly. A stiff woman, still dressed in her scrubs, bends down and addresses the nun in front of her.

"Must you be so impatient?"

Like I have never witnessed, Adam, rather gently, says, "No." He does one better, too. He removes the nun mask, looks the dentist directly in the eyes, and says this:

"I was the one who punched your sign earlier. There was no good reason for me to do it. I'm sorry, Mrs. Dentist Lady."

The stiff woman of—most likely—forty years slips out of sight and leaves the door wide open. Adam stands there, beyond perplexed. She returns. As if the twenty-second vanishing act did her personality some good, she flashes a warm and playful demeanor. She keeps her hands behind her back.

"Pick a hand, any hand," she says.

Adam picks the left hand, and she provides him with a reasonable amount of candy. He laughs. She does, too.

"What's in the other hand?"

The dentist cracks up. She stuffs his bag with another handful of candy. I want to intervene and tell her that no person, let alone a dentist, should be giving a kid this many sweets. Instead, I wait for Adam to join me.

"Other side of the street time."

"Not other side of the street time."

"But you said that I—"

I cut him off here. "Your bag of candy is overflowing."

"So?" He reads my expression then stares at my backpack. "I can use that."

"No, you can't."

"Why? You got drugs or alcohol in there?"

"No."

"I've been taking DARE. I know all about what high schoolers are doing."

I unzip my backpack and show him what's inside. I wish there were something sordid in there. It would impress him and make me look like a cooler person.

Adam tires of looking inside my backpack and steps onto the street.

"Don't even think about it."

"Think about what?" he teases.

"You'll get a jaywalking ticket."

"Jaywalking? Is that like moonwalking?"

"It's much worse. Your parents would be pissed. C'mon. We're not too far from the next crosswalk."

Adam complies with my warning. He leads the way, juggling the candy that's attempting to exit his bag. I glance at the opposite side of the street. The figure keeps pace with us.

E.C. Hanson

Now that I know it isn't some butt-hurt dentist, I have to consider other suspects. But who? Aside from the elderly woman at the crosswalk, who else could there be?

Adam reaches the next crosswalk. He tears into three packages of candy and stuffs the sweets into his mouth. I nearly scold him for doing so, but he is compliant for once in his short life.

"Is that the old bag I pissed off?"

"Okay, totally not okay to call her that."

"What am I apologizing to her for?"

"Well, you made fun of how she walks."

Adam acknowledges this fact with a nod. He watches the silver-haired woman stop oncoming traffic. She motions for the trick-or-treaters to cross. Adam approaches her. While I am proud of his path of atonement, I am upset that the woman is here. If it isn't her, and it's not the dentist, then who is stalking us? Or *what* is stalking us?

The elderly woman bends down and hugs Adam. I shake my head in disbelief. This kid is a charmer when he intends to be. My eyes search for the figure. I cannot locate it. I am relieved. *Is this drama over? Is that as far as the figure will travel?*

As if the gods above heard every word, my questions are answered. The figure appears in between a row of parked cars at the police station. It lifts a small object. I cannot make out what it is yet, but it looks to be a doll of some sort. The figure raises the doll towards the light. It's a poppet of a child dressed in a...Captain America costume.

I vomit in the street. Adam laughs. The elderly woman rushes towards me.

"Are you okay, sweetie?"

I shake my head. Adam isn't laughing anymore. The elderly woman guides me towards the side of the street we have frequented all night. I sit on the wet grass. My pants get soaked; I fear what my ass looks like. Adam offers his best version of a pep talk.

98

"There wasn't that much puke. You'll be fine in, like, five minutes. Maybe less than that."

As sick as I currently feel, the moment provides clarity. I realize I have overlooked a final suspect: Adam's mother. The poppet is too personal for it to be anyone but her. *Why her though?* Well, for starters, she wasn't home when I picked Adam up. Her husband, a burly construction worker, had no clue where she was either. Adam's mother, a massage therapist, has a habit of being elusive. People in town have seen her with various men—mostly well-to-do Southerners—and while the rumors about possible infidelity exist, she always has a slick response for the husband who, for a reason inexplicable to most, is totally devoted to her.

"Text your mother. No, call her. No, FaceTime her."

"She hates FaceTime."

"Do it, or I'll throw all that candy down the next sewer drain."

Adam removes his cell phone and taps a few buttons.

"She's not going to answer," he promises.

I hope she doesn't because it would explain why a figure is stalking us with an Adam poppet in her possession. If it isn't her, I might have a panic attack.

Adam hangs up the phone. I breathe a sigh of relief. I stand, feeling vindicated that I have figured out the identity of the guilty party. I turn to address the figure. It's gone.

"We know who you are."

In a deadpan manner, Adam says, "Are you losing your marbles?"

"I am gaining them, bud."

Adam rolls his eyes, regains control of his massive candy bag, then steps into the crosswalk. I join him. Now I know who's been playing tricks on us, I feel no fear whatsoever for visiting the opposite side of the street.

Adam's phone rings. He shoves his candy bag at me and pulls out his cell.

E.C. Hanson

"She's FaceTiming me."

Before I can respond, he answers the call. His mother, rocking University of Tennessee gear from head to toe, stands in their marble-heavy kitchen.

She is home, which means she is not out here. She is not the figure.

She opens the fridge and removes a bottle of chardonnay. She unscrews it, pours a glass big enough for three people, then takes a sip.

"Everything okay? Did you need me for something?"

I whisper, "Tell her it was an accident." Adam does what he is told. I scan the streets for the figure. I cannot locate it. Then, out of the corner of my eye, I spot the figure near a chiropractor's office. It sits near the entranceway with the poppet. But there is something else in its hand. The figure holds the poppet up again. It has done this move before, so I am not as fazed by it. Suddenly, it shows off a shiny knife, twirls it around, and then jams it into the poppet.

I vomit again, but this time I don't let it escape my mouth. I hear Adam's mother say bye. I look over at his phone and watch her guzzle more wine right before she ends the call.

Thrilled that he made contact and didn't receive some order to come home, Adam walks across the crosswalk without getting consent from me or the elderly woman he apologized to moments earlier.

I cannot let him go that way. This figure wants to hurt him. *What kind of person would I be if I allowed him to walk into certain danger?*

I march after him. When he reaches the other side of the street, I force him to stop.

"Jesus H! Now what?"

I have to do something to save him. Simply telling him that he has too much candy or that I'm not feeling well or that something dangerous exists over here isn't enough to curb his desire to prolong the night in the pursuit of more candy.

100

"This is my last night of babysitting. I got a new job, a better one, so I can't watch you anymore."

The joy rushes out of Adam's face. Even I am shocked by this occurrence.

"You're just saying that," he says as he pushes past me. I notice the figure fifty yards ahead, waiting with the knife and poppet near a wooden bench.

I have to lie. I cannot tell him that I am getting a job in a vet's office because it matches my career plans; I must insult him.

"I am not just saying that. And you know what else? I got a new job because I can't stand babysitting such a bratty and selfish boy. You make me not want to have children."

Adam is stunned. Tears form around the corners of his eyes. Embarrassed, he puts the nun mask back on and walks away in defeat. I feel awful for saying such things, but his life is at stake. I turn to locate the figure. It is nowhere in sight. I turn back to locate Adam. He runs off, with a good portion of his candy falling out of his bag.

I consider heading home, but the guilt overpowers me. I head over to the police station. A bald cop with a ginger goatee sits inside his running vehicle. I wonder if he intends to go anywhere. I wave at him. It produces no reaction. I motion for him to roll down his window. It slides down a crack.

"Yes'm?"

I should tell him about the figure. I should tell him the amount of time Adam and I have been stalked this holiday night. But I don't want to be dismissed. Instead, I put all of my focus and concern on Adam.

"I was hoping you could do me a favor. I was babysitting a boy tonight, and, well, I received an emergency call from my mother. She needs my help getting to the hospital."

"What's that gotta do with me?" he asks.

"I thought, if you weren't busy, you'd be able to follow the kid I was watching and make sure he gets home safe."

The cop sizes me up. He presents a vibe like he has much better things to do than check on a boy. But, to my surprise, he agrees.

"Where's he headed and what's he wearin'?"

I explain that he started with a Captain America costume then switched gears to a nun costume. I can tell that the cop yearns to know why such a costume switch took place; however, he reads my body language and decides that he should let me go to save my mom. Little does he know that my mother is perfectly fine.

As he drives away, I return my attention to both sides of the street. I walk a few steps forward, trying to locate the figure that was on me like white on rice all night.

It is gone.

Minutes pass. I trudge in the direction of Adam's house. I'm not even going to pop in and ask his parents for money. I am merely going to get in my car and go.

After a few steps, it hits me. The graveyard. Adam's stupid song and his disgusting loogie. How could I have forgotten it?

I rush towards the local cemetery, hoping that I can solve the mystery of this frightening figure. I retrace our steps and try to pinpoint the exact headstones we passed. I ascend a hill and pause in front of a series of headstones. None of them stand out initially.

I recall the earlier events of the night when Adam, amped to the max, skipped through this particular area singing, *"Ding-dong, the witch is dead!"* As if the singing wasn't enough, he hocked a loogie on one of the headstones. I didn't think much of it at the time, but I get the chills when I spot a mound of saliva on the headstone of Philomena Montgomery. No big deal, right? Wrong. Philomena Montgomery was reputed to be a witch from the 1900s who cast a wicked spell upon anyone that dared to disrespect her.

Before I can voice the words aloud to express my regret for Adam's inconsiderate actions, someone shoves me from behind. The shove doesn't surprise me as much as the place I land: a hole about six feet deep into the ground. I look up. The figure appears with a shovel. She drops dirt on me. I scream with all my might. It does me no good. The dirt hits my chin, eyes, and mouth. The figure laughs. I beg Philomena Montgomery to stop. She doesn't. She continues dropping dirt on my face. And while I panic over the fact that I won't get to realize my dreams of working in a vet's office or get to say goodbye to my overly conservative, though chill, parents, I take solace in the fact that I saved Adam, brat or not, from this fate.

---

A graduate of NYU, Hanson's work has been published by Smith & Kraus and Applause Books in 8 play anthologies. More than 35 of his short plays have been developed and produced across the United States. His fiction will be published by Collective Tales, Trembling With Fear, Ghost Orchid Press, and D&T Publishing in 2021.

# Waking the Trees

## by Amanda Crum

When the winds came, Marcus stopped to take a breath.

Around him, the trees woke their leaves in a rush—birch and elm and oak, taller than he could see without craning his neck. They marched up the hillside ahead of him and smelled like his childhood in some nameless way, as the air after a storm would always make him think of being seven and walking home from church.

Marcus took a worn red bandana from his back pocket and swiped it across his brow, more out of habit than need. September in Kentucky was a place Floridians only dreamed of, where the trees filtered heat and provided cool respiration. It was a great, collective sighing that raised gooseflesh on his arms, in a good way.

He thought of Tisha living her life uninterrupted in Miami, going out to dinner and watching pink skies in the evening. Maybe allowing a man he'd never seen the shape of to hold a door open for her. When he was younger, two years had seemed like such a long time. Now it was just a single day, repeated over and over, a bridge between then and now. He would never tell her, of course. She had Florida, and he had the Appalachian Mountains. It didn't matter that he sometimes woke up cradling the extra pillow as he had once done her hips.

When the radio crackled static, Marcus pulled it from his belt and sat in a patch of sunlight to answer.

"That you, Stubbs?" he said. "You're breaking up."

"You almost finished in the 12th quadrant?" Stubbs repeated. "There's a storm on the way."

"Maybe another hour," Marcus said, surveying the area of land that had been assigned to him. Orange paint marked thirty or forty trees, designated as a boundary; those affected with disease were given cut marks in teal. Miami Dolphins colors, he suddenly realized, and wished he hadn't.

"Alright, finish up and call out when you're headed into camp. We should be able to get out before the storm gets cranked up," Stubbs said. He was a good man, a fair boss. The safety of his crew was important to him, which made Marcus feel more valued than anything else could.

"10-4."

Hard to imagine a storm breaking the atmosphere when all he could see and feel was warm sunlight filtered through branches. He gathered his supplies into a sturdy canvas duffel bag and slung it over his shoulder. Time to move up the hill.

🐾

Marking trees was a mostly solitary business. Marcus supposed that was what had pulled him to it, that and working outside all day. He'd never been one who could stand feeling closed in or cooped up.

He was surprised, then, when he looked up and found a woman standing on the path in front of him. She was petite but looked strong, bare arms lean and rangy. She wore a dress the color of animal hide. Long dark hair tangled down her back and around her shoulders. From his distance, she might have been 25 or 55. Something about her face seemed to morph in the gently shifting leaf-light, as though she couldn't be pinned down.

"Hello," he said.

She studied him, eyes moving over his clothes and bag, then walked slowly forward, trailing her fingers along the rough bark of the closest tree. She was barefoot. Dirty soles with clinging pine needles.

Amanda Crum

"Do you need help?" he asked.

"No," she said, her face blank. "Do you?"

"I work out here. We're leaving soon," he said. For reasons he couldn't name, it seemed important to let her know he wasn't alone.

"We?"

"My company. They're spread out around the woods, marking trees to be cut down."

She frowned. "Cutting down beautiful living things that have no say in the matter. How do you sleep at night?"

"We only cut down the dead ones, where disease is present," said Marcus. "Do you live out here?"

It was a loaded question; he'd never seen a house, no evidence of anyone. She looked like she'd been living rough for a while.

"I'm around," she said irritably. "What do you do with them? The ones you cut down?"

"A lot of them stay here, in the forest. Birds and frogs and other wildlife put them to good use."

"Why cut them down at all, then? Why not just leave them alone?"

She seemed close to tears, and Marcus found himself feeling badly. He was possessed by a deep shame, and wished he could hide the tools that jutted out from his bag.

"Because if they're allowed to stay rooted, they affect the healthy trees," he said gently. "The entire ecosystem can be thrown off. Likewise, when a young tree is allowed to thrive it can help an older one find nourishment."

"Yes. Trees can communicate with one another. If one is under attack from herbivores, it can release chemicals that tell its neighbors they need to protect themselves. You should stop interfering. Life will always find a way," she said. Her voice trembled faintly.

A sharp crack of thunder split the air, so close that Marcus actually ducked. The storm had arrived, bringing with it the

106

smell of fresh rain. He could see it falling in sheets higher up the mountain. He had wasted too much time with this woman. The crew would be wanting to leave soon. He took out his radio and tried to raise Stubbs, but all that came back was a rash of static and a high-pitched squeal that sent the nearest flock of birds scattering to the sky.

"I'm sorry. I have to go," he said. "Do you have somewhere safe to stay?"

"You'll never get down the mountain before it hits," she said, looking up. The trees had all flipped their leaves upside down in the rushing wind to expose their pale green underbellies, a sure sign of rough weather. "Why don't you come with me? My cabin is just north of here."

Marcus faltered, unwilling to go deeper into the woods when he needed to head the other way. He knew how storms could be on the mountain, though, and there was a significant chance he would get himself lost if he tried to find his way back with limited visibility.

"How far?" he asked.

"Five minutes."

He followed her north, keeping one wary eye on the swirling skies above them. The clouds and taller trees blotted out the remaining sun, dimming the landscape as they walked. By the time her cabin came into view, it was as though evening had fallen early.

She led him inside, into the powerful scents of coffee and lavender. The place was small—just one large room for the living area and kitchen, and the suggestion of a second one just beyond it—but much neater than he'd expected. A large wooden table took up the length of one wall and was covered in jars, boxes, and flowerpots full of growing things. She cooked over an open flame in the fireplace, he saw with some amusement. Truly a woman of the woods.

"I'm Marcus, by the way," he said as she closed the door behind them.

"Trinity," she said.

"You live here by yourself?"

Trinity nodded. "For a long time."

"Doesn't it get lonely, way out here?"

"I prefer to be outside the company of other people most of the time, but when you live amongst nature, you're never truly alone," she said loftily. "I have what I need. It's better here."

"Better than where?"

She moved to the fireplace and removed a kettle from the swinging iron bar just above it. Marcus wondered if any of the other guys on the crew had ever met her and decided against it. They would have mentioned it.

"Seattle," she said. She moved lithely to the table, where a stack of sturdy earthenware mugs awaited. Plucking two from the pile, she filled them with hot water and dipped herbs from a fragile-looking bowl into both. "It's a nice place, but there are too many people. Too much noise. I couldn't concentrate there."

Marcus thought of Miami, where the bustle of the city was life, it was *mana*. And further out, the water provided cool comfort when the sidewalks got too hot. For as much as he enjoyed working alone, he also couldn't imagine being so isolated for long periods of time. Once again, he wondered what Tisha was doing. She was a million miles away from this tiny, strange cabin. The thought sobered him and took his thoughts down a swift and dark path.

The storm hit just as Trinity handed him a mug of tea, a great flood of rain that sounded for all the world like waves pounding the side of a ship. Outside the lone window, their universe went white.

"I'm glad you came with me," Trinity said suddenly, sipping her tea. "I didn't think you would."

"I almost didn't," he admitted. "No offense, I just didn't want to leave my crew hanging. They're probably wondering where the hell I am."

"They won't leave you, will they?"

"Nah, if I don't make it back to camp soon, they'll send some guys out to look for me."

Her face changed then, from slightly worried to appeased. "Good."

Marcus sipped the tea she'd given him. It was surprisingly sweet, not bitter as he was expecting. There were notes of strawberry that reminded him of something familiar, something he couldn't place. She watched him silently, dark eyes roving over his hands as he brought the cup to his mouth.

"You have nice fingers," she said. "Do you play piano?"

It was an odd question, but she was an odd person. Living alone in the woods for years had to have an effect on one's social skills.

"No, I never played any instruments," he answered. "I've always worked with my hands, though. Woodworking, landscaping. Marking trees."

"Those are all jobs connected to nature. Do you enjoy working outdoors?"

"I've never really thought about it, but I guess I do."

"It really takes the bad thoughts away for a little while, doesn't it?"

Marcus frowned. "Bad thoughts?"

She tilted her head, almost playfully. "You know, thoughts of your ex-wife. Who she's seeing, what she's doing. You might think I don't know much about anything, living out here so isolated, but I understand relationships. We always want what we can't have anymore. It's human nature."

Anger surged through him, unbidden. "What do you know about my ex-wife?"

Trinity only smiled, an infuriating non-answer that tugged at his sense of unease. Her left eyelid drooped suddenly in a half-wink, but it wasn't intentional. She lifted her hand and pulled it open wide with finger and thumb, sighing as she did so.

"You alright?" he asked roughly.

"Sometimes our bodies fail us, Marcus. It's inevitable. How old are you, by the way?"

He set his cup down irritably. He was tired of her questions, and the strong tea was churning in his belly. "How old are you?"

Trinity laughed. It was an underwater sound, the burbling reverb of a whale chuckling deep beneath the surface of the ocean. Marcus felt his eyes widen to the point of pain as she suddenly reached into her mouth and pulled out a long, thick, silver wire. It seemed to take forever. The last six inches were covered in a viscous black fluid that gleamed in the bluish light coming through the window. She gagged a little at the end and dropped the wire to the dirt floor, where it lay benignly in the dim light. Marcus recognized it as staking material, the type used to keep young trees from falling over.

"I'm old enough to know that we all need a little help sometimes," Trinity said. "Even a sturdy old oak can fall in a strong wind unless it has support."

"What the hell...?" he breathed, blinking rapidly. His vision was deteriorating, clouding at the edges. The smell of warm tea drifted up and took over. It filled the small cabin, sour as vinegar.

"I can make you forget your sadness," she murmured.

Marcus felt weak. He leaned against the table and felt the side of his hand brush against something hard—a man's pipe, filled with tobacco. A relic from another time, nearly.

"I thought you lived alone," he said.

"I told you," Trinity said, "When you live in the woods, you're never alone."

Marcus felt a sudden and forceful need to vomit. He whirled away from the table and yanked open the door, running out into the lessening rain to purge metallic strawberries. His throat burned terrifically.

When it was all up, he slid against the tree he'd been holding on to for balance and sat down with no grace. His walkie was beneath him, a hard reminder of where he could be, and he struggled to reach for it with trembling arms. It was stuck on his belt loop. He fumbled with numb fingers for a minute, an hour, an eternity, keeping a watchful eye on the cabin as he tried to pry the walkie loose. Trinity wasn't visible.

The walkie wouldn't come free. He turned onto his side, reminded of the time he had the flu and couldn't get out of bed without Tisha's help, and came face-to-face with a pair of gold-rimmed glasses stuck to the tree. No, stuck inside the tree, growing along with it. Embedded in the bark. There was still part of a nose attached. Marcus watched open-mouthed as the sole nostril flared gently. Breathing.

He had no lungs for screaming. Instead, he flung himself onto his stomach and army-crawled on forearms and knees, across wet leaves and prickly branches and sap-sticky pine needles. There were others—a tree with one rapidly-blinking green eye, another with a thick swath of blonde hair growing around the roots like moss.

The blood vessels in Marcus's eyes ruptured as the ones in his heart hardened like quartz. He could only see through a red haze as Trinity walked toward him, an expectant smile on her face. His arms lengthened, thinned, reached toward the sky. His feet rooted, curled into the soft soil where they disturbed earthworms. He stretched beyond his former limits but felt the action only peripherally. It might have been happening to someone else.

In a moment, Trinity joined him. Her lean oak body tilted slightly into Marcus, taking what he had to give. Breathing him in. Rejuvenating. The storm leveled off, peeling away clouds to reveal swatches of sunlight. Rainwater dripped and ran.

Amanda Crum

Later, when the walkie erupted in a burst of static, sixteen trees gently swayed their branches in recognition of something familiar they couldn't quite place.

---

Amanda Crum is a writer and artist whose work has been published in *Barren Magazine*, *Eastern Iowa Review*, *The Hellebore*, and more. She is the author of *Tall Grass and The Day You Learned To Swim*, both of which made the preliminary ballot for the Bram Stoker Award. Amanda currently lives in Kentucky with her husband and two children.

# WHAT DASH DID

## BY VALERIE HUNTER

Dash's older brother left her three things: her nickname, her bicycle, and a promise not to tell anyone what she could do.

He'd given her the nickname early. Harry had been nine and learning Morse code, immersing himself in it with total enthusiasm. Their sister Dorothy, then three, was already called Dottie, so it wasn't much of a leap to call her Dot. Baby Ethel became Dash, a nickname she still embraced.

When Dash was eight, Harry taught her to ride his bicycle. It was far too large for her, but she kept at it because Harry claimed it was a skill everyone should have.

He'd given her the bicycle when he'd left for the army two years later. Then he'd said, "Keep quiet about the plants. People won't understand, and you might get hurt. Don't do it, either, in case someone notices. Promise?"

Dash promised. She always did whatever Harry asked. He was her hero, and the only one she'd ever shown her secret to. If he thought she should keep it hidden, then she would.

The promise had seemed finite then. "We'll figure it out when I come back," Harry said, like the war was a momentary interruption.

It hadn't been. He'd been dead sixteen years now, and Dash was grown, but she still held tight to all three things— the nickname, the bicycle, and the promise.

Valerie Hunter

Harry's death had been the beginning of people leaving Dash. Her father passed away suddenly in '22. Dot—Dorothy now to everyone except Dash—married a banker in '26 and moved to Tulsa. Dash corresponded with her frequently and visited several times a year, but it wasn't the same. Then Mama took sick in '30 and was gone by the end of the year.

After her initial grief, Dash tried not to dwell on it. She'd been left the farm—though it had been mortgaged to pay Mama's doctor bills—the windmill, and a love for the land. Surely someday it would be productive again.

Meanwhile, she had the bicycle. The farm was miles from town, but the bike made the trip manageable. Murdoch was hardly a metropolis, but it had an agricultural college and a bustling Main Street. Even amidst these hard times there was money to be made if you set your mind to it. Dash was secretary to the town's sole lawyer, Mr. Greenway, and she also typed theses for seniors at the college.

For company, she had Alfie, whom she'd first met three years ago. He'd been a little older than the other college freshmen, but no less confused.

"Do you type shorter papers?" he'd asked her.

"The professors accept handwritten, so long as they're neat," she reassured him.

Alfie shook his head. "Mine won't be neat. I'll pay your thesis rate."

His clothes were threadbare, and freshmen essays weren't long. She quoted him a much lower price.

"Could you... fix the spelling? I'll pay extra."

"It's inclusive." Lord knew she fixed enough spelling—not to mention punctuation and grammar—when she typed theses. It wasn't kindness; she just couldn't help herself.

"I've been told mine's especially bad," he warned.

114

The warning was valid. Dash had never seen anyone confuse his b's and d's and p's before, or make every vowel look like an amorphous blob. For the first couple papers she had to ask him to clarify what she couldn't puzzle out herself, but after that she'd grown accustomed to Alfie's quirks. His content was always solid, and neatening up the rest wasn't difficult.

They'd formed a friendship that extended beyond essays. That had been the fall after Mama's death, when the house still felt horribly empty. Dash had other friends, but they were busy with husbands and babies; Alfie fit into her life better. They both understood making do for yourself, finding things to laugh at even when nothing was particularly funny. She invited him to supper frequently because he always looked starving, and eventually Alfie became family. She knew how he was the son of sharecroppers who always worked too hard for too little. How he was intent on doing better for himself. How it had taken him years to scrape together money for college, and three tries to pass the entrance exam.

Dash told Alfie about Harry and the rest of her family, how her father always said the land was everything and she meant to keep it. How she'd tried college for a semester, but the home economics program—the only acceptable major for women—was dull. How she enjoyed working for Mr. Greenway and typing the theses because it kept her mind sharp. She told Alfie everything about herself, except the one thing she'd promised not to.

They did other things together, too, like dances at the college or an occasional movie. When Dot came to visit, she enjoyed teasing.

"That boy's going to ask you to marry him someday, mark my words."

"Dot!"

"What? You could do worse."

Dash didn't tell her Alfie had already hinted about marriage, and she'd headed him off, saying she wasn't the marrying type. Truth be told, Alfie was the only person she *could* see herself marrying, but he wanted a job with the Department of Agriculture or the Farm Service Agency when he graduated. She respected that, but didn't want to leave the farm.

Their friendship remained strong, which surprised Dash. She'd turned down suitors before, and they'd reacted poorly. Maybe Alfie didn't really love her that deeply, which was just as well. She'd enjoy their friendship until he graduated, and then he'd be just another person who left her.

🐾

One February evening during Alfie's junior year, he said with unusual seriousness after supper, "Gotta ask you something."

"So ask."

"Can I farm your land this year?"

She raised her eyebrows. "Why?"

"Why not? It's just sitting there. Judging by your vegetable garden, the soil must be decent, and you've got the windmill for pumping water. I've got a few things I want to try."

"I thought you hated sharecropping."

"This is different. I don't figure you're an unreasonable boss, and we can split the profits even."

After Pa's death, they'd rented the land to Paul Milton next door, but eventually he'd said it wasn't worthwhile. Dash hired someone to do the planting and harvesting then, but she hadn't profited. Last year the land lay fallow. Her job was enough for the mortgage and the taxes, and between typing theses and growing an abundance of vegetables, she'd managed not to starve.

Alfie's offer was generous, and she could use the extra money, even if it wasn't much. She knew he could, too—he had an evening janitorial job, and he'd done farm work previous summers, though it was getting that no one could afford much help. A decent harvest on her land would be a boon to them both.

But the way he was certain the land would produce based on her vegetable garden made her stomach twinge. "I think you'll be disappointed," she said.

"You don't have faith in me?" He grinned, but there was hurt in his eyes.

"This drought's taken everyone's faith."

Alfie shook his head. "I've got ideas. No use planting wheat. I want to try alfalfa, lima beans, crops that don't need much moisture and can still bring a decent return. Will you let me try?"

"If you want to," she said, and he beamed like she'd given him a prize.

Alfie got to work at the first hint of spring. He plowed the fields with the college's draft horses, saying there would be less dust without all the machinery. He did something called contour plowing, claiming it would be healthier for the land. He worked all day Saturday and after classes on weekdays. Dash always insisted he stay for supper before he headed to his janitorial job. She didn't know how he got any schoolwork done, but he must have managed. The junior courses were mostly recitation and practical work anyhow, which he excelled at, and fewer papers. Still, she worried.

"You're working too hard," she chided one evening. The radio was on and they were dancing around the living room to "Build a Little Home," but he kept stumbling.

He held her closer. "I'll be done planting soon. Then I can relax."

"Then you'll have exams," she pointed out. "Hardly relaxing."

117

"I'll get by. The two of us always do, don't we?"

She leaned into his chest, nodding. They always did.

✦

Dash reminded herself of that the following Friday, when Mr. Greenway told her he'd only need her three days a week going forward. "It's been slow," he said apologetically. "You understand."

"Of course," she said, forcing a smile.

"Things might pick up come fall," he added, with the same cheeriness everyone used about these hard times not lasting forever. Dash was well-versed in that tone; she'd perfected it herself.

She spent the weekend calculating how she'd managed. Could she get a second job? Alfie always knew who was hiring; she'd ask him.

Alfie had finished planting, and she hadn't seen him in a couple days. He always came for Sunday dinner, but this week he didn't show up. He finally arrived late Sunday afternoon, deep circles under his eyes. "Sorry about dinner. Forgot I had a botany paper due tomorrow." He held it up ruefully. "Would you mind typing it? I'll pay double."

She took the pages, waving his offer away. "This won't take long. Why don't you nap while I'm typing?"

He collapsed on the sofa, snoring softly within minutes. She typed the essay, a pure mess even by Alfie's standards.

She didn't wake him till half past six. He looked embarrassed when she did, and tried to refuse her offer of supper.

"You need a hot meal in you, or I'll worry you won't make it back to town," she insisted.

By supper's end, Alfie had picked up a little. "Don't know what I'd do without you, Dash. After the harvest I'll take you dancing someplace fancy."

"Sure," she said, putting on the same smile she'd given Mr. Greenway.

"I mean it. Everything's going to be fine. Did I tell you I got a job with Herishen?"

"Another job?" Surely he couldn't stretch himself any thinner.

"Not till the semester's over. Herishen only needs me three days a week, so I'll have plenty of time to work on this place."

"Where you don't get paid," she pointed out.

"The land'll pay me in the end." He smiled, but his voice lacked its previous confidence. He was as worried as she was, both of them clinging to paltry jobs and the hope of a decent harvest.

In the end, she didn't mention Mr. Greenway cutting her days. Alfie didn't need her worries. She'd manage herself.

🐈

By May the air was oppressive, and dust blew across the prairie in waves. Alfie hauled water tirelessly and insisted things weren't nearly as bad here as in the Panhandle, but the crops were clearly struggling. Alfie could put all the sweat he wanted into the land, but it wouldn't change nature.

*But you can*, a small voice insisted.

She could, but she shouldn't. Harry had been right. People didn't like what they didn't understand. It was too dangerous.

She'd told herself this a thousand times before, but now she found herself arguing back. After all, she'd already set a precedent with the vegetable garden.

It had been desperation then, too, and an unwillingness to let the whole farm lie dormant. Why couldn't she have some vegetables? She'd been discreet, toting water from the windmill pond and begging a little manure from Herishen. Still, she knew her vegetables would have looked as stunted as everyone

119

else's if she hadn't infused a little of herself, enough help to be green and thriving.

Visitors commented, but Dash joked about her green thumb and sent them home with tomatoes or cucumbers. No one ever went as far as to call it miraculous. It was easier to accept strangeness than to question it, as long as it wasn't *too* strange.

Maybe she could be discreet with the crops, too. People were used to things growing well on her land, and Alfie was convinced his methods were superior. They both needed the money. Why shouldn't she help things along a bit?

She did it after dark, as nervous as though she was committing a crime. She walked the rows of beans, circled the edges of the alfalfa, sank her toes in the dry dirt beside the corn, humming softly in answer to the songs she could hear, ever so faintly, from the crops themselves. She ran her fingers over a few sad leaves, unsure if it would be enough.

She could barely see what she was doing by the moonlight, never mind whether it had an effect. By the time she went inside, she felt foolish. Of course she hadn't done anything. The garden was the result of hard work and manure, nothing more. Harry had told her to hush all those years ago because he'd known it wasn't real and he didn't want her carted off to the loony bin if she kept insisting she had magical powers.

And that hum she always heard, the way plants sang to her?

Well, maybe she truly was crazy.

Dash lay awake a long time. It was disconcerting to believe something about yourself for so long only to realize it might not be true.

She must have fallen asleep eventually, because then her alarm clock was jangling. She was so used to waking before the alarm that she felt rushed and discombobulated. She didn't even remember the crops till she had mounted her bicycle, and then she almost fell off it.

The fields were a vibrant green, the crops not only healthier but noticeably larger than yesterday.

She wasn't crazy.

Her power was real.

With the glow of this—and the dread of what people might say, because surely she'd gone overboard—Dash righted the bike and headed to work.

🐈

Coming home, Paul Milton and another neighbor stood at the edge of Dash's property, looking at the green fields. They clammed up as she approached, but then Paul said, "Your college boy sure has a way with plants."

"Yep," Dash agreed, and kept cycling.

At supper she told Alfie, "Fields look good."

"I swear everything's twice as big and three times greener than yesterday," he said. "I told you your land's special."

She grinned. "I never doubted you."

After that she strolled around the farm several evenings a week, humming under her breath. She'd ignored the plants' songs for so long, but now they filled her head, each crop a different tune. The alfalfa was upbeat and fast, something to shake her hips to. The beans were quieter, but had a steady beat. The corn was soothing, pretty.

She tried not to overdo. She hummed soft and steady, the crops remained healthy and strong, and she laughed off the neighbors' comments about her college boy and whatever hoodoo he was working.

Then one Saturday Dash awoke to grunting from the front yard, and hurried out, stopping short on the porch.

"Stay there," Alfie called.

She blinked, taking it in. Alfie with a bandana pulled over his nose, his eyes furious. A large mass of something, covered by a tarp, in the windmill pond.

121

She ignored the warning and came toward him. "What—"

The smell of rot hit her. "Don't," Alfie said, but she tugged at the tarp.

A dead mule, emaciated and fly-ridden. Her mind hiccupped briefly, but then she put it together. The mule dropping dead on some poor farm. The farmer hating her or Alfie or the farm's success so much that instead of bothering with the knacker man, he hauled the carcass here to her pond. It must have taken at least two people. Her skin crawled, thinking of them being here while she slept.

"I'll get it out," Alfie said.

It wasn't a one-person job. Dash fetched gloves, and, straining and gagging, they dragged the mule out of the pond.

"I'll call the knacker man from town," Alfie said. "And ask around about who's lost a mule."

"Don't," she said.

He scowled. "People shouldn't think they can—"

"It's not worth escalating."

That evening at supper he had a split lip. She didn't ask him who it had been, and he didn't say. They ate silently, though before he left Alfie said, "Some people are just idiots, Dash. Don't let them get you down."

She nodded, but that didn't keep her from lying awake that night. It would be one thing if the farm's success was mere luck, or Alfie's skill, but it was her. Now she was the one who had to decide what to do next.

Should she stop? A few weeks of drought and dust without her intervention, and the farm wouldn't look impressive anymore. Its strange success would fade from everyone's minds, and their animosity with it.

But why should she let these crops shrivel when she had the means to stop it? Just to placate her neighbors? The same neighbors who'd left that dead mule?

She couldn't let this go any more than Alfie could. She had to protect herself and those crops and the money they'd bring.

122

So she got up and got on her bicycle. It was past midnight, no one around to see. She wasn't sure it would even work if she wasn't on foot, if she was just riding around the edges of her neighbors' fields, humming the crops' song.

However, the next day as she walked to church, all the fields were green. Not as lush and hearty as hers, but enough to have people smiling and talking about miracles like they believed.

She set a schedule after that. Midnight rides on Wednesdays and Saturdays because she didn't have work the following days and could sleep in. She tried to have a specific route, too, but she kept going farther out, following that insistent song.

However, the farther she went, the more watered-down her power felt. The more worn down *she* felt. At first her schedule seemed adequate, but within a few weeks, all the perked up fields were wilting again by the next afternoon.

It was the wheat, Dash was certain. The neighbors grew it in abundance, and it sang the most melancholy dirge. She pedaled and pedaled, and the wheat wailed for her help.

She wanted to wail, too. People were talking. Not about her, thankfully, but everyone seemed united in trying to figure out why the surges and declines of their crops didn't correlate to the weather, why this hopeful oasis only existed in their area. Neighbors stopped calling Alfie "that college boy," and started asking him questions with respect. Not that he had any answers, but he took soil samples to the college, and had a professor come and look.

Dash didn't know what to do. She should've kept her promise to Harry, and now it was too late. She increased her excursions to every other night, regardless of her work schedule. The land needed her.

Exhaustion became a permanent state. Mr. Greenway suggested a vacation, insisting he could get by without her for a week. The seniors whose theses she typed looked concerned when she gave them their papers, saying they hoped she hadn't worked too hard. Mavis at the Five and Dime fussed over her, and told her to see the doctor. Dash insisted she felt fine. Occasionally sheer exhaustion caused her to skip one of her scheduled nights, but not often. She couldn't let the crops down.

The semester ended, and Alfie was working for Herishen. He came less frequently for meals, but he was waiting for her one day when she returned from the office, catching her as she wobbled from her dismount. She shook him off, embarrassed.

"You don't have to run yourself so ragged," he said.

"Don't I?" He of all people should understand. "If I lose this place, what then?"

"I'd take care of you."

"Maybe I don't want taking care of!" she yelled, her fatigue finally exploding. "Maybe I want to manage myself!"

"Of course you do. But it's not worth ruining your health over, not when..."

"When you're here to help?" she scoffed. "You're struggling, too. Besides you'll be leaving next year for some fancy government job, and I'll be alone. I'd better get used to it."

"If that's how you feel," Alfie muttered.

She didn't know how she felt. She was too tired to think. "It is," she said anyway, and he left.

⚓

The week wore on. She saw Alfie from a distance in the fields, but they didn't speak. Dash felt like hibernating for a year, but she kept up her night rides.

She got a concerned letter from Dot. *Mavis says you look like death warmed over. I wish you'd give up the farm. Ernest and I would be happy to take you in. I'd enjoy the company and appreciate your help with the boys. Please think it over.*

Dash surprised herself by actually considering it. A year ago she wouldn't have, but now an orderly life in Tulsa with Dot's family didn't sound so bad. It wouldn't be home, but then, this place wasn't feeling so homey lately, either.

Still, she didn't think she could leave it.

That Saturday was particularly blistering, even after sunset, but Dash went out anyway. She hadn't gotten more than a mile, though, when exhaustion consumed her. She climbed off the bike on trembling legs, sitting beside the road before she collapsed. Her chest heaved, her eyelids twitched, and the cornfield beside her sang a lullaby, urging her to curl up and sleep.

If she listened, would she wake up refreshed? Or would it leech everything out of her, leave her a dried-out husk?

She knew she had to stop this. She couldn't do it anymore. She'd go to Tulsa, make a new life for herself where nothing depended on her to grow.

But even this decision didn't give her the energy to get up.

"Dash!"

A concerned voice rose above the humming. Arms cradled her. "You all right?"

Alfie. Her mind raced for an excuse.

"I couldn't sleep," she murmured. "I went for a ride."

"Liar. You've been nothing but tired for a solid month, yet you keep doing this."

She pulled away, trying to see his face. "You've been following me?"

"For the past week. I was worried."

Her mind spun for a better lie. She'd heard of people sleepwalking; could they sleep-cycle as well?

But she didn't want to lie. Not to him. Not anymore.

"It's me," she said quietly, leaning back against him, ignoring Harry's voice screaming at her to shush. "I'm the one making the crops grow."

She waited for him to pull away, recoil, call her a witch or a lunatic.

He didn't move. "How?"

"It's just a thing I can do. A thing I am. Plants sing to me. I answer. And then they grow."

"Like magic?"

"I guess."

"But…just now? All of a sudden?"

"Always. But Harry made me promise not to use it. Not to tell anyone. He said people wouldn't understand."

"Do you understand it?"

"No."

"Well, that seems like a lot to have to keep to yourself."

Had it been? She'd tried not to think about it until these past months when she couldn't think of anything else.

"Let's get you home," Alfie said, and it dawned on her that he didn't believe her.

She took the flashlight from her pocket, then reached for the nearest withered cornstalk. She caressed it, humming quietly, watching as it greened beneath her fingers.

"I'm not crazy."

Alfie's eyes were wide in the flashlight's glow, but he said, "I never thought you were."

"I had to show Harry a dozen times," she recalled. "I made the flowers in Mama's garden bloom. He couldn't wrap his head around it."

"I'm having a little trouble wrapping my head around it, too, but I still believe you." He paused. "Your ma had a garden?"

She nodded.

"What happened to it?"

"She got sick. It died off." At first she'd been too busy with Mama to remember to tend it, and then it had been too far gone. She'd have had to use her power to revive it, and she couldn't justify that, not for something frivolous.

126

She wobbled over to her bicycle, but Alfie got there first. "I'll pedal."

She was too tired to argue. He cycled, and she listened to all those crops crying for her. "I'm sorry," she whispered. "I can't do it anymore."

She thought they might shriek their disapproval, but they didn't. Maybe they understood.

ᘛ

Dash managed to get inside and into bed, where she slept long and hard, drowning in dreams. In some she was bound to the earth, vines twining around her, insisting she stay. In others her neighbors surrounded her, furious, blaming her as their fields crumbled to dust.

Even when she woke, she was too tired to rise. She lay there, remembering. When she'd first told Harry what she could do, he'd made her show him repeatedly, his expression both fearful and disbelieving. Afterwards he'd always spoken of her powers in whispers, as if they were something to be ashamed of. He explained what people used to do to witches in the olden days, and she had nightmares for weeks, though she'd never told him. He was only trying to protect her.

But now she'd told Alfie, and he'd called it magic. He'd looked at her with wonder and held her like nothing had changed.

She reminded herself she was going to Tulsa. It didn't matter how Alfie treated her. She was leaving, and so was he.

She continued to lay there until she heard noise from outside. Another dead mule? She dragged herself up.

Alfie was by the porch, planting something. "What are you doing?" she asked, blinking in the afternoon sun.

"Last night it sounded like you missed your ma's garden, and I thought you could do with a little happiness. It's just a couple cuttings from the rose of Sharon at the college, but they'll bloom pretty. Maybe next spring we can plant something more."

She didn't tell him she'd be in Tulsa by then, or remind him that he'd be close to graduating. He was giving her something bright and happy and manageable to care for. No sense ruining the moment.

"I figured on harvesting the alfalfa tomorrow," he said. "Should be able to get a couple more harvests before the first hard frost."

She wondered if that success required her assistance. Should she tell him she wasn't sure she could give it?

When he was done, he came to sit beside her on the porch. "Do you want to talk about last night?"

"Not particularly."

"OK," he said like that was perfectly reasonable. "Can I ask you something unrelated?"

She nodded.

"Would you let me farm your land again next year?"

"Won't you have some fancy FSA job by then?"

He ducked his head. "One of my professors let me know that a government agency is unlikely to hire someone who can barely spell."

"He said that?" she asked, her blood boiling for him.

"Not quite so bluntly, but I got the idea. And he has a point."

"Alf…"

"No, it's OK. I've realized I enjoy farming, and that it doesn't mean I'll turn into my pa. Granted it took a few days to sort it all out in my head…" He shrugged. "That's why I didn't know what to say to you last week, when you talked about not wanting to rely on me. But I think I've got the right words now."

He looked her in the eyes. "We help each other out, Dash. I wouldn't have passed freshman composition—hell, any of my classes with essays—if it hadn't been for you. Now, I could

128

be ashamed of that, or I could just appreciate you for the true friend you are." He paused. "And you could do likewise."

She wanted to tell him she did appreciate him, that he was the truest friend she had, the only living person to know her secret, the only person, period, to accept that secret without making her feel monstrous. She couldn't seem to find the words, though, and anyhow, Alfie was still talking.

"And I don't want you thinking I'm only asking to work your land because of what you can do," he said. "I don't want to use you. You make your own choices, but I'd appreciate it if you left the alfalfa field alone this next go-round. I kind of want to see how it does on its own."

She still didn't know if she'd use her magic on the farm again, whether she could manage it without exhausting herself, whether she wanted to risk the neighbors' wrath, whether it would be best to stick to vegetables and flowers. There would be time enough to figure that out. But she knew, suddenly and absolutely, what she wanted to ask Alfie. "What if I said no?"

"About the alfalfa?"

"About you farming the land next year."

She could hear the hurt in his voice as he said, "I guess I'd work somewhere else." He paused. "Are you saying no?"

"I'm saying no to that offer," she said, "and I'm proposing something else." She took his hand. "Marriage. You get me and the farm."

He stared at her. "You're serious?"

She nodded.

He leaned in and kissed her, long and hard. When they finally pulled apart, he said, "You know I'd marry you even without the farm, right?"

"I do." She'd never felt more certain of anything in her life.

The rose of Sharon sang its approval.

Valerie Hunter

---

Valerie Hunter teaches high school English and has an MFA in writing for children and young adults from Vermont College of Fine Arts. Her stories have appeared in publications including *Cicada*, *Storyteller*, and *Colp*, as well as in multiple anthologies.

# DELTA WITCH BLUES

## BY JOE SCIPIONE

The man sat alone on his front porch. Rain battered the protective overhang, playing a steady rhythm against the wood and shingles.

He leaned back in his rocker. In his left hand a harmonica nestled comfortably between his thumb and index finger. A glass half-full with some sort of brown liquor balanced on the porch rail.

As I neared the house, I wondered how many years he'd spent sitting on the porch like that, even in inclement weather. He gave no indication he saw me and instead leaned forward, took his glass, and swallowed a large mouthful. He replaced the glass, brought the harp to his mouth, and played a low, slow blues riff.

The whine of the harmonica cut through the rain. The slow back and forth of the music found me walking in step with the beat as I trudged through the puddle on the path that led from the road to the porch. He played with his eyes closed and gave no indication he knew I was there. Instead, he kept playing, rocking back and forth with the beat of the music. Closer now, I studied the intricate web of creases lining his face like a map and imagined each line to mark another dead-end trail in a protracted life. "Cursed?" I wondered if this was the man I was looking for.

131

The music abruptly ceased. He looked up at me through narrowed slits. "Help ya?" He spoke in a slow, gravelly drawl that matched his playing.

I jumped at the sound of his voice.

"Oh, I didn't realize you saw me." I climbed the steps and joined him. "I didn't want to interrupt. Your playing is beautiful." Water dripped off me and onto the wood planks of the porch. It was rotted in some places, worn in others, but it was good to be under cover out of the rain.

He nodded, and the wrinkles around his eyes and mouth grew deeper. I guessed it was his version of a smile.

"You need something?"

"Ah, yes," I replied, somewhat surprised by his question. "Sorry, I'm a student. Doctoral student actually, writing my dissertation on curses and witch myth here in the area. I was told there was a man down this way who knew about the subject. Road was washed out about a mile back, so I had to walk the rest of the way. You wouldn't happen to have any information on the guy I'm looking for, would you?"

The rain came down harder, drumming a heavier beat against the roof. He exhaled.

"You sure talk fast, son," he said finally. Then for the first time his eyes opened wide enough for me to see them. "I think you're looking for me."

"Oh, I didn't realize. I'm sorry my name is Dennis Nantz, Sir." I extended my hand.

"It's all right." The words tumbled out all at once as if they were a single word. "Call me Chugger. And I guess you better come on into my kitchen if you really wanna hear the whole story. Raining too hard out here, and I ain't got but one porch chair."

He groaned as he got up from the chair, harmonica still stuck in his hand. When he was on his feet, he shuffled across the porch toward the front door.

"Come on this way. We'll sit, and I can tell you a story. Get you a drink."

He was out of breath just getting up, and it was clear he didn't move around too much. I had no idea how old he was, but I guessed he was the oldest person I'd ever met—by a lot.

He pulled open the screen door which sat slightly askew in the doorframe and dragged against the porch when it was halfway open. Chugger stepped around the door and into the house.

"Just give it a tug closed," he said as he shuffled forward. I followed and yanked on the door that first squeaked then slammed behind me.

He stopped and lit a candle, then set it in the front window of the house; it was the only light in the whole place.

I turned to follow Chugger. The shack was hot and muggy, and most of the windows were closed, no doubt on account of the rain. The floor, its planks as worn as those of the porch, creaked and groaned as we passed a threadbare recliner on our way to the hall connecting the front room to the small kitchen at the back of the house.

Chugger dropped his harmonica on the sagging wooden folding table and left his glass there too, then reached up and grabbed a second glass and an unlabeled bottle of what looked to be the same brown liquor he'd been drinking.

"How old are ya? What did you say your name was again?"

133

"Dennis, and I'm 24, Sir."

He collapsed down into the kitchen chair and motioned at the empty one opposite him. He poured the brown liquid into both glasses.

"Bourbon's all I drink nowadays. Been a while since I had anything else." He pushed one glass to me. "Don't be calling me 'sir' anymore. Name's Chugger. I've had that name for a while now and I don't plan on changing it anytime soon."

"Yes, yes. Of course. Chugger."

I took the glass, and he raised his to me. Our glasses touched, and I took a small sip. Chugger took a considerably larger one. The alcohol burned on the way down and warmed my stomach.

"Now listen. I ain't never told anyone this story. And might just be the mood I'm in, or the bourbon, or the fact that you came a mile down this road in this storm to talk to me. But I got a feeling you're the right person to hear it. Whatever the reason is, I'll tell you my story. But it can't ever be published or nothing. You can use it as reference or however it is you college kids do, but can't repeat the story or use my name. Understood?"

I nodded.

"Alright then, drink up and listen up, and no questions 'til I'm done. Got it?" He took another large swallow. I did the same and listened as he told me his story.

🐾

They gave me the name Chugger when I started playing the harp years ago. Been playing the thing every day ever since. Most people learn to play a musical instrument when they're younger but me, I never even picked up the harp until I was almost 30 or so. Can't be sure any more on account of the years running together like they do. Anyway, after that, I realized I needed to learn and play the harmonica. Even though I was older, I picked it up pretty quick.

We had a lot of them blues joints around here, so I got to playing at a few of them some nights after work. It was at one of those shows where I met the woman that led me to this curse. I was maybe 40 years-old then and waiting in the wings to get on stage. I was on last even though some of the other fellas that went on before me might have been a little better than me. They all played guitar, too. But I was fairly well-known around here back then, and people would wait to hear me, even though I was the only one to play just the harp.

So anyway, I got on stage—it was a rainy night, kinda like today—and I had my bourbon and my harp and I just sat there and started playing. Before long I had the place rocking, tapping their feet and singing along. It was one of those nights when I was just in a groove. Everything I played sounded perfect. The harp was loose. The crowd was lively and into the whole show.

Toward the back of the room, I noticed a woman, younger than me but not by a lot, with an even younger woman next to her. Mother and daughter, I supposed—perhaps a younger sister—because they looked so similar.

I'd always been a single man, never could be tied down, but if a beautiful woman caught my eye, well then, you know sometimes I had to see if I could make some time with her. This woman, let me tell you, she was the most beautiful woman I'd ever seen. She just so happened to be in my age bracket, too, so you know I had to go talk to her. At least so I could learn her name.

135

After the last song, I stood right up, because she was near the back of the room. I didn't want her to make a quick exit, so I rushed back there. Even left my drink on stage. Just carried my harp through the crowd, sneaking in and around people trying to clap me on the shoulder and yammer on about what a great job I did.

When I got to the back, she was still there. I flashed her my best smile, and she returned it. Her companion, the younger one, she didn't look very happy.

"Hello," I said. "People around here call me Chugger. On account of...you know." I held up my harp.

"I get it," she said and raised her eyebrows at me. I think I fell in love right then. It was a shot from Cupid's arrow. From that moment on, I never wanted to be a single man again.

"Mary Sue." She extended her hand. I took it and kissed the top of it. "This is my daughter Margaret."

"Nice to meet the both of you." I offered my hand to Margaret, but she turned away, a disgusted look on her face if I ever saw one. So, I returned my attention to Mary Sue. "Would you care to stay after for a drink? Musicians have a spot in back. We can drink away from the crowd if you want to go someplace quiet to talk."

She declined but told me she'd be back around the next time I played—without her daughter. I told her I understood, and I usually played that joint a few times a week. It wouldn't be hard to find me.

We said our goodbyes, and she was out the door and on her way. I was certain I'd never see her again.

But the next week I was sitting on the same stage, in the same joint blowin' the same tune on the same harp. I looked up, and there she was. Alone this time, from what I could see. I finished my set but didn't have to push my way to the back of the room. When I stepped off the stage, she was there waiting for me.

"Must'a liked the music if you came back for more," I said.

"Something like that." She smiled, and I fell in love with her all over again. "Sorry about my daughter last time. Her father died, and she doesn't think there should be any other men for me."

"She's protecting her mama. I get that. Come on back here, and we can talk."

I led her through a door and into the back room. A few other men were back there drinking with their families. I greeted them as we passed. Introduced Mary Sue to them. But it was too busy for my liking. Mary Sue and I went out back and sat at a table beneath a single lantern.

The night was warm, muggy even, and the crickets serenaded us as we talked.

The world passed around us. We drank a little, laughed a little, but mostly I just wanted to be with her. To talk to her and learn about her. Just spending time with her when it was just the two of us was enough for me.

When the lantern burned low, and the joint had emptied out, we finally stood up and left. I walked her home and gave her my schedule for the rest of the week. We made plans to meet up after every one of my upcoming gigs.

I walked home that night thinking about how I was going to marry this woman. I'd never felt about a person the way I did about her, and I was sure she felt it too. There was a connection I'd never had before. As a forty-something year-old man, to feel like that for the first time—I was happier than I'd been in my life. I started hoping I'd get to see her more than just at my shows.

Two nights later, I was playing at the same joint. So, I knew she knew where it was and wouldn't get lost on the way there. All night I had my eyes glued to the front door, waiting for her arrival. She'd said she'd show up early so we could talk before and after I played. But as the night wore on, I never saw that beautiful face.

Finally, it came my turn, and I went and did my thing. I wasn't really into it, just went through the motions. I didn't care. My priorities had shifted, you see. I wasn't caring about the music. I was caring only about Mary Sue, and she wasn't there.

I finished my set and flopped down on the bench in front of the joint with a bottle of bourbon, just drinking right from it. No glass or nothing. When the place totally cleared out, I stumbled the few miles home and passed out in bed.

Next night was a repeat of the previous one. I watched the door all night waiting for her face to light up the room, but I never saw it. The same with the show after that. By then I'd given up hope. Maybe she'd changed her mind, or something came up and she had to leave town unexpectedly for some reason or other. Problem was, I'd never know what happened. I consigned myself to the fact that there was nothing I could do, and I moved on.

At the next gig there was a glimmer of hope. It wasn't Mary Sue I saw at the back of the room when I looked out from stage, but her daughter, Margaret. She didn't look happy, but she made eye contact with me. When I finished my set, I went right to her.

"Is your mama okay?" I asked before I'd even got to her.

She shook her head. "No, what did you do to her?"

"What do you mean? I walked her home the other night. She was fine. Planned to meet again."

"She hasn't left bed since. She told me where you were tonight before she fell back asleep. Wanted to know what you gave her to drink."

"Same stuff I had. Same stuff I always have." I pointed to my glass still sitting next to the chair I sat in on stage.

"Well, she's sick. Maybe dyin'," Margaret said.

My heart dropped. I'd only spent a few hours with Mary Sue, but in that moment I knew I couldn't bear to live without her.

"Can you take me to her? I didn't do anything to her. I just want to help."

Margaret sighed, and fixed her gaze on me, probably studying me to see if I was telling the truth. I was, but didn't know if she believed me. Eventually, she nodded.

"Come on," she said and stormed out.

We walked in silence. She'd never taken a liking to me, and her mother was sick. I didn't want to make it worse by talking to her, so I kept my mouth shut.

We ended up at a small shack not far from where I lived. Back then I didn't get out much. It was work and then home at night, so I didn't know my neighbors unless I saw them after a performance.

The place was dark. She led me through the door and into a small back bedroom. Margaret lit a lantern. I saw Mary Sue

139

asleep in the bed, wrapped in blankets, but she didn't look sick to me. Looked the same as she had the last time I saw her. Still, it was strange to see her vulnerable like that.

I stood back, and Margaret knelt next to the bed.

"Mama, your friend is here. He really wanted to see you." She put her hand on Mary Sue's forehead.

Mary Sue rolled over to face her daughter. Her eyes fluttered open.

"What friend?"

"The harmonica player, Mama. Remember?"

"Chugger? He mighta got me sick."

"Yeah, him. He says he didn't, though. He was worried about you, so he came."

"Alright, I think I'm okay to talk for a minute, Margie. Can you get him a drink?"

Margaret nodded and stood up to leave the small bedroom. I took her place, kneeling beside the bed. I realized at that moment I didn't know Mary Sue all that well, though my feelings for her were strong.

"I'm sorry you're sick, but it wasn't anything I gave you."

"I know," she said. Her voice sounded weak, but what I saw with my eyes told me different. "I just couldn't think of what else it could be."

Margaret came in with a glass and handed it to me.

"Drink up," Mary Sue said, "and then we can talk."

I took a big mouthful and swallowed. It felt warm in my throat, like bourbon, but it didn't taste like it. It was brown, though, and strong as hell.

"What is this?" I took another mouthful, swishing it around this time before swallowing, hoping to taste more of it.

"Just something to keep you still." Mary Sue, she sat up in bed, a grin so big on her face, it nearly split the skin off her skull.

"What, you're not—you're not..." I stammered.

"Sick? No, sorry. I'm not. I hate doing this to you, because I really do like you, but there is no other way around it."

"What do you mean?" I tried to stand up, but my legs were frozen in place. I could feel them, but they wouldn't move.

I heard Margaret come in behind me but couldn't turn my head to look at her. Mary Sue rolled over on her side and looked over my head at her. Mary Sue's lips narrowed, and her eyes hardened. The warmth in those beautiful eyes I fell in love with was gone, replaced by something sinister.

"Help," I said but knew in the back of my head it was useless.

"He's ready," Mary Sue said. From behind my frozen body, Margaret handed her a plate. At first, I couldn't see what was on it, but she lowered it onto the bed right in front of my face. It had a small glass bowl in the middle of it. Inside the bowl something was burning, and white smoke wafted up into my face.

"Chugger, I really am sorry. I did like you. I still like you. But if I'm going to be rid of this curse, I need to pass it on to someone else. Unfortunately, you're that person."

Mary Sue started to speak in a language I'd never heard. Margaret stood behind me, saying the words along with her, chanting. Mary Sue stopped, then blew the smoke right into my face. I tried to hold my breath for as long as I could, but that just made me take a bigger breath in when I finally inhaled.

"I'm sorry it has to be this way, Chugger," Mary Sue said again. Even as they poisoned me, I couldn't be mad at her. I was sure there was a good reason for her doing what she did. I sucked in another breath, and my eyes watered. A third breath, and the room spun. After that, everything went black.

When I woke up, I was on the floor of that same room. Nothing felt different, and I could move again. I coughed a couple times, still feeling smoke in my lungs that was no longer there.

"Chugger," a voice I recognized as Mary Sue's called from somewhere in the darkness. "I feel terrible. If you want me to explain why this happened to you, I will. But even if you don't care about the why, you should at least know *what* happened to you."

"Explain then," I groaned and rolled onto my side.

"I was cursed, 'the waning' they call it. Margaret isn't my daughter. She's my twin sister. We're the same age, her and me. I look older because of the curse. The only way to rid myself of that curse is to place it on someone else, and that has to be you. I'm sorry about that. But along with the curse, I've given you a gift, because I do like you and I want to help you."

"You could have helped by doing this to someone else," I said.

"No, I couldn't. Something told me it had to be you."

"What's the gift then?"

"The gift is simple. The waning can only exist in one person at one time. If you find another to take this curse, then you'll be free of it. But you have to find the right person. I can't tell you how to find them Chugger—when you meet them, you'll know."

✴

"We spoke for a little while after that. I was tired, exhausted. She helped me home. I held her hand, in spite of what she'd done to me. She'd cursed me but also given me a chance to get out of it, and a chance to be with her again. Not in this body you see here, but in my younger one, the one I'd been in when I first met her. Mary Sue had given me that chance. I was thankful for it, and I loved her. We never really lost touch after that."

Chugger fell silent. He'd recounted most of his tale staring down at the silver harmonica that lay next to his arm on the worn wooden table, but now looked up at me. He turned his empty glass in his hands.

I couldn't say why, but I believed his curious story. "So, it's true then. You've actually been cursed. This will be great for my research."

"I've been cursed. Yes, I guess you could say that." Chugger let out a low laugh, but it seemed to stick in the back of his throat.

"You think, I mean, it sounds like to me that they were witches, right?" I was enthralled with the idea of finding someone who was actually cursed and who had been in contact with witches.

Chugger nodded, "there's been rumors about witches down here for as long as I can remember. But the truth is they

143

keep to themselves and blend in, so no one ever knows if the stories are true or just myths."

"Until you have a story like yours." I said, shocked and still trying to process what I'd heard. I always suspected at least some of the myths about witches might hold true, but I didn't doubt Chugger's story for even a moment.

"Right. I didn't tell ya the end of it, though, but I guess there's just a little more. Last chapter of the story or something."

"Please finish."

"I still played my gigs for a while until all the joints near here closed up. If a club wasn't within walking distance I didn't go. I was getting old so fast, you know. Made it hard for me to get around after a while." He paused and pushed his glass away. "Mary Sue and Margaret, they never went far, you see. I'd see them from time to time. When I ran into them, they always looked the same. I told Mary Sue every time I saw her that I wanted to be with her. Those witches became my friends. They promised they'd keep an eye on me as I got older and weaker.

"And if I ever felt the time was right, if I had a visitor that I *knew* was the right person, they could help me get young again, look like myself again. All I needed to do was light that candle in the front window over there. When they saw it, they'd come in and help me switch the curse to someone else."

My eyes widened when I realized what Chugger was saying. A sound came from behind me, and I moved to look but was frozen in the chair. I shifted my eyes back and forth trying to see who was there, but I knew. It was the witches.

"Oh, no," I said. My voice shook. "You're doing this to me?"

"It's not the end of things, son." Chugger released a throaty chuckle. "Eventually someone will come along, and you'll know they're the right person, and, well, you know what to do with that candle when you find them. When we see it, we'll be right along."

Two beautiful women about my age appeared from behind me. They didn't introduce themselves, but I knew their names.

"Relax son," Chugger said. "I lived with this for a long time, but you'll survive. You want to be an expert of witchcraft in the Delta? Here's the ultimate field study."

I knew he was right, and crazy as it might sound, I didn't protest. I wanted this.

"It's alright, hun," one of the women said. "One day you'll be free from the waning, just like Chugger." She placed a plate down in front of me, lit a match and dropped it into the small bowl at its center. Whatever was in the bowl caught fire, and a plume of white smoke wafted up into the air. Chugger smiled, leaned forward, and blew the smoke gently into my face. On either side of me, Margaret and Mary Sue chanted words I didn't know and couldn't even begin to describe.

I coughed and inhaled more smoke; I began to lose focus. Chugger, the table, everything around me blurred. I fell toward, but my fall was slowed. One of them must have caught me before I hit the table. The last thing I saw was Chugger's harmonica.

When I woke, the rain had stopped, and the sun shone in through a tiny window. I was still in Chugger's kitchen, laid out on the floor. The scent of mold and smoke still hung in the air. Feeling hungover, I rolled to my side and coughed a few times. Eventually I got to my feet, but my legs felt heavy, and I had to force them to move. The plate with the remains of the burned substance was still on the table, as was Chugger's jug of hexed bourbon and the empty glasses.

Chugger was gone, though, along with the two witches.

I collapsed into a chair, processing what had happened. The longer I sat there, the older I felt.

A few minutes later, I rose and ambled out of the house. I made my way back up the road to my car, happy I didn't have to trudge through the rain this time.

I was alone, somewhere in the Mississippi Delta. I had a list of things a mile long I wanted to accomplish before I grew old, and, I realized, not a lot of time left to get them done. As I rounded a turn in the road, the unmistakable sound of a harmonica wailed in the distance.

———————

Joe Scipione lives in the suburbs of Chicago with his wife and two kids. He is a Senior Contributor and horror book reviewer at Horrorbound.net. He has had stories published in several anthologies including *Stories We Tell After Midnight: Volume 2*, *Satan is Your Friend*, and *Trigger Warning: Hallucinations*. His debut novel *Perhaps She Will Die* comes out summer 2021. When he's not reading or writing you can usually find him cheering on one of the Boston sports teams or walking around the lakes near his home. Find him on twitter: @joescipione0 or at www.joescipione.com.

# A Picture's Worth

## by Peter Lundt

*New Orleans, 1951*

The photograph came to me as an inheritance—a bequest made from one generation's black sheep to the next—through an uncle I'd been led to believe died in WWI, but who, I'd come to learn, led a long and happy life, if happiness is to be gauged by wealth amassed and adventures undertaken. A seemingly miserly gift, the image, featuring a neoclassical folly in an anonymous garden, was an ambrotype, an early form of photo created by mounting a negative on a black backing.

I'd been drinking all morning at Lafitte's when a new arrival—a solid block of a man in a cheap suit cut from wool both far too shiny for respectability and far too heavy for the city where he found himself—darkened the door. He had just enough of an air of policeman about him, the moment he crossed the threshold, my companion, a bored gigolo who'd reached an age that precluded him from exacting too great a toll for the pleasure of his company, slid from his stool and slipped out the side exit.

As the man lumbered toward the bar, pushing back the brim of his fedora and wiping his brow with a kerchief, I blended the gigolo's deserted bourbon with the dregs of my own. I averted my eyes, though I kept the arrival in my periphery.

He dropped his heavy, scuffed briefcase onto the bar, then opened it and riffled through the contents. A moment later he stood at my side and tossed on the bar before me a decade old mugshot of myself, clipped to it a report of the public indecency arrest that instigated my swift decline.

"Wesley Donovan?"

I sipped my drink and focused on the bar. When I didn't respond, he pounded the photo with a thick, square finger. "Is this you?"

If he'd come to arrest me, it seemed unlikely he would take the time to reminisce.

If he intended blackmail, he arrived far too late. Widow Haydell, the landlady at the hole of a rooming house on Toulouse, had fleeced me for another week's rent—last week's—hours earlier. That left the change in my pocket, tips I earned the night before playing piano at the Monteleone. The trio of coins would cover my bar tab if I made the drink in my fist my last.

Besides, I had no more secrets left.

I looked from the large hand to the photo to his face. "It used to be."

He offered me an envelope upon which my name had been written in a firm, if flowery, script. I broke the seal and removed a letter, typed, and signed by a man named Pool. I read the message, not fully comprehending, not yet able to understand the uncle I'd believe dead before my birth had, in fact, only expired shortly after the New Year and had named me a beneficiary in his will. Pool's letter explained that my uncle had employed the services of a news clipping agency to keep track over the years of the dour Southern family from which he'd been ejected. Pool, a lawyer acting in his capacity

148

as executor of my uncle's will, hired the detective now at my side and armed him with a dossier of those articles to aid him in his search.

I looked up at the man, he handed me the meager file of clippings.

About half the cuttings consisted of announcements of births and marriages, as well as obituaries annotated in a careful hand—I assumed my uncle's own—to set the record straight on the points where eulogizing had blunted truth. To my surprise, the remaining articles were about my younger, better self: the school board's approval to push me up a grade, news of awards for various achievements, mostly academic, including a mention of a scholarship offer to study ancient languages—for which I'd shown an aptitude from early childhood—at an Ivy League university, and a second to study music at a renowned New York conservatory. The former I gratefully declined, and the latter accepted with great enthusiasm. I'd often wondered whether if I'd taken the other path, if I'd still end up just as this man found me, a New Orleans libertine and wastrel, half drunk at noon and considering advances being made to me by a cut-rate hustler.

I pushed the clippings aside and turned back to the letter, rereading its final lines once and then again. "My client, your uncle, wanted me to stress the following to you. What he's left to you might, at first consideration, strike you as an inconsequential keepsake, but if you have any of him in you, you'll be quick to divine its worth. Regardless, whether you discern what your uncle perceived to be the item's intrinsic value, or if you, and I quote, "will take after his dullard father," you are now the item's sole rightful owner."

"All right, then." I turned my focus on the detective. "You've found me. It's mine, so let's have it."

Peter Lundt

He returned to his bag and produced what I at first took to be a red velveteen box, but after he placed it, this time with care, on the bar before me, I realized it was a kind of folding case, about eight inches by six. I hooked the top corner of the cover with my index and began to ease it open. The skin on my arms turned to gooseflesh, and for a blink I paused, hindered by a preternatural fear that I was about to loose something dark upon the earth. I felt a flash of anger towards myself and my sudden superstitious turn. I flicked the cover open.

No genie flashed before me. No devil appeared in a puff of smoke. My eyes fell to a black and white image of a circular colonnade, a 'monopteros' I'd later come to learn, situated in a garden so neglected the wild had nearly reclaimed it.

A weatherworn folly stood at the edge of an encroaching wood. I looked to the detective for explanation, only to catch sight of his broad shoulders as he ambled from the bar.

🐱

"Didn't he find you, then?' My landlady called after me as I mounted the stairs to my room. The woman insisted her boarders address her as "Widow Haydell" with an air of pride that suggested she felt she'd won the title by pushing her husband to an early grave.

I paused on the step and looked down at her.

"The big fellow. In the suit. Could've been a Bible salesman, could've been plainclothes vice." She waddled closer to the stairs and grasped the pineapple-shaped finial. "Either way, I doubted I'd see you again." Her eyes dropped to the case in my hands. The curiosity in her gaze at first annoyed me, then inspired me. I rushed down to join her at the base of the stairs.

150

"Yes." I clutched the case to my chest. "He found me." I hesitated, holding off long enough for her to decide I intended to hide the man's identity from her. Then I shamed the matronly devil by speaking the truth. "He was a detective, you see…"

Caution rose in her eyes, and I could feel her steeling herself to evict me.

"A private detective, I should say."

I bit my lip and studied her features.

"And what does this you should say 'private detective' want with you?"

"It's only…" I hesitated, stringing her along. "Can I trust you to keep a secret? Only for a few weeks?"

"A few weeks?"

"That's how long the detective said it would take to settle probate." I saw the question forming on her lips. "Probate. The final disposition of my uncle's assets."

"Assets," she echoed the word. This one she understood.

"Yes." I let a look of joy light up my face. "It seems I'm about to come into a great sum of money." My joy faded to embarrassment. "Only I'm still short for now. Just for a few weeks. Until probate is complete."

Her eyes narrowed as she grew wary.

"I'm hoping," I continued, "to make a business proposition to you. If only you'll let me stay on 'til I have the cash in hand, I'll pay you double, no, triple your usual rates."

She snorted her contempt. "Sure, you will."

151

Peter Lundt

"No, really," I said, holding out the case and easing its cover open. "This was taken in the garden of the estate I'll be inheriting. It looks like Uncle has let it go to seed." I moved to close the cover before she remarked on the age of the picture, but she reached out, almost touching it though stopping short. "It'll take some work to bring it back to its glory."

"Queer little statue," she said, pointing. I turned the picture and held it up. I hadn't noticed any statuary, only the folly, but now after having it pointed out to me, I could see it quite clearly. Visible at the center of the structure, peeking out from between two of its Ionic columns, stood a statue of Faunus, the shaggy woodlands god with horns crowning his head and cloven hoofs instead of feet. The statue's sudden appearance, for it seemed as such, unsettled me. I closed the cover without giving the widow the chance for further inspection.

"I'd start with that devil," she said. "Get him out of the garden first."

"I'll have to see the whole of the estate before making any decisions, but you may be right."

She took a couple of steps back and brought her hands to her hips. "Ten times."

"I'm sorry?"

"If you're going to be as rich as you're saying, I'll let you stay on until your..." She searched for the word.

"Probate," I offered.

"Yes, your probate. Only, I want ten times the usual. And if it turns out you're lying to me about the money, I'll see to it you catch up with your uncle and that devil of his in hell." Her

152

face flushed, and her eyes contracted into obsidian dots. "Agreed?"

"Agreed." I went back to the stairs, her flinty stare pushing me up each step.

🐈

The patrons that night were few and tightfisted, most not even bothering to acknowledge my tip jar even when they made requests. I poured the coins into my hand, and without looking, shoved them into my pocket, cheered by the feel of a pair of silver half dollars. I kept my hand in my pocket, jingling the coins at every corner as I made my way along Royal. I walked on automatic, finding myself at the Lalaurie Mansion before snapping to and realizing I'd overshot my destination. I turned back, then followed Ursulines to Bourbon.

I entered Lafitte's to find half the clients, but twice the misery as the bar I just left. Eyes rose to take me in. Eyes lingered. But I was here for the drinking. I felt them fall away as I focused straight ahead. A drink, my regular, slid down the bar to me, and I reached into my pocket for a coin. My fingers found one of the half dollars, and I pulled it out and dropped it beside my drink.

"Cut me off when that's gone," I said.

John, the bartender, picked up the coin and tilted it toward the light. "What the hell is this supposed to be?" He handed it back to me. A woman in profile on one side, on the reverse a horse prancing on letters I took for Greek. He leaned over the bar toward me. "Looks old." He lifted his chin and called to someone across the bar. "Bill, come take a look at this."

I recognized this Bill. He owned an antique store on Magazine Street.

Bill examined the coin. "Interesting. Where did you come by this?"

"My tip jar." I produced the other from my pocket. "There were two of them."

"I'm certainly no expert, but I would say that's quite a tip. Greek. Ancient. I'm guessing they're well over two-thousand years old. Not too worn. I suspect they'd be worth around two hundred. Each." He returned the coin to me. "If you'd like I can introduce you to a collector friend."

◖

I knew myself well enough not to risk more than the one drink. With the coins gripped tightly between my fingers and my hands shoved deep into my trouser pockets, I rushed back to the boarding house on Toulouse. I tried the door, relieved to find it unlocked as I'd missed the Widow Haydell's curfew. I wouldn't have to face another of her tirades for waking her to let me in.

The ground floor was dark, unusual as she made a habit of leaving on a nightlight for her own comfort and convenience. Even less ordinary was the weak light shining down the staircase from above.

I climbed the stairs, taking care to tread lightly. The long hall was silent, save for the raucous snores of a fellow tenant and the discordant pings sounding from the washroom's leaky faucets. The light, I realized, emanated from my own room, my door standing half-opened. I eased down the hall and glanced around the doorframe to catch a glimpse of the trespasser before deciding to commit to a full-on confrontation. I saw no one. I stepped into the doorway, and found the room empty and, at first glance, undisturbed. I closed and bolted the door behind me. Only then did I spot the ambrotype on the floor, lying cover open and face down. I'd stashed it in the room's battered armoire, tucked in with my undergarments.

I bent over and snatched it up, worrying that the glass protecting the image might have shattered in the fall. I flipped the case over and froze. The glass held, but the picture almost stopped my heart.

In the image, just before the folly, stood the Widow Haydell, eyes opened wide in panic, her mouth gaping into a frozen scream. As I studied the scene, an almost liquid darkness seeped in from behind the picture, surrounding her and drawing her deeper and deeper in, until she was gone, and the folly, without its statue, stood alone.

I closed the case and set the ambrotype on the bed.

I reached into my pocket and jingled the two ancient coins.

———————

Peter Lundt eschews most things Internet, especially social media, preferring to save his "likes" for his dog. Peter enjoys running, writing, napping, and—hate if you must—vegan cuisine.

# TELLING SECRETS

## BY JAMES ALLEN GRADY

"What you doin', Granny?" the boy asked from the cabin's doorway, his bushy brown hair fluttering in the breeze whistling up the remote East Tennessee holler.

"Oh, just straightenin' up, Tommy," Agnes said, with a big toothless smile at her baby boy, the great grandson who had saved her life. Then she returned to wiping down the counter with a tattered old rag.

"Why?" Tommy persisted. The place was as clean as it ever was. At thirteen, he now felt he should know such things.

Agnes glanced at him. "Well, if you must know," she said, pursing her lips, "we havin' company later."

"How you know?" he asked.

*Always another question,* Agnes thought. *That curiosity!*

A pang wracked her heart at the thought of how tall he was getting. Almost all his baby fat was gone, and those long, willowy, tan legs...

*Time flows like a river: its surface so calm, but step into and you feel its irresistible power.*

"Granny?" he asked, alerting her that she'd been 'traveling,' as her grandmother had called it.

"Well, I just got an itch," she said. Seeing the flash in his intelligent, fiery eyes, Agnes said, "Rooster told me."

"Who's Rooster?" Tommy asked.

She laughed heartily—it was a reasonable question. She was acquainted with no fewer than three Roosters.

"Rooster come down from the hen house and give two long crows on the porch," she explained. "Means company today—two folks, to be exact."

Tommy's brow furrowed. His granny had tons of sayings and remedies and knew the weather and how to birth babies. Women from town sought her out for such.

"Are you a witch, Granny?" Tommy asked.

Agnes was taken aback: Tommy had always been inquisitive and insightful, but she'd always expected he would be older before he asked that question.

"I ain't nothin' but a backwoods holler granny," she said. "People come to me, 'cause I know secret things...'"

"So, you *are* a witch?" Tommy asked.

Tommy didn't seem afraid. But then again, Agnes had never read him fairy tales about evil witches either. Those characters she replaced with wicked stepmothers or evil sheriffs.

*The real terrors of this world*, she thought.

"It's as good a word for us as any, I reckon," she said, sighing.

"Us?" Tommy asked, eyes now sparkling with interest, a smile creeping onto his face.

"The *women* in my family been granny witches since...forever, I guess. My mawmaw used to tell me 'bout the olden times—" Agnes cut that terrifying thread short. "But...guess it dies with me."

"But Aunt Sally and Cousin Rita?" the boy said, confused.

"Ain't interested," she said, waving it off and turning to resume cleaning. "Got no women to pass it along to."

Appearing at her shoulder—oh-so-recently he stood at her elbow, and that pang returned—Tommy said, "Why's it got to be a girl?"

Agnes considered Tommy carefully and said, "I guess 'cause birthin' babies and helpin' women...ain't a man's place."

157

"I mean, gotta be stuff a boy can do, right?" he asked, his eyes pleading.

*You waited three generations to train somebody up*, she thought. *You gonna tell this boy he c'ain't have it?*

"Plenty," she said. "And ain't no harm in you knowin' 'bout women's things either, is there?"

✦

"That lyin' rooster's lucky," Agnes said to Tommy in the late afternoon. "If I could afford a new one, we'd be havin' stew tomorrow!"

The boy laughed and said, "What do people come here for, Granny?"

"Lots of thangs," she said. "You seen 'em come get me to help with babies often enough."

Tommy *had* seen her leave many an evening, only to return the next morning. Sometimes, when she was gone even longer, he worried she'd died, leaving him all alone up this holler, and that they would take him to live in one of those places. Even thinking about it, his stomach recoiled in fear.

"Some folks come for medicine," she said. "Things I cook up from those roots and things we collect."

"Medicine for what?" Tommy asked.

"Everything from somethin' for their movements to somethin' that'll make their peckers stand up," Agnes said, chuckling at the last, having forgotten for a moment she was talking to her great-grandson.

*Guess that's why we pass it down to our girls*, she thought. *Easier to talk to them about peckers.*

Tommy's eyes went wide, and her chuckle turned to a cackle. "If you wanna learn, Tommy, you gonna hear your ol' granny talking to you about shit and peckers and punaners."

Hesitantly, he nodded, and she was secretly pleased he didn't recoil from the topic.

"A lot of people come feelin' down…lifeless," she added. "We can help."

"How?" he asked.

"Got some plants what can ease it up," she said. "And gotta talk to 'em 'bout what's goin' on. Might have somethin' for that too."

She went on, explaining some people came looking for protection, others to change their luck with the law or the ladies; some wanting to have babies, others to usher folks to the great beyond ahead of schedule.

"I don't deal in that kinda shit," she added about the last. "Anything you do, Tommy, make sure they's good in it, far as you can see. Or, if not, at least make sure someone deserves what they about to get."

From outside, they heard a man's voice, loud but still distant, and a softer voice responded.

"Good thing I ain't kill't that bird," Agnes muttered and stood. "Listen in if you want, just act like you ain't."

Tommy followed his grandmother onto the porch.

"Howdy, there," a tall man in a grey casual suit and a fedora called.

"Howdy," the old woman replied with a wry look. But Tommy didn't notice the man, or even his grandmother's glance down at him. He was transfixed by the tall boy walking a few steps behind the man.

"You know him?" Agnes asked softly.

Tommy nodded but volunteered nothing.

"What can I do for you?" Agnes called.

"I come to talk with you, ma'am," he said.

"What's your name, son?" she asked. "And who's this handsome feller with you?"

"Lloyd Chambers, and this is my boy, Max," he said, removing his hat and giving her a quick nod. The man's dark hair was thinning but had very little gray in it.

He asked, "Mind if I come on up?"

159

"Come on," she said, moving to sit in her favorite rocker. "Take a seat."

"Much obliged." The man grabbed a chair a few feet from her and turned it to face hers. As he sat, he nodded at Tommy. "Mind if we talk private?"

Agnes said, "Tommy, you give me and Mister Chambers a moment."

"Max, make yourself scarce," Lloyd said to his own boy, who shot Tommy a glance as he wandered out into the yard to sit in a tire hung from a strong old oak branch.

"I figured this was about your boy, since you brung him," Agnes said.

"Nah," the man said, "we was just out this way...givin' him a lesson, and I didn't want to leave him in the car down at the road."

"It's treacherous down yonder." Agnes nodded, then sat waiting for the man to get to the point.

After a long silence, he said, "I got a problem, and I was told you was the woman what could help...remedy it."

"Depends on the problem," Agnes said sagely. "They's a lot I can do, and they's a lot I c'ain't..."

"My daughter's pregnant, out of wedlock." He removed his hat and rested it on his knee. "She's only sixteen. Ain't no need for anyone to ever know."

Agnes stopped rocking and gazed out into the distance. "Who sent you up here?"

"My housekeeper Ellie Mae said you was a, well, that you knew these sorts of things."

"I reckon Ellie Mae didn't exactly know what you was after?"

"No." Lloyd's eyebrows arched. "I told her the missus might be wantin' another one—havin' trouble. C'ain't have the truth getting' out. How'd you know?"

"If she knowed, she would've saved you the trouble." Agnes started to rise. "Get on outta here. Ain't nothin' I can do for you."

"Please, ma'am." Lloyd put a hand on her arm to stop her. "She don't need this kind of trouble—"

"Well, she gots it now," Agnes said. "But they's some folks round 'bouts these parts that ain't got my worries. Just tell Ellie Mae you need to put a scare on somebody, your bossman or whoever. Sure, she knows somebody..."

"You're the best granny around. I just want the best for my little girl."

"Well, I'm sorry, but no," Agnes said more firmly.

"She was attacked by... Well, I'll spare you the details, ma'am," Lloyd persisted. "She's innocent in all that, and all the responsibility for this is mine."

"And mine." The old woman sighed. "I c'ain't *just* do this. I need to consult—"

"Consult?" Lloyd asked. "Consult who? Ain't nobody here but the boy, and he don't—"

"Why'd you come see me?" Agnes punctuated her question with a pointed look. Seeing the man about to protest, she held up a hand. "The cards. The spirits."

He nodded to show his understanding. "Need me to do anything?"

"Just sit there. I gotta get the cards and some tea." She hurried inside, making sure the door latched behind her.

"What's going on, Granny?"

She was mumbling to herself when Tommy spoke, making her jump. "Jesus, child." She rested a hand over her racing heart. "Nothin' to concern yourself with, boy." She turned away and began searching for the deck of playing cards she used for divination purposes.

"Granny, you promised to," Tommy said.

"I know what I said, damn it," she grumbled. "But there are things..."

"There are things I can do, you said." Tommy's eyes blazed with an unnatural light.

Agnes stopped suddenly and calmed down.

*Man can wait,* she thought. *Chambers needs me, I don't need him.*

"Why'd you look like the devil done walked up a few minutes ago?" Agnes asked.

Tommy blushed. "I *hate* him."

"Hate's a strong word."

"He picks on me," Tommy said. "Calls me names. Pushes me."

"Still, hate?"

"I don't guess so, but I really, really, really don't like him none."

*That blush again,* she thought. *Later.*

"Then you ain't gonna like what I'm gonna ask of you," she warned. "But you want to help, you gotta do it."

"What?" he asked cautiously.

"I need you to go out there and take that boy down to the creek and ask him about the baby."

"Do what?" he asked, raising his voice so she shushed him.

"Just ask the boy why his daddy come see your granny 'bout the baby. If he don't know nothing, tell him must be about an animal and let that be the end of it."

"Okay, Granny." He paused hesitantly. "Do I have to take him down to the creek?"

"There or leastways out from under his daddy's eye."

"Okay." Tommy's confusion at the necessity of separating Max from his father showed on his brow.

"Go on now while I keep lookin'! Run out like you're goin' to play."

"They're in the drawer by your chair." Tommy opened the door and bounded out into the yard.

Agnes, now a bit confused herself, walked over to the side table and opened the drawer. Inside were her cards, wrapped in a tattered old piece of silk. She looked over her shoulder though the open door and...

*Stop with that for now you old fool,* she thought to herself, *or you'll be travelin' sure 'nough.* She wished Lloyd would just disappear. She felt like she needed to travel on this one. *Later.*

She grabbed some tea and put the kettle on to boil. "Would you like a cup, Mister Chambers?" she called loudly.

"Much obliged," the man called back, not moving to enter, for which she was thankful. It would be uncomfortable to have to stop the man at her threshold without warning.

Tommy slowed as he approached Max Chambers, and the boy barely looked up at him.

"Hey, Max," Tommy said, trying to will his voice not to quaver.

Max barely grunted but did glance up now.

"You okay?" Tommy asked genuinely.

When Max looked up again, there was rage in his eyes, but it was just as quickly extinguished by Tommy's expression of concern rapidly mingling with fear.

"Sorry." Max stood, causing Tommy to take two quick steps back and gasp.

"I, uhm," Tommy said, growing confident Max was not going pounce on him. "I'm goin' down to the creek to play. Wanna come?"

"Sounds like baby stuff," Max said automatically. Seeing Tommy frown, he quickly added, "What's there to do down there?"

"I look for rocks and plants and things for granny," Tommy said. "Sometimes if it's warm enough, I go swimmin'."

Max's face transformed as he smiled suddenly. "You got your own swimmin' hole?"

Tommy nodded. "I'm the only one who ever goes out there."

"And you'd let me see it?" Max asked.

Tommy smiled. "Sure."

Max fell in beside him as he started for the woods. A year older and at least six inches taller, Max could easily have outpaced his younger classmate.

"Why's your granny need that kinda stuff?" Max asked when they'd walked a few minutes in silence.

"For her work."

"Yeah, but what—" Max began.

"What's your daddy want from her?" Tommy cut him off.

Max fell silent for a moment. "Medicine. That's what he said anyway. I asked him why he'd come to an old mountain woman for that, and he said it was 'cause she's a granny who knows things."

"That's what she uses the stuff for."

"Oh," Max replied, an uncomfortable silence falling between them.

Tommy sensed it was now or never. "Do you know what kind of medicine your daddy wants from Granny?"

"Nah," Max said. "He said it was something 'bout 'goat'?"

"Maybe gout?"

"What's that?" Max looked like he was trying to recall his father's words.

"I don't know," Tommy said. "I just remember teacher talkin' bout how Thomas Jefferson had 'the gout' when he was... No, it was Ben Franklin."

"Could be."

"I heard them talkin'." Tommy gave Max a quick glance. He didn't want to turn Max sour. He'd taken enough punches from the big boy already.

Max looked curious though.

"Your daddy said somethin' about a kid," Tommy said. "A baby?"

"I just found out about that."

"Who's havin' a baby?" Tommy asked, but Max raced ahead.

When Tommy caught up with Max, he found the tall boy staring at the stream. Almost a river, it flowed over rock piles as it snaking its way down the mountain. From where they stood, it ran flat along the edge of the mountain for a few hundred yards before resuming its descent.

"This is so cool," Max whispered. "Bet nobody but you's been out here in practically forever."

"Granny comes a foraging with me sometimes, but besides her…" Tommy shook his head as his words trailed off.

"Where's the swimmin' hole?" Max asked, his happy enthusiasm forcing Tommy to put aside his mission for the moment.

Tommy pointed. "Just through the trees."

"Let's go," Max said, and started walking fast. Tommy had to jog to keep up now. "No way!" Max exclaimed before Tommy could see where he was looking.

Some moss-covered boulders along the mountain side of the swimming hole were piled right next to the deepest water. The pool was easily thirty feet long and twenty feet wide, probably bigger, and the water moved fast enough you couldn't see the bottom from where they stood.

"Is it deep enough to jump in off those rocks?" Max asked.

Tommy laughed. "I wouldn't go headfirst just in case, but yeah."

Max bit the inside of his lip again, this time as he struggled against his excitement. "Can we?" he finally asked, exhaling what seemed like a long-held breath.

Tommy wanted to say no. He wanted to demand explanations for Max's change of demeanor. He wanted to be angry.

"Go ahead," Tommy said.

Immediately, Max kicked off his shoes and put his socks inside them. Then he looked over his shoulder and asked, "Ain't you comin' in?"

"Nah," Tommy said.

"You sure you don't mind?" Max asked.

Tommy shook his head, and Max quickly started unbuttoning his shirt. Once he'd removed it, he grabbed the bottom of his undershirt and started to lift it over his head.

Tommy tried not to watch, but as soon as the white shirt was in front of Max's face, his eyes were locked on the lean boy's muscular torso. While his arms were brown, his torso was pale—milky white. And there was the novelty of the caramel-brown hair below his navel and under his arms, where Tommy himself was still mostly smooth. When the shirt tore free of him, Max's bushy brown hair was a mess of waves and curls, and he shook his head from side to side, causing it to settle easily back into place.

Tommy ripped his eyes away for a moment, but Max turned away from him to remove his jeans. Max had to repress as gasp when the boy turned, not because of the boy's lovely form but because of the angry red stripes and sickly brown, yellow, and blue splotches that covered Max's back and the back of his thighs.

Max seemed to sense Tommy watching, so he quickly stripped off the pants, tossed them aside, and ran to the edge of the pool. Now Tommy's attention *was* on the boy's rippling legs. Then Max jumped, drawing his feet up to his chest and crashing into the water with a great splash.

When he surfaced, Max was giggling like all his cares had been washed away. Tommy had not yet heard of the River Lethe, but if he had, his amazement at the transformation would have had a concept to match.

"Come in," Max called loudly.

"Tommy blushed and shook his head. But he took off his shoes and socks, and walked to the edge, sitting on a rock and lowering his feet into the water.

Max dove deep into the pool, Tommy figured trying to touch bottom and then emerged further away. He repeated this process a few times before turning toward Tommy and swimming confidently, gliding through the water with only his head and butt, clad in white briefs that may as well not have been there when wet, breaking the surface occasionally.

Max emerged and gasped, running a hand over his wet hair to push some of the water back, and still that smile shone.

"You swim good." Tommy almost said, "look good" and was glad he caught himself. He didn't want to die out here—not right when his granny was finally going to tell some secrets.

"Thanks," Max said, still short of breath. "I took lessons at the town pool."

"Are y'all rich?" Tommy asked. "Sorry, that was—"

"Don't worry about it." Max's face grew a bit more somber. "I guess we are?"

"We ain't," Tommy said, laughing.

Again, the silence grew awkward as Tommy sat looking down at Max, who floated in the water, his side brushing Tommy's leg. Tommy couldn't decipher the look the boy was giving him.

"Why're you so mean to me at school?" Tommy blurted.

Max looked away. "I ain't."

"You are," Tommy said. "Then today—"

"I'm mean to everybody." Max's voice quavered. "It ain't just you—"

"It's worse with me, and your buddies seem—" Tommy fell silent as he noticed Max's jaw was clenched and his fists had balled up beneath the water.

Tommy saw Max follow his gaze and relaxed his hand with an embarrassed look.

"I don't know." Max averted his eyes. "I don't mean to, but I just get so pissed at you."

"But I ain't never done nothin' to you," Tommy said.

"I know that." Max seemed intent on not meeting Tommy's gaze. "But I started because everybody picked on you. And the more I done it, the madder and madder I get…"

"You mad at me now?" Tommy asked.

"A little." Max finally was able to look back at Tommy. "But no. I usually ain't 'til the guys egg me on and I lay into you. Then it's just…"

"Usually ain't?"

Max blushed bright. "Sometimes I look at you in class and just get mad."

"Why?" Tommy asked.

"I don't know," Max began harshly, before blushing. "I don't know."

Then he pushed off from the rock with his powerful legs and sped off through the water like a fish, stopping at the other side of the hole, putting his arms on the ground and leaning over so his forehead was in the dirt.

"Max," Tommy called. He felt a kind of dread for which he had no context—and a part of him longed to reach out across the expanse of the water with his very spirit. "I'm sorry."

"Aaagh!" Max yelled at the top of his lungs, a primal cry that showed Tommy a deeper place than he had ever seen in a soul.

Tommy pulled his feet out of the water and walked around the swimming hole. Max never looked up as he approached. Tommy sat and put his feet back in the water. His hand trembled as he placed it softly on Max's wiry shoulder.

Max looked up at Tommy, his green eyes glistening and red. Then, they turned angry. "If you ever tell anybody—"

"I ain't gonna," Tommy said. "I would never."

Tommy saw Max's rage evaporate, as the big boy's shoulders slumped.

"I'd deserve it if you did," Max whispered.

"No, you wouldn't."

Tommy stared into Max's eyes, and felt the boy look back into his, into him. For a moment, Tommy thought Max would recoil from his touch, from his gaze, as he felt the muscles in the boy's back tense. Then, he felt Max begin to tremble, and Tommy so wanted to make everything right for Max.

Tommy was young, but he had long known not everything could be made right. But for Max perhaps something? Tommy felt a radiant warmth—lacking heat—emanate from his own hand, and Max's shaking stopped.

But then Max started to cry and settled his forehead down on Tommy's bare thigh, beneath the leg of his shorts. Tommy put his hand on Max's head and stroked it gently until the boy grew quiet.

"I'm sorry I'm such a big baby." Max wiped the snot from his face with his arm.

Tommy's whole body tingled when Max's hand wiped the spot on his leg that was still wet with tears.

"You ain't," Tommy said. "Somebody hurt you. Maybe that's why you—"

"Yeah." Max looked away. "Can we just play?"

Tommy removed his hand from Max's head and lifted his own t-shirt over his head. Then he stood and turned away, to remove his pants and underwear, before jumping in.

"Skinny dippin'?" Max laughed through his sniffling.

"I don't want to walk that far in wet underwear," Tommy said. "Not like yours hide anything anyway now." He blushed, realizing he'd admitted to looking.

"Ain't got nothin' I want to hide." Max plunged beneath the water, reemerging half a minute later with his briefs in hand. He swam to the edge to wring them out and hung them over the rock to dry. "You're right about that, though."

Tommy gulped as Max swam his way. Max dipped beneath the surface and tugged on Tommy's leg to pull him under. But he didn't hold him down or try to scare him, so they both surfaced, laughing, their chests inches apart.

Feeling the tension rise, Tommy swam off, and the two of them played tag in the pool for a half-hour. Then Max swam toward his underwear and Tommy's clothes.

Tommy called out, "You ready to head back?"

"No," Max said wistfully. "I wish I never had to leave, but if I keep my father waiting…"

Tommy swam up behind Max so close his chest came flush with the boy's battered and bruised back. Tommy willed his body not to betray him as he examined Max.

"Did your father do this to you?" Tommy asked. From this close, he could see old scars that looked like the healed stings of a whip cracking on flesh.

Max nodded, and Tommy put his head down on the back of the boy's shoulder. It was now Tommy's turn to cry.

Max turned slowly but didn't push Tommy away, and Tommy wrapped his arms around his schoolyard nemesis.

Chest-to-chest, other things to other things, Tommy shook as he whispered, "I'm so sorry."

"You ain't done nothin'." Max put his own arms around the smaller boy.

"I can just feel," Tommy whispered. "I…I…"

Max squeezed Tommy tight, then he leaned down and kissed Tommy softly on the lips. It wasn't passionate, but it wasn't brotherly, and again Tommy did feel all of it. He now realized this wasn't a new ability, or an anomaly. He'd just never put two-and-two together—that he'd inherited a gift, and a curse. This time, he knew why Max had hit him, why Max got mad at him. What he saw could have pleased him— but it just made him sad.

"I'm sorry," Max whispered, starting to panic. "Please don't tell any—"

Tommy kissed him back, and this time there was fire—of the sort only two naive teens in moment of unexpected discovery could muster.

After that, they held each other for a few moments more, before silently collecting their clothes and starting to dress, watching each other openly. This silence was not awkward at all.

As they walked from the clearing, Max would occasionally smile at Tommy, until he worked up the courage to ask, "Can we go swimmin' again sometime?"

"I'd like that," Tommy said. "And if you ever need to get away…"

"Thanks," Max said. After a few hundred feet he asked, "Did you do somethin' to me?"

"I," Tommy began to stammer, then fell silent. He *thought* he might have done something to Max. "I didn't do nothin' to you…"

"I didn't mean something bad," Max said, and Tommy warmed at the thought the boy meant to reassure him. "It's just my back doesn't hurt as much."

"Must be the water," Tommy said.

"Your eyes are strange, sometimes—"

Tommy felt a shiver rising up his spine as he met Max's gaze. "Water's good for—"

"Yeah." Max nodded. "The water."

"I forgot to ask." Tommy changed the subject. "Who's having the baby?"

"My mom," Max said. "She's been trying for a while."

The talked occasionally all the way back to the clearing and arrived just in time to see Lloyd Chambers walk off the porch carrying a small bag.

"Come on, boy," Lloyd yelled at Max. "Got what I came for."

Max shot Tommy a sheepish smile over his shoulder as he jogged over to his father. Tommy smiled back and walked slowly over to where his granny still sat, cards laid out on a table next to a cup of tea drained down to the leaves.

"Guess you don't hate him no more?" the old woman said with an amused chuckle.

"Never did," Tommy reminded her.

"So, his momma's havin' the baby, and his son's got the devil in him 'cause his pa beats him?" the old woman asked.

James Allen Grady

"Did he tell you?" Tommy asked.

"Nah, I knowed it sure 'nough."

"If you already knew, why'd you—"

"I needed you to see," Agnes said, "to understand…this power is real."

"When I touched him, I could feel it all, Granny," Tommy said. "I could feel where all his meanness comes from. And I think I may have made him better. Maybe some?"

"Could you now?" Agnes had only meant for him to see what she could do. He would discover something from the boy that she already knew, and she could gradually initiate him into the more peculiar parts of the work.

Now they had discovered that he'd been unintentionally wielding the gifts, and that changed the shape of things. There was a bit more urgency in his training—and most alarming to her, she had foreseen nothing of it in her travels.

He nodded. "And when he kissed me," Tommy rushed on, the words tumbling from his mouth before he could retrieve them. He stepped back from the woman, terror in his eyes.

Agnes nodded, smiling. "Go on."

"Most of all, I could feel why he gets mad at me, more than anybody else," he concluded.

Agnes knew she would definitely be traveling soon, for guidance and strength. *But not now. Now he needs you.*

"So you got the healing touch *and* the true sight." She nodded. "Guess we do gots to train you up."

He looked at her sheepishly. "I said he kissed me."

"I heard you boy." Agnes held up and hand and closed her eyes, drawing a deep breath.

*Lord, God,* she thought, *if ever there was a time to be able to seek guidance.*

"I'm sorry." Tommy bit his lip and stood on the balls of his feet for just a moment.

"I just ain't ready to talk 'bout that yet. I'm an old woman, and I don't know what to say…'cept I love you."

The boy sighed in relief, and, as a couple of tears rolled down his cheeks, his eyes flashed fire—this time she was sure of it, sure she'd seen all three colors in his iris blaze like little sun-rings today.

With a meek laugh, he said, "Well, if you're going to train me up, you gotta be comfortable with your grandson talkin' about peck—"

The old woman cackled with delight but held up her hand. "Lord, child, my heart!"

Then she leaned back in her chair and said, "So you want to know what he come for?"

Tommy nodded.

"He told me a man attacked his daughter and he needed a tonic to fix her it so's that baby ain't born."

"But it's his wife's—"

"And she wasn't attacked, neither." Agnes shook her head, eyes narrowing. "I don't know whether it's his, but he sure 'nough tryin' to use me to kill his own wife's baby."

"But he left with," Tommy said, horrified.

"I told you we don't deal with that shit, boy… I give him a charm and a dream tonic for her. 'Bout to have me a nice long talk with Missus Chambers tonight up where spirits mingle."

"You gonna do anything 'bout Mister Chambers?" Tommy's eyes reflected the impact or Max's injuries on his heart. "Wish you coulda seen Max's back."

"I didn't need to see, boy—not with my eyes, anyway." Tommy looked at her, expectantly waiting for her to continue. "I'll do what needs to be done to protect that child too. I hope she handles it, though."

"Even if it means bad magic?" Tommy asked.

James Allen Grady

"Ain't no bad magic," she said. "Ain't no good magic neither. They's just good people and bad people, and the people standin' between 'em."

Tommy nodded. He knew who his granny was.

———————

James Grady is the Managing Editor of *Out & About Nashville*, Tennessee's oldest and largest LGBTQ+ monthly magazine. He lives in Nashville with his husband, boyfriend, and three big dogs, and is often found locked in a tiny room trying to write. He is currently finishing a novel set in 1950s Appalachia—following one young woman's journey to escape the trap her mother created for her—and beginning another building off the characters introduced in this volume.

"THE TOMATO WITCH"
Heather Scheeler

# Jezebels and Harlots

## by B.F. Vega

I remember as a child after church, on the days there were football games going on at U of L., my family would load into our station wagon the instant social time let out and start the hour-long trip from E-town to Louisville. Just north of Fort Knox, where 31W skirts the banks of the Ohio River, my mom would turn and say, "Avert your eyes, young ladies."

My little sister and I would dutifully turn our heads to look at the river. But sometimes I would dare peek in the other direction. The building we were not allowed to see was a large square with no windows, no hayloft, no big doors, but painted like an old barn. Even when I didn't look, I would know we were passing it because my mother would mumble the words "Jezebels and Harlots."

After high school, I moved to Humboldt State in California. It took me almost a month to realize why it felt so different. I finally realized the air is different in California—it's not as heavy as in Kentucky. I know scientifically it has to do with the influence of the Pacific Ocean, but the more time I spent away from home, the more I started to believe that maybe there was something beyond the scientific explanation.

I was originally there to study botany. I took my first folklore class to satisfy a requirement. I was prepared to dislike it, but the first time the teacher said the words "granny witch," I could feel the oppression of air weighing down on me, with thunder rumbling in the distance and lightning bugs sparking arcane codes. Just those words felt like home. I was hooked.

My specialty became the feminine in the use of magic. I traveled the world meeting different magic users and folk healers, but it wasn't until I was in Jordan doing research on biblical witches that I learned about Jezebel. I had known Jezebel was a prostitute, or harlot as my mother would say; I didn't know Jezebel was considered the first witch.

One night in Jordan, almost two decades after leaving the heavy air of Kentucky, I was lying awake in my tent. The cooling dry air felt as different from the banks of the Ohio River as Mars was from Earth. But, the smell of campfire smoke was fading, replaced by the scent of Kentucky sweet grass and bourbon. The air turned warm, and sticky. It settled on me like a blanket, and I felt again what I had felt in that first folklore class. The air was calling me. The next morning, I booked a flight to Louisville.

I hadn't told my family I was coming. I had a hazy idea of surprising them, but when I landed and rented a car, I knew I was going to be making a stop my mother would not approve of.

ꙮ

*J&H Gentlemen's Club*—the building added a neon sign in my absence. A dozen women, cigarettes dangling from their lips, lay about in various stages of undress sunning themselves. I got out of the car, and the woman who was nearest the door lowered her sunglasses to take a better look at me. She pushed them back into place and leaned her head back so she was looking into the open door.

"May! Company!" She took a drag of her cigarette and turned over.

A woman about my age appeared at the door. She wore a long blue cotton sundress that left her shoulders bare. Her amber hair was pulled up into a messy bun. Her skin glowed slightly in the sunlight, and, as I got closer, I saw her eyes were the green of pine needles. She loitered in the doorway, not moving or speaking until I stood before her.

I extended my hand. "Hello, I'm Dr. Katherine Pence-Grey."

She looked at me, and a slow smile stole across her face. "I'm May," she said before adding, "Now to what do I owe the pleasure of an eminent Doctor of folklore and sociology visiting my residence?"

"You know who I am?"

"Sweetie, I've read your books. I disagree with some of your conclusions, but why don't y'all come in? I can't imagine you are still acclimatized to our humidity."

I followed her into a cavernous room filled with small round tables and stools. A bar ran across the wall nearest the door. Opposite was a stage with three metal poles running from the stage deck to the ceiling. She didn't stop but headed toward a door in the back of the room. I followed her into a hallway that could have served as a bordello set from an old Hollywood western. Plush red carpet ran under my feet and up a steep staircase with a gracefully curving railing of mahogany. I didn't notice most of it at the time, because I knew from the moment we entered that there was an A.C. unit somewhere. It was at the base of the stairs.

I stood still, letting the frigid air dry some of the stickiness my hair had acquired during the short walk from my car to this point.

May snickered. "Sweetie, we need to get you re-acclimatized, if you are going to be any use to me." She then proceeded up the stairs before I could ask her what she meant.

The gaudy bordello decor continued throughout the whole upstairs hallway. May led me to a door that opened into what was clearly her office. Here, the Persian rug underfoot was exquisite. The understated paneled walls and modest sconces seemed to belong to a home in the Hamptons, not a strip club in Kentucky. She sat in a leather chair behind her mahogany desk and gestured for me to take one of the upholstered wingback chairs in front of it.

"Iced tea?" she asked.

"With sugar?"

"Girl, you have been away from home too long." She arched one perfect brow as she pressed an intercom button.

While she requested a pitcher of iced tea to be sent up, I looked behind her at a large bookcase jammed with everything from *Physica* and a collection of *Hippocratic Corpus* to *The Botany of Desire* and a copy of *Gray's Anatomy*. The shelves held curios as well: an old mortar and pestle, a cornhusk doll, and a box of willow wood.

"You're a witch," I said.

She laughed. "I've been called worse, but yes, I am a witch. I come from a long line of witches. And I need some help." At that point the woman came in with the tea.

May waited until I had my first pull of true Southern sweet tea before continuing. "What do you know about your Aunt LueEllen?"

"My mom's aunt?" I asked, taken aback, "Um, only that we used to go out to her cabin the day after Christmas to bring her some gifts and provisions. How do you know about her?"

May ignored my question. "Did you ever go in the house?"

"No. I mean, I don't think there was running water. She had an outhouse."

"How was the Jordanian desert?" She asked offhand.

"How did...?" I started to ask but stopped. May was trying very hard to appear all-knowing, but two could play at that game. "You use the strip club downstairs for income and sexual energy to enhance your spells."

May's lower lip dropped open for a moment, and both her soft-angled eyebrows rose before she said, "You don't mess around do you, Katie? And yes, witchcraft doesn't really pay

179

the bills. The strip club was a win-win you could say." She nodded at me and continued, "Okay, I suppose I should be straight with you?"

"That would be appreciated." I smiled.

"I know you know what a granny witch is. Your great aunt LueEllen was one. So was her daughter, who is your mama's cousin and my mama. For that matter so, was your mama's grandmamma and so on all the way back to Katherine May Reynolds."

"We're cousins?" I asked in disbelief. "My mom always used to call this place 'Jezebels and Harlots'. We weren't even allowed to look at it when we drove past."

"Yeah, her mama got in big with the Baptists. I think your mama wanted to be one of us and—"

"And she was reminding herself why she wasn't." It made sense. "You said you needed my help?"

"Yes. As I'm sure you know, there are very few true granny witches left. My ma first opened this place as a school to teach more, but it didn't do well financially. She left when I decided to apply for our liquor license. We still keep in touch, but I haven't been able to get a hold of her for a week now. I drove down to her place, but I couldn't get past her gate. I was at a loss when I saw you in my mirror."

"You scry in a mirror?" The practice of scrying had always fascinated me.

"That's what you latch onto?" She shook her head so that the messy bun on top of her head moved like a pom-pom at homecoming.

"Well, I assume that you sent for me—somehow— because you need a family member. My mom wouldn't come within 100 miles of this place. My sister doesn't believe in magic. That leaves me, who at least knows witchcraft in the abstract."

"So, you'll help?" May asked, leaning back in her chair and studying her cuticles intensely, as if they held the secrets of the universe.

I paused for a moment to wonder how genuine her nonplussed act was. "I'm not a witch."

Almost instantaneously she replied, "You have our blood."

Now it was my turn to sit back and take in my own dirt encrusted nails. This reminder of where I had just come from gave me an idea. "Can I write about it later if I change everyone's names?"

"If you didn't change everyone's names, your mama would kill you, then call my mama to resurrect you so she could kill you again," May said looking directly at me and not moving a muscle as she waited for my reply.

I nodded my head sagely. "Well, then we should go find your mama. You have no idea how bad mine is when she's blocked from doing what she wants."

"Thank God," May said as her shoulders sagged. The realization she hadn't been sure I would help erased any doubts I had about her or what I had just agreed to.

🐈

The next day, we drove down to the far western corner of Kentucky. We turned onto a dirt road that led into the swampy delta of the Cumberland River. May pulled up to an old wooden gate set between two pine trees, got out, and tried to open it. I saw a little spark like a firefly lighting, and she jumped back blowing on her fingers. I got out, walked up, and opened the gate with no problem. I shrugged at her, and we got back into the car.

We arrived at a large cabin with a porch running the length of the front. I got out and walked up to the front door. I tried the knob.

"Key?" I yelled back.

"There is no key," May shouted through her window.

"Well, the door is locked." I gestured for her to come try.

She eased out of the car, seeming to brace for another shock. But none came. She shrugged, walked up beside me, and tried the door. "It's locked."

"I know. I tol—" A black cat appeared from nowhere and jumped into my arms. It started bumping its head on my chin and mewing.

"Claudius?" May examined the cat.

"Your mom's?"

"Yeah. He's not an outdoor cat."

I focused on the pet. "Where is May's mama?"

Claudius licked my nose, then jumped out of my arms. He ran to the side of the house, then stopped. He mewed at me, and I swear I heard the words "come on" in my head.

I shrugged and started to follow him.

"You can talk to animals?"

"No. But we have to start looking somewhere."

"You can talk to animals," May insisted. "Nobody in our family has been able to do that since our great-grandma."

"I can't talk to animals. Like I said, it's a good place to sta—" I broke off. Claudius had stopped running and now sat on top of the ground-level entrance to a cellar.

In my head I clearly heard, "Took you long enough."

May stepped forward and grabbed the handles as Claudius jumped away from the doors. These doors opened easily. "Bring a flashlight," May said, "unless you want to summon a league of fireflies to light the way for us."

I rolled my eyes and pulled out two flashlights, handing one to her. We descended a flight of steps into an old earthen room. I almost tripped at one point when Claudius ran between my legs.

In the tiny room I saw a door I presumed would lead up into the kitchen. I started toward it, but May held me back.

"Hang on. Ma usually has a ward on this door." She pulled a small vial of an inky liquid from her pocket and mumbled a few words in what sounded like French over it. She then flicked some of the liquid on the door. I heard a pop, like a circuit tripping, then the door just swung open to reveal a perfectly normal set of steps.

At the top of the stairs, another door opened onto a compact kitchen with an old-fashioned cast iron stove and a teal melamine table. Claudius immediately deserted us for his food bowl.

We started looking for May's ma by going toward the front door. A dining room and living room space took up the entire front of the house, though the dining room had been transformed into a workspace. A large metal table held battery operated electronic scales and a neatly arranged display of vials with metric measurements, and a bookshelf filled with books on herbalism stood beside an ample built-in cupboard. I knew granny witches were herbal healers, but I never suspected one had such modern equipment. It was an interesting contrast to the unpainted living room with its bare wood walls, wicker furniture, and an old rag rug that had seen better days.

May caught my expression. "Ma spends on what's important to her."

I nodded. It made sense. From the living room a short hallway with three doors ran toward the back of the house. The one on our right led back to the kitchen via a small laundry room. The one immediately in front of us opened on a tiny but incongruously modern bathroom. To our left was a small bedroom. We opened the door to the bedroom and were momentarily blinded by the surprisingly intense glare of the now setting sun as its light shot in through a curtainless window. May gasped.

A woman in a long white cotton nightgown lay on the bed. I didn't need May's reaction to know it was her mother. At first, I thought she was dead; she lay absolutely rigid, her arms crossed over her chest, and her open eyes fixed on the ceiling. It looked like someone had laid her out to be buried, but as I drew nearer, I saw her chest moving ever so slightly.

May shook her. "Mama!" She looked up at me. "We need to get her to a hospital!"

"I agree." I pulled out my cell phone, then realized I had no service. "Is there a house phone?"

May nodded. "In the dining room."

I hurried back to the workspace and found the phone in one of those old-fashioned wall niches. I picked it up, but, as I feared, heard no dial tone.

"What did I expect?" I said out loud. This happened in every horror movie I'd ever seen—of course, it would happen here and now.

Claudius came into the room and mewed at me. In my head I heard, "Look out the window." I stared at the cat instead.

"You are talking to me aren't you?" He gave no answer, instead jumping up on a cushion placed in front of the window. He batted his paw on the glass and looked back at me. I walked over to look out. At first, I didn't see anything unusual, but as the last rays of the setting sun hit the driveway, a woman stepped into view. Swirling black shadows surrounded her. I knew what she was. I had met my share of Bokor. I ran back to the bedroom.

"May," I yelled.

"What?" She looked up, still cradling her mother. "You went to call an ambulance."

Pulling on her arm and trying to avoid tripping over Claudius, who was suddenly underfoot, I tried to speak, but realized my throat had gone dry. I swallowed a few times before getting out, "They can't help us."

May opened her mouth, but I didn't give her time to get a word in. "I need you to put the strongest ward you can on all the doors to the cabin immediately. I think I know what is wrong with your mom."

To her credit May didn't argue. She released her mother and dashed to the workroom. I followed on her heels.

She opened the large cupboard, revealing a fully-stocked pantry of herbs and other ingredients.

She didn't reach for any of these jars or bottles, but instead pulled out a large drawer at the bottom. Inside were boxes, bottles, and bags all neatly labeled with skull and crossbones and Latin names.

"What am I guarding against?" she asked.

"Bokor." I said, and she stopped what she was doing to turn and look at me. Her eyes were wide, and the color drained from her face. She ran past me to look out the window. I joined her to find the Bokor now stood directly facing the cabin. The shadows had fanned out to ring the building.

"Waiting for nightfall." I drifted back from the window.

"Lauralie," May said in a near whisper then added, "I need your help."

I nodded. She quickly gathered ingredients and threw them into the mortar and pestle. She pulled a small grimoire from her pocket and pointed to a recitation in Latin. "Out loud, until I tell you to stop." She handed me the book.

I started reciting as she ground the ingredients in time to the rhythm of my words. Once she'd reduced the mixture to a mash, she joined in the chanting and brought the mortar over so we could both touch it. I didn't surprise me when Claudius joined us and placed his paw on the mortar.

Something like static electricity shot through my body, starting at my feet and running to the top of my head, then down again through my arms and out of my hands. As soon as I felt whatever it was leaving my body, May stopped chanting and nodded.

185

May grasped the pestle. "I'm going to go apply this. You make sure every door and window is locked. Magic is great, but sometimes a good old-fashioned deadbolt is better."

We split up. She went into the cellar, and I started examining all the windows. The shadows, darker than the enveloping night, had drawn closer. I dragged the heavy coffee table in front of the door for good measure.

Once I'd secured all the doors and windows, I turned to the cupboard and started searching for ingredients I prayed I was remembering correctly. When May entered the room, I was already mixing the antidote I had been taught in Haiti.

"Who the hell is Lauralie?" I tapped the spoon on the rim of the mixing bowl, causing it to chime. "Why is she outside with a legion of shadows? And why has she been trying to change your mother into a zombie?"

"Is that what's wrong?" May's brows knitted together, and her pupils got so large her pine green eyes took on the color of an inky forest. "What did she do to her?"

"It's a potion. A poison really. You have to administer it over a certain period of time. Then you gotta trick the Yoruba into turning their gaze from you. If you do it correctly, you end up with a servant who is capable of performing your bidding, but who no longer has free will." I paused to look her squarely in the eye. "There is zero history of Bokors or Vodou in Kentucky. The witchcraft here is of Scottish origin. So, dear cousin, who the hell is out there and why?"

"She used to be my best friend, but…" May spread her hands in a hopeless gesture.

I let it drop. At the moment, I had more pressing concerns, and I didn't trust her to tell me the truth anyway.

"I need some of blood. For the mix. Human."

May nodded and, as I suspected she would, retrieved the vial of the almost black mixture from her pocket and held it out to me. I put three drops in the mix and prayed it was enough before returning it to her. As she was putting it back into her pocket, I said, "If I had known we were dealing with blood magic, I wouldn't have helped."

May had the grace to be suddenly interested in the floor. "I know. But I couldn't open the gate. It took a family member to get me through."

I nodded in understanding. "How the hell did Lauralie get through?"

"I think the ward might be very specific," May said, having moved from an interest in the floor to an intense study of the wall over my head so that I couldn't meet her eyes.

I bemoaned the fact that I didn't have the gene to arch a single eyebrow. Now would have been a great time to give her back some of the aloof treatment she had given me back at J&H. I was about to say something cutting when I noticed the tears on her cheeks. I decided not to ask why her mother set a ward against her. I carried my mixture back to the bedroom and held it over May's mom. "Elegba, a little help. Please."

"That's not a spell," May said.

"No, it was a prayer." I answered, "We need all the help we can get. Besides, I've always been partial to Elegba." I poured a little bit of the mixture in the hexed woman's mouth. The mixture caused her skin to flush purple down her throat and, I guessed beneath her white gown, to her stomach. I waited until the purple hue died, then dripped a few more drops into her mouth. This time her lips took on the purple hue, and her veins grew more prominent as the mix worked its way into her bloodstream.

A banging on the front door startled me, and I tipped a little more in than I meant to on the third try. May's mom choked and coughed and blinked. Her irises, which had been brown and a little cloudy, now shone a fierce lavender. The banging at the door continued and was joined by pounding on the glass of the windows as well. The entities gathered might be shadows, but they had force.

May sunk onto the bed, "That was the most powerful charm I know."

"I hope the doors hold." I answered and looked up at the window. A face that could have once belonged to a woman looked back at me, its features distorted beyond any semblance of humanity. Her lips bulged like they had been stung by a hundred bees. I could make out no nose, and her eyelids looked like they were glued into the open position. I screamed.

May screamed, too, and ran into the other room to get the little bit of the remaining ward. She sprinted back in with Claudius right on her heels. They slammed the door behind them just as the sound of splintering wood coming from the living room announced something had breached the cabin. May quickly dabbed some of her ward on this door, then ran to the window where the initial woman had been joined by two others, each at different stage of decomposition.

May smeared the ward all around the window, knocking a rosemary plant off of the ledge as she did.

I'd just managed to drag a heavy dresser over to block the door when I heard Claudius in my head, "She will need the Bible from the bottom drawer."

I didn't even question it. I yanked open the dresser's bottom drawer and pulled out an old Bible. I turned and placed it on May's mama's chest under her hands.

The woman blinked again, then her hands unfolded from each other to clasp the book. She sat up and looked at me. She coughed once and said, "Katherine Anne Grey, you look just like your mama."

She looked around seeming to take stock of our situation then spotted her daughter. "MayLynne I thought I told you that you were not to step foot in this house until you gave up that black magic garbage."

"Ma...mamma," May stammered, "I was wor—"

"It was my fault," I said giving May a shut-up glance. There were more important things to deal with than a family argument. "You were ill, and I needed her help."

At this point Claudius jumped up on his mistress and started purring. I heard, "I got this." He then turned and jumped into my arms, purring even louder.

"Well, if Claudius trusts you, then I do too." The woman reached out to take the Claudius back and said into his fur, "Call me Rachel. If I know MayLynn, she hasn't even had the decency to tell you my name." She turned to glare at her daughter, and as she did, caught sight of the creatures outside her bedroom window.

"Jesus H. Christ! What are those?"

"Um," I said, struggling to find the least distressing way to summarize and failing, "at a guess I think they're damned souls being manipulated by a Vodou Bokor who has summoned them by sacrificing their own soul to a demon."

"Straight to the point. Just like your mamma." Rachel said. "Okay, I don't know how to deal with Voodoo, but I do know demons."

"Technically," May started, "it's not Voodoo—"

"Girl, if I wanted your opinion," Rachel snapped as she climbed out of bed, "I would have asked for it."

A massive blow hit the bedroom door and jiggled the dresser.

Rachel dropped Claudius, who ran under the bed. "They're in the house?"

"Yeah." I nodded. "It might be best to wait until sunrise when the Bokor's power weakens unless you have a secret stash of the herbs you'll need?"

"No." Rachel laid her bible on the bed, and Claudius pounced on it.

In my head I heard, "Open it." I crossed to the bed and sat beside the bible.

It was old—easily late 1700's—and everything, from the worn hand-patched leather creased by generations of fingers, to the barely visible gilt of the words K. Reynolds on the bottom of the front cover, showed that this book had obviously been passed down and treasured through the generations. Claudius jumped off the book as I moved to open it. I flipped to the front where there was usually a space for recording births and deaths. I'd guessed right about its age. The first entry was "Katherine May Reynolds b. 1750 Edinburgh." It struck me as odd to see only women listed. I traced the line down to the bottom where my birth, my sister's, and May's had been recorded. May's name had been crossed through and beside it someone had written "Harlot." I could hear my mother's voice from all those years ago, Jezebels and Harlots. I now knew that for her the word served as a kind of ward, a way to remind herself nothing good would come of giving in to the family's legacy of magic.

The pounding on the door stopped cold, and a voice on the other side called, "MayLynne, I know you're in there. I can feel your blood!"

"Go away, Lauralie," May yelled, the polished woman of the world I'd met at Jezebels and Harlots now gone.

I wasn't sure if she was more scared of Lauralie and the shadows, or of her mother who spat out the name "Lauralie," and glared at May with such intensity, it wouldn't have surprised me to see her burst into flames.

"What do you want?" I called.

"I want May. She was supposed to join me in my soul debt if I helped her get her stupid little school back into solvency. Who would want to be a simple healer when there is real power in the world? I taught her the magic of blood and sex. She owes me." Lauralie screeched through the door.

I don't know if Rachel would have hit May, but I grabbed her hand just in case. "No. Wait." I glanced down at the family Bible. "Family. Granny witches are family. Their mortal family

190

and their church family are what make them different from other paths?"

"Yes," Rachel answered me also looking at the Bible.

"Rosemary." I pointed to the plant lying on the carpet.

"Of course," Rachel said, walking over to snap off three sprigs of rosemary. She returned and handed me a sprig saying, "Your grandmother's blood protect you."

"And you." I replied solemnly.

She then turned to May.

"Mama, I'm..." May started, but her words were cut off by the tears. She wiped her eyes with the back of her hand before looking straight into Rachel's eyes, "I'm sorry. I was so worried, and then Lauralie, and it's my fault, and I didn't know, and—"

Rachel stopped the river of words rushing from her daughter. "Your grandmother's and my blood protect you."

May hugged her mother tightly before returning the benediction.

Rachel hugged her back before turning to me.

The dresser was really rocking now, and I knew it would only be a few more moments before Lorelei was in the room. I linked one arm with Rachel and the other with May and held out the rosemary sprig between my clasped hands. The other women did the same.

The dresser gave way as the door broke free of its hinges. Shadows flooded the room but stopped like they'd hit a brick wall when they got within a foot of the rosemary sprigs. Slowly they started to dissipate. As the black inkiness of the shadows cleared, I could make out Lauralie in all her dark glory.

Hair that was probably once a rich auburn was coated in mud, woven into braids and pulled back into a bun secured with two long thick needles penetrating the empty eye sockets of a cat's skull. Her cheekbones and long nose seemed supernaturally sharp when contrasted with the deep purple hollows of her cheeks and eyes. Her traditional grey robes were

191

richly embroidered with jewel toned thread depicting the disfigured faces we had seen at the windows as if she had woven their souls into her garments as mere adornments.

"A little sprig of rosemary can't save you." The words slithered out of her cracked lips and crawled onto our faces, slipped through our nostrils and wriggled down our throats, sucking the breath from our lungs.

None of us replied. Instead, as one, we stepped forward and encircled the Bokor.

Rachel started the Lord's Prayer. I followed, and then May. As we chanted the prayer all of us touched Lorelei with the rosemary sprigs, causing her skin to hiss like water dropped on a hot griddle. She threw her head back and let out a long drawn-out howl before collapsing to the floor, her power gone.

✔

I honestly think Lauralie expected to get away with what she'd done; there isn't a specific law against using dark magic to turn someone into a zombie. It came as a shock to her when the sheriff, a patient of Rachel's, arrested her for breaking and entering, trespassing, and poisoning.

No one was more surprised than May though, when I broached the idea of turning J&H into a school once again. This time with the power of my academic expertise and the help of some of my colleagues who were especially good at grant writing, which is its own type of magic.

We never talked about Lauralie or what brought May and Rachel to the point where Rachel had created a protection spell against her own daughter. To speak of something is to give it power, and we all needed to focus our power on healing magic if we were going to bring the Katherine May Reynolds Center for Appalachian Cultural Studies to life.

Still, sometimes a crow will land outside my window and caw at me. Whenever it happens, May and I scry together in her mirror looking for another young woman whose misuse of magic has taken her down a dangerous path. We send the Kentucky air to summon her, and once she's arrived safely at our school, the crow disappears until next time.

I have named him Elegba.

———

B.F. Vega is a writer, poet, and theater artist living in the North Bay Area of California. Her short stories and poetry have appeared in: *TL;DR Nope 2*, *Nightmare Whispers*, *Dark Celebration*, *Dark Dossier Magazine*, *The Cauldron Anthology*, *Extreme Drabbles of Dread*, and *Haunts & Hellions*. She is still shocked when people refer to her as an author—every time.

# GRANNY WITCH

## BY RACHEL COFFMAN

Adeline crept across the mountainside ridge, working to stay one step ahead of the unseen presence behind her. Her eyes darted, the deep shadow snaking into her own as the bile began to rise into her throat. The familiar dread crawled across her skin and settled over her like a layer of pond slime. Ahead she could see her granny waving her forward, but as she got closer to her safe presence, the image faded, leaving her grandmother's help just out of reach. Her desperation peaked and she found herself drenched in sweat as she jolted back onto the path, winding its way into familiar surroundings, and ran all the way home.

🐈

As she watched the sunrise from her kitchen window, she rubbed her eyes and shuffled toward the counter for her morning coffee. Her insides still quivered as she tried to shake off last night's familiar experience. For as long as she could remember, her dreams had been a glimpse into the future, sometimes downright confusing and unreadable, but other times clear and exact moments in time. Lately, she'd been experiencing similar situations while she was awake. As a young girl, she remembered her granny explaining how to read the vague dreams and premonitions, but her grandmother had been gone so long most of the knowledge had faded away over time. Granny had been the only person in her life who'd understood her draw to magic. She'd long since learned to keep her gifts to herself and rarely spoke of them with anyone.

Her memories of life in southeast Kentucky tugged at her heart. It had been nearly 13 years since her mother's death, when her father had moved her and her brothers to the small town on the outskirts of the Great Smoky Mountain National Park. She'd graduated from the University of Tennessee with a botany degree and spent her days giving tours and working at the Tremont Institute. Lost in thought, she admired the spring morning from her kitchen window.

Startled back into reality by her obnoxious ringtone, she smiled at the name on the screen. "Hey, silly girl. Aunt Addy can't wait to see you this afternoon." She laughed at the mumbling banter of her two-year-old niece until her brother Sean took the phone.

"Hey Addy, when do you think you'll get here? I'll be at work, but Tom and Ella are excited to see you. Tom says he's leaving me with the baby and taking you out on the town this weekend, so be ready."

"I'm heading out in about an hour, so I should be in Asheville around eleven. You know, Tom doesn't have to take me out. I'm perfectly content chilling at home with you guys."

"Of course, you're content doing nothing; that's why Tom is taking you out. You've had a shit month, and Tom is excited to take you to a new gallery downtown. I think he's going stir-crazy trying to balance being a stay-at-home dad, while still finding time to paint, but God forbid I bring up getting a nanny."

"Leave the man alone. You are lucky to have someone who puts his family first."

"Then do me a favor and take his grumpy ass out tonight."

🐾

The spring wind whipped her hair as she took in the picturesque shades of green and wildflowers through her windshield. Her favorite playlist blared, and she looked forward to seeing her family, but she hadn't been able to shake the dread that wiggled its way around in her stomach. Anxiety and depression had been constant companions most of her life, but she hadn't felt this kind of foreboding since right before her mom died. It made her nervous, like the emotion was a precursor to something tragic. Pushing back her unease, she put on her best auntie smile as she pulled into Sean's driveway to see Tom and Ella waiting for her on the porch.

"Who is this little girl? She can't be my Ella; she's too big." Addy pulled her suitcase out and kicked the car door shut.

"It me, Aunt Addy. I big girl now," giggled her niece, running to hug her legs.

Adeline hugged her brother-in-law and swooped Ella into her arms, covering her with kisses. "I've missed you guys so much," she said, "how can it have been two months since I've seen you?"

Tom met her at the bottom of the stairs with a mimosa, and she gratefully accepted the drink. "So, spill it," he said.

"Spill what?"

Tom's amber-brown eyes looked into her tired face. She'd never been able to hide anything from him. In college, she'd often gone to Tom with her problems instead of her brother.

196

They shared an unspoken sense the others didn't understand. He was the only person who didn't question her uncanny ability to know what would happen before it happened. His gran in Louisiana had raised him and taught him to see and understand with more than his eyes.

"Girl, don't even try. I can smell the sadness on you. Tell your favorite brother-in-law all about your troubles."

Addy laughed despite herself. "You suck, you know?" She took a long pull from her drink and fell into the sofa. "It's the same shit. Another guy weirded out and ghosted me, work has been awkward, and I spend more time in the mountains than I do with actual people. And the dreams are back."

"The ones where you are being stalked by something?"

"Yup, and my granny is there again, trying to tell me something, but she's gone before I can get to her. And this feels darker. Remember how I told you about the overwhelming fear and dread I felt before Mama died? It's like that again. I feel something pulsing inside of me, like my energy is twisted up. I swear, sometimes I feel like I'm cursed. The shit's even bleeding into my waking life now."

"I can feel something's off with you. When we're out tonight, I have a friend I want to take you to meet. She's a healer of sorts. If anyone can see if you're hexed, it's her."

"I was joking about the curse, Tom."

"Joking or not, she'll be able to help."

🐾

After dinner, Addy and Tom strolled around downtown Asheville until they ran into a wall of energy sending shivers across her skin. A few steps later, they were standing in front of a small shop called *Granny Magic*. Soft light poured from the windows, and a plump woman in her late 60s with long gray hair milled around inside. Before they had time to touch the door handle, the shop owner turned, focusing her sharp gaze on Addy.

A bell tinkled as Addy and Tom entered the store. Tom stepped forward, introducing the women. "Addy, this is my friend Mama Jean. Mama, this is..."

But before he could finish his sentence, Mama Jean interrupted, "So, you're my expected visitor. The spirits been tellin' me someone special was gonna come into the shop today, and aren't you special indeed." She measured the girl up and down, her deep blue eyes glinting with curiosity.

"I'm sorry," Addy questioned, "special?"

"Very," said Mama. "How long have you known you's a witch?"

Addy glanced sideways to Tom, "You must be mistaken, I'm not a witch."

"Interesting," Mama hummed. "You definitely got some strong magic inside of you. Probably what initially drew that nasty one to ya."

"Excuse me?" Addy balked, "I will not let you speak to my brother-in-law that way."

A loud, bubbling laugh exploded from the odd woman, and a knowing smile crept across Tom's face. "I'm not talking about this pretty boy. Tom and I have been friends for years. I love that one." She winked at Tom. "Nah girl, I'm talking about that mean-ass spirit that's been following you around since you was a youngun. I know you done felt him near ya. There's no way someone as strong as you ain't feelin' that."

Addy stepped closer, smelling the patchouli wafting off the older woman. She looked around, noticing the oddities surrounding her. Several empty hornet nests hung over a shelf of glass jars filled with various dried herbs, while candles and beeswax lined the walls. Inside the shop windows were several boxed beds growing an excellent selection of familiar fresh herbs. She saw teas, grinding pedestals, rows of books on the history of Appalachia and magic, along with every crystal you could imagine. The place smelled amazing. And behind the counter was a small, private room.

"That's where I do card readings and work healings on folks. Why don't you step back here, and we can talk about why you came." Tom nodded his approval while Mama Jean flipped the "Open" sign over, closing the shop for the night.

The three walked into the backroom. Mama sat across the table from Addy and Tom. Addy spoke first, "You know, this all seems a little crazy."

"Crazy's relative. Let me ask you this," said Mama. "Do you ever get feelins' about things, like you already know what is gonna happen?" She acknowledged the shock in Addy's eyes. "I bet sometimes you even dream about things that come to pass."

"Sometimes."

"I bet there's been a lot of chaos in your life—bad relationships, an overall unhappiness with everything, a disconnect from family. Am I right?"

"Things have been messed up since my mom died, but I don't see how that relates to anything."

Rachel Coffman

"At some point in your childhood, you opened a portal, and something attached itself to you. It's been causing chaos ever since."

"But how could I have opened a portal? And a portal to what?" Addy asked.

"Portals are like kinda like doorways to other realms or time periods. There are plenty of ways to open 'em. Sometimes, people open doors by playing with spirit boards or other practices of trying to communicate with the dead. Occasionally, someone's magic is so bright it punches through when they get agitated or frustrated. Repeated tragedy in a single location can cause a crack lettin' spirits slip through. Any of that sound familiar?"

"I've had the sight, as my granny used to call it, since I was young, which sparked an interest in paranormal. My friends and I made spirit boards and tried to hold seances when we were young."

"There ya go. Messin' around with that stuff, you managed to pick up somethin' ugly. I'm willing to bet it had something to do with your mama's death too."

Addy felt the color leave her face, and a wave of nausea swelled in her stomach. "You mean, something I did caused my mama's death?"

"You wasn't the cause of your mama's death, sweet girl. You was just a child. Your granny seen what you were when you was little. Didn't she ever talk to you about your family's history? All the women in your family have had a touch of healing powers, but I bet they ain't seen nothing like you in generations."

"My granny died several years before my mom. I was only 9 or 10, and then we lost my mom," said Addy. "The only thing I know about my mom's family is they immigrated from Ireland to the hills of Southeast Kentucky. My granny did know about my dreams and visions, but after she died, Mom told me not to talk about it outside the family."

"I'm sorry for your loss, but that makes sense. You weren't old enough to practice the healing arts before your grandma died and probably didn't come into your full powers until puberty. She's always with you, you know? Your granny."

"That's part of why we're here; I've been seeing her again in my dreams. I'm always running from a dark, ominous shadow, and when Granny tries to communicate with me, she can't. If she's always with me, why doesn't she talk to me?"

"I'd say it's the shadow stopping her. Once you get rid of that foul ghoulie, your grandma will be able to communicate," Mama Jean reassured her. "Did you ever find the family's book of healin'? Some people might call it a 'grimoire' or a 'book of shadows.' It's probably archaic, may have even come over from Ireland, full of the knowledge of the women who have come before you. It'll have their workings, yarb knowledge, remedies, and notes from every witch who kept the book for the next generation. Find that book, find your magic, and get rid of that attachment."

"It's that easy? Just read an old book, and suddenly I'll have powers? What if I can't find the book?"

"Look through your mama's stuff. The book will find you because you need it. They always find their next sitters. And no, it's not as easy as just readin' the book. You'll have to open yourself up and have faith in ya ancestors; embrace your natural gifts. Then you'll have to read and learn, but I'd say it

201

won't take ya long. If you don't find the book, come back and see me. I'm not as strong as yer folk, but I have a few tricks up my sleeve."

🐾

The next evening Addy sat in her living room, staring at the woods outside. She loved living on the perimeter of the Smoky Mountains. As a forest ranger, her dad had taught her to navigate hiking trails and identify natural threats. Her mom had taught her the basics of herbal medicine, and Addy had since learned to identify almost every plant in the region. She would have never tied that to magic; she'd just always felt at home in nature. She swirled her chamomile tea and breathed in the steam. Before she changed her mind, she stood and walked outside.

Weather had taken its toll on the old barn behind her house. The wet grass stuck to her bare feet as she lugged the heavy, misshapen door to the side. It had been a long time since she'd looked through her mom's things. The initial pain of loss had dulled to a constant ache, but the barn smelled like her mom. Tears pricked at the corner of her eyes as she surveyed the eclectic belongings. With a deep breath, she exhaled, "Hey, Mom."

She ran her fingers across a pink velvet chaise her mom had inherited from her granny. She laughed when she plopped down, only to have a spring rip through the fabric and snag her jeans. Standing back up, the velvet split further from dry rot. She moved on, looking through box after box. By the time she had finished, she'd found three dresses, a sweater, and an open envelope of incense she'd take back in with her. But there was no old family book. Something caught her attention as she turned to leave; the pink fabric she'd ripped was moving. A mouse scurried out of the chaise when Addy smacked the spring, revealing the corner of a worn book. "Oh, come on," she said, "you have got to be kidding me."

She pulled the volume from the sofa and gently dusted the leatherbound cover, revealing the name Ó Canáin below what looked like a star. The book was massive, worn pages tucked into it. With the sun beginning to set, she carried the heavy heirloom into the kitchen, setting it clumsily on her grandmother's round oak table.

She slowed her breathing, using the grounding techniques Mama Jean had showed her at the shop. As her mind cleared, Addy lifted the engraved leather cover. The first section of the text was in what she recognized as Gaelic, with English words scratched along the margins. The following section seemed to be a translation of the first, telling the story of Ava Ó Canáin. The book's purpose was to record Ava's experiences moving from Ireland to Kentucky while keeping her Irish traditions alive. It explained how foraging in Appalachia wasn't unlike that of her homeland, once she learned the plants and their healing properties. She'd sketched and labeled each, listing a variety of purposes below.

Addy thumbed through Ava's rules of magic, a list of the pagan holy days, and spells. She flipped ahead, finding it morph into a combination of old and new religions. Sewn into the spine were animal hide envelopes labeled to hold various spells, healing practices, and hexes. In the back of the book, a family tree listed each generation of witches and their gifts. It was there she saw her name written in her grandmother's handwriting. Addy's powers still listed as "exudes great strength, although still undetermined."

♌

She spent the next couple of weeks scouring the pages, trying to familiarize herself with the information within. She'd gathered the herbs, stones, and woods mentioned, storing them in a room she'd set aside to "practice" her magic. And although she felt she understood the subject matter from an intellectual standpoint, she didn't feel any familial connection. She didn't feel any power or magic within the words. Frustrated, she decided to go to bed.

Addy woke up, and fear immediately choked her sense of logic. Eyes darting around her bedroom, she couldn't move her body or speak but could see the dark shadow on top of her, forcing her into the bed. She fought through the panic, focusing and forcing out words she'd found in her grandmother's book. "Darkness out; only light is welcome here."

Jolting up, she grabbed her chest and gasped for breath. Fear gave way to anger, and she shouted into the still room, "Leave me alone!"

She heard a faint whisper, "He'll be back soon, Adeline, so listen and heed my words. Take the book and go to the mountains. You will find the strength you need in those ancient mountains. Use that strength to find me, and we will end this evil, once and for all." It was her grandmother's voice. It had been so long since she'd heard it, Addy was surprised she recognized her, but she knew in her bones it had been her grandmother talking to her.

Addy threw on a jacket, laced her hiking boots, and headed out the back door with her granny's book. She knew the familiar path through her backyard, past the barn, and into the woods like an old friend. Her eyes adjusted to her surroundings, the moon dark, preparing for its next lunar cycle. Unsure where to go, she tucked logic away and focused on her gut instincts. Her ears popped as she fully opened, letting intuition lead the way.

Each of her five senses sparked to life. Hands held out to embrace the night, the cool dew kissing her fingertips as they brushed the leaves on each side of her. The mixture of earth, honeysuckle, and sweet pine sap called her forward, reminding her of her youth. The whinny of a screech owl called her deeper into the woods until she found herself in a clearing next to a crick.

Immediately she knew she'd found her destination. Following the book's instruction, she spun clockwise three times before entering the space she intended to work within. Her grandmother's quilt billowed onto the damp ground, Addy set down the book, and shed her jacket, socks and shoes. In a stone circle between the quilt and the brook, she built a fire, tossing Mountain Ash branches into the flames to protect and open her psychic powers. Then, sitting on a large boulder, she plunged her bare feet into the stream, shrieking at the shock of clarifying cold. She waded into the rushing mountain water, wearing only a white cotton nightgown, and plunged herself completely, emptying her thoughts and grounding her energy.

Using the berries from the mountain ash bush, she blew on each, creating a circle of protection around her working space. Dripping, she strode back to the quilt and laid on her back, toes in the grass, and stared at the canopy above. "I purge my doubt in the waters of my ancestors. I ground myself in the knowledge of all those whose blood, love, and sacrifice have supplied sanctity to this all-knowing earth. I draw on the magic of the Appalachian Mountains which I call home. Come forth, sisters of Ó Canáin and show yourselves. Share your

205

ancient wisdom and pass forth your magic to the daughter before you."

Addy smelled electricity in the air just before lightning streaked across the sky above. She stood, at once letting go of all doubt and focusing on the magic within her. Within her circle of protection, women of all ages began to materialize, holding hands with various smiles of mischief, determination, hardness. Directly in front of her, two women stepped forward. The first she immediately recognized as Granny and tears flooded to her eyes. The other woman's simple plaid dress and apron were in contrast with her masculine worn leather hat.

Her grandmother clapped her hands together and cackled with delight. "I knew you had it in you, Sissy! I ain't gonna lie, though; I didn't realize you had *all this* in you."

"Granny?" she asked.

"Yes, darlin'. I've been trying to get through to you for years, but that pissant misogynist was givin' me a run for my money. But you've been learnin', and you've confused him for now. We won't have too long, but enough time to send that interloper back to where he came from."

Unsure what to say, Adeline turned within the circle surveying each woman with curiosity. "How can this be real, Granny? Is it true, am I a witch?"

Beaming with pride, Granny said, "Sissy, you have a power stronger than anyone in our bloodline has seen since," looking at the woman next to her, "well, since our Granny Ava."

Ava stepped forward, laying a cold hand on Addy's cheek. Her face shone with warmth and satisfaction as she softly spoke, "Hello, Adeline. We've been waiting for you to find the magic. Did you know your prophecy was revealed even before I left my homeland of Ireland? A formidable mountain witch unfamiliar with magic, traditions stolen by the hands of premature death. But your granny saw it in you and never gave up reconnecting you with your heritage."

"The malicious attachment I've been told about, how do we banish him? Was he the cause of my mother's death? Was it my experimentation with things I didn't understand that brought him here?"

Her granny stepped forward again, "This attachment is not your responsibility to bear, Sissy. Your blossom into womanhood drew an angry spirit from a previous life, hungry to use your awakening power to finish what he hadn't been able to during his lifetime. Your mother had shunned the practice, writing off our family's gifts as superstition, so when he used your energy to advance on her, she was ill-prepared. And you know the result. Startled by his aggression, she stumbled back, knocking herself unconscious, tipping the candle that would engulf her life in the process."

"However," Ava interjected, "it is your responsibility to rid yourself of him. It's time to break his stronghold and send him back to the hell he came from."

Addy felt anger bubble to the surface, and along with the intense emotion came a warm wind, flaring the fire within their circle. "What do we do? I want him gone...now."

"First, we must draw him into our circle, so you need to move the berries to open a path. Then you must call him to you. A witch hunter feeds himself with narcissism and ego, so taunting should work easily enough. Once you have him, we will close the circle, and you will recite this incantation."

207

Immediately, the book flipped open to the page needed. Its letters shone so Addy could read them even in the night. "These mountains are full of longstanding knowledge and have magic from many religions and cultures before and including us. Use that power and fire to purge the land of his vile energy."

Addy gathered her courage, and a section of the mountain ash berries and stepped back into the broken circle. Suddenly, she saw the familiar shadow slithering along the outskirts of her ring of protection. "What's the matter spirit," she mocked, "afraid of a few women in the night? Afraid we'll find out about your impotence; prove you once and for all to be the lesser sex? In this era, only weak men attach themselves to and prey on prepubescent girls. Why not come out of the shadows and play with a real woman?"

The retribution was swift as a wind blew by, opening a gash on Addy's cheek. But before he had time to run, the granny witches closed the circle, trapping him with the victim of his decade of torment. The shadow swirled violently, finally solidifying into a dark mass, nothing recognizable but the traditional Puritan hat. They circled each other while her sister witches chanted. Addy gathered the blood from her face, smashing it with the berries in her hand and spitting in the mixture.

As she worked the mixture, infusing her magic and intent, she taunted her nemesis further. "Nothing to say for yourself, little man?"

"I have no fear of you, filthy woman. The Devil still sleeps in your bed, tainting your soul and disgracing your name. You were not strong enough to defeat me then, and you will not be strong enough to defeat me now," he spat.

She laughed. "Don't ever underestimate a southern Appalachian woman." She focused on her work. "With this blood of mine, drawn by your hate, and the protective berries of these wise mountains, I break this connection." Addy jolted forward, swiping the mixture into the angry creature's shadowy face. Before he could react, she thrust her hands into the fire. "I banish you and your hostile intent from this world. Find yourself surrounded by strong women intent on keeping you far from these mountains and from my kinfolk." Staring into the spirit's soul, she clapped her hands three times in the fire as the mixture burned from her uninjured palms. A wave of magic knocked him back, dispersing his essence into the forest night like ash.

With the spirit gone, the ghosts of her ancestors solidified around the circle. They each began speaking with enthusiasm and gratification, but Addy's granny stepped to the center of the ring, raising her hand. "I know you all have so much you want to ask and share with our newest witch, but don't forget we are on mountain time now, and mountain folk never find themselves in a hurry. Tonight is just the first of many times we have with our sweet Adeline." The women settled down and smiled at the youngest among them. Ava stepped forward, kissing her heir on the forehead, then shimmered out of visibility.

Adeline wrapped her arms around her grandmother, and exhaustion hit her so hard she almost lost her footing. "I'm not ready for you to go," she said, "I have so many questions."

"Sissy, I've been in your dreams since I left your physical world. After tonight, we will have hours to reconnect. Your magic is unlike anything our family has seen in generations, and although your mama didn't believe in our power, she taught you about nature and holistic healin'. You're so much more prepared than you think you are, my child. The family is always around; you just need to come to the mountains to find them. This moment was just the beginning. Go rest, and we'll get to the real lessons tomorrow."

After her granny had left, Adeline gathered her belongings and put out the fire. As she walked through her backyard, she felt her mama in the barn and smiled. The doors to her house opened as she approached, and after she set everything down on the coffee table, she plopped onto the couch and said smiling, "Hey, Mom."

---

"Granny Witch" is Rachel Coffman's first published work. She is a self-proclaimed introvert continuously thrust into an extroverted world, which is how she found her love for writing. Rachel's true magic is her ability to create illusion through words, and her excellent multi-tasking gifts allow her to establish order within chaos. Often labeled a wife, mother of three, seeker of the paranormal, whiskey aficionado, eclectic witch, or horror movie fiend, Rachel finds the word conundrum a better descriptor of her existence in this crazy universe of energy and ideas.

# Rise of the Mother Bear

## by Indigo Giordana-Altú

The joys of life were soon to be suffocated by yet another economic recession. Kiara had come to know hardship and trauma were not respecters of persons, but the doom and gloom stories of the big world also didn't faze her much. Occasionally, she drifts into wonder over how the nation came to such a state. She surmised it could be the collective negative energy and poor choices that snowballed throughout history. After all, thoughts, words, and actions are conduits of power. With the current events of late, it was surely the verge of the great denouement that would soon throw all into a survival-of-the-fittest competition.

Kiara resolved she would not panic with the rest. She was unusually tranquil most of the time and planned to stay that way. It always served her well.

Even in that moment, she sat content on her front porch. Kiara was odd in many ways and one of few people who truly enjoyed a hot humid day beneath Carolina blue skies. Her floral dress stuck like cling wrap on her sweating umber skin. A chorus of frogs sang off-key. The air smelled like dust. It meant rain would be along soon to cool everything down. There was nothing like it.

"Mama!"

Jayden's voice hit her like a hammer striking hot iron on an anvil. Kiara's eyes snapped open and fought the blur of sleep to focus on the tablet her six-year-old shoved in her face.

211

"What is it?" she asked with slight disinterest as she shifted in her chair.

"I was a lucky ninja, and then the screen went black," Jayden whined.

Kiara sighed. "Give it here."

All it needed was to be plugged in. A part of her wanted to lie and say it was broken so he would come out of the virtual abyss that was surely siphoning his lifeforce. She wished she had never bought it, but, as Jayden pitched at the time, all the other kids had one. Truly, she couldn't care less what others had, but Jayden had a charm about him. His sapid voice and big hazel eyes were capable of bringing those around him to servitude.

Avoidance wasn't her strength. She was being pulled in by Jayden's gaze that was full of expectation for her to make everything better. The pools of tears already started to form, so she chose not to disappoint him with her antics.

Kiara gave Jayden a calming hug and led him to take a few deep breaths. She guided him into the house and introduced him to the magic of the charger. When the pad finally had enough power to turn on, Jayden's outburst was so full of joy and love. Those tiny arms wrapped around her neck, and Jayden's plump lips planted a big kiss on her cheek that made her choice worth it.

Since it was clear rest wasn't in the cards for her, she ventured out to the front yard to harvest some more leaves and flowers from her hyssop shrub. Her stock was running low, and she'd promised a weekly brew for her neighbors. Everyone who lived on her road swore by her teas, insisting they were what kept them at full health. Some reported not getting so much as a throat tickle when the trees erupted and blanketed everything with thick yellow pollen. Every year it looked like a golden version of Mt. Vesuvius's bombardment of Pompeii.

Hardly anyone appreciated spring, but Kiara, of course, loved it. Kiara used the most unexpected ingredients, including birch tree pollen, for brews, tinctures, and powders. She had become a living legend in that town. With a population of just over three hundred people, she supposed that wasn't saying much, but her neighbors' constant marveling made Kiara smile inwardly.

She often wondered how they would feel if they knew it had little to do with anything she concocted, and more to do with the secrets that had been passed down her line for centuries from one matriarch to next. White magic was in her blood. Once she understood a person's life, if they had good intentions, she did everything she could to help them. Some people loved to refer to her practices as "New Age," an idea she found to be ridiculous. It was all as ancient as could be, but people had gotten too lazy with all their conveniences, to keep up with it.

Deep down she wanted to shout it from the rooftops so all people could rise to their highest capability, but she wasn't going to tempt fate by sharing too much. She learned a long time ago how people in the Bible Belt reacted to anything that didn't fit their antiquated, 18th-century ideals.

As for her small town, forget being branded as a witch— it was bad enough to most she was a single mother. They let it pass for their own benefit, but she still knew that beyond their smiles to her face, there was talk behind her back. One thing the people were good at was picking apart other people's lives and spreading gossip like wildfire. But she and Jayden were better off on their own.

🐈

Jayden's father, Ryan, almost always carried a dark aura. It wasn't there when they met, but it grew over time. The more fixated he got on money and things, the darker it grew. It consumed him so much he stopped looking at Kiara with love, fixating instead on the possibility of turning her into a cash cow. They constantly fought over her refusal to abuse her gifts, and because she never charged anyone for her remedies.

She never had a need for much. The house was left to her by her mother, and she was content just living off the land. Here and there she would sell quilts or knitted baby clothes she made, but that was about it.

She rued the day she allowed Ryan to see her knowledge went beyond how to use the elements. Kiara knew the secrets of psychokinesis, astral projection, and so much more. She just really never had a need to use any of those aspects of the power herself. After Ryan found out, he was so full of *why don't you do this* and *why don't you do that* or *nobody would know* moments. She refused him when he wanted to put her on social media and bring the whole world to their doorstep. When that idea fell through, he actually tried to convince her to teleport in and out of a bank vault. Kiara was as strict as she had been taught to be and would never harm anyone for selfish gains.

When she couldn't take it anymore, she insisted Ryan move out of her home. He didn't go without an argument, but the police assured him that since he wasn't Kiara's legal husband, he held no claim on her property; he had to go. He tried to use the then unborn Jayden to stake his claim, but they clarified it didn't matter if she was pregnant with his child.

She hadn't seen Ryan since the day she sent him away.

🐈

Day turned to dusk.

Jayden finally had a desire to play outside, though she was busy cooking their dinner. After her many refusals as she couldn't go outside yet to look after him, she gave in because of that thing Jayden was so good at. Before he went out she listed at least twenty *don't do's* and said she would be watching from the window.

As she said she would, Kiara repeatedly glanced out her kitchen window. Several times they had exchanged a smile and a wave from the distance. She was just about done with her rendition of his favorite dinner—chicken fried steak, mashed potatoes, and sugar snap peas. In between all the frying, draining, mashing, and stirring, she paused to check up on him again.

Kiara was relieved to see Jayden off the tablet and out there square dancing with the fireflies. He reminded her of herself. After she stared a little too long and allowed her heart to balloon with pride for her sweet handsome son, she realized the gravy was scorching. She yanked the pot off the stove and mumbled chastisements to herself for ruining it and having to start again.

After scrubbing the pot, she got her butter, milk, and flour to mingle once more before adding shakes of salt and pepper. Whisking the mixture, she mused on how something so simple could require such attention to come out just right. It was more persnickety than some of her herbal tinctures.

The sound of a car door slamming and tires rolling over gravel caught her attention. She removed the pot from the stove and stepped out with her heart pounding.

Kiara looked around. She saw no car. She saw no Jayden.

"Jayden!" she called out over and over, hearing her own desperation grow until reality gut punched her. She wailed as she went running barefoot down the road, and neighbors popped out of their homes one by one, peering like inquisitive meerkats.

When her feet suffered all the abrasions they could handle, she collapsed in the middle of the road.

Someone had kidnapped her son.

Indigo Giordana-Altú

Kiara hated herself. For all her teas and tinctures, her healing spells, and her other witchy ways, she never worked to develop the one ability that might have kept Jayden safe. She hadn't developed her clairvoyance and never saw it coming that, in all muck of the world, her son would become the next Amber Alert flowing to people's phones and television. Now, hungry for something new, reporters sounded almost enthusiastic as they spoke of the abduction of her son.

Kiara felt a sting in her heart as she heard her son's name being spoken, then remembered how they never found that girl from Shelby or that little boy out of Roseboro, both of them missing now twenty years or more. What wreaked worse havoc on her brain was what she discovered in the two days since it happened. There were hundreds of thousands of known missing kids in the country. When she learned this, Kiara knew, as much as she trusted law enforcement, she had to do something herself to make sure Jayden didn't stay missing forever.

Kiara tore through the house. She grabbed books with spells, mixed this, that, and the other, lit candles, chanted, or simply sat on the floor sobbing. Neighbors tried to check on her, but whenever she saw their solemn faces appearing at her door with trays of food she did not ask for, she would use her Mana to send them away. They were oblivious to the craft when they each turned with extremely dilated pupils and walked away like puppets on strings. She needed to think and could not deal with trite expressions of sympathy.

The police had turned first to Ryan, considering him as Jayden's biological father, a prime suspect. But he told them he probably wouldn't even recognize Jayden, let alone kidnap him. The police found no signs of Jayden, so they took Ryan at his word and moved on. With an earnest face, Ryan asked them to keep him updated.

216

She paced the house, trembling with the fear of the ticking clock she was up against. She didn't know who had Jayden. A molester? A human trafficker? A murderer? She glanced up at the space just above her kitchen cabinet where she stored a few of her dried herb satchels to keep them out of Jayden's reach. Here she stashed all things that should only be used by experienced practitioners, the true wise ones. Some of the dried plants, such as jimsonweed, were deadly, but she also kept stimulants like betel nut up there.

Kiara climbed on her stool and took them down. She looked at the bags as though they were her one true savior. A powerful brew was soon created.

When she was finished, Kiara carried the potion to her incantation room and placed it on an altar. She sat before it, chanted, rocked, and begged her ancestors to help her with the problem at hand. She drank the brew. A white light outlined her body before it absorbed into her. She caught sight of her eyes in the mirror; they were no longer dark brown but purple.

She stood and reached for a small bowl filled with a mixture of juniper, mugwort, tonka, sage, and other elements of protection. She sprinkled the blend in a large circle, then laid down in its center of it. She rested one hand over her heart and one over her belly.

Again, she chanted. Suddenly her body stiffened, her back arching up. A vision of Jayden came to her. He was crying in a darkened room. An unfamiliar woman, with brown knotted tresses and tribal tattoos covering her bronze skin, slapped him. Someone she couldn't quite make out through the haze held a mobile phone out toward Jayden. The phone was recording Jayden's terror. Then, Kiara's breath caught as she heard the distinct voice of Jayden's father.

Kiara's recognition of the location became clear. They were at Ryan's late grandmother's house in Ahoskie.

"I said do it again, you little freak," Ryan screamed at him.

Jayden sniffled, "No. Mama said not to."

217

He barely got the sentence out before the woman struck him again. Reacting under the pressure, Jayden sent a glass sitting before him flying across the room where it shattered against the wall.

Kiara could hear Ryan celebrate and shout about how rich they were going to be. Fury burned within her. She snapped out of the vision and sat up. Deep down, she knew the right thing would be to call the police and let them know what she discovered, to let them handle it, but the scorned woman, the adrenaline-filled mother, and powerful witch within her took over instead. It was an internal alliance for vigilante justice.

Kiara stood with arms outstretched and called on dark forces she never had before. Within seconds, she skipped the inventions of modern man and teleported to the room where Ryan and the woman held Jayden captive. She knew her intentions were brutal. As her son shouted with gladness to see her, she enchanted him to fall into a sleeping state.

The tattooed woman jolted and grabbed a nearby butcher knife, but Kiara's magic ripped the weapon from the woman's grip and sent it spiraling down with great force into her foot. She screamed out in pain.

Black veins pulsated from beneath Kiara's skin. Before their eyes, she shifted into a large bear. She growled and slapped the woman with her large paw, sending her and the butcher knife that impaled her foot flying backwards. Another swipe of the paw left five gashes across the woman's face as she writhed in pain.

Still in her animal form, Kiara gnashed her teeth and chased after Ryan who had not been man enough to stick around. By the time she got outside, he was already halfway down the road in his car. She changed herself into a falcon and got ahead of him.

Kiara landed and morphed into her human form. She stood, looking at Ryan dead-on as he chose to accelerate in her direction. She closed her eyes and extended her palm as she chanted. Both his wrists broke. He hit the brakes as he agonized. He was no more than twenty feet away from her. Kiara walked over and used her power to rip the car door off. It flew through the air and crashed down onto the road, sliding and pushing up dust clouds. Unable to even unbuckle himself, Ryan begged her not to kill him.

Kiara laughed. "Kill you? As much as you deserve it, I'm no murderer."

"Then what are you going to do?" He panted with his hands dangling from their hinges with knotted bulges beneath the skin.

She uttered a spell, "We never met. You will forget. Wherever you go, no son shall you know. In this moment, your eyes go blind. Riches you shall never find. Today and forever more, I untether you from Jayden and me. So mote it be."

Ryan's eyes changed to a cloudy gray as he called out for help. He couldn't see anything and had no idea where he was.

Kiara disappeared and stood before Jayden who was still peacefully sleeping under her spell. She glanced down at the strange woman whom she had never met before. She was clearly in pain from the wounds Kiara had inflicted on her. They were serious—she was bleeding out. The woman started praying what seemed to be a Catholic prayer and, at one point, Kiara thought she heard the woman refer to her as the devil.

For a second, Kiara thought of turning back into a bear so she could maul the woman for having laid a finger on Jayden, but Kiara's mother's voice came to her, reminding her of the dangers and pitfalls awaiting those who lived in the shadow ways.

Kiara extended her palm toward the woman and healed her wounds. Still, she had no desire to make them pretty; she left the claw marks as keloid streaks across her face. She chanted a spell to erase the woman's memories of Ryan; then, without caring if the woman would be welcomed, Kiara sent her back to her people.

Indigo Giordana-Altú

Kiara scooped Jayden into her arms and transported them both to their own town, leaving Ryan's grandmother's house in flames that eventually turned it to cinder. Once in the safety of their home, Kiara left Jayden sleeping for the rest of the night, while she contacted police and neighbors to share that she found him. They all had many questions about Jayden's whereabouts during his time of being missing, but she was able to enchant them just enough to send them off to pursue other interests.

All she wanted was to focus on loving and raising her son with a more watchful eye. To be sure of it, she cast a spell to help her do so for the rest of her life. The next morning, she knew the gift had been bestowed upon her. She arose with the pulsating of a new larger energy within. She undressed to shower away anything she still needed to shed away to keep her path clear. That is when she noticed something new. On her skin, she now bore a mother's mark, in the shape of a bear.

———————

Indigo Giordana-Altú, a member of the Horror Writers Association, has a background in penning stage plays, film scripts, short stories, poetry, news features, and research articles. She has an affinity for mystery, drama, and horror. Often her stories highlight the human condition, encourage personal reflection, and inspire positive living. Indigo is NC born and Cali raised. Though she moved back to NC over 25 years ago, she only recently found her happy place in the NC Coastal region. Indigo is an ambivert who will dance in the rain, hug a tree, talk to animals, and simply love others authentically.

# HAZING NIGHT

## BY ROWAN HILL

"You eat bullfrogs? Straight up gross, girl," Janet gasped out between laughs, Marie also chuckling. The two rounded the University's Econ building on the wide path and fell in with other students waiting for the pedestrian signal to cross the street.

"I swear on sweet baby Jesus, taste just like chicken. A wet, ugly, Arkansas chicken," Marie countered with a smile. Further down the wide, oak-lined street, a large Ford truck, horn honking and blinkers flashing, turned the corner. Loud country music blasted through open windows as it crept through the intersection, allowing everyone on the street a good look at the pair of naked men, bodies painted red, in the flatbed. The pledges shielded their privates with signs that proclaimed '*Sigma Phi Party 9 pm*'.

"Y'all so lucky you pledges are girls," Janet said, eyeing the truck. "Could you imagine being a pledge and doing that shit? At least when sororities do it, we do it in private."

Marie, a freshman, and current pledge nodded but didn't totally agree. She'd done some strange things during the four weeks she'd been running the hazing gauntlet. *Strange*. She sighed as the truck rolled out of sight. The hazing would be worth it. She needed this. Chi-Alpha was everything, would open doors Marie didn't even know existed, here in Mississippi and elsewhere. She could handle a little strangeness.

A coarse tickle ran down the length of Marie's bare upper arm, and a shiver shot down her spine. She turned to see the hulking figure of Richard Adair, the university's star linebacker, standing behind her. An ugly smile twisted his beautiful lips as Marie's lungs locked up on her.

"Goin' to that party, Marie?" His eyes traced her curves beneath her pastel yellow sundress. She clutched her books tighter to her chest, shifting her backpack. Janet gave her a curious stare.

"Stay away from me, Richard," she said, trying her best to keep her voice from cracking. She turned away.

He gave a disturbing laugh in reply, and she felt her long brown hair shift on her back as if he had fondled it. They'd missed the walk signal, and the caution flashed. Marie linked arms with Janet, and they strode away from the towering man, merging into the band of stragglers just reaching the other side.

He called out to her through the crowd, "I'll see you later, Marie."

The girls turned the block and found themselves alone on the wide pathway.

Janet broke the silence. "So, Dick Adair, huh?" Marie released a long-held breath, and a look of comprehension dawned in Janet's eyes. "What'd he do?"

A day after it happened, Marie relayed in tears an abridged version of her near assault to another Chi-Alpha member but hadn't spoken of it since. She shivered at the memory of Richard's darkened car. Still, she couldn't stop herself from assuming a light tone. "We went on a date, and he and his wandering hands do not understand the word 'no'." Horror merged with empathy on Janet's face, the look bursting through Marie's airy facade. "No," she said, "I got outta there quick, but I had bruises for weeks." Marie was confident Richard just thought of her as a poor farm girl from South Arkansas, with no one nearby to help her if she got into trouble. Expendable. "Never again. He's lucky I didn't call the cops on him or file a report with the university."

"Lord, huh? The Adairs are old money, too. Probably woulda been water off a duck's back."

Marie nodded. Another reason why she needed Chi-Alpha. Support. Sisters to help while she was an eight-hour drive away from her mama. The two girls turned onto Sorority Row, and the Chi-Alpha house came into sight.

An opulent, white colonial mansion, large columns framing the front of the three-story building, it was a world away from the little two-bedroom farmhouse Marie left in Pine Bluff. She needed this. Her mama would be so proud, pledging the oldest, richest sorority in Mississippi. The jobs she could get, the opportunities available. Every alum of the blue-blooded sorority at the chapter either married a CEO or became one herself.

Janet placed her hand on Marie's shoulder as they mounted the steps. "Don't worry, Pledge." Her mouth tilted up into a one-sided, sly grin. "Once you're in, assholes like Dicky Adair won't be a problem." She released Marie then turned, opening the front door to reveal a flurry of activity.

A riot of pastels, the unspoken dress code of the house, whizzed everywhere as young women, carrying bundles of dark material, signs, and other crafts, ran through the foyer to the kitchen, to the living room, or to the meeting area. Marie's eyebrows arched in interest. It was supposed to be her last day of pledging, the final hazing night when the Council would decide if they would open up their pearly, pastel-ridden gates to her.

"Pledge!" Marie's temporary moniker resounded from above. She looked up to see two women gliding with unnatural grace down the grand staircase.

Samantha Belle, Chapter President. Her blonde locks, cut into a stylish bob, brushed the shoulders of her lilac-colored sweater set with matching capris and heels, the color pairing perfectly with the light tan she received summering in Cape Cod. She held a clipboard, a smile displaying her perfect teeth as she read from it. If Marie ever thought of someone as charming, it would be the legacy member Samantha Belle from Georgia.

The voice that had called her, though, belonged to the shorter, stouter Vice-President, Penelope Brown. She, too, wore a sweater set identical to Samantha's in all but color. An austere dark rose cashmere strained to cover Penelope's square shoulders.

Penelope stepped in front of Marie. "Daydreaming, Pledge?"

Marie snapped to attention. "No, High Mistress!" Janet gave her a pitying smile, but exited the foyer, leaving Marie to her fate.

"You gonna pull that poor-girl-wandered-into-the-wrong-house routine tonight, Pledge?"

Marie shook her head emphatically, "No, High Mistress!"

Samantha now came up beside the two, smiling at the pair. "Ready for tonight, Marie?" Her gentle Southern drawl reminded Marie of Scarlet O'Hara. Samantha touched her forearm lightly, and Marie almost sighed with the contact.

Marie nodded. "Yes, Grand Mistress."

"This month hasn't been too hard now, has it? You excelled in all your tests."

Marie glanced down to her arm where Samantha's soft, dainty hand lingered.

"No, Grand Mistress, it was fine. But I've never done tests like those before, so I'm not sure how I did."

Samantha tilted her face upward and gave a light, captivating laugh. "You have a lot of potential, Marie. I look forward to tonight," she said as her hand slipped from Marie's arm, leaving Penelope to deal with her. Marie watched Samantha's well-toned back turn the corner, then finally gave Penelope her entire attention.

"I swear, Pledge," Penelope said, "if you fuck this up tonight, you will be finished at this campus."

Vulgarities were rare in the demure and genteel house, and Marie blinked twice. "I'm sorry?"

Penelope crossed her arms. "Tonight's your final ordeal, noob. The 'will they or won't they' crap comes to a finish." She leaned forward to whisper in Marie's ear. "Tonight, we see if you got the balls to stick with us or if you bale quicker than a farmhand on harvest week." She pulled away to reveal a mischievous grin. "Now get out back and make sure Capra and Capella are nice and clean. I want to be able to see my reflection in their horns."

Marie nodded and curtsied, as required, then left the lobby and passed through the house and out to the large backyard bordered by a towering forest. She spotted the only other pledge already in the penned area near the tree line where the two male goats lived.

"Hey, Casey." Marie stepped inside the pen.

The other potential member had a pet comb in her hand and was sitting on a stump next to a goat. "Can you believe we still have to do this? I mean, I thought 'mascot duty' was cute the first week, but after five, it's getting reeeeal old."

Marie grinned and led the other goat to a place where she could sit and brush its coat.

"Naw, it's not so bad. Much easier than farm work I'm used to. Heck, even when pledging is done, I still might come take care of these two handsome boys." She scratched the large goat on its brow. "At least these fellas don't shout 'Pledge!' at me."

Casey tossed the comb on the ground and stood, brushing the short goat hair off of her cashmere sweater and matching skirt. "Can you take over here? I've gotta get my nails done before tonight." She held her hand out for Marie. "Working on this pair has them all dirty and scratched up."

Without waiting for Marie to respond, she opened the gate and whispered a quick goodbye, sneaking around the side of the house so as to not get caught. Marie sighed and turned back to the goat she was brushing, scratching his head simultaneously. The last month hadn't been too hard, not if you really needed the prize at the end. Not if you were hungry for it. Starving.

The strange hazing rituals she'd gone through weren't nearly as bad as she had anticipated. A few card-guessing games. A couple strange scavenger hunts. Only one night where she gave blood, and another when they dissected frogs and hamsters. The sisters wanted to see how much gore she could take. Marie had grown up on a working farm. It'd take a lot more than rodent guts to make her bow out.

As she began to gently scrub the goat's horns, a faint echo of what sounded like a scream came from beyond the trees. Marie gazed out into the dense Mississippi woods, still steamy and thick with crickets and cicadas. She strained her ears over the insect chirping to try to make out the sound again.

The thick felt rubbed softly against her eyelids, while tiny stones and pine needles pricked the soles of her feet. Marie walked blindfolded and barefoot over the forest floor. As she predicted would happen, her toe stubbed against a root, and she tipped forward, stopping herself from falling at the last second. The cloak draped around her body gaped open, and the warm night air caressed her naked breast.

Other than the occasional direction, Penelope remained silent as she led the way. Marie had accepted all the walking conditions as Penelope demanded them, only hesitating when she told her to get naked.

There hadn't been any nudity at any point in the hazing. The act flew in the face of the sorority's veneer of primness. But after a second under Penelope's stare, Marie unzipped her dress and pulled down her underwear, accepting the proffered black cloak. She looked to the room's doorway expectantly.

"Will Casey meet us there? Wherever we're going that is."

"She will not." Penelope's said with fast, clipped words.

"But—"

"Casey put a manicure before duty. She's out. Now shut up unless you want to join her."

The sole pledge, then, whittled down from ten at the start of the month, Marie continued to follow Penelope through the woods in the midnight hour. She guessed they'd been walking fifteen minutes when she heard faint singing, or chanting, from ahead. She didn't recognize the song, but the laconic and eerie character of the words gave her a chill. Marie's heart started to beat frantically in her chest at the sudden sinister quality of her hazing. Everything so far had taken place in the house or on campus. There had been little secrecy to the process; Marie had only been blindfolded at certain parts of their other hazing nights.

The chanting grew louder, more frenetic, with each step over the rough forest floor until the chorus reverberated around her. Two strong hands gripped both of her arms, pulling her to a stop.

The chanting abruptly ended, and the blindfold slipped away from her face. Marie's lips parted in shock. They stood in the middle of a ring of burning torches, a surreal glow enshrouding the cleared space. Tall pines surrounded the open area, firelight shone and flickered on them, creating deep shadows. On the ground were the naked bodies of the sisters, bent over their knees, hands splayed wide with arms stretched out to the circle's middle. Marie drew a sharp breath, the air catching in her lungs when she noticed who was in the center.

The sorority's two docile goats stood next to a kneeling, bare-chested man. Shadows danced across his sweaty chest. Even though a blindfold covered half his face, she recognized Richard Adair. His chiseled, footballer body was alert and taut. His lungs pulsed up and down as he drew ragged breaths. A long, curved dagger pierced his shoulder, the punctured skin swollen and bleeding.

Marie felt her cloak fall away. She was as naked as the other women of the circle. The High Mistress stepped closer to Marie, filling her sight. Penelope, also naked except for a thick, black lace collar with sharp, bulky edges that contrasted with her pale skin.

"You ready, Pledge?" she calmly challenged.

Marie licked her lips and nodded uncertainly. She looked across to Richard Adair. His beautiful chest shining in the soft glow. He looked ethereal with his tan skin and large frame. The dagger protruding from his shoulder. The stream of blood painting his pectorals and abs.

Penelope locked eyes with Marie and crossed into the inner circle. Without speaking, she went immediately behind Richard and snatched off his blindfold. She gripped his head on either side. Her fingers splayed as far down as his cheeks, nails digging into his flesh. He cried out, then began sobbing. The two women broke their gaze, Penelope's focus falling on Richard, and Marie's eyes following.

As if he had been commanded, Richard began to speak, his voice quavering. "I...was going to...get off that night...whether you wanted to or not," he paused, and a lump, thick and bulging formed in Marie's throat. She wiped a tear away as he spoke. "I'd done it before...I knew how to keep you still," he sniffed, and drool seeped from the side of his mouth.

Marie had forgotten to breathe and sucked in air. Memories of his attack washed over her. The click when he'd activated the car's child locks snapped in her ears. She felt again the heat of his oily hands forcing their way under her clothes. Smelled his hot, moist breath, a sickening mix of mint and draft beer, puffing on her face. The sparks she'd seen when he bashed her head against the window shot up once more before her eyes. The nauseated disorientation that followed the blow, and the bitter taste on her tongue.

He wouldn't stop. He wouldn't listen to her. Wouldn't even talk. Now, he wouldn't stop talking. "If that university rent-a-cop hadn't strolled closer, I wouldn't have chickened out and flipped the lock." Richard ended his confession with a sob and tried to lean over his knees. Penelope gave a violent jerk to his head again, and he stilled.

Marie stood there for an age, eons, feeling all eyes on her naked body, but only Richard's gaze unnerved her. It felt like she was still vulnerable to him, like he was still in control.

A delicate finger trailed along Marie's nape, then followed down her shoulder. A soothing touch. She turned to see Samantha Belle standing beside her, with perfect, coiffed hair and a knowing grin on her face. Samantha wore a fine, black lace collar and nothing else. Marie's eyes glanced down her statuesque body.

She cupped Marie's face, a thumb wiping away the stream of tears. "Marie," she whispered, saying the name with the French inflection her mama always hoped for, "are you scared?" Samantha curled a strand of Marie's hair around her finger.

Marie nodded. "Is this a joke? Another hazing prank?" she asked, trembling.

Samantha gave her a pitying look. "No jokes, Marie. You have to trust me. I'll take you out of there." She leaned in and whispered like a lover sharing secrets. "Let me take you away from that life, Marie. Let me free you from that little town where you were raised, where you would die. That dying, little, incestuous town." Samantha pulled away and her hand came up. She snapped her fingers, and a single flame flickered to life in the palm of her hand, a smooth, effortless gesture.

But powerful.

And Marie could feel that power.

"Let me pull you from the bayou, Marie. Let me give you something more."

A fat tear dropped as Marie's worst fears whispered themselves to her, taunting her that she'd never escape her little Arkansas town. Not really. She'd die within its limits. Die there just like her beautiful mama would. Spend eternity buried in an ugly, treeless cemetery with only a flat grave marker, the kind a riding mower could pass over without stopping, as witness to her existence.

Samantha moved aside, revealing Penelope and Richard. Penelope snatched him by the hair and yanked his head up. He spoke, "Even...even after you escaped, I...I still think about how I could get you alone. I know where your math class is. A place I could take you where we wouldn't be found."

Marie tasted bile in her mouth, though Samantha's sweet voice rang in her ear. "So many opportunities, Marie. Let me give them to you. Let me give you what all our sisters enjoy. Have enjoyed for centuries. Mama will be so proud."

The naked coven sisters began to chant, a soft chorus that silenced the sounds of the forest. Marie's body was drawn to Richard. A magnet to his savagery.

"I...still think about you," he cried. "I don't know why."

"Marie, let me help you, let me give you everything. And all you have to do is give me him. Take him out of the world. Be a force for good. Be good with us," Samantha crooned.

Another step, louder chanting, escalating adrenaline running through her veins.

"I could tell you're a virgin." Richard was now sobbing through his words. "I've never had one before."

Penelope wrenched the dagger from his shoulder, and he screamed at what Marie sensed to be a searing agony. Marie couldn't take her eyes off his lips, his gaping mouth. The chanting grew louder, fierce. In a trance, she drew closer to him, his confession fueling her anger, her disgust, and, despite knowing she'd done nothing wrong, shame. Warm mud

230

squished between her toes as she stepped before him, the loud chanting now burying his sobs.

Marie focused on his face, and their gazes met. His eyes were red-rimmed and flickered away as she heard a *bleat* from one of the goats, its body hitting the ground with a solid thud. Richard kept talking through his blubbering, and Marie felt a fresh wave of hot liquid wash over her feet, as hot as the fire in her veins. Livid, vengeful fire.

"I wasn't scared of being caught...the others never said a word..." Marie felt something cold and metallic slide into her palm, her fingers willingly clenched around it.

"Think of all the things we could do together, Marie," Samantha whispered, her voice floating on the dark night. "Think of all the things you could be."

Richard sucked in a breath and struggled to free himself from Penelope's grip. "I just keep thinking about how tight and warm you'll be..."

Marie felt the dam holding her back from her vengeance break. The chanting grew frenzied as she cocked her arm back, and with an anguished scream, brought the blade down, stabbing the hollow above his collarbone. A spurt of hot, arterial blood hit Marie's breast. She pulled the blade out, then brought it down again, over and over. Penelope released Richard's hair and the body collapsed. Marie's breasts, coated and dripping in the blood shot from his body, rose and fell in the cool air. Her hands shook with the rush.

The chanting stopped and gentle hands guided her away from the two bodies, Richard and the goat, lying in the circle. Their blood had pooled into the middle and the sisters crawled forward, moaning as they clambered into the mixed blood. Marie watched in a daze while her new sorority sisters began to lick and drink from the dirty pool, a swath of naked flesh and tangled limbs rolling over one another, trying to access the sacrificial blood.

Rowan Hill

"And one for Azazel," Penelope's voice rose above the circle. Marie saw her slap the living goat on its hindquarters, sending the beast scurrying off into the night wood.

Samantha drew up beside Marie. "You did wonderfully." She tucked a lock of Marie's hair lovingly behind her ear. "You're going to make an exemplary addition to our coven. We're going to clear this old Southern campus of all the filth, Marie."

Marie nodded absentmindedly, watching as naked bodies, covered in maroon, viscous mud writhed and convulsed. Janet's dirty, marked face flashed in the mob, her expression one of wildness as she slithered. The backs of the sisters had begun to bubble, sharp, geometric shapes pushing out from between their shoulder blades.

One of the girls cried out in ecstasy, arching her slender form. From above one shoulder blade, a black bone erupted. It pushed itself out, longer and wider, another on her other side following. Other girls twisted their bodies, and Marie saw the same ebony bones emerging from all of them. They cried, moaned, whimpered in pleasure and pain until one of the black bones finally spread and revealed a fan of beautiful, long black feathers.

All the wings opened simultaneously, the cries now turning to ones of elation. The wings began to beat, flap themselves against the earth and muddied soil, the bodies they were attached to hanging limply. Looks of exultation and excitement on all their faces as the mass of sisters now began to rise off the ground, lifted by their conjured limbs.

They rose higher and higher through the ring of trees, the torches casting shadows on their bodies. Their laughter grew fainter as Marie, transfixed, watched them from the ground. One by one, they began to fly out of the circle, away from campus, and deeper into the Mississippi woods until Marie could only hear faint whispers of their laughter.

Her breath had calmed, and the daze had nearly left her as the adrenaline faded, replaced by a chill over her naked body. She looked around the circle, the carcasses of the goat and Richard still lying prostrate, their bodies no longer bleeding.

Samantha Belle rounded her, a broad stream of dirty blood now ran down her chin and trailed down her neck. Penelope, also with foul blood smeared across her cheek, approached and the two sorority leaders led the new coven member together to the middle. Samantha gave Marie a smile wide enough to make the girl blush.

"Welcome, sister. Welcome to your last home," she said with her charming drawl, her grace not even marred by the blood now on her chest.

She gave a laugh of relief and groaned with pain and pleasure as black bones lined with thick feathers erupted from her back. Marie stood still, watching in shock until the wide wings began to flap and Samantha Belle took to the sky as if it was natural to her. Her gentle giggle floated down on the breeze long after she had flown away. Penelope remained, her ebony wings already erect and waiting. She gave Marie a smaller, tighter smile.

"Yes, well done," she said as if loathe to give the compliment. The demonic wings began to flap, and her athletic body began to lift off the ground, following the Coven's Grand-Mistress. She turned to look over the macabre scene once more, a dazed Marie still standing in the middle, naked, cold and left behind as the newest member. Penelope called out over the flapping of her wings before she took to the sky,

"Now, clean this mess up, Pledge. I want this sacrificial circle spotless by morning."

Rowan Hill

---

Rowan Hill is an author currently on hiatus as an ESL Professor and living on a volcano in Sicily. She loves writing flawed female protagonists and have found they work well in extreme environments. She has writing credits with Cemetery Gates, Kandisha Press, and now Curious Blue Press, all of which can be found on her website writerrowanhill.com.

# CRISSCROSS GIRLS

## BY RUTHANN JAGGE

When you live in rural South Texas, spring means you need to be careful outside. Creatures start to creep, slither, scurry, and crawl awake, and you don't want to be the first thing that gets their attention. It can also mean that other regularly staid things tend to be a bit easier to rile up. That's not always a bad thing.

It had been a miserable winter. A never yielding overcast hid the sun, but had given no rain in months. Shades of grey where there should've been green made everything at the old farm look even more run down and depressing. The air smelled musty, like dust and old fertilizer.

In general, people tend to take rain for granted, but you understand it's pretty much the main topic of conversation when you live in the country. Mother Nature isn't prone to bargaining, and she doesn't play fair. Rain, or the lack of it, is the cause of many problems. When it doesn't fall, livestock gets sold and the land goes back to the bank. Wells run dry. Equipment breaks down, fences fall into disrepair, and there isn't money to mend either. Hand-me-downs get another patch, and you eat a lot of beans for dinner. Some drink more than usual, and women keep their heads down to hide bruises. It isn't pretty, but it happens during such times.

Folks get desperate. Lines at government offices and at banks grow long, as people dig their heels in deeper and sign away more of what they don't have. They gamble on better days, believing that if they can get through this rough patch, they will turn things around. Hope replaces logic for some, because it's all they have.

On a particularly dull afternoon, seventeen-year-old Beatrice "Birdie" Montrose decided she had enough of being cooped up. It was a school break, but everyone had to do their share when crops were planted and pulled. They were always dumping or spraying poison on the row crops. There were animals to feed and seasonal incomes to be made, so you did it all for the sake of the dirt. School breaks just meant hard work with no pay for most of the young ones; Birdie had to spend all her time helping in the fields or catering to her annoying younger brother.

Birdie went out to walk in the farthest plot, looking for things that might have come up in the heavy red dirt the last time the old machines plowed through it. She found some treasures: old silverware, a lucky horseshoe, and even a few arrowheads she glued to a board and hung on her wall. Last month she found a heart made of tin with the initials "L M" meticulously scratched into the soft metal and a hole punched through. She ran a piece of string through the hole and wore the heart around her neck. Birdie didn't own anything else that was shiny.

Birdie had to walk further than usual from the house and barns to find a sweet spot. The wind was sharp, and her rubber muck boots were old and sloppy. Walking between the furrows wasn't easy; the old dirt was hard and clumpy, and you could turn an ankle if you weren't careful.

The place originally belonged to her maternal grandfather, Jude Mathis, but she never knew him, and her mother, Anna, had no love for the man. Jude married her grandmother Leticia to get her land, and she ran off when Anna was young because he was terrible to her. Some claimed Jude Mathis got rid of her on his terms.

The once lush farm was dry and barren after Leticia had gone, and Anna's life with her father was cold and hard. The only love she knew came from a kind older woman down the road. Her father hired Tom Montrose to help one summer, and Anna married him in the Fall. She hoped for a better life with the handsome young man, but it never happened. He had no other ambitions; Tom worked on the farm and in time began mistreating her as well. When grandfather Mathis died, he left his daughter nothing but his worn-out red dirt. Her dreams were long gone, and Anna's marriage had soured like the parched fields in the hot Texas sun.

Birdie wasn't having any luck today, and it was getting chilly, so she headed back to the house. Her ten-year-old brother, Jacoby, would use her absence to stir trouble if he grew bored. Jacoby was born small with asthma and didn't do much of anything for fear something might bring on an attack and result in an expensive visit to the doctor. Birdie had to pick up the slack and do everything Jacoby couldn't or wouldn't. She hated the boy and often felt guilty because he was her brother, but he went out of his way to make life miserable for her.

Her father doted on Jacoby, and recently had started taking his son to the "Monday Night Meeting," where a select group of men gathered to drink coffee and discuss "important things." These men were the real decision makers in the community. The tight-knit group of local farmers invited Tom to join them when Jacoby was born, and he'd been proud to finally be included. He was respected now; having a son made all the difference.

A dust devil fired up to Birdie's left—odd, as it wasn't the season for them. The tall, spinning cones of dust usually only kicked up on scorching summer days, but the drought made many things act strange.

237

She moved closer as it started to rise. She saw colors in the dust as it swirled in the dull light. It gave off a smell like old rusty metal or a handful of warm pennies. Birdie wrinkled her nose as drops of something sticky covered the front of her worn denim jacket. She slapped at the dampness, but it stung like fire ants biting her hands. The dust devil whirled faster like it was trying to pull her in closer, or maybe knock her over. Birdy knew she should run but couldn't.

It wrapped itself around her. She stood at its center struggling to breathe. She heard voices, then something pushed her hard from behind. Birdie felt water seep into her old boots as a large puddle slowly formed around them. Water filled the deep cracks of the field where she stood, and her head began to spin. Her skin felt like it was sliding off, and the moment everything went dark, she figured this must be what it felt like to die.

🐾

Anna didn't notice her daughter was gone until she didn't hear the girl in the kitchen getting things ready for dinner. She'd spent most of the afternoon trying to make a few of her old things fresh so Birdie could wear them. She knew how to use plants to dye them brighter, simmering the worn clothes in a large pot then carefully hanging them to dry. It pained her Birdie didn't have anything pretty, but there was never any extra money.

She didn't want to ruminate on her shortcomings as a mother yet again, so she grabbed a sweater and went out to the field, squinting for a glimpse of the girl and loudly calling her name. Dusk was falling, and she tripped over the dry clumps of field dirt in the gathering dark.

When she found Birdie, the girl was lying on the ground in what looked like mud. *There's been no rain so, how?* Anna thought. Birdie was whimpering, and Anna struggled to help her to her feet. Her skin felt hot. "You are burning up. We need to get you in and dry, and, oh damn, I hope I don't have to call the doctor. You know how angry that would make your father."

Birdie gazed at her blankly, like she heard Anna speaking, but the words made no sense. She didn't seem to be able to stand on her own. Anna was petite but strong from years of hard work; she tugged her daughter up and dragged her back to the house.

Anna got the girl into a chair and brought a cool cloth for her head. Birdie looked a little better, but her face was still flushed. Anna slid off her daughter's jacket and gasped.

Both of Birdie's hands had deep marks on them, dark red like fresh burns and running in a jagged pattern through the middle of each palm. Anna dropped to her knees. She licked her finger and made an X on the girl's forehead, fighting back the tears. She didn't fear for herself as her life wasn't worth much anymore, but she did for her daughter, who still mattered.

People told stories about things gone wrong in the past, about the women some called "witches," killed for having a mark on them.

*The things we bury will grow.*

Birdie's brother Jacoby walked into the room, munching an apple and smirking. "What's the matter with her? I wanted something to eat an hour ago, and she wasn't here to fix it. Bet she was out meeting a boy doing you know what." His eyes narrowed, and he grunted like a pig, but his mother stood in front of the girl, blocking her hands from his sight.

She snapped at him. "Get your stinking butt out of here before I throw you into a pot for dinner." She knew he'd run to her husband the minute his truck pulled in, anxious to cause trouble for her girl. *Not today, you brat.*

He left, tossing the apple core onto the floor, grunting and laughing.

Ruthann Jagge

"Honey, we have to go upstairs," Anna whispered to the now conscious girl. She guided her daughter into the small room they only used for company or when someone was sick. She could tend to her there.

Birdie didn't seem scared; if anything, she appeared elated, going on about how sweet the air in the tiny gabled room smelled. Anna brought a cream for healing and bandages for her hands, along with a glass of water the girl said tasted delicious.

Anna regarded her daughter, more concerned by Birdie's near delirium than the wounds on her hands. "I'll tell your father you were helping me cook down onion skins for dye and the pot lid slipped. If he wants to see you, don't say a word, and don't ask any questions. I'll come up after they leave for the meeting." Anna heard her husband's old diesel truck grinding up the road and dashed down to greet him.

Jacoby, true to his nasty nature, got to his father first. "Mama yelled at me, and Birdie didn't fix my food." Anna saw he even managed to squeeze out a couple of crocodile tears.

Tom scowled at Anna as he walked into the kitchen holding the boy's hand. "Was there a problem here today? Don't I have enough to worry about without coming home to this?"

Anna rattled the plates she was setting on the table and explained that Birdie had a small accident while they were doing busy-work, and she'd be perfectly fine in a day or so. "I'm sorry I snapped at you, Jacoby," she said aiming a tight smile in the boy's direction. "I was trying to help your sister. You want her to be okay, don't you?" The boy sniffled and grunted again, but the matter seemed settled for now. The three of them sat down to eat. Anna mentioned the girl was resting, so she'd take her up something later.

"I hope she can make herself presentable by Saturday night." Tom held his knife and fork pointed at her like weapons. "They have something over at the Adderly's, and

240

we're going. I didn't raise her to keep her, so she needs to get out and mingle."

At that moment, Anna knew he held no love for his daughter or her. She was pregnant with Birdie when they married, and he liked to remind her that "he gave up a lot" when he "did the right thing by her." He also claimed the land and property left to her, and Anna had to make do with very little, including his affection.

Anna hoped to send her daughter to the small junior college not far away. She was a good student and wanted to be a teacher. Classes would start again soon after planting, and she knew Birdie wanted to try for a scholarship. If Birdie could get out, continue her education, perhaps she could have a very different life to Anna's own.

"It's Monday Night Meeting, Dad," Jacoby's voice cut through Anna's pondering. "I can't wait to go, can you?"

Tom smiled at the boy. "Yep... it should be a good one tonight. There's some stuff we need to talk about."

Tom shoveled a forkful into his mouth. "I was at the feed store, and Joel Adderly told me some things that could be important. You know what we talk about is important." Tom nodded to no one in particular, chewing his cornbread and beans. "Damn it, Anna, is it too much to ask for a chunk of meat in the mix once in a while?" He knew very well there was none in the freezer, but Anna knew better than to argue. She promised she'd see about getting some turkey next week, or maybe some venison.

Tom and the boy ate quickly and left nothing. They didn't give a second thought to Birdie, so she put a napkin over half her food for the girl. She gathered the dishes, staying clear while Tom and Jacoby got ready to go.

"Don't bother waiting up," Tom said, leading Jacoby out the door. "It's going to be a long one tonight."

When they were out of sight, Anna ran upstairs with the food and another glass of water. The girl was awake, sitting on the bed, humming softly to herself. Anna noticed Birdie's eyes were glassy. "Please eat a bite, and then we can talk." She sat on the edge of the bed and held out a forkful of the beans.

Birdie turned her head from the food her mother offered and reached for the glass of water. She maneuvered it to her lips between bandaged hands. "This is so delicious. I can't even describe it."

Anna felt the girl's forehead—she was still burning up. "Let's get you into something easy so you can rest. I can't call the doctor unless your father says so, and you know he won't. You need to try and sleep this fever off."

Birdie struggled with her shirt because of her hands, so her mother gently pulled the cheap cotton blouse over her head. Anna fought back the tears when she saw a red X like a brand on the young woman's back. "Oh, my sweet girl." She noticed the tin heart shining on a string around her daughter's neck. "Where did you get that? Did you make it?" She hoped some boy working in the fields hadn't tried to beg favors from Birdie in exchange for a scrap of metal.

"I found it in the dirt and thought it was pretty. See? Someone put their initials on it."

Birdie turned to her. Anna saw the scratched-in letters "L.M."

Anna recognized those initials and was stunned. She closed her eyes for a moment and remembered her beautiful mother wearing a silver heart around her neck. Birdie looked so much like her. Anna wondered if she should take the tin heart away, get rid of it before Tom laid eyes on it. She reached out but couldn't bring herself to remove it from around Birdie's neck.

She pulled up a chair and watched over her daughter until the girl slept, then drifted off to an uneasy rest next to her.

Anna and Birdie sat on the steps watching the heat waves fade with the setting of the sun and waiting to leave. Birdie looked beautiful but sad in her blue dress. "I don't want to go, Mama," she said. "I don't like all those people, and Father will be drinking."

Anna knew her daughter kept to herself, except for a few girls from school. "I can't tell him no this time, Birdie. His mind's set. Please do this without a fuss, then we can start thinking about your college, okay?"

Tom and Jacoby came out of the house. "Let's get rolling." Tom bounded down the steps. "Don't want to be late to the fun." Both he and Jacoby seemed in good moods as they helped them into the old truck. Anna hoped it might not be such a miserable night after all.

Tom navigated into a spot among the long row of trucks parked in a field at the Adderly place. He lifted a hand in greeting to a group of men standing under a tree, drinking.

"You go find something to eat." Tom nodded toward the house. "All the women are over there."

A large bonfire blazed on the other side of the field. Anna and her daughter joined the group of females at the wooden table covered in platters of food. Anna didn't know the Adderlys well, but they'd lived down the road as long as she could remember, so they counted as "neighbors." June Adderly was a mousy little woman with brown lifeless eyes, and dull brown her hair she always wore pulled back into a tight knot. Living so far out in the country made socializing hard. At least Birdie seemed glad to see her friends from school.

The number of men heading across the field toward them had grown much larger now. Anna guessed there might be music or dancing. Maybe the men at the Monday Night

Ruthann Jagge

Meeting decided it was time for a little fun and casual get-togethers were an accepted way to meet new people. She noticed, though, none of the young men were hanging around the girls. This seemed unusual. She made her way over to Birdie who was chatting with her friend, Nan.

The group of men formed a circle around the table. "You all stay right where you are," one of the men announced. "We've got a little something planned."

Several young women giggled and smiled, but as the circle closed tighter, Anna noticed a few of the men had ropes, while others carried axes, large knives, or hammers. A few of the youngest held lengths of heavy metal fence pipe.

Joel Adderly, a large, homely man in jeans and a tight plaid shirt, grinned broadly. "Now you all know we meet on Monday nights to discuss important things. A while back, I caught a whiff of something we needed to discuss. You women have been holding out, and it's high time we take care of that." Tom clapped him on the shoulder as he went on, "One of you witch bitches has the dowse on her, and we're going to find out who that is real quick. We've worked our asses off in this shitty dirt without any rain or water long enough, and now it's your turn to pitch in or else."

Anna grabbed Birdie's hand and thought to run, but the men surrounding them stood almost shoulder to shoulder. One of the younger men tossed a rope around Nan's neck and pulled her back hard. The dark-haired girl clawed at the rough rope and tried to scream.

Birdie moved toward her friend, but Anna caught hold and held firm. Another man picked up Nan's feet, and together they carried Nan, kicking and thrashing, to the bonfire. The circle around the women came in even tighter, and Anna could smell the alcohol as the men leered and laughed and nodded at each other like they were agreeing.

"Hell yeah, Adderly," a rough voice called out. "Let's show them we aren't playing around."

244

Joel Adderly jumped up on a table. "I found a book my wife hid from me." His voice took on the emphatic singsong of a radio evangelist. "Oh...by the way...did you notice her dumb-as-dirt self isn't here tonight? That's because I tore the skin off her then crushed her skinny bones into meal for the field outback. Finally got some use out of her." The men laughed, and Adderly called out, "Toss her in, boys. We'll get this party started."

The group of terrified women screamed as the strong young men lifted Nan's slim body high into the air and flung her deep into the center of the blaze. She managed to run out, shrieking madly with her dress in flames, but they pushed her back in with sharpened pitchforks. The rest of the crying woman scrambled frantically, but axes, hammers, and knives shone in the light, raised and ready.

One of the men sliced deep into Joann Carter's arm, and she dropped to the ground, spraying blood. Birdie clung to her mother. Anna spun her daughter around, intending to shield her long enough to break through the circle. Birdie was fast, and if she could get even a few steps ahead... Anna stopped. Her husband and her son moved in quickly to block her movement. Tom shoved her back hard, and Jacoby laughed as he pointed his small knife at his sister. Anna released Birdie and stepped between her and her husband. "Tom...stop this, please. You can't let this happen."

Tom narrowed his eyes. "No, you stupid bitch, I want this to happen." He spat at Anna and took another swallow from the bottle he clutched. "Who do you think came up with the idea anyway?" Anna turned away, unable to look at him.

From his perch atop the table, Adderly continued, "Now, my wife had this old book. Her grandmother kept notes and made drawings in it. Stuff about water-witching and how to do it. How she could find water and make it rain. How to hold the rods and bring the damn water right up from the ground." His

Ruthann Jagge

words were met by raucous cheers. Adderly took a swig from
a proffered bottle, then handed it back.

"When I was taking care of my wife, she told me alla you
ungrateful bitches knew about these things, but decided against
sharing because you didn't like us much. She told me how your
grandmothers got pissed off because their husbands took their
land from them. How they got together and did nasty things:
they cursed the damn dirt and all the men, that's why we didn't
have sons to help work it." Adderly was on a roll. He wiped
the whiskey dripping from his chin. "She said they made some
filthy deal with the Devilman to hold back the water and the
rain, unless they chose to bring it. She said there was one of
you—I'd half-skinned her by then—who still knew how to do
it right here and now."

He gazed down hard at them all. "Now tell me, ladies,
does any of this ring a bell for you?" He paused as if awaiting
a response. When none came, he shifted his focus to one of
the younger men. "Ed, grab another one, will you?"

Ed Mayne flung a rope around the neck of a tall blonde
girl. She violently thrashed and choked as it tightened. "We can
do this all night, ladies. Hell, I've got a barn full of whiskey and
nothing but time." Another burst of cheers. "None of you are
going anywhere until we find out who the water witch is."

Ed dragged the girl into the group of men. "This one's
pretty," Ed called up to Adderly.

Adderly signaled with a nod to a young man wearing a
stained straw hat and holding a large hunting knife. The man
laughed, grabbed a fistful of her shiny hair, and forced a kiss
on the girl. He drew back, and with a fast flick of the blade,
sliced off her nose, leaving a gaping hole. He jabbed the knife
down hard into the girl's chest, hooting as he sliced upward.
As she bled out, one of the older women fainted to the ground,
and Anna saw John Evans kick her hard with his dirty boot.

"Now, if you all don't knock off that howling, it's only
going to get worse," Adderly announced like he was the voice

246

of reason rather than a monster…one of the monsters. "We've discussed this matter every damn Monday night for a while and planned lots of things we can do if y'all don't play nice." He surveyed the women with contempt. "Now, which one of you is the bitch that can pull water? Point her out, and we might let a few of you stick around. We still gonna need someone to make dinner, right boys?" Adderly's eyes picked Anna out from the crowd. He climbed down and advanced on her, the circle of men opening just enough to let him pass.

He slapped Anna's face so hard she saw sparks. "And you with your whore mother, Leticia Mathis. She was in on all this too, before old Jude tied her ass to a wagon and ripped her clean apart. I am thinking you and your darling daughter deserve special treatment tonight. We've got a couple of nice sharp stakes out back to plant you on, so you can rot for fertilizer."

Anna struggled to think straight. She saw Jacoby standing next to the man she'd thought was her husband, but she no longer cared about either of them. Birdie was all that mattered now. The thin girl stood quietly, her strawberry hair glowing a deeper red in the light from the bonfire.

🐾

Birdie clutched the little tin heart on the string around her neck, whispering to herself as if in a daze. She turned to face one of the younger men and softly said, "John Sizeman, I know you from school. I've seen you looking at me. Give me that thing in your hand."

The short, chunky boy stared at the ground. His lower lip quivered as he handed her the metal fence pipe he'd been clutching. He tried to leave, but another boy roughly shoved him back into the circle. "You fuckin' pussy! I hope she cracks your stupid skull wide open."

"I don't care if she does," John said. "I think I deserve it."

247

Ruthann Jagge

A few of the men pushed forward to take the pipe away, but Birdie held tight to the length of metal. She whispered words she knew she daren't say aloud, and the fence pipe slowly split, both ends bending out until the pipe took the shape of an X.

"I knew that girl was off," her father spat the words at her mama. "I told you she wasn't right in the head."

Birdie ignored her father, but shared a knowing glance with her mother. Birdie walked, holding the pipe, breaking through the circle of men. She could smell their hatred but also their fear. She closed her eyes and let the metal rod guide her away from the bonfire and into the field of dry dirt. Vibrations ran through her body as the piece of metal, now a dowsing rod, twitched ever so slightly up and down, left then right.

A dust devil whirled to life nearby, but this time Birdie wasn't afraid. The men followed, roughly holding onto most of the women, dragging them along. But the women were calm now. Birdie looked back for her mother to find Joel Adderly gripping her tightly in one arm and holding a hammer in his other hand. Her father and brother stood at his side, staring at her, their mouths agape. She closed her eyes as the dust flew higher. She felt the ground beneath her feet crack wide open. She heard a gentle voice in the wind, "Hold tight, my girl, this is your dirt!"

Water bubbled up from the ground, rushing into the deep cracks. Lightning pierced the sky, and rain fell hard. She heard a man yell loudly, "You were right, Adderly. This witch can pull water."

They men released the women and all but the Sizeman boy raced in toward her for a better look, yelling, "Hell yeah!" and "Bet your ass!" They were so full of themselves, they never noticed the women forming a circle around them, grasping each other's hands and chanting softly. The words the circle spoke came to them from the women who'd gone on before them, the women who'd sworn their revenge. Their men might

248

have murdered them for dancing with the Devilman, but not before they cursed the dirt and the husbands they hated for taking the land and love that was rightfully theirs.

The men, laughing and dancing in the water streaming over the field, started sinking until they were in knee-deep, firmly stuck in the fresh mud. Shouts of joy turned to terror, as the more they thrashed and fought, the deeper they sank.

Birdie could hear Adderly and the others shouting out threats against them, but none of the men could break free. The cursed land held them captive. Her brother and father held on to each other, struggling to break free. "Anna, help me," she heard her father cry out, but her mother didn't even flinch; she remained in the circle with the other women.

Birdie's hands felt like they were on fire. She pointed the metal pipe in the direction of the bonfire. It burned out of control now, the flames kicking up high as they roared and crackled over the wet dirt. The fire raced forward to engulf the men.

🐱

The women calmly waited until the screams died out, until the fire left nothing but ash and the stench of deaths. Birdie fell to the ground, still alive, breathing rapidly. As she fell, the storm faltered, and the waters receded. Anna rushed to her daughter as the rest of the women slowly moved about, waiting for the bones of their horrible men to cool, so they could grind them into a fine meal that would feed their dirt.

The girl's clothing was in tatters. Through them, Anna could make out a faint red X, the mark of the Water Witch, burned into the girl's back. Her daughter was one of the "Criss Cross Girls," just as Anna's mother, Leticia Mathis, had been. Anna saw the tin heart bearing the initials "L.M." still dangled around Birdie's neck.

Ruthann Jagge

Anna wondered if her girl would be okay. She would take good care of her, but the rest, well, that would be between Birdie and the Devilman. She would have to strike her own deal when the time came.

———————

Ruthann Jagge writes dark speculative fiction and horror. Her stories are influenced by extensive travel and an appreciation for homegrown horror and superstition. She grew up in Upstate N.Y., where the month of Halloween is always celebrated in style, and currently lives on a rural cattle ranch in Texas with her husband and his animals. She's a contributor to several popular anthologies and is working on her first full-length novel. An avid reader in all genres, she also enjoys reviewing books for Women in Horror and other authors she admires.

"SUNDAY & PETER"

Heather Scheeler

# THE WITCH AND THE WAIF

## BY RIE SHERIDAN ROSE

Barbara Yeager sat on the porch of the split-level treehouse she called home. Her architect had called it eccentric, but she loved it. Especially the stilts, ending in taloned bird feet, holding up the upper story—she'd really had to fight for those.

She took a sip from the martini in one hand, while manipulating a small glass sphere from one finger to another—like David Bowie in that movie with the goblins—on the other. It kept her hands supple. You never knew when that might come in handy.

Bored, she concentrated her focus, narrowed her eyes, and the ball rose six inches above her hand to dance on the wind. As she set down her empty glass on the side table, a maidservant appeared from thin air and refilled the martini. Barbara smiled like a contented cat. It was good to be queen—at least of this little corner of Texas.

Looking out over the well-trimmed lawn, she saw a cab pull up to the iron gates. A remnant of her old Goth girl days, the fence was a twisted fantasy of wrought-iron bones, topped with skulls wired with LEDs for the evening. Few people dared the massive gates with their skeletal hinges and jawbone locks. She was impressed this one had.

The girl who stepped out of the taxi was gorgeous—if you liked the pale, blonde, fashion-model type.

The stranger lifted a suitcase from the back seat and approached the gate timidly, took a deep breath audible clear across the yard, and pushed the button on the intercom beside the gate. Languidly reaching a blood-nailed finger to the box on the table beside her, Barbara answered the buzzer.

"Yes? What do you want?"

"M-Ms. Yeager? My name's Lisa. My stepmother sent me."

"And who might your stepmother be?" Like pulling teeth with this one.

"Um...Lily Carson. She used to be the widow Blackwell..."

"Oh, yes. 'Lily Wears Blackwell' we used to call her at the country club. Come on up, dear." She pressed another button on her console, and the gates swung open with a theatrical creak. She grinned, as Lisa slid between the wings of the gate as quickly as possible, taking care not to make contact with the iron, not even with the skirt of her dress.

*For the best,* Barbara thought, glancing down at the console. *I forgot to turn off the juice. That could have been messy.*

Stretching like a cat, Barbara rose to her full heel-enhanced height and stepped to the edge of the porch to await her visitor. She thrust out her perfectly-manicured hand to the girl.

"Welcome, Lisa. I'm so glad you could come. I've been looking forward to meeting you ever since Lily called. I understand you're looking for summer employment?"

The girl blushed crimson. "Yes, ma'am," she mumbled. "Papa's away a lot, and there isn't enough money to send all three of us to school. Penelope and Nicola are older, of course, so it's only right they get their tuition paid first."

*With your father's money, no doubt. Lily always was good at sniffing out a payday.*

She smiled at the girl encouragingly. "Well, I'm sure we can come up with something for you to do around here. Let me give you a tour of the house. Introduce you to the crew."

"That would be lovely, Ms. Yeager."

"Call me Baba. All my friends do, and I've a feeling we're going to be great friends." She slipped her arm through Lisa's. "Tell me more about what Lily's been up to."


By the end of the tour, Lisa had relaxed a bit, and was chattering happily about her dream to become a kindergarten teacher.

"Of course, I'll have to work my way through. Penny is going to study abroad in Paris, and Nicky wants to go to medical school, or law school—I don't think she's come to a final decision yet."

*Whichever one wastes more of your Papa's money, I bet*, Baba thought to herself. *I haven't even met Penny and Nickel, and I can tell they're selfish brats, just like Mama Lily.* "And you want to shape little minds, is that right?"

"Oh, yes. I do so love children."

"I think you'll fit in around here quite nicely. Now, what I really need is a personal assistant to handle all my crazy cravings and keep track of my social calendar. Does that sound like something you might be interested in?"

"Yes, Ms. Yea—Baba. Very much so."

"Good. Salary is five hundred a week plus room and board. With a bonus at the end of the summer if your work suits."

"That's incredibly generous, ma'am…"

"Don't worry. You'll earn every penny. Now, do you need any help collecting your things?"

"Oh, no, ma'am. I've just got the one suitcase. Lily thought it would be best to come prepared."

*I'll just bet she did. Probably has already turned your bedroom into a home gym or something, the selfish cow.*

"Well, then, I'll show you to your room."

Baba liked the girl. She was sweet-natured and unselfish—gods only knew how she managed it with that wicked stepmother of hers. They'd have to try and toughen her up a bit without ruining that lovely disposition.

🐾

Lisa couldn't believe her luck. Lily had made it sound like she was going off to be eaten or something. Instead, Baba was a peach.

She looked around her room for the summer. It was twice the size of her room at home, and was light and airy, nestled in the trees at the top of the house with a lovely murmur of leaves in the breeze. It was the work of a minute to put her clothes away. Her few books looked lonely on the shelf above the desk, but maybe she would splurge a little once she got paid.

She lifted the porcelain doll out of its nest of pillows and placed it in the center of her bed. It was the last gift her mother had given her, and it was a source of much comfort as she cried herself to sleep under Lily's cruel regime. "We're home, Kukoka. We must do our best to please Ms. Baba. This opportunity is too good to waste…and you know Lily would love it if we crawled home with our tails between our legs."

She imagined the doll's answer—*Don't worry, Lisa. Things will look better in the morning. Get a good night's sleep and the dawn will bring delight.*

It was something her mother often said to her when she was little. Kukoka's imaginary voice even had her mother's slight Russian lilt to it.

Lisa hugged the little doll tight, and then went down to find her employer.

The rest of the afternoon was like being in the presence of a Fairy Godmother who was half whirlwind. First of all, Baba was dismayed to find out Lisa didn't have an iPad or a MacBook.

"We must remedy that at once. How can you keep track of my calendar if you don't have anything to keep it *in?*"

"I have a phone," Lisa murmured, holding out her cell phone.

"My dear, I don't even know how you can make phone calls on that thing," Baba *ts*ked, gesturing her into the silver Tesla. "Upgrade in progress."

The car leapt out of the garage like some great cat, flying down the road far faster than Lisa felt entirely comfortable with.

"You'll get used to my driving," Baba called over the roar of the wind. "I admit, it can be a little intimidating at first."

Lisa just nodded, clutching her seatbelt in white-knuckled hands.

By the time they pulled up in front of an Apple store she'd gotten fairly used to Baba's wild ride. But when the older woman breezed into the store calling for the latest versions of laptop, tablet, *and* phone, she felt she must protest.

"Ma'am, that's not necessary—really."

"It *is* necessary, Lisa—really. Information is the heart of my business. I need you to know what is going on every moment of every day. If I need you to call Tokyo for my next Tarot reading, I need you to have a phone that can do that. If I need you to schedule a dinner party for twelve of my closest friends, I need you to have the internet at your fingertips to find a venue, plan a menu, order place-cards, whatever. I need you to have a computer that can handle the job. I want you to have the flexibility to carry a tablet everywhere you go. Do you understand me?"

"Yes, ma'am," she whispered, dismayed she was already being lectured.

Baba slipped a finger under her chin and raised her head. "My child, don't look so disheartened. I've far more money than I know what to do with, and I see something interesting in you. I plan to nurture it. Part of that will be to make sure you have the tools you require to make your job—and my life—easier. Do you understand me?"

"Yes, ma'am."

"Good. Now, come pick out the cases you like."

ᵔ

Baba stifled a sigh as Lisa picked out plain white models of all her new devices. No matter how she sweet-talked the girl, she couldn't convince her to try a bit of flair or style. *Poor little mouse probably hasn't had anything new of her own since her mother died.*

After seeing Lisa ensconced back in her room with instructions to familiarize herself with her new toys, Baba retreated to her inner sanctum to make a phone call of her own. *This* one wouldn't require Lisa's assistance.

"Hello, Lily? It's Baba, darling. Yes. Yes, she arrived just fine. I think we'll get along famously. She's a perfect little lamb, isn't she? We'll have to do something about her wardrobe, of course…oh, no—I just want her to look the part of my assistant. Her clothes are all so…worn, aren't they? Heavens no, dear. I'm not asking you to provide for her." *After all, you've made it abundantly clear you consider it a waste of money…* "I just didn't want you to be surprised when she brought home a bit more luggage than she left with. Anyway, I'll let you go now. Lisa and I will be fine. You won't recognize her when she comes home." *Not if I have anything to say about it.*

She hung up the phone with a satisfied smirk. Lily would be stewing for weeks about how unfair it was Lisa should get all the nice things one of her own daughters "deserved" instead.

257

She pushed the intercom button on the wall. "Lisa, dear, are you hungry?"

The tentative answer made her wince. "I could eat a little...if you're ready for dinner. Is there something I can do to help?"

"No, dear. Cook is very protective of her kitchen. On her day off, we're on our own, but tonight, you're my guest. Put on something nice and come down as soon as you're dressed. I'm expecting friends."

"Y-yes, ma'am...or I could eat in my room if you'd rather..."

*Poor little mouse. She's so afraid of being hurt.* "No, dear. I particularly want you to meet these friends. Best dress."

She released the intercom button before Lisa could protest further. Now, she needed to make a list of things to shop for tomorrow. She was determined to return Lisa to Lily in a completely different shape than she had found her.

🐾

Lisa pulled out every piece of clothing she owned and studied the woefully small pile. Denim skirts, T-shirts, jeans, a couple of nice blouses, and one A-line black dress. Not much choice there. It was wear the dress or coordinate separates, and she got the impression Baba would be distressed by denim at dinner. At least the dress was silk.

It had been bought for Nicky but wouldn't zip over her ample charms. Lily had thrown a tantrum and tossed the dress at once, but Lisa had rescued it from the trash bin and tried it on. It fit her perfectly, and it was her go-to if dressing up was required.

But now it felt dowdy. She was embarrassed to wear it in Baba's lovely home—especially to meet her friends.

Her eye caught sight of Kukoka lying on the bed, and she could hear the doll's voice in her head. *Don't despair, Lisa. It's*

258

*always darkest before the dawn. You don't need diamonds to shine. Be yourself, and all will be well.*

"Thank you," she whispered, slipping into the dress. "You always make me feel better, Kukoka."

She hurried now, braiding her hair into a shining crown on the top of her head. She pinned a rhinestone brooch into the braid in a whimsical moment. The glass jewels caught the light and made reflections dance across the walls.

Lisa added a touch of makeup to her pale features and tilted her head at her reflection. *Not bad. Not bad at all. Maybe not Baba beautiful, but I won't be a disappointment.*

With a little wave to the doll, she went downstairs to meet the guests.

As she stepped into the living room, she almost turned around and walked back out again. It seemed Baba's guests were all young men. Supremely attractive, young men.

A pale, blond fellow who looked like he'd be equally at home on the cover of *Rolling Stone* or *Time* magazine lounged against the buffet, swirling a drink in one hand. A redhead with a mischievous twinkle in his green eyes sat on the back of the sofa telling some story that called for extravagant hand-gestures to a black man with a goatee and a shining golden earring. The listener laughed aloud, his voice musical as bird-song.

"Ah, there you are, Lisa," called Baba from her throne-like chair. "Come and meet the boys. Nigel over there," she said, waving an arm toward the black man, "just popped in to say 'hi' and meet you. He's got to bounce for work."

Nigel came up to Lisa and took her hand, bowing over it, then planting a lingering kiss on the back. She felt her face burst into flame as he murmured, "It's a pleasure to meet you. Alas, I must go. Maybe we can meet for lunch someday? If Baba lets you go that long." He winked at their hostess, then released her hand. "Really, Lisa. I hope to get to know you better soon."

"Go on, now, you," Baba scolded, making shooing motions. "Those warehouses won't watch themselves."

Nigel snapped a salute and left.

"Nigel's my night watchman," Baba explained, coming over to take Lisa by the arm. "Now, let me introduce you to the others. This is Michael." She laid a hand on the redhead's arm. "He's my gardener, and jack-of-all-trades. And that divine dilettante across the way is David." She waved at the blond who rippled his fingers in return. "He's my dresser in the morning. I'd be lost without him. He's the only one who can get me all put together at the crack of dawn.

"Now, let's go eat before it gets cold, and Cook refuses to make any dessert for a week."

Baba let go of her arm and went to commandeer David's. Michael offered his own arm in exchange.

"Such a lovely lady must have an escort to the table." His voice had a touch of Irish brogue. She was a sucker for an accent.

"Indeed," she replied, taking the proffered arm.

Dinner was a delight, as David proved quite the wit, telling wickedly pointed stories that soon had Lisa laughing with the rest. She'd never dared to laugh at home—not if Papa were gone, and he was gone so often. It had been nearly a year this time, and Lily swore he wasn't ever coming back, lamenting the injustice of having to raise his daughter as well as her own girls. No matter that Penny was nearly thirty, and Nicky twenty-five.

"Do you like to ride?" Michael asked, startling her out of her musings.

"What?"

"Do you like to ride? Baba has a world-renowned stable, and I'm sure she could spare you for an hour or two now and again." He glanced at Baba.

"Excellent idea! The horses don't get nearly the exercise they should. You can have her from two to four every afternoon, Mickey. That's when I take my nap."

"But I've never ridden," Lisa answered, panicked by the thought of an animal that large running away with her—or worse, stepping on her.

"No problem. Mickey's an excellent teacher. And I bet I have a habit you can wear."

"Can't I just wear jeans?"

"If you'd rather, sweet. It's up to you. But she can't ride tomorrow, Mickey. Tomorrow I've a full day planned."

"I should be saying goodnight, then," Lisa murmured. "I still have to figure out some of the programs we downloaded this afternoon if we have appointments to keep tomorrow. It was lovely meeting you both."

With a last glance at Mickey, she fled the room before Baba could stop her.

Baba watched her go, clicking her tongue. "That girl's going to take a lot of work, Mickey mine...but I do think she might have a wee bit of a crush."

"Baba, don't be mean. She's a lovely thing, and you don't need to be forcing nothing on her."

"I won't...promise. But I must do what I can to break her out of that shell she's trapped in. Her wings will atrophy if she doesn't learn to fly." She turned in her chair. "David, dear...did you have a chance to make that phone call I asked you to?"

"Oh, yes. I'd nearly forgotten. Quentin Carson has been conducting business in Hong Kong for the last several months, but—when I apprised him of the current situation—he promised to wrap things up as soon as possible and return home to Houston. He'll be here no later than the Fourth of

Rie Sheridan Rose

July. That gives you about six weeks to meddle before Papa takes over."

She wrinkled her nose and stuck out her tongue at him. "I never meddle. I just facilitate an outcome."

"I see."

"Well, come on, boys. Let's let the maids get to work. Tomorrow is a long day. Come and tuck me in, David."

"My pleasure, mistress." He held out a long-fingered hand to her.

She took it, shivering a little in anticipation of what those hands could do.

"I'll make sure everything's locked up," Mickey said, with a grin. "You two enjoy yourselves."

"We will," Baba replied, dragging David toward the stairs.

After a very pleasurable evening spent with David and his extremely skillful hands, Baba saw him off to bring in the dawn. She lay in her nest of pillows and contemplated what to do next.

Mickey would be a fine match for Lisa. He was charming, financially stable, and handsome as the dickens. The girl was obviously attracted to him. Of course, Lily wouldn't approve at all, because Mickey wasn't the sort to put up with her manipulations. He'd soon set her straight. And, with the father coming home as well, Lisa's future could be a thing of beauty.

She stretched sensuously and climbed out of bed to dress. Something simple yet expensive for today, she decided. She was going to take Lisa shopping, and then to lunch at the swankiest place she knew. If they happened to run into Lily and the girls...well, she could arrange that.

🐈

"Oh, my heavens...is that Kukoka?"

Lisa whirled at the sound of Baba's voice in the doorway.

262

Her employer sank down on the edge of the bed and picked up the doll. "I remember when I made this for your mother to give to you. She worried so, and she knew she was ill. She wanted to leave a piece of herself behind for you." A sad smile flitted across Baba's face. "There was a true lady."

"You knew my mother?"

"Oh, yes. We were dear friends. I can't believe Quentin filled her place with the likes of Lily." She put the doll back on the bed. "Are you ready to go, dear?"

Lisa nodded, feeling like a poor church mouse in her serviceable black slacks and tunic compared to Baba's radiant silk ensemble.

But looks were soon forgotten on the wild ride to town.

Lisa finally managed to breathe again as Baba pulled the Tesla into a parking space on a street lined both sides with upscale boutiques. Yesterday's shops had been mostly electronic in nature. Today, it was all couture.

Lisa had never seen such clothes in her life. And Baba insisted on an entire new wardrobe for her.

"After all, my dear, you're going to be my spokesperson when I can't attend to something or need a break from my obligations. I need you to be the image of class and elegance. And I'm afraid Lily has stunted your growth in this area." Baba looked over the top of her Dolce & Gabbana sunglasses with a disapproving frown. "You can't go around dressed like an orphan if you're supposed to be my representative. Now, come."

Resigning herself to the fact Baba would always get her way, so it was better not to argue, Lisa swallowed her sigh and followed her mistress into Chanel.

Baba picked up a blush pink pantsuit and held it to Lisa's chest. "The color is nice on you...but it is a bit too sweetness and light. We want you to give the impression of cool competence that can crush your enemies on a whim. More like

263

this, I think." She held up a peacock blue jumpsuit with gold accents. "Go try this on."

Lisa took it reluctantly but had to stifle a gasp when the fabric contacted her skin. It was soft as a cloud and ran through her fingers like water. When she stepped into the dressing room and tried it on, it was like slipping into a second skin. The image in the mirror was not her usual shy, mousy self, but some exotic water-dragon—ready to take names and kick ass. She had never worn anything that made her feel so alive before.

"Come, come. Let me see," ordered Baba from the floor of the showroom, and Lisa strode out of the dressing room, giving a little twirl to her employer.

"Yes!" Baba cried. "That's just the thing. It's scrumptious on you. Now, go and get your things, we have a lot more shopping to do."

"Of course. It won't take me a minute to change—"

"Who said anything about changing? You'll be wearing *that* out of the store." She gestured to the jumpsuit.

Despite herself, Lisa's heart rose. She knew she shouldn't succumb to Baba's wild decisions, but she did love the outfit so.

"Hurry along, dear. We have a schedule to keep."

By the time Baba called a halt for lunch, they both had several bags in hand, and Lisa had an entire new wardrobe from the skin out. She'd also gotten a haircut and complete makeover. She kept sneaking glances at herself in the window reflections as they passed, marveling over the fact it was truly *her* image.

Baba stored their bags in the trunk of the Tesla and waved Lisa in. "Come on—I'm hungry as a horse. Let's get a bite to eat before we get back to it, shall we?"

Lisa still couldn't get over the fact there was no real engine on the car, just a front storage trunk as well as a smaller one in the back. It was as if it were magic—though she knew it was really electric. Having learned the futility of protest, Lisa slipped into the passenger seat and belted herself in.

"What do you think of this car?" Baba asked her, a slight frown between her brows. "It's served me well, but it's several years old now. I think I'll get a new one. Why don't you take this one?"

"I could never afford the payments," Lisa demurred.

Baba burst into gales of laughter. When she finally regained control of herself, she replied, "Oh, darling—it's paid for. All it would cost you is the insurance."

Lisa ran a hand over the upholstery. It *was* a beautiful car, and she'd never had a car of her own. *If I'm to be Baba's assistant, I can't go around looking like a bum...* "All right," she answered reluctantly. *I'm not so sure I should be getting so far into Baba's debt.*

"Good. Now that's settled, we'll have Mickey take us car-shopping tomorrow. Always good to have a man along to kick the tires and distract the dealer while we pay attention to the important stuff."

Lisa found herself smiling at Baba's enthusiasm. And the idea of spending more time with Mickey didn't hurt either.

Baba turned to Lisa. "You aren't going to like this, darling, and I'm terribly sorry about that, but it really can't be helped."

Lisa frowned. "What is it, Baba?"

"Before we go into lunch, there's something you should understand. I'm a very unusual woman. In fact, most of my friends call me a real witch, though some of them spell it with a B."

*Intriguing.* Lisa settled back in her seat. "Just what are you trying to say, Baba?"

"I'm always trying to fix things, especially for the people I love—and I'm very fond of you, my dear. So, I invited Lily and the girls to meet us for lunch at one of Houston's swankiest eating establishments." The last words were all in a rush.

265

Lisa sighed. "Well, at least that isn't as bad as I was afraid of. Honestly, I think I can handle them now. I just have to remember what you've taught me."

"That's my girl." Baba patted her knee. "Let's go show the Dragon Lady what a beautiful swan you are."

🐈

Baba was exceptionally pleased with Lisa's response. Her little mouse had come quite a long way already. She couldn't wait for Lily to see. By the time summer was over, Lisa'd be a real force to be reckoned with.

But for now, the important thing was to give Lily her comeuppance.

"You ready?" she asked Lisa.

Taking a deep breath, the girl nodded.

"Then let's do this."

Tossing Lisa the keys to the Tesla, she said, "You can drive home."

Arm-in-arm they walked into the restaurant. Baba saw Lily across the room, and gave her a finger wave.

"Look, Lisa dear. It's the whole gang, come to say congratulations on your new job." She made sure all three could hear her. "So good to see you, Lily, and you must be the Penny and Nickel I've heard so much about." Turning to Lily, she said, "Too bad you don't have a Dime to go with them."

Lily's eyes narrowed, as if trying to decide whether or not she'd been insulted. "So nice to see you again, Barbara. I do hope Lisa is behaving herself. It was so nice of you to offer her a job, otherwise I don't know how else she could go to school this fall. There's just so little money to go around."

"Money's such a dreadful thing, isn't it? But you just can't live without it. Lisa's proving invaluable. I don't know what I'd do without her." She turned to Lisa. "What time is that appointment this afternoon, dear?"

Lisa whipped out her new tablet and brought up the calendar. "3:30, ma'am."

Baba hid a smile at the envy that flashed across the stepsisters' faces at the sight of the state-of-the-art machine.

"We should probably go ahead and order then." Baba gestured Lisa into the seat beside her and settled herself comfortably. "Order whatever you'd like, dears, this is my treat."

Penny and Nicky immediately began whispering over the menu.

Lily set hers aside with a brittle smile. "I'll have whatever you're having, Barbara."

Baba turned to the waiter, hovering nearby. "Dinner salads for myself and the lady, then. Lisa dear, you *must* try the lobster, it's to die for."

"Sounds delightful," Lisa murmured, handing the waiter her menu with a smile.

"I'll have that too," ordered Penny imperiously, "with a side of shrimp scampi."

"And I'll have a ten-ounce sirloin, medium well, with a loaded baked potato, and three dinner rolls." Nicky was practically licking her lips in anticipation.

"Oh, to be young, and not have to count calories, right, Lily?" Baba sighed theatrically. "But those days are gone for the likes of us."

Lily huffed. "I don't know what you're talking about. I'm the same size now I was in high school."

Baba raised an eyebrow at Lisa, and Lily's face reddened.

"One of the reasons I asked you here today, Lily, was I was wondering if your other girls might like a job as well. Of course, I only need one assistant, but there are other positions I need to fill."

Eyes shining, Nicky leaned forward. "Oh, yes please, Mama. Look at the lovely things Lisa has gotten."

Penny shrugged. "I suppose it would be nice to have some spending money for Paris."

"That's settled then. We'll expect you tomorrow, and Lisa will tell you what to do."

The stepsisters looked less pleased at that possibility.

The rest of lunch was uneventful, and when goodbyes had been said, and they were once more in the Tesla, Lisa turned to her with a raised eyebrow. "Just what have they gotten themselves in to, Baba?"

Batting her lashes—the picture of innocence—Baba replied, "Well, we really do need more help around the house. Mickey has been telling me he needs someone to muck out the stalls, and Cook would like a new scullery maid..."

Lisa burst into laughter. When she could finally control herself, she shook her head. "Baba, the way you magically put people in their place, I think you've earned that title of witch honestly."

They laughed all the way home.

———————

Rie Sheridan Rose multitasks. A lot. Her short stories appear in numerous anthologies, including *Killing It Softly* Vol. 1 & 2, *Hides the Dark Tower*, *Dark Divinations*, and *On Fire*. She has authored twelve novels, six poetry chapbooks, and lyrics for dozens of songs. She tweets as @RieSheridanRose.

# ALLEGATIONS OF ALCHEMY

## BY LAMONT A. TURNER

Rupert itched all over. It had been three days since he'd set out on the Rigolets in the old pirogue, and he hadn't set foot on land since. His plan had been to take the Rigolets to Lake Pontchartrain and escape into Orleans Parish, but by the time he'd figured out which direction he needed to go, he'd sobered up enough to see the flaws in the plan. Instead, he'd drifted along the edge of the swamp, waiting for the swelling in his ankle to go down.

Fortified by the oxycodone he'd stolen from the woman whose husband he'd just murdered, and the twelve pack of beer he'd taken from the back of his pick-up, he'd hardly noticed the hunger, or the blisters the Louisiana sun had baked into his back after he'd been foolish enough to fall asleep with his shirt off. The insects, however, had been impossible to ignore. Horse flies bit into his flesh and buzzed in his ears, while mosquitoes made white welts on his red skin. The welts bled when he scratched them, summoning even more horse flies to the feast. It had gotten so bad, he'd considered escaping into the water, but was afraid he wouldn't be able to pull himself back into the boat.

Rupert shook the last three pills out into his palm, swallowed two, and dropped the third back into the bottle. His sense that he wouldn't have made it this far without the pills was balanced by the knowledge his desire to have them was what led him to his current situation. He hadn't been interested in that woman at the bar. She would have been pretty but for the swollen lip and black eye that marked her as a hard luck case, but Rupert knew enough to stay away from the ones who came in crying. Somehow, she'd latched on to him, though, sobbing out a litany of the woes inflicted upon her. Rupert heard only bits of it, his concentration focused on the television mounted on the wall behind the bar, until she mentioned the arthritis in her hips and the trouble she'd had finding a doctor understanding enough to give her the right prescription.

That was where it had all gone bad. He should have just walked away instead of going home with her. He shouldn't have taken her to bed, or smashed her husband's head in after the man walked in on them. There was no way he was getting out of there without a fight, but pummeling the man with the dumbbell he'd found at the foot of the bed had been a mistake. He should have just walked away, but he was drunk, and naked, and had twisted his ankle fighting the man. He'd brought the weight down on the man's face again and again, not stopping until the screams of the woman on the bed finally jolted him back to human consciousness. His animal rage replaced by a robotic numbness, he'd dressed, grabbed the bottle of pills off the nightstand and left the woman in her bathroom sanctuary. He could hear her calling the police through the door.

"Help! Somebody please help!" The voice wasn't a memory. It was there now, drifting out from the swamps. Rupert swatted the mosquitoes away from his ears and held his breath. At first he heard only the sound of the water lapping at the sides of his boat, but eventually the plea came again, this time punctuated with a scream. Realizing it was the voice of a child, Rupert threw himself over the side of the pirogue and waded into the swamp. He moved as quickly as his ankle and the soggy earth would allow, keeping his arms up to brush back the branches from his face.

As he came to a small clearing, he found himself face to face with a young girl with her back to a tree. Her blouse quivered with the pounding of her heart while she frantically kneaded the coarse fabric of her skirt between trembling fingers. Behind her, rutting in the moss with its black snout, a large boar made grunts like the cruel chuckle of some monster closing in on its prey.

The girl jumped and started to scream when Rupert crept up to put his hands on her shoulders. Realizing she was blind, he laid a finger across her lips and shushed her.

"It's okay," he whispered. "It won't bother us as long as we don't bother it."

"What is it?" stammered the girl.

"It's just a wild pig," Rupert said, taking her hand and leading her into the thicket. "It won't follow us through the brambles." When the boar was out of sight, he sat her down on a fallen pine and leaned against an oak tree to take his weight off his throbbing ankle. "What ya doing alone out here?"

"I was fetching some berries for my grandma when I got too far from the cabin and my eyes stopped working. Then I heard a sound and got scared. I thought it was the *loup-garou*."

"What's being away from the cabin got to do with your eyes?" Rupert asked. "You say'n you left your glasses back there?"

"I'm blind," said the girl. "Been that way since birth. My grandma uses her magic ta make it so I can see, but it only works long as I'm not too far from her."

"Magic? You say'n your grandma is some kinda witch?"

"She just knows a lot of things regular folks don't," said the girl. "She learnt about Voodoo from her ma and would have passed it down to mine if she hadn't died. She said she's gonna teach me when I gets ta be old enough."

271

"Whatever you say, kid," Rupert said, wanting to sit, but afraid he wouldn't be able to get back up if he did. "Any chance your grandma might have lunch ready if we can find her?"

"She don't take to strangers much," said the girl, "but I'm sure she'd be grateful if you brought me back ta her."

"Well, it shouldn't be hard to trace a blind girl's path through brush this thick," Rupert said, noting the tracks they'd left in the soft earth. "Hopefully your friend back there has wandered off already."

⚓

Aided by the plumes of white smoke visible whenever there was enough of a gap in the trees, and the scent of venison, it hadn't taken Rupert long to find the girl's grandmother's shanty. Situated on a patch of high ground, the clapboard hovel stood on four-foot stilts in the shadow of a dilapidated barn.

"That's gotta be your grandma's place," Rupert announced. "I can't imagine there's too many people squatting way out here in the middle of nowhere."

"That's it," the girl shouted, letting go of Rupert's hand to race across the clearing and up the steps of the shanty while Rupert stared in disbelief. How did she do that? She couldn't have been faking it, he thought. He was sure the girl had been blind. He was still trying to make sense of it when the girl reappeared on the porch to wave him on.

"You can see?" he asked as he reached the stairs.

"Told ya I could," the girl replied. "I just had ta get back in range of the magic."

The porch rail wobbled as Rupert leaned on it, dragging himself up the stairs. A missing step revealed a fat nutria rat gnawing on a bone. He felt his stomach churn as the stench of decay wafted up, temporarily overpowering the scent of cooking meat coming from the doorway above.

"This is the man who helped me, Grandma," the girl announced as Rupert stepped into the shack. An old woman, her face barely visible under the ratty shawl draped over her head and shoulders, looked toward Rupert and nodded. Rupert let go of the door frame he was using to steady himself to wipe the drool off his chin with his sleeve, and then toppled over, passing through the floor to land in a pile of bones. The bones shifted under him as he struggled to get up and escape the rats that scurried from the darkness, crawling up over his legs toward his face.

᷾

Something wet and cold landed in Rupert's lap as he sat up. A boney hand on his chest pushed him back down and returned the wet rag to his forehead.

"Best lie still," said an unfamiliar voice. "You been through a lot. Gonna take time ta get yer strength back."

Rupert started to ask about the rats, but gazing past the figure hovering over him, he saw the floorboards where he'd fallen were intact. "A dream," he muttered, holding up an arm and finding it free of bites.

"I wouldn't be surprised if ya was dream'n bout hell fire with that fever ya been run'n," said the voice. Rupert looked up and tried to make out the speaker's features in the dim light of the fire from the hearth. The shadows darkened the lines etched in her brown skin, making her face seem impossibly withered. Rupert thought she looked like a mummy until she turned her head so her watery eyes caught the reflection of the fire, causing orange flame to dance in the deep sockets. For a brief moment, she seemed animated with demonic fury, causing him to wonder if his eyes had glowed like that as he'd wielded the dumbbell.

"How long was I out?" he asked, noting his skin was no longer on fire. He held his hand before his face, searching for welts, but the dim light revealed none.

273

"You was out fer the better part of the day," said the girl coming into view as the old woman went to answer the summons of a bubbling caldron suspended over the fire in the hearth. "It's getting on midnight."

"I remember. You were blind," Rupert said, sitting up and throwing off the coarse blanket, only to yank it back over himself when he realized he was naked. The girl giggled.

"Your clothes are still on the line outside," she said. "They was all wet and nasty when grandma pulled 'em offa you."

"I'm grateful you all took care of me, I really am," Rupert said, watching the old woman stir the caldron. "but I got some place I gotta be. If you'd be kind enough ta fetch my pants, I'll be on my way."

"Ya got some place ta be?" asked the old woman. "Maybe them police helicopters that's been hover'n round all day might help ya get there."

"What makes you think those helicopters have anything ta do with me?" Rupert asked.

"I guess ya expect us ta believe you were out here in the swamps, look'n like you'd spent the last week wrassel'n with gators, 'cause ya needed ta git some exercise," said the old woman. "It might be ta yer advantage ta squat here for a spell."

"I guess I could use some time ta rest up," Rupert said, remembering his previous escape plan had consisted of serving as mosquito bait while slowly dying of thirst. "I'd still be obliged if I could have my pants, though."

The girl nodded and rushed out to retrieve his clothes, leaving Rupert alone with the old woman and the unfamiliar odor seeping from the caldron.

"What ya cook'n?" Rupert asked, sniffing at the smoky air. "I could empty that whole pot, even if it does smell like burn'n tires."

"This ain't gumbo, boy," the old woman said, dropping something into the caldron that threw up plumes of blue smoke as it sizzled. "I'm make'n gold."

"I don't much care what you call it," Rupert said. "I'm going to eat it, as long as you don't have any objections."

"You won't be hungry much longer," the woman said. "After today, you'll never be hungry again."

"You got a crystal ball hidden in that apron?" Rupert asked, gesturing at the girl who had just returned with his pants to turn around so he could put them on. Forgetting his ankle, he put all of his weight on it as he stood, but there was no pain. He sat back down and examined it. The swelling was gone.

"What kinda witchcraft you use on me?" he asked. "There ain't a scratch anywhere on me."

"'Tain't witchcraft," responded the girl. "Witchcraft ain't real. My *mémère* used Voodoo ta fix ya up."

"Call it what you will," Rupert said. "It comes from deal'n with the devil."

"Yer half right," the old woman said, dipping a ladle into the caldron and scooping something that glittered onto a wooden plate. "I had ta go outside my religion ta make this. For this, I needed the help of yer devil."

Rupert stared at the steaming gold nugget on the plate she held out to him, thinking it couldn't possibly be real. It was nearly as big as a baseball.

"It's real," the woman said, reading his thoughts. "An' ya ain't gotta worry 'bout steal'n it. It's yours if ya want it."

"I don't get ya," Rupert said. "Why would you—"

"Cause I always pay fer what I take," the woman said.

"You think I'd be dumb enough ta trade my soul for a lump of gold?" Rupert shouted, dashing the plate on the floor.

"Yer soul!" the old woman cackled. "What would I want with that? I need a strong back, not no stained up spirit."

"You expect me ta believe you'd give me a fortune ta patch the holes in your roof?" Rupert said. "I woulda done that for a bowl of stew."

"I was think'n of somethin' more long term," the woman said. "There's a lotta work ta be done 'round here."

275

"Get the devil ta chop your wood," Rupert said. "I'll take my chances with the helicopters." He pushed the girl aside and had taken a few steps toward the door, when he recalled the old woman's prophecy. She'd said he'd never be hungry again. He decided that could mean one of three things. He could be rich, he could be getting regular meals in prison, or he could be dead. He turned and looked at the gold nugget still on the floor. If he left it, that would leave only two of the possible outcomes, and they weren't the two he wanted.

"I'll take your gold, witch," he said, rushing over to scoop it up, "but I won't be hanging around here with it."

He could still hear the old woman's laughter as he plunged into the swamp at the edge of the clearing. It was dark, and the swamps were difficult to navigate even during the day, but he had to get back to his boat. If he could make his way back to Old Spanish Trail without being spotted, he could call someone to pick him up and get him across the lake. He wasn't alone anymore; the lump of gold in his pocket would buy him all the friends he needed. Once he was in New Orleans, he could arrange passage to Texas where he could lose himself, or even travel on down to Mexico and live like a king.

Nearly blind, he plodded on, keeping his left arm over his face to ward off the branches while feeling the air before him with his right. It was a clear night, and though there was no moon to light the way, he knew enough to gauge his location by the position of the stars. As long as he kept going in the right direction, he'd come upon the water, and, hopefully, his boat.

He had almost succeeded. He'd nearly reached the water, when he saw a glow up ahead. Pulling back the branches, he saw the glow came from a spotlight raking the shore. They'd found his boat. He let the branches swing back and ducked down as the light fell on him.

"Damn," he muttered through gritted teeth. He'd have to go back and try to persuade the old woman to hide him. He didn't like the idea of threatening a child, but if she thought the girl was in danger, she might go along with it. Staying hunched over, he turned and started back, but tripped over a cypress knee, landing face first in the ankle-deep water. The light came back.

Rupert lay there on his stomach, afraid to move, his chin still in the water. The light did not move. It stayed focused on the trees above him. Could they have heard the splash? Were they piloting the boat to the shore at that very moment? He raised his head just far enough to take in what the light revealed. There was no path he could take without pushing his way through the thick brush. They would be sure to hear him if they set foot on shore.

As he looked around, two pinpoints of light in the clump of cypress less than a foot from his head caught his attention. He recognized the snake that was peering at him as a cottonmouth just before the light shifted away, and he felt a stabbing pain in the hand he'd brought up to protect his face. He had no choice now. He could either turn himself into the men in the boat and hope they felt inclined to get him help, or he could head back to the shanty. The old woman had fixed him up before. He would force her to do it again.

The old woman was waiting for him on the porch as he stumbled into the clearing. The pain in his hand made it hard to think but he was aware enough to avoid the missing step as he dragged himself up the stairs while she watched his progress, a satisfied grin on her withered face.

"You have ta help me," he said, collapsing at her feet as he finally reached the porch.

"It's too late," she said. "There's nothing can be done. Besides, a deal's a deal. You got the gold, an' I got me a handyman."

Lamont A. Turner

Rupert stood under the hot Louisiana sun, the gold nugget suspended from his neck scraping against his bare chest as he raised the axe. Images of a dumbbell smashing into a bloody face flashed before his eyes as he brought the axe down on the log, but they didn't mean anything to him. All he knew was he had to do as he was told. He didn't eat, he didn't breathe, and he didn't sweat. He worked until it was time to go stand in the corner of the shanty to await the old woman's next order. He couldn't remember enough to have any regrets, or to appreciate it that the mosquitoes no longer bothered him at all.

---

Lamont A. Turner is a New Orleans area writer and father of four. His work has appeared in numerous print and online venues.

# BLACKOUT

## BY ANGELA M. SANDERS

Margo DuBose raised her head from her pillow and, suppressing a groan, let it drop again. Light seeped through the bedroom's blinds, along with midsummer birdsong. The pillowcase next to hers was smooth. Preston hadn't come to bed. Again.

She rolled onto her back. Preston's army buddy had dropped by for dinner—she remembered that. She'd started with a gin and tonic, a ladylike size. Preston always told her gin was a woman's drink. Lilac, the girl who helped in the kitchen, mixed it and handed it to her without meeting her eyes. As if what Margo drank was any of her business, stupid girl. She even had the nerve to bring up the woman out at the old Keir place. Said she could help with certain "problems," if she wanted.

Margo pressed her splitting skull. Something had gone wrong last night. A different kind of wrong. Lilac had something to do with it—or did she? She'd been squirrelly lately, avoiding eye contact.

Before dinner, the men had opened a handle of Jack Daniels. Preston made their drinks—two ice cubes, whiskey, a splash of water, stirred five times. Even now Margo could hear the glug, the spoon on crystal, the satisfied first swallow. The men's gazes followed Lilac through the kitchen door. They ate cold chicken and potato salad and talked about Eisenhower's policies on communism. As a councilman, Preston always postured himself as the big man in the know.

Night had fallen, and fireflies sparked the darkness. Lilac was slow with the gin and tonics. Margo could have sworn this time she'd been careful not to overdo it with the cocktails. At some point, Preston's buddy left. Margo had a faint memory of his dark blue Chevy backing out from under the big oak out front.

She closed her eyes and tried to recall the rest of the evening. The clearing up, locking up after Lilac. It was no good. She couldn't remember.

Margo heaved herself from bed and made her way to the bathroom. At least she'd had the wits last night to wash her face and undress. She fumbled for aspirin and pushed open the bathroom window in the hope that fresh air would blow the fog from her brain. Usually, the pristine tile floor and marble countertop, all the way from Carrera, Italy, soothed her. She'd made the right choice in marrying Preston. She was someone important in Macon now.

She smoothed her hair and caught a glance of her fingernails in the mirror. Some kind of dark crust clung to her right hand. She took the soap to it and examined herself as she scrubbed. Her features were thickening, not with age, why she was barely thirty years old, but with alcohol. Yes, Margo told herself for the hundredth time, she'd stop drinking. After the election, maybe. Preston would be so much easier to live with then.

Where was her husband, anyway? She looked into the guest bedroom. No Preston. She almost passed it up, but on second thought poked her head into the nursery, painted daffodil yellow for the children they hadn't yet had. He wasn't there.

Downstairs, the kitchen was empty. No Lilac, either. Margo pounded a fist on the counter. "Where is everyone?" Her words echoed. "Lilac? I want my coffee."

The girl should be here by now. Had Margo fired her?

Margo pushed into the dining room. Last night's dishes covered the table, a fly making breakfast of the potato salad. Picking up speed, Margo crossed the entry hall to the drawing room, then through to Preston's den. Chances were he'd slept on the couch again.

"Preston?" she said as she rounded the corner.

Her husband was there, all right. Sprawled on the couch, just as she'd guessed.

What she hadn't anticipated was the knife in his chest.

🐈

"Mrs. DuBose." The woman stood, hands on hips, at the front door of the old Keir place. The mongrel behind her growled low.

Margo's fingers ached from having clutched the steering wheel so tightly. That white-handled knife up to its hilt in Preston's chest. His head at an angle nature didn't intend. As loathe as she had been to drive out here, a place no self-respecting lady would go, Margo hadn't known where else to turn.

She wasn't ready to call the sheriff. Not until she knew for sure what had happened last night. Maybe the woman would know where to find Lilac. Maybe, then, Margo could get some answers.

The woman's house needed a coat of paint and probably more than that, but the garden thrived in tidy rows with odd things placed between them: a silver spoon here, a baby's shoe there. A circle drawn in white ash near the black-eyed Susans. Behind the house was an abandoned pecan orchard and a stream likely fetid from the mill.

"Ma'am?" The woman said.

She didn't even know the woman's name. "Good morning. Have you seen Lilac?"

The woman stepped forward, shutting the dog in the house. Her hair was pale blond—or white, it was hard to tell, making her age impossible to guess. She dried her hands on her apron. "No. Why would I?"

"There's been a serious incident at the house, and I believe Lilac was involved." Margo's words sounded unnecessarily formal, especially here. She lightened her tone. "I need to find her."

The woman stared. "Ailith Keir. That's my name."

That explained her taking over an old farmhouse so creepy that locals avoided it at night. She was kin. "Mrs. Keir."

"You said it was serious. You've notified the sheriff?"

Margo shifted her handbag to her other arm. "No. Not yet. I don't want to alarm you, but it will be much easier if Lilac turns herself in. I'll talk to her before she makes things worse. It's the Christian thing to do."

"Is it?"

Although she'd scrubbed them clean, Margo curled her fingernails into her fists and raised her chin. "You'll understand if I don't go into details."

Margo had her story. Lilac had wanted Preston's attentions. She'd killed him when he refused her, and Margo would find her and make her confess. Lilac could barely pluck a chicken, let alone kill a man in cold blood. Still, Margo would point out, rage could make a person do just about anything.

"I see," Ailith said. Her eyes were pale, too, like opals. "I'm sorry I can't help you." She turned to go back into the house.

"Wait." Margo reached out, touching the back of the woman's calico blouse, worn thin from years of washtub and clothesline. She yanked her fingers back as if she'd brushed a hot skillet.

Ailith turned to face her.

Margo snapped open her purse and held out a thick wad of green bills. "I need your help."

Ailith ignored the cash. "I already told you, I haven't seen her today."

The strain was too much. The years of drugstore perfume on Preston's shirts, the hangovers, the empty cradle. Now this. Preston's buddy had been at dinner. He'd know that only Lilac and she were home. No one had broken in. The knife had come from her kitchen. If Lilac could prove her own innocence, Margo was sunk. She had nowhere to turn. No one in this town would take her side against Preston's.

"They say you help people," Margo said.

"I do. Those who need it. Those who can't get help elsewhere."

Margo's words came as barely a whisper. "I don't know what happened last night. My husband is dead. Can you help me?"

Ailith's stare drilled into her. The wind picked up, chiming the bells nailed to the porch's soffit. "Killed?"

Margo nodded.

"I see." Ailith reached for the cash. "Wait here while I get some things."

◢

In the midday sun, the DuBose house looked starched and innocent. Inside, it was clear by the dishes crusting in the heat on the dining room table that Lilac had not returned.

"Where is he?" Ailith said.

Just feet away, in the drawing room, was the liquor tray. A splash of gin would set Margo right. Not that she normally drank before five o'clock. Not more than a sip or two to take the edge off of the night before, anyway.

"No," Ailith said. "No drinking. Close the blinds partway, as you do when it's hot like this. Everything is as if normal today, do you understand?"

"Okay. Can I have a glass of water?"

283

"Fine. No liquor, though." She pointed through the room to the arched entrance to Preston's study. "He's through there?"

Margo nodded. Her gaze swept the drawing room and all the things she loved—the gladioli in the Lalique vase from Preston's grandmother, the Persian carpet walked on by governors, the silver-framed photos of Preston and her with important people. How did it come to this? She shouldn't be letting a woman she wouldn't even nod to at the grocery store order her around her own house. Yet what choice did she have?

When Margo returned to the darkened study, Ailith had lit a squat beeswax candle on a saucer. She was pinching herbs into a black bowl and murmuring words in a language Margo didn't understand. Ailith worked as if Preston's body were no more than a collection of throw pillows.

"Stand out of the way," Ailith said. "Behind me. Are you strong?"

Margo stared at Preston's strangely twisted neck. He'd never sneer at her again. He'd never curse at her when her monthlies came with no sign of a baby. "Pardon?"

"Do you faint easily?"

"No," she said.

"Under no circumstances are you to leave where you stand now. Do you understand?"

Margo nodded. "What are you going to do?"

Ailith ignored her. "This will last only a few minutes. You'll have your answer. You'll know exactly what happened last night."

She tilted the candle and lit the bowl of herbs. A thick blue smoke smelling of skunk and burnt eucalyptus curled upward. She lifted the bowl to her lips and blew the smoke toward Preston's body. Beyond the reach of her breath, the smoke seemed to travel of its own accord. It shrouded Preston's face.

"What is—?" Margo started.

"Hush." Ailith reached into a leather pouch and withdrew dried petals the vivid orange of a sunflower and sprinkled them among the other herbs. "See how little blood there is? He died when his head hit the table. The knife was extra."

Margo forced herself to breathe evenly. This couldn't be her life. She was watching someone else's life. If only she could wind back time, way past last night. She might have married Roddy and lived near his parents' farm. She never would have touched alcohol. No, she wouldn't have the home and the status, but she wouldn't be here, right now, either.

The smoke curled, wisping over Preston's chin, circling his nose, and washing his forehead. One eye snapped open.

Margo inhaled sharply and she grabbed the edge of the desk, knocking over a paperweight. Ailith stood her ground.

Preston's eye was bloodshot with whiskey. The other eye appeared crusted shut. His head stayed in its unnatural bend, still dangling on the couch's arm. On one hand, a finger lifted. It was like watching a marionette of bloody flesh tugged by a novice puppet master.

"Councilman DuBose," Ailith said. "Can you hear me?"

Preston's jaw dropped and a growl escaped.

Margo steadied herself against the desk behind her. This couldn't be happening. Her pulse throbbed in her ears, and she strained to catch her breath.

"Councilman DuBose," Ailith repeated. "Tell us what happened last night."

The bloodshot eye swiveled to Margo. Her trembling grip on the desk's edge tightened. "Her." His jaw flapped grotesquely. His arm raised and finger pointed. "She did it. Bitch."

"What did she do?" Ailith spoke as if she were a stern teacher talking to a fussing child.

"Lilac." He laughed—just his mouth, not his eyes—and a teaspoon of blood burbled at the corner of his lips. "She asked if I was intimate with her. 'Intimate.' That was the word she

285

used." A drop of blood followed the angle of his chin to his jaw.

"And then?"

"Said I was a disgrace. She was crying." His laugh flashed to anger. "She pushed me."

"You can't do this to me," Margo said, her voice low at first, then rising in pitch. "I stood by you. For ten years I did right by you and made you look good. Then you—"

"Shut up!" Ailith elbowed her back against the desk. For such a slight woman, she was strong. "I said, stay back. Away from the herbs. We only have a few more seconds."

Already the smoke began to curl upon itself and retreat. The blue leached away, and it smelled sweeter now.

"You're no good to me," Preston said, his voice dropping like a phonograph running slow. "Couldn't do the one thing you had to. Lilac didn't have a problem getting with child. Didn't take more than a few times, either."

Margo lurched toward her husband, and Ailith grabbed her by the shoulders, hurling her into a chair. "Stop. This is dangerous. Listen to me."

Behind her, Preston lay inanimate again. His eye remained open, but his arm had flopped to the couch. He was dead, she reminded herself. He'd never hurt her—or anyone—again.

"Lilac is pregnant. Preston did it," Margo said.

"Yes."

"Last night. I remember now. He was sending her to Atlanta to—to fix it."

"She's going to stay with kin, instead. She's keeping the child."

Bits of the night were coming back. Yes, they'd fought. She'd pushed him, and he'd fallen. Hit his head. She hadn't known if he was dead, but she hadn't been willing to take the chance he'd survive, so she'd fetched the knife. She glanced at Ailith. How did the woman know about Lilac?

The clock on the mantel ticked in dim study. Ailith leaned against the doorframe and watched her. At last, Margo spoke. "As far as anyone is concerned, you may have killed him."

Ailith tilted her head, her expression neutral.

Margo gestured toward the French doors separating the office from the drawing room. "Your fingerprints are on the handle." Yes. This was it. As she spoke, her confidence grew. "A woman like you detests men with power. You killed him."

"Is that so?"

"Who are they going to believe, anyway? Me, or you?"

Without saying a word, Ailith drew a handkerchief from her apron pocket and wrapped it around the knife's handle. She pulled it from Preston's chest. His torso lifted slightly with the effort.

"You won't accuse me. Not as long as I have this." She laid the knife in her carpetbag. "What's more, Lilac will need money to care for her child. You'll give it to me."

Ailith lifted her bag and calmly left the office. She stopped at the liquor tray and took the bottle of gin by its neck before continuing through the entry hall.

That was it, then. Margo's mind rushed ahead to the trial, to the probable conviction. Her house and her position wouldn't matter then. Preston had been popular, and his behavior wouldn't be an excuse for murder. That's how men were. Besides, he'd known the judge personally. She sickened to think of the jury's pitying glances and the stark jail cell.

She blindly followed Ailith to the kitchen. "What are you going to do?"

Ailith uncapped the gin and poured it down the sink. "Do you have a shovel?"

"Why?" Margo asked, her eyes on the juniper-scented liquid filming the sink. Bits of brown herb stuck to the porcelain. She drew her brows together. She hadn't noticed the herbs last night among the ice cubes and wedges of lime, but they'd been there all along. Of course, they'd been. She

287

pictured Lilac handing her a gin and tonic, beaded with condensation, on a silver tray.

Margo glanced at Ailith's carpet bag, then to the woman herself. Now it all made sense.

Ailith rinsed the sink and washed out the bottle. "Time to take care of your husband, don't you think?"

———————

Angela M. Sanders writes the Witch Way Librarian cozy mysteries and the Joanna Hayworth vintage clothing mysteries. As Clover Tate, she wrote the Kite Shop cozy mysteries. When Angela isn't at her laptop, she's often rummaging in thrift shops, lounging with a vintage crime novel and her shelter cats Squeaky and Bitsy, or pontificating on how to make the perfect martini. www.angelamsanders.com.

# COMEDIC TIMING

## BY LINDSAY PUGH

Miz Cackle rides the gentle curve of the road hugging the west side of the estate, heading toward Route 40. Nana Chuckles has sent her with a list for Piggly-Wiggly and the apothecary. Gentleman Giggler is drifting on a cloud over the Atlantic right now, and when he arrives he'll crave ginger ale and fried chicken. Also on the list: lemons, Splenda instead of cane sugar because Nana Chuckles suspects she's pre-diabetic, Cheerios, and hamburger for Lil Dragon. Miz Cackle offered to let Lil Dragon ride shotgun, but he was more interested in a nap this morning. He usually likes the apothecary, where he plays with the owner's cat Mitzy under Miz Cackle's supervision, after a careful occlusion spell to make a little dragon look like a big house cat.

Nana Chuckles is laughing out the nuisances in the mansion this morning. She was dressed in a cheerful red bandana and brewing tea at eight. "Good morning, Cackle," she said. "I've left you a list for the store. Can you take the glade when you come back?"

"Banshees again?"

"Yes, there's a couple of them. I'll need you to remind them we agreed they'd stay in the caves, away from the hiking trails."

"Department of Forestry coming through soon?"

"Two weeks out. Lots to do before then."

"I'll find a new joke book while I'm out."

The library is lined with humor books, worn, pages dog-eared, clever jokes underlined and starred, bad ones crossed out. Reader's Digest pages have been torn and pinned to the walls. Nana Chuckles favors limericks and Miz Cackle likes puns. The magazine pages are intermingled with notebook paper, with their own jokes and funny moments transcribed. They travel occasionally to comedy shows and write down the best lines to reread and chuckle at later.

Miz Cackle smiles and nods at the people in town, who always vaguely recall her as a neighbor but can't place when she moved to Elmswood. The magic of the house relaxes them as they see her, and she often has a good joke for them in the dairy aisle. When they walk away, it's hard to recall the features of her face, just the kindness in her eyes, the smile lines on her face. She's her old nana's caregiver, they recall. How old is old nana, anyway? Seems limber still. Sixty or so, maybe.

🐾

*Nana Chuckles?*
*Hm?*
*Do we age?*
*You're wondering why I haven't died yet.*
*Nana!*
*It's the work, dear. It keeps us suspended, in a way. We're aging all the time; you just couldn't tell without a microscope.*
*So will you——?*
*No time soon. When the work no longer needs me.*
*What if I need you?*
*I'll be here as long as you need me, dear. As long as I have something to teach you, and you have something to teach me, I'll be here.*

🐾

Most Thursdays Miz Cackle goes to the second-hand bookstore on Tuttle Street. They have a good humor section, and they also have Sam Smirk, the clerk who Miz Cackle is very afraid she is falling in love with.

"Anna!" Sam says when she walks in, beaming. His smile is like a sunrise. He is the only person to call her by her first name in a hundred years.

"Morning, Sam," Miz Cackle says.

"Did you like *Good Omens?*"

"Nana and I both loved it."

"Great!" Sam is still grinning. "Can I help you find anything else today?"

He always asks, and she always says yes, to spend a few golden minutes with him, even though she knows she'll only make herself love him all the more.

Whenever the phone rings at home, she knows it's Sam. He's the only one she's ever given the number. She almost never lets herself answer, but she looks forward to the pitiful bleating of the outdated corded phone that crackles when you pick it up because of magical interference, because it is a sign Sam Smirk still hopes.

Every so often, she toys with the idea of a forget-me-spell, to make Sam's fondness for her fade like an old photograph, so he never steps outside of the dance they're doing, and she never has to tell him no. But she doesn't want the phone to stop ringing, or to forfeit the personal book recommendations, the jokes he prints out for her.

She tries not to think of consequences and hopes this can be enough.

🐈

Gentleman Giggler's arrivals and departures are always unpredictable. A wind will whoosh into the kitchen, and Nana Chuckles will look up from her crossword and smell the air. "He's coming," she'll breathe, exhilaration stealing across her face. "Cackle, Gentleman Giggler is coming!"

The following days will be a flurry of cooking and tidying. The mansion will have faded somewhat in the time he's been gone, and everyone knows it; Nana Chuckles and Miz Cackle forget to do things like empty the gutters or repaint the baseboards. But they'll gather fresh bouquets and turn over the mattresses to help. There's more of the work, too, so they can have time to sit and talk uninterrupted by howls and complaints from the trees. And trips to town for his favorites. Miz Cackle wonders if Nana Chuckles works so hard to welcome Gentleman Giggler to make him stay longer or make him miss home more when he flits off.

Gentleman Giggler arrives on his cloud and drifts down slowly, so as to make an entrance. Nana Chuckles stays in the kitchen until the heel of his boot has touched the soft earth, then she darts outside in her nice green dress Cackle got her one Christmas. Gentleman Giggler is wearing his velvet suit jacket and a silk tie. He considers it one's duty to always look presentable. They gaze upon each other radiantly for a moment, then he offers her his arm, and she takes him into the kitchen for a cup of cider to ease the wind chill.

Miz Cackle and Gentleman Giggler have a cordial relationship. He considers her like a pet Nana Chuckles keeps to stave off the loneliness, albeit a useful one, like a cow or a horse. She finds him pompous, but he makes Nana Chuckles so overjoyed when he visits. Nana Chuckles is the neutral zone between them: both want her to stay happy, and therefore, they tolerate each other.

The one thing Miz Cackle knows Gentleman Giggler likes about her is that she's a good cook. He inhales the fried chicken every time, and every time he conveniently forgets who made it.

"It's dazzling, my love," he says to Nana Chuckles, who reminds him, "All thanks to Cackle!"

"Right," he says dismissively. It makes Miz Cackle grit her teeth, but she holds her tongue. Mostly. Sometimes she can't help it.

He's talking about dragons tonight, the mountainously large ones in the Himalayas. "It could've had me for an appetizer in a moment," he tells Nana Chuckles.

"Wouldn't be much of an appetizer," Miz Cackle says quietly. Lil Dragon snickers under the table. Both Nana and Gentleman Giggler ignore her.

Lil Dragon doesn't seem to much like him either, which amuses Miz Cackle. Gentleman Giggler is always trying to befriend Lil Dragon so he can study him closer. Lil Dragon is exceedingly rare as a specimen; pygmy dragons nearly always die in the wild when their mothers stop catching food for them. If it weren't for Nana Chuckles, Lil Dragon probably would've gone the same way. Nana Chuckles came home with him in her arms, clinging to her sweater like a lost kitten. She'd found him in the Dragon Caves on a routine census check. He was unusually small, even for a pygmy, and she'd decided to take him home with her, provided his mother agreed. Busy with four other normal-sized babies, she did. "One day, you'll find a stray that won't follow you home," Miz Cackle said.

"You did," Nana Chuckles retorted, and like so many things she said, it made Miz Cackle laugh.

🐈

She found the forest before the house, on one of the long walks she took at odd hours. At the time, she felt like life was dragging her behind it by her skirt. Part of it was the war, the bodies with the last name CACKLE on their tombstones. But even before the war, before her father and brother shipped off, Anna Cackle suffered from what folks called melancholy.

Nana Chuckles told her later that guardians usually found the forest first. "The forest calls you because it knows you already," she said. "It let you go off the path and see it as it really was."

It felt like a fever dream. The trees were older than they should be, she realized. They looked like they'd been rooted since the beginning of time. The branches hung like the shoulders of old women at the end of the day. There were no signs of rabbits or deer, no chittering of squirrels, but she didn't feel alone. She found herself holding her breath. She should've been cold, in her thin shawl, but the sunlight filtering down was somehow enough. She found a waterfall and dipped her feet into the pool. Bright lights wove in and out of the trees, the fairies the first creatures bold enough to steal peeks at her. She accepted their presence absently. It had felt so natural. The forest recognized her as its kin.

Nana Chuckles emerging across the clearing was as sudden and as expected as a sunrise. Nana Chuckles was wearing a floral dress, an oversized straw hat, and old boots smeared with mud. Her hair was a peculiar shade that seemed to glow silver and amber all at once, age and youth intermingled. She looked like she never stopped smiling, and Miz Cackle's sadness cracked apart just enough.

"Come for tea," Nana Chuckles said. She strode past Miz Cackle without another look, her straw hat bobbing decisively. Miz Cackle laughed just a little at the sight, and Nan Chuckles called back, "There's the spirit!"

❧

*Tea's brewing. You have questions.*

*Endless ones.*

*Curiosity is the best way to learn. Let me show you. Tell me something that makes you laugh. Anything at all.*

*Alright. There's a suffragist. A man says to her, 'Women have never produced anything of value to the world.' So she says back that women's chief product is the men and told him he could decide whether they had any value.*

*A chuckle, a warm, throaty noise, rose out of her and wrapped around Miz Cackle like a knit sweater. As she laughed harder, Miz Cackle couldn't help but laugh, too, and their voices wove together beautifully, a harmony that blended so easily. The night twinkled with them. As they quieted again, Miz Cackle realized she felt better, somehow, like she had dropped a weight to the ground and stretched her muscles.*

*Did you—?*

*You and I did together. That's my magic, darling. Laughter is the best medicine.*

*Can you teach me how?*

*Maybe. It's not easy work. There's sacrifice involved.*

*I know about sacrifice.*

*Ay, I know you do. We'll see, yeah? Tea's ready.*

🐱

Gentleman Giggler's cloud jaunts take him worldwide. He observes the magic of the world and reports back. It's very important work, both he and Nana Chuckles assure her, and it informs their own methods on the home front, but Miz Cackle wonders why he's the one that has to do it. He hops from portal to portal and talks to their guardians, and he sends letters back to them that smell like mountain air. Nana Chuckles carefully saves them all and records their knowledge in what they call the "How-To Book." The How-To Book is a green gingham book labelled "Favorite Recipes," which they both get a kick out of. It is somewhat organized into Creatures, Spells, Potions, and Laughter Magic, though sometimes Nana Chuckles will accidentally write an entry about werewolves next to a Smile Persuasion Spell. Theoretically, it is for their successors, whoever the portal chooses and sends their way next.

295

Lindsay Pugh

Miz Cackle loves the house, the rickety Victorian contraption it is. Nana Chuckles says it manifests into the perfect home for its inhabitants, so they must not need central heating after all. It's painted the color of a whelk shell, with vivid violet shutters. Two turrets stand against the sky, and smoke plugs stalwart out of the chimneys. The wraparound porch has a swing and rockers, and a big window that opens into the kitchen so they can talk while they cook. Miz Cackle's room has a little balcony she grows poppies on. This is a life she never knew she was destined for.

🐾

*Where are you from, Nana Chuckles?*

*Oh, I've been from everywhere. I've gone wherever the portal needs me to be. I found it first in Ireland, or maybe I should say it found me. It's a bit hard to explain, but there's a world beneath this one, and a world above, and a world beside it and around it. Anything you've ever read about is real, and a lot of things you haven't read about are real, too. We keep the balance between them all, between the human world and the magical ones.*

*Are there other portals? Other guardians?*

*Many, yes. And there are many others like me. They all have their different methods of guardianship. I just find laughter the easiest to bear.*

*Why do you think the portal brought you here?*

*I think it brought me to you.*

🐾

Nana Chuckles and Miz Cackle have discussed several times if it's worth the risk to invite Sam into the world. It's the closest they get to fighting.

"Smirk," Miz Cackle will say meaningfully.

"Could be a coincidence," Nana Chuckles says.

296

"Could be a sign," Miz Cackle says.

And round and round they go.

See, Nana Chuckles is right. It's hard to know whether the portal will accept Sam as one of them, whether he has the right joy in his bones to become a guardian. Miz Cackle would have never thought she had that capacity on the days she sank into her bed and couldn't eat. But Nana Chuckles knew when she saw her in the forest.

If she's wrong, the house may expel him by force, and crush him in the process. He could lose his mind or even die, and all because she was wrong? Miss Cackle can't risk him. Sam likes comics and to cook, and he is full of life that should never extinguish.

And so she dreams of a world where she could leave the house or he could stay in it, and they could laugh the world into focus together, with Nana Chuckles and Lil Dragon close around. But she never could leave, and she could never ask him to come.

ᶾ

*You have to be invited by a guardian to join. If you'd like, cross the threshold, and I'll bless you, and you'll be part of the guardianship.*

*Miz Cackle stood on the steps and peered into the house, so stately, ancient like the elms themselves. The firelight spilling out invited her closer to the only joy she'd felt in months.*

*What if I can't be like you?*

*You can, dearie. It takes a special person to see the world as it is, the layers of time and place and thought. You have it. I'll just leave the door cracked and get back to my work, hm? You can come in if you like, and if you don't, I understand.*

*She did.*

🐾

Gentleman Giggler leaves after nine days, longer than usual. Nana Chuckles quietly kisses him on the porch, and Miz Cackle watches from the kitchen and holds Lil Dragon in her arms and scratches his neck. He murmurs, unsettled by Nana Chuckle's uncharacteristic somberness. "It's all right," she says to him.

Gentleman Giggler mounts his cloud. They make eye contact, and Miz Cackle nods. He nods back. These are the terms of the agreement. She will pick Nana back up again. She's been stockpiling limericks. Nana Chuckles comes back in and comes to pet Lil Dragon. She lays her head on Miz Cackle's shoulder.

"Do you want to hear a limerick?" Miz Cackle says.

"Of course, Cackle," Nana Chuckles says. "Who do you think I am?"

🐾

Miz Cackle sits defeated in her rocker, thinking again of what could be if she could truly let herself love Sam Smirk. "It's all right, little one," Nana Chuckles says, pulling her close. Miz Cackle burrows her face into her shapeless linen dress. It smells like the house: tea and bread, vanilla candles, mystery and magic. Miz Cackle has never known anything else so well or been so known in return. The house's bones are her own. Nana Chuckles is right.

"It's not fair," she says into Nana Chuckles's skirt.

"I know," she says. "It's not fair the menfolk wander and come home when they please, and you and I stay here and tend to the forest, but it's what is."

"Don't you get tired of being left?" Miz Cackle says.

Nana Chuckles smiles. "It doesn't matter if I get left. I have the house, and the trees, and Lil Dragon, and, most importantly, I have you."

Miz Cackle wipes her eyes and sits up. "And I have you."
That almost feels like enough.

🐈

And then comes the day that Sam decides he's tired of
dancing and breaks the pattern of steps. Miz Cackle is
perplexed when there's a knock. There are so rarely visitors to
the house, and they're usually fae who rudely barge into the
house to complain about other fae without bothering with a
perfunctory knock. It's too late for the mailman. She thinks
she's imagined it at first, until she spots a blue Honda Accord
out the window. The same car she has seen parked outside of
the bookshop. The horror dawns slowly.

"Nana Chuckles," she yelps, and Nana darts over. "What,
dearheart?"

"He's outside," she whispers, and Nana knows what she
means.

"I have to tell him to go," Miz Cackle says. "And he'll
never want to see me again."

Nana Chuckles is silent as Miz Cackle walks to the door
just as Sam timidly knocks.

"Hi Sam," she says, opening the door just a crack. Lil
Dragon tries to peek out, but she nudges him aside with her
foot. They don't bother with cloaking spells here, and Lil
Dragon is quite clearly not a tomcat now.

"Anna," Sam says. "We got a new shipment, and I saw
some things I thought you'd like."

"Isn't that sweet?" Miz Cackle says, too high, her voice
alerting Sam, whose eyebrows crinkle with confusion. "Let me
just come out on the porch with you."

"Well, I was hoping to see your house," Sam says. "Your
room, maybe." He blushes. "Not like, agh, I meant—and meet
your nan?" He shifts to look behind her.

"You can't," Miz Cackle cries.

"I'm sorry, I—" Sam looks at his hands. "I must've misread the situation," he says. "I thought there was something between us. I'll…I'll just go."

"No, there is, I—" Tears are choking her now, and she wants so badly to let Sam inside. "I want to let you in."

"So why don't you?" He asks, finally starting to sound angry, and she gapes, unable to explain the complexity of the world they inhabit and how he only sees one of its layers. Could he ever see them all? Could he stand it, or would he stay on the run from it, like Gentleman Giggler, in love with magic's fun but not its sacrifices?

Nana Chuckles nudges her aside, gently, so they both stand in the doorway, the door wide open, letting the smell of vanilla candles trickle out.

"What Cackle means," Nana Chuckles says with a meaningful look, laying a hand on Miz Cackle's arm, "is that you have to be invited in."

"Oh. Well, can I come in, then?" Sam says, shifting the books in his hands. Miz Cackle looks at Nana, who nods, and Cackle understands the stakes she is putting Nana through, how she is asking Nana to restructure their world again in an unpredictable way. She looks at Sam, with his floppy hair and nervous smile, and she aches with a longing to see him at the breakfast table.

"Yes," Miz Cackle says, opening the door and readying herself to say the blessing as he steps over the threshold. "Yes, come in. I'll make some tea."

---

Lindsay Pugh lives in Richmond, Virginia, with her partner and two tabby cats. She enjoys writing magic realism and urban fantasy, and reading anything she can get her hands on. She has been previously published in *Parhelion*, with upcoming work in *Allegory Ridge*'s spring anthology.

# ACKNOWLEDGMENTS

Special thanks to Pat Allen Werths, my not-so-secret secret weapon, Eric J. Guignard for his patience and guidance, and my more sociable half, Rich Weissman, for encouraging me in yet another venture.

# ABOUT THE EDITOR

J.D. Horn is the Wall Street Journal bestselling author of the Witching Savannah series (*The Line, The Source, The Void,* and *Jilo*), the Witches of New Orleans Trilogy (*The King of Bones and Ashes, The Book of the Unwinding, The Final Days of Magic*), and the standalone Southern Gothic horror tale *Shivaree*. A world traveler and student of French and Russian literature, Horn also has an MBA in international business and formerly held a career as a financial analyst before turning his talent to crafting chilling stories and unforgettable characters. His novels have received global attention and have been translated into Turkish, Russian, Romanian, Polish, Italian, German, and French. Originally from Tennessee, he currently lives in California with his spouse, Rich, and their rescue Chihuahua, Kirby Seamus.

304

CPSIA information can be obtained
at www.ICGtesting.com
Printed in the USA
BVHW042029150421
605035BV00009B/981

9 781736 620700